ALSO BY WALTER STOVALL
Presidential Emergency

THE MINUS POOL

WALTER STOVALL

Wyndham Books
New York

Published by Wyndham Books
A Simon & Schuster Division of Gulf & Western Corporation
Simon & Schuster Building
Rockefeller Center
1230 Avenue of the Americas
New York, New York 10020
WYNDHAM and colophon are trademarks of Simon & Schuster
Designed by Stanley S. Drate
Manufactured in the United States of America
Printed and bound by The Book Press, Inc.
1 2 3 4 5 6 7 8 9 10
Library of Congress Cataloging in Publication Data

Stovall, Walter.
    The minus pool

    I. Title.
PZ4.S89Mi   [PS3569.T673]   813'.54   79–27816

ISBN 0-671-61040-6

1

Mr. McManus, a small man with a nose as flat as the blood of a ghost, was expecting a glorious day. It had started promisingly. At 5 A.M., for the first time in three months, he had taken a leak standing up. Then came the phone call. An hour and a half later he was still on his feet. He was breathing without strain and gazing down from his living-room window. Across the street, in the dim dawn, a razor-thin rain punished the leafless trees of Central Park.

He regretted the rain. It would exaggerate the panic of Freddie Dee when he found the invalid missing. Freddie Dolan had rolled him around in a wheelchair since the middle of August; he was asleep in a small room off the kitchen. At least Freddie Dee won't call the cops, Mr. McManus said to himself as he walked tentatively to the closet in the front hall of the enormous apartment. The thought comforted him. He slipped on a heavy raincoat, muffler, and hat. He selected an umbrella, the expensive one, and quietly let himself out. He wanted to make certain he didn't arouse Freddie Dee.

Leaving Freddie Dee a note was out of the question. Mr. McManus hadn't written a note to anyone, including his wife, his mother, or his children, in more than forty years. He hadn't lived to the age of seventy-four, he reflected as he summoned the elevator, by writing notes. He was confident that Freddie wouldn't have figured out what to do by the time he returned.

The elevator door slid open. The uniformed attendant gasped in astonishment. "Jesus, Mr. McManus! Does Freddie know you're—"

"It's okay, Jerry," said Mr. McManus. He was aware of the tremble in his voice. He felt his dewlap jiggle against his muffler as he spoke. It had grown disproportionally large against his shrunken neck. "Time I was on my feet again. Under my own steam, you know?" He pressed a ten-dollar bill into the elevator attendant's hand.

He stepped carefully from the elevator. He noticed himself in the gilt-framed lobby mirror. The image he had seen as he shaved was reaffirmed. The bushy brows above his reptilian eyes, set in a nest of wrinkles, were ivory white. His once ruddy face was chalky. The flesh drooped from his cheeks. His nose was no longer a token of brutal nobility; it was a node of ravaged gristle and bone. He looked *old*. He even imagined an odor of urine about himself despite the copious amounts of talc he had applied after his shower.

He made his way through the lobby. He was mindful not to let the umbrella touch the marble floor. He did not want to give the appearance of using it as a cane.

The doorman was equally startled. "Blessed Mary and Joseph, Mr. McManus! I had no idea you was up and around. . . . Not going out alone, I hope. Sidewalks are thick with ice."

Mr. McManus advanced gradually toward the door. "Doctor's orders, Mike," he lied. "Need a light stroll." Into the doorman's hand he unobtrusively placed a twenty. "If Freddie comes looking for me, tell him to relax. Tell him not to come looking for me. I'll be back soon."

"Better let me whistle you a cab," said the doorman anxiously. "This is no kind of day for a man in your condi—" His face reddened as he caught Mr. McManus's glance. "The weather's rotten," he finished crisply. He cast his eyes at the mat beneath his feet.

"I need the exercise," Mr. McManus said with a tight smile. "Believe me"—a quaky chuckle "—I need the exercise." He pulled his kid gloves over his thick hands. The knuckles were prominent, the thumbs painfully stiff, the skin mottled.

He descended cautiously to the sidewalk. He stood for a moment under the canopy. He looked up and down the street, Central Park West, without moving his head. It was deadly cold. He saw nothing unusual. But he felt unsure. He knew that an elderly party such as himself, taking his first mincing steps since a thunderous heart attack, would have to be especially alert. He took a slow, deliberate, deep breath. He exhaled apprehensively. He saw the puff of moisture. He was still breathing easily. So far, so good. He smiled tightly again. His exhilaration was holding up. He bunched his muffler about his throat.

Mr. McManus started walking downtown. The rain had nearly stopped, so he kept his umbrella furled. The wind had slackened. It had grown lighter, but the sky remained leaden. There was a distinct threat of snow. The sidewalk, as the doorman had warned, was thick with ice.

He was not wearing rubbers. He never wore them. He thought they were inelegant. It was just as well, he thought. The fear of slipping—and breaking a hip or worse—would keep his gait at a pace that wouldn't exhaust him.

The street was all but deserted. Rare for a Monday morning on Manhattan's Upper West Side but not unheard of in December weather like this. An occasional jogger. A few well-bundled people walking their dogs. Here and there an early riser with a briefcase. A few taxis. A bus or two.

A few blocks south of the Museum of Natural History he turned. The side street was lined with converted brownstones. Their windows showed Christmas decorations. A few of the buildings were nursing homes. Mr. McManus avoided looking at them.

The ice on the side street was less thick. He quickened his step a fraction. It felt good. He realized acutely that his graceful strut—the style he had affected when he first climbed through the ropes as Kid Sweeney and had retained until a coronary occlusion had nearly killed him—was missing. But it felt good.

At the corner of Columbus Avenue he stepped into a candy store that sold newspapers. He sat down on a stool at the far end of the counter in front of the telephone booth. Symphonic music blared from a transistor radio. Mr. McManus was the only customer.

"Cup of tea, Leo." He said it familiarly, as if he had never been away. He hung his umbrella on the counter, pushed back his hat, and leaned forward on his elbows. He had not allowed Freddie Dee to roll him to his customary haunts. He did not want long-standing acquaintances to see him in a wheelchair. It would have been humiliating.

And conceivably dangerous.

The man behind the counter was pale and bald. He was the owner. He wore an apron and a heavy shirt, sleeves rolled up. On the inside of one forearm were four crudely tattooed blue numbers. He looked up in mild surprise. It was as much emotion as his face had registered since 1945. Until three months ago Mr. McManus had come to his candy store to buy the newspapers and a racing form every day since he opened it. He came at approximately the same time every day, but never the same time two days in a row.

Word had circulated in the neighborhood of Mr. McManus's seizure. It was said that Mr. McManus probably would not recover. The candy-store owner had received the news with a sympathetic but distinct shrug and gone about his business.

He turned down the radio and drew a cup of boiling water. The reappearance of a dead man was, to him, no big deal. He occasionally thought that was what he saw when he noticed his own reflection in the chrome-plated urn. He put a spoon and teabag on the saucer and placed it before Mr. McManus.

"Want the papers?" His voice betrayed no interest or curiosity. The question was as far as he was prepared to go in the way of acknowledging Mr. McManus's infirmity. Mr. McManus heretofore had fairly swaggered in, grabbed the newspapers and a couple of scratch sheets with one hand, and begun tearing through them furiously as he plopped them on the counter.

"Not today, Leo. Thanks." He dipped the teabag delicately in the hot water. The crockery cup was chipped on the handle. It looked dirty where the glaze had worn thin. "I want the phone for a while. Can you put up the sign?"

The owner immediately reached under the counter. He withdrew a frayed, gray slab of cardboard with the words "Out of Order" printed on it haphazardly and a wire loop through the top. He affixed it over the coin slot of the telephone in the booth behind Mr. McManus and returned to his spot on the opposite side of the counter.

"You dealing the line?" he asked, leaning close, in a low voice that hinted of anticipation.

"No." Mr. McManus placed the soggy teabag on the saucer. He gingerly grasped the handle of the cup. He lifted it slowly several times, testing to see whether he had the strength to bring it to his lips. "Just setting a meet— Guy I haven't seen in a while."

"Oh," said the owner in a tone of resignation. He moved off toward the other end of the counter. He had felt a twinge of eagerness when Mr. McManus asked for the "Out of Order" sign. It was a sensation he had felt every time he had received Mr. McManus in his store (which, until three months ago, had been every day, except when he closed in observance of Yom Kippur, for thirty-five years). It had sparked in him what a doubtful man would call hope. It had enabled him and his wife to make a good deal of money.

Mr. McManus managed to sip the tea and lower the cup to the saucer without dropping it. He remembered his image in the lobby mirror. His bottom lip drooped and his blue eyes shone with the glassiness of oblivion. A casual observer would have taken him for merely another of the neighborhood's legion of barely breathing old geezers.

For the moment he was thankful for his crumbled face. It would serve as a shield against Leo, against the other customers who would soon be drifting in for their morning papers. He wanted to look harmless, weak, obsolete. He wanted no one approaching him or, for some reason, offering to be solicitous. He wanted to be ready when the phone rang.

Suddenly a huge man, obviously young and in a hurry, pushed his way in. He took a seat near the door, at the opposite end of the counter, facing Mr. McManus. He wore a skimpy black raincoat over an old lightweight suit and a white shirt open at the neck. But he clearly was not a derelict. Nor did he appear to be suffering from the subfreezing weather. He had freshly cut dark hair and what seemed to be a military bearing.

A damned funny way to dress on a day like this. Mr. McManus observed under his thick white brows. At the same instant he caught the man eyeing him with a furtive but unmistakably photographic glance.

"I would like an egg of cream," the man said. He spoke with an accent that made his order come out as "agacadeem." He had what Mr. McManus called an "olive oil" complexion and was on what Mr. McManus considered, from a lifetime of experience, very bad terms with the English language.

"A what?" said the candy-store owner as he accepted change from another customer who bought a newspaper and departed.

"An egg of cream," the huge man repeated in the same garbled fashion. He spotted the tattooed numbers on the owner's forearm. A pained look of recognition momentarily altered his nervously resolute expression. Then it vanished.

"Ah. *Du vilst ein* egg cream?"

A hint of a smile appeared on the man's mouth. He seemed about to reply in Yiddish when something told him not to.

"An egg of cream," he said again, unsmiling and somewhat impatient.

"You want an egg cream," the owner said disdainfully. He knew the customer understood Yiddish. He was offended that he refused to speak it. He drew chocolate syrup into a glass, poured it half full of milk, and carelessly topped it off with a splash of carbonated water. It was a bad egg cream. He knew it. Ordinarily he eased the carbonated water into the glass over a spoon held under the tap. This customer, he decided, was a *zhlub* who wouldn't know the difference.

The man tasted the drink. It was an item usually sought in the summer months. He grimaced.

"*Is zu kalt*," he said angrily.

"What do you mean, too cold?" snapped the owner. So *now* the *schmuck* speaks Yiddish, he thought with irritation. So let Mister Smart Guy talk to himself. "You ever hear of a *hot* egg cream? Thirty cents." The standard price was a quarter.

The man dropped the change on the counter. A quarter and five pennies. He took a last, almost casual look at Mr. McManus and left without tasting his egg cream again.

Mr. McManus contemplated the scene behind his empty gaze. An obvious foreigner dressed like he should be in Florida but can't afford the plane fare busts into the joint and gives an old man the eagle-eyed once-over. He orders an "agacadeem" when it's cold as hell. First he won't speak Yiddish and then he does—to complain about the quality of an egg cream, a New York variety of chocolate soda that he clearly had never tasted before. He pays for it in exact but complicated change, a transaction that a transparently recent arrival like this would have to ask help on. Again the Yiddish. Mr. McManus didn't understand much of it in conversation, but he knew this man didn't learn his on Orchard Street.

"Leo," he called out and motioned with a nod. His voice was stronger. He found he could hold the teacup without difficulty. "Bring me a cigar."

The owner withdrew a box from a space beneath the showcase. It was new and contained twenty-five Havana Montecristos. He imported them illegally for Mr. McManus from Geneva. They cost $75 a box, for which Mr. McManus paid the candy-store owner $100. They arrived, unhindered by U.S. customs, in packages marked "Unsolicited Gift. Value Under $10."

Mr. McManus knew the value of a good cigar.

"The egg cream guy," he said as the owner held the box open before him. He took several cigars and gently stuffed them under his heavy raincoat into the breast pocket of his jacket. Then he selected one for now. "Ever see him around before?"

"Never," replied the owner. He closed the cigar box.

"What do you think?" He deftly bit off a minuscule portion of the head of the cigar. He preferred to pinch the end but was no longer able to because of his arthritic thumbs.

"What do I think about what?"

"The guy who asked for the egg cream."

"He knows from nothing."

Mr. McManus removed the band and stuck the cigar in his mouth. The owner (himself a nonsmoker) set the box aside and produced a book of matches. He struck one and held it up, scarcely allowing the flame to touch the tip. Mr. McManus inhaled evenly, in short puffs, twirling the cigar until the end glowed uniformly. It was his first since his heart attack.

"Is he a Puerto Rican or what?" He exhaled the smoke softly.

"A Puerto Rican? Him?" The owner sounded astonished. Had near-fatal illness robbed Mr. McManus of the thirty-five years of experience he had gained from coming daily to *his* candy store? "He should live so long. Are you kidding?"

"A Jew?"

"Of course a Jew. But a *plosher*. An Israeli *plosher*, I might add. Also an unimportant *plosher*, I would guess. A pickle-factory *plosher*." The owner stood back and looked directly at Mr. McManus. "A man who is important doesn't act important. Know what I mean?"

"An Israeli? How do you know he was an Israeli?"

"Have I been to Israel eleven times? Does my brother live in Tel Aviv? *He's* a *plosher*, my brother Morris. They're all *ploshers* now, Israelis. Arrogant bastards. Believe me, he was an Israeli, the egg cream *nudnik*." The owner made his way back to the showcase and shoved the cigar box into its space underneath. "Who *needs* it?" he muttered.

Mr. McManus made another mental note. The shabbily dressed stranger was an Israeli. He rolled the cigar smoke from cheek to cheek as he wondered why he was being checked out. He did not pursue the speculation. The guy was an Israeli. There are lots of Israelis. The Montecristo tasted very good. Excellent, in fact.

The telephone rang in the booth behind him.

Mr. McManus cautiously slid off the stool and stepped inside. He sat down gently and lifted the receiver.

"Who's sitting?" croaked a low voice.

"Nobody," replied Mr. McManus. "Better try Queensborough Park."

There was a pause and then the low voice again. "Kid?"

"Yeah."

"Kid, this is Billy."

"Yeah, Billy. You called, remember? Early."

"I'll be out front in twenty minutes. Black Rolls. A Phantom. You haven't seen it yet. You make it okay?"

"I'll make it. If I made it to Leo's, I can make it to the curb."

"The young guy. What's his name? Dolan's kid. The guy who's been, you know, helping you out. You ditch him for a while?"

"It's okay, Billy. I'm alone."

"You're *what?*"

"See you in twenty minutes. In your new Rolls," he said and hung up.

Mr. McManus buttoned his heavy raincoat. He grasped the handle of his umbrella and walked slowly toward the front. "Thanks for the sign, Leo." He paused at the end of the counter. "And the cigar." He slipped a twenty-dollar bill across the formica top. "Like I said, I ain't dealing the line. But I'm talking to some people. Some action later, maybe. I'll see how the day goes with my bum ticker. If I hear anything, I'll drop by and we'll lay it and love it. You do me a favor?"

The owner nodded.

"A young guy, not too bright, he's been giving me a hand. If he should happen in, you don't know me. Okay?"

"Know you?" There was a note of resentment in the owner's tone, as if he had detected a lessening of Mr. McManus's confidence in his descretion. "Have I ever known you?"

Mr. McManus smiled thinly to convey that he was aware of the owner's injured pride. "No offense, Leo," he said kindly. "I just wanted you to know. I been under the weather. The kid's been giving me a hand. I'm out alone and he don't know. He might get jumpy, come around asking questions. See what I mean?"

The owner, his sense of esteem restored, nodded again.

Outside the gloom was thickening. It would be snowing soon. The moist wind was spiky and insistent. It slashed the faces of the deliverymen as they briskly unloaded their cases of goods from double-parked trucks and carted them into the stores and shops that lined the street. Christmas trees bound with cord crowded the sidewalk in front of an adjoining florist.

Mr. McManus chose a spot that had been salted and scraped clean of ice. It was beside a grimy gumball machine. He took tiny puffs on his cigar. He was careful not to lean on his umbrella. He was happy to be outside despite the bitter cold. The candy store had begun to draw its throng of morning customers. He didn't feel up to contending with the nervous intensity of a crowd of newspaper buyers on their way to work.

He relished the taste of his cigar, the way a child relishes a sweet he has been told will ruin his teeth or spoil his appetite. The difference between his cigar and a child's forbidden chunk of chocolate fudge, he reflected, is that an old man knows his life can be measured by the intervals between good cigars.

One of the deliverymen, a boy, caught Mr. McManus's eye. He was short, with thick, bowed legs and a perfect Roman nose. He moved with a kind of cute nimbleness as cases of soft drinks were lowered to him from the side door of a truck. Mr. McManus was fascinated. The kid could have been Billy Light, give or take fifty years.

Mr. McManus, by temperament, abstained from reminiscence. But the kid taking the cases from the truck looked so much like young Billy Light that it startled him. For the moment he forgot his health, and the bleak weather meant nothing to him. The delivery took several minutes. He was still captivated when the kid, with insouciant agility, swung into the cab of the truck as the driver pulled away. Mr. McManus was relieved to see him leave. The flight of retrospection the scene had launched was beginning to annoy him.

It was an old story. He hadn't thought of it in years. A hell of a lot had happened since, Mr. McManus mused as he surveyed the accumulating traffic on Columbus Avenue. The years of boxing. The glut of experience that taught him to ask no favors of fate. Marriage and children. The war that erased forever his fear of close calls. Lots of money. Legalized sports gambling. And, now, a glimpse of the end.

Feathery snowflakes swirled about him. He tugged at the collar of his heavy raincoat, gathering his muffler under his dewlap against the heightening wind. He tossed what was left of his cigar into the gutter. The strength in his legs was ebbing. He pondered whether to step back inside. Presently a black limousine with New Jersey plates detached itself from the flow of trucks, taxis, and buses and drew up to the curb.

"You shouldn't have stood outside like that," admonished Billy Light. The car moved slowly toward the Broadway intersection. "Not alone." They were seated side by side in the rear. A glass partition separated them from the driver, a young man Mr. McManus did not recognize.

Mr. McManus stared inconspicuously at a crumpled newspaper on the floor. It described the pervasive fear cast over the city by a homicidal menace known as the "elephant gun killer"; the press had invented the label because the victims—five in all, in the last two and one-half months—were shot with the same high-caliber rifle. Notes had been sent to the newspapers warning that the killer would strike again; they were signed "Finger of God." The murders took place late at night in Manhattan; the victims were light-haired young men, shot from moving cars.

Billy lectured on. "I said you shouldn't be outside. Not in weather like this." He was plumper—and healthier looking—than Mr. McManus. His face retained an aquiline beauty despite its age and prevalent puffiness. Billy Light, like Mr. McManus, had arrived at adulthood as a boxer of encouraging expectations; he was born Nathan Leitstein in a dismal tenement on Sheriff Street, several blocks from the Pike Street cellar where Mr. McManus himself was born; he learned to fight because he had to and went on to improve his skills among a set of furriers' apprentices. They had abandoned their boxing careers at the same time—at the same moment, in fact, in the same gin mill—and resumed their identities as McManus and Leitstein. They clung to the habit of addressing each other as "Kid" and "Billy."

"How's the wife?" Billy asked. They passed Lincoln Center and headed downtown. The high, vaulted portico of the Metropolitan Opera house at the rear of the complex was veiled by snow. They seemed to have no destination. Just going for a spin while they talked.

Mr. McManus took his eyes off the newspaper. "Florida," he replied wearily. "The place in Gulfstream Park. Grandchildren with her. Christmas, you know. I'll try to get down myself if I'm up to it."

His expression became vacuous. When his heart attack struck him down, he had insisted on solitude. He calculated that his chances of survival would be much improved if he isolated himself from the excessive attention a family is driven to devote to a stricken member.

When he was released from the hospital, he acquired Freddie Dee, a bumbling young hoodlum temporarily in need of sanctuary, as a caddie and quasi-protector.

"How'd you get away from Dolan's kid?" Billy asked at length.

"Left him asleep," replied Mr. McManus after a moment in his quaky voice. He was still alert but tired. Too tired, in fact, to ask Billy what this was all about.

The car rounded Columbus Circle and crept onto Fifty-ninth Street. Billy eyed him with interest. "Don't take this wrong, Kid," he said abruptly, "but I got to try one on you." He shifted slightly to face Mr. McManus. It was not apparent that Mr. McManus had heard him. "How many seconds are there in 1,813 years, 7 months, and 27 days?"

Mr. McManus inclined his head a fraction. His eyes were still opaque. He was silent a moment and then answered wheezily, "527,234,384,000."

Billy donned a pair of half-moon glasses and studied a slip of paper he had plucked from his breast pocket. The answer was correct. His grandson had worked it out the night before on a pocket calculator. He had given the boy the gadget as a Chanukah gift. His mouth nevertheless drew tight.

"Mind if we do another one?" he asked anxiously.

Mr. McManus shook his head. His face remained immobile.

"What are the factors of 36,083?"

"None," said Mr. McManus irritably. The glaze vanished from his eyes, and he squinted angrily at Billy. "Is this what you got me up for?" His voice was gaining strength. "To do vaudeville routines?"

Mr. McManus had one of those minds that could execute incredible mathematical exercises in mere fragments of time. Once, while waiting for baseball season to begin, he had performed as "The Amazing Dr. Kauntem Ahgin" on a bill headlined by Sophie Tucker at Loew's State. The act failed. Mr. McManus lacked stage presence and the producer canceled him after three nights.

Billy's face fell. It was what he had been afraid of. The heart attack had damaged the Kid's brain. It happens when you get to be his—our—age, he thought sadly. He stuck the slip of paper back into his pocket. He fingered his half-moon glasses.

"I said the answer is none," Mr. McManus repeated through clenched teeth. The quaver in his voice had receded.

"It's okay, Kid," said Billy patronizingly. "We'll have a nice drive.

Then I'll drop you off. Maybe we should call your guy, Dolan's kid, let him know you're okay. The rest can wait. No need to bother with it now."

"God damn it!" Mr. McManus shouted. "I said the answer is none. 36,083 is a prime number. Prime numbers don't have factors, you moron!"

Billy swiftly withdrew the slip of paper again. "What's 2 to the 42nd power plus 1?" he demanded.

"4,294,967,297," Mr. McManus shot back. "That's not a prime number, *either*." They approached Fifth Avenue. The downtown vista was strung overhead with holiday lights. Through the snow they looked like muted pastel buttons. "You get it by multiplying 6,700,417 by 641." He sank back in his seat. "You know what you can do with that piece of paper. Now, for Christ's sake, will you tell me what's doing?"

Billy studied him over his half-moon glasses. His original evaluation might be off, he decided. The Kid's brain seemed okay. Still . . .

The brake lights flashed on the car ahead of them. The horses rigged to the hansom cabs across from the Plaza snorted moisture.

"See those lights?" Mr. McManus pointed a gloved finger at the car ahead. "Light travels at 186,000 miles a second. It takes 36,918 wavelengths of light to give the impression of red. You know how many wavelengths have to hit the human eye for you to see red?"

Billy looked at him in wonder. His doubts were fading.

"444,433,651,200,000," Mr. McManus said triumphantly and stripped off his gloves. "*Now* will you tell me what's doing?" He pulled a cigar from beneath his heavy raincoat and lit it.

Billy removed his glasses. His misgivings dissolved. If the Kid had survived with his preternatural computing faculties intact, the rest of his mind must be all right, too. "Turn up Madison," he ordered the driver through the intercom phone. He switched off the instrument and lit a cigar of his own.

"I had a call last night," he said between puffs. An apartment building of Edwardian design with bronze lampposts slipped by on the right. The snow accentuated its age. The traffic thinned as they drove farther uptown. City trucks were spreading salt on the streets. "Some people want to use the bank."

A number of years ago Mr. McManus and Nathan Leitstein had obtained a license to operate a small bank in Switzerland. They often had occasion to deposit, withdraw, and conduct other transactions on extremely short notice. The speed—and profound discretion—they needed was frequently illegal at banks in their own country. Their bank was called the Commercial and Claims Bank. It was located in Basel. The managing director was Herr Lemmer, a cautious man with the gloomy, distant look of an unsuccessful priest. Mr. McManus tolerantly suspected him of narcotics addiction.

"So?" Mr. McManus wished Billy would get to the point. "It's a bank. Anybody with money can use it. Something wrong with the money?"

"I can't say."

"Why not?"

"There's so much of it."

"How much?"

"A hundred and fifteen million." Billy sighed and added, "Dollars. Which, when you smooth it out, is a lot of money."

Mr. McManus's eyes came into total focus, as they had when he watched Billy's *Doppelgänger* unloading the truck outside the candy store. "Whose money is it? Where'd it come from?"

Billy took a thoughtful puff on his cigar. "I don't know whose money it is." There was a trace of hesitation in his deep voice. "But the guy who asked is an Israeli. He does a lot with Israel Bonds. He said 'we' a lot, so I don't think he was talking just for himself. He called from Jerusalem. Things are pretty screwed up over there, you know. By the way," he added, his voice rising to a point just above the chest register, as if he were gripped by some psychological crisis he was unwilling to acknowledge, "he's already been in touch with Lemmer."

Mr. McManus's expression relapsed into vagueness. But his mind was popping with questions. Why, he wanted to know—but dared not ask Billy's opinion at this time, for a number of long-standing reasons—did an Israeli take the trouble to look him over not a half hour earlier? Why did an Israeli from Jerusalem, who wasn't "talking just for himself," want to put more than a hundred million dollars in their Swiss bank, and where did he get the balls to approach Herr Lemmer with that kind of deal without checking first with him or Billy?

"Give me the scoop," Mr. McManus mumbled. His face remained a blank.

"What should I tell him?" Billy asked with decidedly strained nonchalance. "The guy who called." Then suddenly he blurted out,

"Lemmer's in town. He got in late last night. After I got the call from Jerusalem. He called from the airport. He sounded scared. Scared shitless. He said he didn't want to make a move until he talked it over with me. With us, I mean. I didn't have a clue he was here until he called. I swear I didn't."

Mr. McManus inclined his head toward Billy. Had he been fit, he would have sneered and cursed Billy for trying to pull a fast one. As it was, he conserved his energy and smiled crookedly. "Where is he?"

"At the apartment."

"Let's speak to him."

Twenty minutes later they were in a small but comfortable apartment near the top of a fortresslike complex in the low Thirties a block or two from the East River.

"The coffee will be ready in a few moments," said Herr Lemmer. He was a lean man with an apprehensive air that made him cheerless in almost any setting. He conveyed the impression of a butler pressed into service while his employer was on vacation and forced to render service to guests whom he disliked. The apartment, in fact, was owned by Nathan Leitstein, who maintained it as a *pied-à-terre*.

"You ever done business before with this guy?" asked Mr. McManus. "The guy who called you?" He was seated on a low sofa next to Nathan Leitstein. Herr Lemmer had taken their hats and coats with melancholy courtesy when they arrived.

"Not to my knowledge," replied Herr Lemmer, taking a seat opposite them. His tone was petulant. His pinched face betrayed a lack of sleep. Outside the window behind him the snow was falling harder. "A cursory review of the records turned up no trace of the man's name. Only his mention of Mr. Leitstein as a reference disposed me to entertain further discussion of his proposal. I should point out that we in Switzerland have vivid memories of the scandal a number of years ago occasioned by transactions initiated by citizens of the state of Israel. If you will recall—"

"The bank that got burned," Mr. McManus interrupted, "we all remember that."

"Ruined, sir," said Herr Lemmer balefully. "Ruined."

Nathan Leitstein leaned forward and placed his palms on his knees. "Any reason we shouldn't take the money?"

Mr. McManus listened closely. He thought he detected a nuance, a smugness perhaps, that implied Billy Light could answer his own question.

Herr Lemmer put his hands together and touched his chin. "The proposal raised a number of questions," he said sadly. "Questions that I believed would have been indiscreet to moot on the telephone. That is the reason for my visit."

"Is the money hard or soft?" Mr. McManus was impatient. He knew Herr Lemmer was stalling, but he could not understand why Billy Light had portrayed him as panic-stricken. Apart from the fact that he was here and not behind his desk in Basel, Herr Lemmer was in every respect the steady, unadventurous banker Mr. McManus had always known him to be.

"I have no way of knowing," Herr Lemmer replied, as if he had been asked whether the fruit in a nearby bowl were ripe or green; those who wanted to know such things would have to find out for themselves; he did not eat fruit; it was an irrelevant question.

"Then let's take it," said Mr. McManus. "Tell the guy who called that you're expecting the money. But accept it only as a time deposit. Let's see. At 2 percent on a hundred and fifteen million over three months that's—"

Nathan Leitstein frowned but kept silent.

"He is not interested in a time deposit," Herr Lemmer put in curtly.

"What's wrong with a time deposit?"

"The gentleman who telephoned asked for a special account. He was emphatic on the point."

Mr. McManus's bushy brows knitted. "You can't put dollars in a special account. Not even a hundred and fifteen million of them."

Herr Lemmer folded his arms across his chest. "The gentleman proposed to leave the money in the account for one day and then withdraw it. At which point it would be brought here."

"Here? To New York?" Mr. McManus made no effort to conceal his astonishment. "He told you where the money would be going? How the hell do they—whoever 'they' are—think they can move that much cash? In one day?"

"They are willing to pay an extraordinary commission." There was a trace of defensiveness in Herr Lemmer's voice. "In addition to the normal interest, of course. Frankly that was my paramount consideration."

"An extraordinary commission?" Mr. McManus lit a cigar. "How extraordinary?"

"Seven hundred and fifty thousand dollars to the bank," Herr

Lemmer replied at once, "and two hundred and fifty thousand dollars each to you and Mr. Leitstein."

"How much for you?"

"That, naturally, must be decided by you and Mr. Leitstein."

A soft ring emanated from the kitchen. It was the electric timer attached to the coffeepot.

"Excuse me, gentlemen," said Herr Lemmer. He rose and left the room.

Nathan Leitstein shifted and glared at Mr. McManus. "What if it is cash?" he said in an angry stage whisper. "Who cares how they move it? I don't *want* to know. What about those God damned commissions? That's all that counts with me."

"What the hell's wrong with you?" snapped Mr. McManus. His eyes blazed with contempt and binomial certainty. "You're thinking like Lemmer, looking for a cheap way to get your laundry done free." His face broke into a half smile. "Don't be mean to yourself. What do those commissions add up to? When you think about *all* of it? Think about it, Billy, for Christ's sake. One hundred and fifteen million iron men. That's what's up for grabs. I say to hell with the seven hundred and fifty thousand for the bank. I say to hell with the two hundred and fifty grand apiece for me and you. It's just juice we don't have to squeeze. I say let's take a shot at the big one."

Nathan Leitstein stiffened a moment and then relaxed and brightened. He clucked and shook his head. "Kid, I swear to God, not only can you draw a bead on something nobody else can see, you can *hit it*."

Mr. McManus grinned slyly and puffed his cigar. "Like a guy who can rewrap a new shirt and not have any straight pins left over?" He wanted to make certain Billy understood he wasn't taken in by flattery.

Nathan Leitstein shrugged. He understood.

"I'll get Lemmer off the hook, right?"

Nathan Leitstein nodded.

Herr Lemmer reappeared. He was carrying a tray laden with cups and a carafe of coffee. He poured and distributed the cups and resumed his seat.

"We had a chat, me and Mr. Leitstein, while you was out," Mr. McManus began; he ignored his coffee, "and here's what we decided. The deal sounds good, but it's too flashy. Somebody's bound to notice that much dough moving into one place and out of it the next day. If somebody notices, they'll start asking questions. A couple of back numbers like us are too old to be answering a lot of questions. From the Swiss or the feds. Got me?"

"I understand," replied Herr Lemmer in a tone of sorrow of the sort heard from a factory owner who locks out his workers in the belief that they will make trouble when he announces a wage cut.

They talked at some length about the difficulties that lay in store for depositors—and bankers—who played recklessly with discretionary accounts in Swiss banks.

"What you do," Mr. McManus said finally, "is get on the phone to the bank. Tell your people to tell the guy who called, the Israeli, to get lost. But tell him polite. And tell them to keep quiet about the whole thing." He looked at Nathan Leitstein. "Have I skipped anything?"

Nathan Leitstein shook his head.

"We'd better get going," said Mr. McManus, rising laboriously to his feet. "Thanks for taking the time to fly over. I'd like to stick around for a while, but I'm still on the mend. There'll be something for you. For the trouble you went to. Me and Mr. Leitstein will show our appreciation. Like always. Have a nice trip back to Basel."

Herr Lemmer saw them to the door. He gave them their hats and helped them with their coats and shook their hands. His outlook had improved a fraction at the news that he would receive a bonus for his pains despite his conviction that his employers had denied themselves a mellow opportunity to interpret the Swiss banking law creatively and make a considerable amount of money. He let them out and went straightaway to the telephone.

In the elevator Mr. McManus said to Nathan Leitstein, "Get in touch with your guy in Jerusalem. It's probably the same guy who called Lemmer. Tell him the deal's off with the bank. Thanks but no thanks. Something like that. String him along. Try and make him drop a hint on how else the money might be moved."

"They got a habit of gilding the pill, these Israelis." Nathan Leitstein's face constricted a trifle. "They talk and talk about one thing and all the time they mean something else."

"Look." Mr. McManus leaned against the elevator wall. "Let him know we get the idea. We figure him and his people was using this bank quickie to put the shake on us, right? To get us parked outside and then suck us in. Tell him we're extremely wide open to a proposition. Let it slip, if you have to, that we know his bloop to

Lemmer was highly irregular to say the least, and if word of it got to certain authorities he would have a damned tough time ever cashing another check in Switzerland. But don't lean on him. Don't scare him. Give him a fact or two and let him figure it out. We got to let him know we're ready to play. And we want his money out in the open where we can see it."

The elevator deposited them at the enormous glass-fronted ground floor.

They drove up First Avenue. Mr. McManus was nearly exhausted. He slumped against the seat and closed his eyes. Nathan Leitstein told the driver to turn west on Ninety-sixth Street and then said, "I'll call him first thing I drop you off." He looked at his wristwatch. "I'll be in touch the minute I get word."

The snow was dense and beginning to drift in the rising wind. The car made its way slowly along the winding, trenchlike transverse road through Central Park. They emerged on Central Park West and turned south. Traffic was clogged. It wasn't only because of the snow.

"No," said Mr. McManus wearily. "I'll give you a call. In an hour. I got to lie down. Rest for a while. You be at 1407?" Billy nodded. They were within a few blocks of Mr. McManus's apartment building. "First day on my feet, you know." Billy nodded again.

In the distance the dull glow of pulsing colored lights was visible. As they drew nearer it became apparent that the lights were atop a dozen or so police radio cars. The sound of a Klaxon could be heard. An ambulance was maneuvering its way from the other direction as rapidly as the chaotic traffic and heavy snow would allow.

The turmoil turned out to be immediately across the street from Mr. McManus's building. There was a huge crowd of curiosity seekers. At least half the police on hand were engaged in restraining them. Mr. McManus noticed that his doorman and elevator attendant were on the fringe, tiptoeing for a peek at what happened.

Mr. McManus reminded Billy that he would telephone in an hour. He allowed the driver to open the door for him. As the car pulled away he let his cigar fall into the dark slush at the curb. He stepped up to a burly uniformed policeman who was part of the crowd-control detail.

"What's going on?" he asked. He clutched his muffler to his throat.

The policeman was a good foot taller than Mr. McManus. He looked down at the pale, shrunken man. "Nothing to worry about, Pop."

Mr. McManus gritted his teeth. He felt his chest tighten for a fraction of a second. "Did I say there was anything to worry about?" he snapped. "I live in this building. I want to know what the hell is going on across the street from where I live."

The policeman was disconcerted. He had noted the Rolls Royce that dropped this little guy, driver holding the door. He glanced over his shoulder at the building. It was old and elegant. Like this little guy. It was obvious to him that only people of affluence lived there. Possibly people with clout downtown. This little guy might be one of them.

"Guy shot across the street," the policeman said crisply and added, just in case, "a kid really, young blond guy on his way to work. Hole in him like this." He made a wide thumb-and-forefinger circle. "I just got here. The call said he was hit by a rifle from a moving vehicle."

Mr. McManus remembered the newspaper on the floor of Billy Light's limousine. "The 'elephant gun' character?"

"Could be," answered the policeman. "If it was, it was his first time in daylight."

Across the street ambulance attendants worked to strap the victim onto a stretcher. Television crews and newspaper reporters rushed forward, multiplying the confusion. Oozing blood discolored the snow.

Mr. McManus grunted a word of thanks. He eased his way through the spectators who were vying for vantage points under the canopy at his building entrance.

Muttered speculation had it that the "elephant gun killer" was a crazed black. "After all," said an indignant white woman in the shoulder-to-shoulder mob on the steps, "he signs those God damned notes 'Finger of God,' doesn't he? It sounds just like something they say in those churches up in Harlem."

A middle-aged black man who was almost at her elbow took exception to this statement. A vehement argument broke out between them over the merits of racial grievances. It ended when the black man declared, "You never been to a church in Harlem in your life!"

The lobby was deserted. Mr. McManus sat down across from the nonworking fireplace and peeled off his gloves to await the elevator attendant. He was breathing effortlessly, but he was worried about incontinence. It had been more than two hours since he urinated. He was growing gloomy at the thought of wetting himself. That would be unendurable.

To take his mind off his bladder he thought about his family. He decided he was strong enough for the trip to Florida. And the rigors of Christmas celebration. Airline reservations would be a headache. He would have Freddie get on it the minute he got upstairs. He supposed he would have to take Freddie along. The problem was how to keep Freddie away from his family. He absolutely would not tolerate Freddie at his family's table for Christmas dinner. . . .

He felt a hand on his shoulder. He looked up and saw a stranger. A man no larger than himself but ages younger, with close-cropped red hair and one hand in a pocket of his overcoat.

Mr. McManus surmised he had been hiding in one of the small nooks off the lobby. Perhaps the one where the doorman concealed his pint of rye.

"Would you be so kind as to accompany me to the lift, sir?" said the man in an accent Mr. McManus couldn't place. Australia? Scotland? With his free hand he grasped him by the elbow to raise him to his feet. Mr. McManus knew better than to try and resist.

The small stranger operated the elevator lever. Halfway up he took his hand from his pocket and displayed a Mauser HSc seven-round .32 caliber automatic. He leveled it at Mr. McManus. His ruddy outdoors face was impassive.

The elevator opened opposite Mr. McManus's apartment, which occupied the entire wing of the building. The door was open. Down the long hallway, in the living room where he had stood anticipating his "glorious day," he could see seven men. All but one were white. They wore jackets and ties. The single black man was dressed in work clothes. What appeared to be a toolbox was at his feet.

One of them was at the window. He was watching the activity fourteen floors below. He had a deep Mediterranean complexion. He remarked that the police were interviewing witnesses.

Sprawled legs forward on the huge sofa were Freddie Dee and a young woman. They were stark naked and bound hand and foot and gagged with adhesive tape. Mr. McManus guessed that Freddie had had the woman in his room overnight. One of Freddie's eyes was eggplant purple and swollen shut.

The small stranger nudged Mr. McManus in the kidney with his Mauser. He trudged into the apartment.

The intruders were standing at near attention. Three or four of them shot occasional glances at the nude woman. They curled their lips in tight vicious smirks.

Not the black man. He looked straight ahead. His heavy-lidded eyes were fixed on something—anything—elsewhere in the room.

The swarthy man at the window turned briefly. He gestured with two extended fingers. Index and middle. One of the others detached himself to return the elevator to the lobby. He did not reappear.

A short, stocky man with a roast-beef face and bristly, granite-gray hair stepped forward.

"Sit down," he snarled at Mr. McManus and motioned peremptorily toward a chair by the sofa. "Please," he added, modifying his tone to thick, unctuous menace. Then he jerked his head toward the man with the pistol.

"Put away your *houtieslayer*, Piet," he commanded in the same unaccountable accent. "Now!" The red-haired man nodded stiffly and slipped the weapon inside his overcoat.

Mr. McManus ignored the squat man. He sat in a chair against the other wall. The toilet was next door. He feared he would have to go at any minute. He would not have sat where he was told, anyway. He had reached the point in life where he was extremely hard to frighten. These men might kill him, but they would not scare him to death.

Then fury overtook him. Here he sat, he thought, enraged, marched into his own apartment with a gun at his back, in his heavy raincoat, with his hat still on, for Christ's sake. He was even holding his God damned umbrella. Which he promptly flung to the floor.

"What's doing?" he shouted. He tossed off his hat and squirmed out of his raincoat. He glared at the man with the roast-beef face. "I said, what the fuck is doing?"

The veins bulged in the squat man's forehead. The nostrils of his flat nose flared. Otherwise he did not move.

"Look!" Mr. McManus continued to shout. "I don't know what you hooples want. But if you want it from me, you'd better tell me what's doing. Fast. There's no telling how much time I have. I'm sure you know that. Besides"—he got up slowly and put his hand on the door to the toilet—"I have to piss."

The others lunged a half step in his direction but halted as the squat man raised one palm to the level of his granite-gray temple.

"When I come out," said Mr. McManus; he opened the door, "I want to know which one of you hooples was in touch with Nat Leitstein. And which one talked to my bank." Then he looked narrowly at the squat man. "I want them"—he pointed with his free hand at the nude forms of Freddie Dee and the woman—"untied, fully clothed, and on their feet. Where I can see them without straining my eyes."

He was closing the toilet door when he felt someone gently shove in behind him. It was the black man.

"Jesus," he muttered. The black man eased the door shut. "Is taking a leak in private too much to ask?"

"*Ekskuus, baas.*" The black man took up a position that allowed him a view of Mr. McManus's face in the medicine-chest mirror. He wore an enormous wristwatch, which he touched continuously with his other hand.

"What?" Mr. McManus was mystified. Was this man speaking a language or just making a noise? "You say something to me?"

"I'm sorry, my *baas*, sir," came the deep, monotonous reply. "Orders. I'm to stay with you until you have relieved yourself. Major Espensheid's orders." He sounded self-conscious and abjectly apologetic. His voice made a click sound at the end of certain syllables.

Mr. McManus unzipped his fly and began the process of relaxing until his waste fluid flowed freely. It took time. At last his urine spattered in the bowl. He tried to place "Major Espensheid" in the framework of the morning's events—the call from Billy Light; the poorly dressed Israeli who scrutinized him in the candy store; the word from Herr Lemmer that somebody wanted to store a hundred and fifteen million dollars in their Swiss bank and bring it to New York the next day; the daylight murder in front of his building; the stranger who held the automatic on him.

He shook himself and rezipped. He resolved as he washed and dried his hands to have this Major Espenwhatsit make some God damned sense out of this. He glanced over his shoulder. He noticed that the black man was unarmed. He also noticed that the man was totally ill at ease.

"Boo," he said. The black man gave a start. Mr. McManus noticed that, too. This guy is scared to death of white men, he realized, even a shaky old codger like me. He was amazed. He hadn't seen that in years.

"I'm done, snowball," he said. Mr. McManus never employed racial slurs except for effect. He was one of those exceptional North American white men who managed to avoid racial prejudice without abandoning his eye and ear for racial differences. In this case, since the black man was not carrying a weapon and virtually trembling, he figured that anything he did to worsen the state of the man's already wretched nerves would be to his advantage—one less threat to worry about, since the white men did not seem so fainthearted.

He turned and faced the black man. "Open it," he ordered.

The black man moved swiftly, instinctively, and whipped open the door. He did a half bow as Mr. McManus toddled out, and returned to his spot by his toolbox.

Mr. McManus sat down heavily on the chair outside the toilet. He still did not fully trust his bladder.

Freddie Dee and the woman were unbound and ungagged and seated side by side on the sofa. Freddie had on trousers and a T-shirt; tufts of jet black hair sprouted from the neck. The woman wore jeans and a sweater; she was blond and, it turned out, had a delicately beautiful face; she was smoking anxiously. Both were shoeless.

The man with the short red hair was behind the sofa. He held his *houtieslayer* at the back of Freddie's neck. The squat man— presumably, Mr. McManus thought, Major Espensheid—was standing over the woman. His pouchy face was drawn in contempt.

"I will not be insulted," he cried in his barely intelligible accent. "Only a *sedelose vrou* smokes . . . cigarettes. I will not have it in my presence!"

"What in hell are you talking about?" The woman hunched her shoulders and sucked her cigarette.

More accented English, Mr. McManus noted.

"He is telling you that only women of loose morals smoke cigarettes. He is offended. Deeply offended." This from the swarthy man at the window. He spoke in dispassionate tones. His English, too, was accented but easily understood, like the woman's.

The squat man shook with rage. "Stamp it out this instant!" he shouted; his red face glowed. "Do you hear?"

The woman drew her arms across her breasts and took in inconclusive puff. She tilted her fine-boned face toward the squat man. "Fuck yourself, *nebbish*."

The squat man seized the cigarette. He was about to hit the woman with the back of his sunburned hand when the sound of sirens and Klaxons penetrated the room. Everyone except Freddie, the woman, and Mr. McManus jerked his head toward the window.

"They're leaving," said the swarthy man, holding back a curtain, "the ambulance, the police, the journalists. Everyone."

He strode to the center of the room and looked around him. He gestured with two fingers to the man behind the sofa, who brusquely reholstered his automatic; then to the squat man, who stepped back and clasped his hands behind him. The others relaxed a fraction too.

He turned to Mr. McManus.

"We are businessmen." He was taller than the others, and exuded self-possession. "I apologize for the circumstances of our introduction. We wanted to impress you. To make certain that you understand we are serious. Serious businessmen. Our information is that you have exceptional qualifications in the realm of speculative ventures. Is that correct?"

"What business are you in?" Mr. McManus looked at him dubiously and concluded he was witnessing a second-rate Mutt-and-Jeff game (a police tactic to obtain cooperation; a suspect is first threatened with violence and then offered coffee and doughnuts as a token that the detectives are honorable and have his interests at heart). He did not believe for an instant that these men were genuinely connected with business.

"We are primarily investors. For what we believe to be a singularly generous arrangement we wish to engage your services for—"

"I'm no stockbroker," Mr. McManus interrupted calmly. He lit a cigar. "I can put you in touch with several. The best money can buy. They'd be happy as hell to get their hands on your arrangement. But before I turn you down flat, I want to know who called Nat Leitstein. I want to know who called my bank and who wants to hide all that money in it."

"Make this *dwaser ouman* understand he is to answer questions, not ask them." This was the squat man. He was bouncing heel-to-toe. "Or shall I do it?" He bared his teeth and ground a bulky fist into his other palm. The swarthy man shot him a hard glance, and, after a moment, he dropped his hands.

"Mr. Leitstein was contacted by one of our associates," the swarthy man went on. "The same with your Herr Lemmer. Because of the amount of money involved, we anticipated that he might be hesitant. We also anticipated that you might be hesitant. We know of your reputation for caution. We thought it best to visit you personally. To see if an accommodation might be reached. My colleagues and I operate on the theory that habits can be suspended for a time for the right price and the right proposition."

Mr. McManus exhaled a gust of smoke and decided against disclosing that the money—was it the same money?—would be turned down by the Commercial and Claims Bank. He studied his cigar. He had to hand it to this guy—he's primed. At length he said, "I've heard a couple of figures. Seven hundred and fifty grand. Two hundred and fifty. What habits would I have to break to get that?"

"Perhaps I should not have suggested that we want you to break your habits. On the contrary what we wish—and are willing to pay handsomely for—is an adventurous, somewhat unorthodox use of your expertise."

Mr. McManus sighed and glanced at Freddie Dee. He knew Freddie wasn't too sharp—the kid's father had told him so—but he had no idea he was stupid enough to allow these gorillas past the front door. Freddie had put up a fight (his swollen eye vouched for that), but that, to Mr. McManus, magnified his brainlessness. Probably humping the bimbo when the bell rang and rushed to the door without thinking—about anything—he concluded and gave Freddie a disgusted look.

He turned back to the swarthy man. "What's the deal?"

The swarthy man smiled complacently. "The deal, as you call it, depends on whether you agree to participate. Without your agreement there is no deal."

Mr. McManus felt the blood rush to his pallid cheeks. "Deal?" he shouted angrily. "I don't know how you hooples are used to doing business. But I don't do business unless I know what's doing. Got me? I know what's doing—I mean everything—or I don't make deals. I don't even discuss deals." He rose slowly. He got an ashtray and returned to his chair. "Especially I don't discuss deals with a bunch of hooples that bust into my apartment packing heat and spread my people out buck naked in broad daylight. Hooples that slap people around and don't take the trouble to introduce themselves." He crushed his cigar in the ashtray and set it on the floor. Outside the snow had eased and the light had broadened to a leaden glare. "I don't know where you hooples come from. Wherever it is, they don't teach you much manners."

The swarthy man pointed two fingers at one of the others, who snapped open an attaché case and withdrew a cream-colored folder. The swarthy man took it and handed it to Mr. McManus.

"Read this," he said sharply. "When you've finished, I think you'll be in a position to reevaluate your stubbornness."

He folded his arms and added smugly, "It's rather long, but, I think, comprehensive. I'm sure you will find it interesting. I did. If you begin to tire, I'll read aloud. There are sections I enjoy immensely."

Mr. McManus opened the folder. He looked at the cover page. There were two short paragraphs. The top one he recognized as Hebrew. The other was in a language he couldn't identify. He guessed both said the same thing.

He licked his index finger and turned to page two. It was in English. Across the top was the legend, LEITSTEIN/McMANUS.

It was, as the man said, interesting.

Jackie Dolan sat in the bleak, unheated kitchen of a ground-floor apartment in the Flatbush section of Brooklyn. He squeezed a lumpy pimple on his pitted cheek and stared at the heavy rifle. He should have cleaned it by now. The unyielding pimple preoccupied him. He was sick to death of cleaning the rifle every time he fired it. The Jew demanded it. The Jew would be there any minute. Just like always. Even though it was snowing sideways.

He was afraid of the Jew. The Jew was as big as a bear and, Jackie did not doubt, just as mean.

Abruptly he gave the pimple a rough, hopeless rub and lifted the rifle from the table. It took some effort. It was a custom-built .375 H&H magnum mounted on an old FN Mauser action. It weighed more than twelve pounds.

His hands were numb and hard from the cold. He tried to detect signs of rust. That was what the Jew looked for first. Rust.

He couldn't concentrate. He glanced desperately at the litter of steel wool, cotton patches, and tiny oil cans. He looked for the cleaning rod.

Where was the God damned cleaning rod?

He jerked his head about the room, once even at the ceiling. Forlornly, he forced back the bolt. He eyed the empty chamber. His hands began to shake. "Fuck it," he said aloud nearly dropping the rifle, and pushed back from the table.

The refrigerator contained nothing but a few cans of beer. Jackie popped one open. He took a deep gulp as he dragged himself into the living room.

It was small and bare except for the mattress he slept on and the arbor press he used for reloading cartridges. Cartons of bullets, patching paper, and powder were scattered about. A pharmaceutical cylinder of amphetamine tablets lay nearby. A fifth of rye, half empty, stood at the head of the mattress.

He sloshed two fingers into a glass and tossed it back with a shudder. He chased it sloppily with beer and plopped his bony body cross-legged onto the mattress. He was about to resume his pimple squeezing—he would be forty the day after Christmas and had more acne than when he was twelve, he reflected bitterly—when the familiar bolt of pain riveted his right shoulder. It was recoil sensitive from firing the H&H one-handed from a car window.

The apartment was intensely cold. The Jew had promised to buy fuel but hadn't, Jackie brooded and had more to drink. He had promised to at least buy an electric heater, but he hadn't done that, either . . .

". . . You'll be back with your stick in Ovamboland before you really begin to notice the cold," the Jew had told him three months ago. "What does it matter to a troopie like you, slotting *houts* in America or along the Kunene River? Members of Uitmoormag understand they must accept unusual assignments, do they not?"

"Sure," Jackie replied immediately. He was sipping a bottle of chibooli beer in a shed at the Grootfontein airstrip. He had just stepped off the Dakota. He managed to mask his exhilaration. At last he had a sense of *belonging*.

The feeling came over him that morning when Major Espensheid himself flew to the forward base at Ruacana Falls to summon him. Major Espensheid was a member of Special Branch with duties related to the Bureau of State Security; he also was commander of Uitmoormag. He accompanied Jackie on the flight from the operational area but remained silent after introducing him to Captain Zanin.

What turned the trick, although Jackie lacked the imagination to perceive it, was the language. He was gladdened almost to tears when Captain Zanin addressed him in English. It wasn't American English, but it was English.

Jackie had been in South Africa for four years, three in the army, but scarcely spoke or understood a word of Afrikaans. In the army (the *Verdedigingsmag*, the Defense Force, he was constantly reminded) he caught on quickly that to speak English was to be identified as a *rooinek*, a "Brit," a species of human hardly more tolerable, to an Afrikaaner, than a Kaffir.

He felt excluded, nearly repudiated, when he was posted to Uitmoormag. It was an odd lot of old soldiers from former French,

Belgian, and Portuguese colonies. They were able to speak to each other in any number of languages, and they easily understood the Afrikaaner officers. Jackie was the single American. He was roughly the same age as his fellow Uitmoor troopies. But he wasn't an old soldier.

Jackie was assigned to Uitmoormag because he was one of nature's necessary fools. He came to South Africa because he had heard it was a white man's paradise. The immigration authorities told him that the computer technology he had learned in the U.S. Air Force would land him a secure job. With his savings he bought a modest, pitched-roof house in Alberton. He was hired by an electronics factory, and he and his wife applied for citizenship. They enrolled their sons in an Afrikaans-speaking school, acquired two Bantu servants, and, as a final act of conformity, renounced Roman Catholicism for the mathematically ruthless theology of the Dutch Reformed Church. Jackie advanced to assistant foreman at his job and believed he was in the manager's favor —when one day, after eight months and no warning, his place was given to a young Afrikaaner who had completed a training course in West Germany. Jackie was dis-illusioned for a time, but rather than go on the dole (he believed a white man had no business accepting public charity), he joined the army.

The army. It had been Jackie's secret dream as long as he could remember. Not any army. A special army. A daring, dedicated, tough army. An army with a mission. A *white man's army!*

"A bit long in the tooth for regular active service, aren't you, Mr. Dolan?" asked the dour recruiting officer, mercifully in English. "Training's extremely difficult. You understood I said active service?"

"That's what I'm looking for. Active service," Jackie replied solemnly and added with a grin, "I always wanted to take a shot at a nigger."

The recruiting officer, a reservist, pulled a face; it had nothing to do with the racial views he strongly shared with the pimply, unem-ployed man before him; he knew the fate of men such as Private Soldier Dolan; he had no use for men who joined the army for a purpose.

Jackie was transported by bus with a batch of younger men, all on the two-year intake, to a base near Pretoria. His wife agreed it was the best thing. After preliminary training, which he found not as "extremely difficult" as the recruiting officer had warned, he volunteered for the Special Action organization. For the extra pay.

Special Action training was unique. He thought it would devastate him. He mastered all the weapons—it was natural enough; he had belonged to a gun club for years—but the physical rigors were excruciating. He couldn't run fast enough, board a hovering helicopter fast enough, or react fast enough in unarmed combat. Worse, since the commands were delivered in Afrikaans, he couldn't understand fast enough. At the end of the course everyone but Jackie was sent to Israel for parachute training—and he was handed over to Uitmoormag.

Uitmoormag (Slaughter Force in English) was known in the Defense Force as the "hobo regiment." Its hardened, disreputable foreigners could as easily have been in prison as in the army. In their first action—to Jackie's astonishment, in support of an irregular formation of blacks in the Angolan war—one troopie, a Belgian, was flogged across the small of the back with a cane. He had drawn a knife on an officer who ordered him over a footbridge believed to be mined.

In an "antiguerrilla" operation in Rhodesia they were laughed at by a black unit. "You never nail a terr like that, slope," an Ndebele sergeant of the African Rifles admonished Jackie after warning him to make less noise in the bush. Earlier in the day, the sergeant cautioned him against dabbing water from a stream on his face. "That water full of the *bilharz*. Get in those sores on your face, kill you before sundown. Whyn't you crunchies get back downsouth, look after your own? Think you can kill Africans better than we can? Hah! We been killing each other for a thousand years. . . . Go off on a spot of leave. Have a taste of mother's best graze. But steer away from the flat dogs."

"The flat dogs?" Jackie was bewildered.

"Crocodiles, crunchie!" the black sergeant howled.

For political reasons unfathomable to Jackie the South Africans pulled out of Rhodesia. Uitmoormag bivouacked near Ruacana Falls in South-West Africa. They made daily forays across the frontier into Angola; they were told that the Ambo tribesmen might be SWAPO partisans intent on blowing up the hydroelectric dam. The day Major Espensheid arrived to fetch Jackie, the men had surrounded an Ambo village thought to be infected with cholera and infiltrated by Cubans. Their orders were to shoot anyone who tried to leave. Medical help was not expected.

". . . It's a joint operation," Captain Zanin was saying in the airstrip shed at Grootfontein. "All aspects compartmentalized. That means you know only what you're told and do only as you're ordered. Orders will come from me and me only. Is that understood?"

"Yes, sir," Jackie answered crisply.

"Do you know why you were chosen, Dolan?"

Chosen. He, Jackie Dolan, had been chosen. "No, sir," he said in a near whisper.

"Because you were reared in America. New York City. Would you say you are acquainted with New York City? All of New York City, the public buildings, the traffic arteries, the subways, everything?"

"Yes, sir!" Jackie cried. "I come from Cannon Heights—that's in the Bronx; it's my old neighborhood. The folks moved to Bay Ridge—that's in Brooklyn—after my old man retired from the department. My grandpa lived in Inwood—that's in Manhattan. Me and my wife lived in Middle Village—that's in Queens—before we came here. To Alberton, I mean. My brother, Freddie, he used to live in Staten Island. He's in California, now, Freddie, and he would—"

"Read this, Dolan." It was Major Espensheid, speaking in English for the first time Jackie could remember. He had been slapping his thigh with a rolled-up newspaper. He popped it into Jackie's hand and left the shed.

The newspaper was English-language. Jackie read.

The general strike by blacks throughout South Africa was in its sixth week . . . the mining industry had nearly closed down . . . the bottom had fallen out of South African gold stocks . . . manufacturing plants were running at 20 percent capapcity . . . foreign investment was down 80 percent . . . drought threatened crop devastation . . . mass arrests and numerous executions had had no effect on black resistance . . . bombings occurred daily . . . the police were author- ized to open fire on any assembly of more than three black males regardless of the circumstances . . . the prime minister had been given war powers; he said there was absolutely no doubt that the disorder was communist inspired . . . cabinet ministers were quoted; in sum, they said: Every measure necessary, no matter how harsh, would be applied to break the back of the "revolution" and restore the peace and prosperity of Afrikaanerdom.

Major Espensheid returned. He carried an enormous rifle mount- ed with an expensive scope. He handed it to Jackie and retrieved his newspaper.

"We're at war." He slapped the front page with the back of his thick hand. "Make no mistake of it. The Kaffirs are making their bid. The Griquas, too. Of course, they will be stopped. *We* will stop them."

He flung the newspaper to the earthen floor. "That"—he pointed to the rifle— "will be waiting for you in the States. Of course, the scope will be removed. No need for that on this mission. You'll take special care of it, won't you, Dolan? It's from my personal collection."

"I'll make certain he does," Captain Zanin interjected sharply. . . .

And he did, Jackie thought dejectedly in the freezing apartment. That fucking Jew was worse than any Afrikaaner stick leader about cleaning weapons. Jackie blew on his hands and rose wearily from his mattress. He returned to the kitchen and began cleaning the rifle.

The whiskey and beer steadied his hands but did not ease his spirit. His hatred for Captain Zanin gnawed at him. That fucking Jew, that sheenie bastard, had lied to him. He had told him he could visit his brother, catch a couple of ball games. Then he had ordered him to stay in this rotten apartment until he was told otherwise. And the other lie. *That* was the worst. That fucking Jew.

What the hell, he thought as he reassembled the rifle, today was the last time. No more Captain Zanin after today, he sighed in alcoholic gloom.

He heard a key in the front door. Brisk footsteps and Captain Zanin appeared. He seemed to Jackie to increase in size each time he returned. He had a bag of hamburgers from a fast-food restaurant, which he set on the drainboard at the sink. He stamped the snow from his plain shoes. He seemed unaffected by the cold, although he was wearing only his habitual black raincoat over an old summer suit. His white shirt, as always, was open at the neck. He picked up the rifle and inspected it.

"Rust," he snapped. "There." He pointed to the trigger guard. "And there." A spot on the barrel. "Make smaller pads of steel wool. Use a finer grade of oil. Apply it liberally. And *rub*, Dolan!" Captain Zanin's English was more accented than on that scorching day at Grootfontein. "But don't be overzealous or you'll rub away the blueing. Your Major Espensheid wouldn't like that, would he?"

Jackie tried to make light of the demerit. "Okay, Captain." His speech was slurred. "Plenty of time, right? This was the last job, right? Want a beer?"

Captain Zanin braced himself in a fluid, authoritative motion. He placed his hands on his hips. "You are still operational, Dolan. You are still under my orders. My personal orders. There has been no stand-easy. Prepare the weapon for operational conditions."

"You said today was the last time," Jackie whimpered. "I was counting on that. You don't know what it's like, being laid up in this shit hole, going out only when you tell me. Going out and zapping a . . ."

He couldn't bring himself to say it.

"A white man?" Captain Zanin's bronze face beamed with contempt.

"Yes, God damn it! A white man!" Jackie fingered the raw pimple. He avoided Captain Zanin's eyes. "Today made six guys. Six white guys. *You lied to me!* You said it would be niggers."

He reached down and seized a day-old tabloid newspaper. The headline read, "Elephant Gun Killer?" Under it was a composite police sketch of a stern, round face with Negroid features.

"What the hell is this? It says witnesses told the cops the guy looks like this. It don't look nothing like me. It says the newspapers been getting letters signed by the 'Finger of God.' I haven't sent any letters to the newspapers or anybody else. What is this 'Finger of God' shit?"

"You must read up on your geography, Dolan," replied Captain Zanin sardonically, "if you want to be a good Afrikaaner. Finger of God is a rock formation north of Keetmanshoop. It is something of a tourist attraction. Like some of the sights in the Grand Canyon. Have you visited it? I have only seen photographs."

"The Finger of God?"

"The Grand Canyon."

"I never been anywhere except to Germany in the Air Force. I thought I was going to get out to California to see my brother." Jackie sounded bitter again. "Why can't I take a couple of days off? Fly out to see him? You said I could." He refrained from again saying that Captain Zanin lied to him; he was not at all sure how Captain Zanin would take it a second time. "Why not, for Christ's sake?"

"You have no money. Also you are still operational. This may be New York City, but for you it is merely an operational area. Besides"—Captain Zanin's tone was even more sarcastic— "it is possible that the police at any moment could receive a more accurate description of this murderer. They could receive it before you had a chance to board a plane. Do you understand?"

Jackie nodded. He swallowed hard to hold back tears.

"You are to remain here for further orders. In the meantime tend to Major Espensheid's weapon. And try not to poison yourself with the *bronfen*."

"The what?"

"The *bronfen*. The whiskey, Dolan," he mocked. "Cheer up. The next contact"—this was Captain Zanin's term for victim— "may be a *svartz*."

Jackie looked puzzled. He understood no more Yiddish than he did Afrikaans.

"A *svartz*, Dolan. You know, a *hout*, a Kaffir," Captain Zanin said from the kitchen doorway. "A nigger."

Jackie heard the door close and the lock turn. He squeezed angrily at his cheek. The pimple was the size of a small vegetable.

He looked without desire at the bag of hamburgers.

That fucking Jew, he thought, that Hebe.

He walked back to the living room. He hoisted the bottle of rye and took three violent, unchased pulls. Then he collapsed on the mattress.

How much do the cops really know? he wondered foggily.

He had a momentary urge to break discipline and try to find his old man. Jesus, old Charlie would be floored. He would ask him to call some old friends in the department to see if the bulls were close.

The urge passed. He lost consciousness.

2

Mr. McManus was suddenly weary. His chest constricted, and, oh God, did he feel it.

He felt in his jacket pocket for an aspirin tin that held several digitalis tablets. He told the swarthy man he wanted a glass of water and his slippers.

"My feet are wet," he said wheezily. "I don't want to catch cold on top of everything else."

The swarthy man signaled with his two-fingered gesture. One man disappeared and returned with a crystal goblet filled to the brim. Another followed with his slippers.

Mr. McManus downed the tablet and handed the stemmed glass to the swarthy man.

"Be damned careful with that," he said. He kicked off his shoes, removed his socks, and nestled his feet into his slippers. "My wife will have your ass if she comes back and finds one of those broken."

He waited until he was breathing again without pain. Then he returned to the LEITSTEIN/MCMANUS folder on his lap.

It was a dossier, written in the special, elliptical language of a civil servant or a lawyer. Despite phrases such as "able to maximize income during economically depressed periods" and "employs innovative methods to restructure financing," Mr. McManus sensed that someone had compiled damned near—but not quite—the total "book" on him and Nathan Leitstein.

Rendering the cant into plain English, and filling in the history as he went, he read this story:

Nathan Leitstein was spotted as a comer one afternoon in 1926. A trainer who had grown up in the neighborhood happened to be back on family business. It was the day of the first Dempsey-Tunney fight.

Young Nathan, a lightweight, was knocking the bejesus, bare-knuckled, out of a rangier, heavier boy in a vacant lot near Chatham Square. The fight had been arranged by a Second Avenue restaurant owner. For reasons Nathan was unaware of, the heavy money was on his opponent. Between rounds his second whispered that a big shot from uptown was in the crowd.

That was all it took. At the sound of the restaurateur's spoon against a garbage can cover, Nathan waded in—hitting hard inside and away; making the other boy miss his long and short punches; putting together flashy combinations that gave the impression he was better than he was; above all, avoiding hard shots to his face.

And it was over. Nathan "Billy Light" Leitstein, winner by a knockout.

The man from uptown had a few words with the restaurant owner and then took Nathan aside.

A few hours later, across the East River in North Brooklyn, a young undefeated featherweight billed as Kid Sweeney limbered up in his corner at the Ridgewood Grove Sporting Club. It was his twenty-sixth professional fight. His opponent was a few years older and the betting favorite.

Kid Sweeney got inside fast and threw a storm of punches. Most of them landed solidly. The older boy at once resorted to moving away. He clutched as often as he could and jabbed when he thought it might make Kid Sweeney miss a punch.

Which seldom happened.

Kid Sweeney attacked unremittingly—with a stinging left hook to the other boy's body that crashed a split second later against his jaw; if the other boy slipped the left to the jaw, he caught Kid Sweeney's uppercut like a shot.

The fight, the second on the evening's card, was stopped after three rounds. The favorite, who was behind but showed no signs of being hurt, did not meet the fourth-round bell.

Kid Sweeney's nose was bloody and slightly broken. He was

bewildered but asked no questions. He sponged off under a cold water tap, dressed, and caught a ferry back to Manhattan.

He dropped by the cellar on Pike Street. He split his eight-dollar purse down the middle with his mother in exchange for a rubdown. He had lived in the cellar until he quit school to fight full time. He then boarded a subway for the Upper West Side where he lived in a rooming house that catered to young boxers.

The next morning at six sharp he was about to begin his roadwork on the cinder path around the Central Park reservoir when he was shocked to see another figure panting and shadowboxing his way down the track. He was shocked because he had always been the first out for roadwork. The figure appeared to be his age and height but a few pounds heavier. Kid Sweeney fell in alongside him.

"You mind?" His body was stiff from the night before. His breathing was a trifle labored.

"Nah," said the other boy. He was gasping violently. "My *ugh* first *ugh* day. Never run *ugh* before. Could do with *ugh* some company."

"You established?"

"No."

"What name you fighting under?"

"I don't know. *Ugh*. Name's Nathan Leitstein. *Ugh*. They call me Billy Light. *Ugh*. You?"

"Kid Sweeney."

"That your name? *Ugh*."

"Name's McManus."

"Can't talk anymore. *Ugh*. No wind yet. *Ugh*."

They made several laps and left the park. Kid Sweeney figured Billy Light had gotten carried away and done more roadwork than he could stand on his first day. The guy will collapse in his room and miss his rubdown at the gym, he thought.

An hour later Kid Sweeney walked across the floor of the gymnasium. It was a cavernous shell in the West Fifties. He was astonished. A thick, bandy-legged fighter was working with a fury on the heavy bag. His blows were showy but relentless.

It was Billy Light. His concentration on the bag was total.

"That new guy, Billy Light," said Kid Sweeney. He stretched out on a table for a trainer to rub his legs back to elasticity. The room reeked of liniment, disinfectant, and sweat. "Did anybody tell him he needs a rub after his run?"

"Tell him?" The trainer was a thin, sallow man with hairless arms and hands. "I rubbed him a half hour ago. He was at the door when I got here, this Billy Light. Wouldn't take no breakfast. Wanted to start. I give him the big bag. Wants to work a round his first day. A regular animal."

Mr. McManus paused. He looked around the room. All eyes were on him. Except Freddie Dee's and the girl's. Freddie stared anxiously into space. The girl twisted a strand of blond hair and inhaled the latest of a chain of cigarettes.

"You." Mr. McManus said sharply to the squat man. "Empty this." He pointed to the ashtray.

The squat man glanced about him and then complied.

Mr. McManus lit another cigar.

For several years Kid Sweeney and Billy Light fought and, more often than not, made short work of their opponents: the Kid as a featherweight who took two punches to get in one; Billy as a lightweight whose preferred method was to stall and then charge in with his varied stock of punches, thus allowing him to win numerous short fights and break about even on longer ones. Admittedly, many of their opponents were men on the way down who had never been very far up to start with. But they managed to compile commendable records and move beyond the twenty-five-dollar-a-fight category.

They frequently fought on the same card. At the Coliseum in the Bronx, the Star Casino in Harlem, the Broadway Arena in Brooklyn and other poorly lit, sweaty "clubs" so wretchedly ventilated that the tobacco smoke hanging over the ring was as much a burden as the men they were fighting.

Occasionally fights were organized for them in other cities.

"You ever wonder why the God damned rounds are so short in joints like that?" Billy Light asked. They were on a sultry, almost airless train back to New York from Baltimore. He had lost a split decision and earned thirty-five dollars. Each time he had started to put his combinations together, the bell clanged, leaving the other man on his feet.

"Short?" Kid Sweeney, too, had lost a split decision. He was favoring his right eye. His opponent had rock-hardened the bandages under his gloves with gypsum plaster. He was also trying to shake the effects of a barbiturate that had been slipped into his water bottle. "You call those rounds short? I could've swore they lasted an hour."

"Guys from New York," interjected the withered second with a face like a Tenth Avenue manhole cover, "they always get short rounds when they're busting the hometown boy and long ones when the hometown guy's hot." He extracted a toothpick from his vest and shoved it between his teeth. "That's what it's all about in them places. It don't matter. The promoter was owed a favor. It was tough money, but the guy ain't owed anymore."

The Kid and Billy persisted. Gradually, doggedly they expanded their reputations. But their personal paths diverged.

Billy Light was taken over by a sponsor, a bootlegger who operated a string of blind pigs. He left the rooming house for a furnished apartment. He fought as often as ever but trained at a camp in New Jersey.

Kid Sweeney continued to train at the same gym, assisted by the same seedy second, and remained under the monotonous management of the gymnasium owner.

They seldom appeared on the same card and followed each other's career chiefly through the newspapers.

They met again in 1933, fighting each other. They were "underneath" on the card at the second Ross-Canzoneri fight. The Kid had to put on ten pounds to qualify as a lightweight. Billy Light was the favorite, 5 to 2.

"Billy Light's big time now," his manager told him. "He ain't won nothing big, but he's big time. You take Billy Light, you got a title shot."

The manager added begrudgingly that the fight was worth $300 to the winner and $100 to the loser. He was a corpulent man who bulged out of the narrow jackets and short, cuffed trousers he wore in an effort to stay in fashion. He axiomatically hated to tell a fighter how much a fight was worth. He feared that the boy would not fight for less in the future. In this case he knew Kid Sweeney could use the winner's share and concluded that the prospect of a title shot would intensify his aggressiveness.

The fight was at Madison Square Garden. The crowd was principally interested in the main event. The men and women in the ringside seats talked of John Dillinger, Adolf Hitler, Carl Hubbell's fastball, and how much they should invest in a new play called *Tobacco Road*. They were still taking their places when Kid Sweeney and Billy Light mounted the steps for the final preliminary match.

Kid Sweeney as always went in storming. Billy Light as usual attacked in fits and starts, trying to control the rhythm of the fight.

In the middle of the third round Billy abandoned his advance-and-retreat style. He stood flat and punched and landed straight rights to the Kid's head. Sighs of approval arose here and there—Billy Light had never hit so hard. Then, before the round ended, Billy returned to form, closing and withdrawing, and Kid Sweeney recovered, despite a bleeding nose and an eye that was beginning to swell.

At the bell the Kid hurried to get in close. Billy, unaccountably, stood his ground. Within seconds the Kid was able to bash a left hook against Billy's ribs. Billy avoided the subsequent left to his jaw—and wound up with his head locked in the Kid's angled elbow. The Kid immediately swung his right uppercut. He knew the blow hadn't landed cleanly. He thought Billy had slipped it.

But Billy was on all fours—and remained there until he was counted out.

There was no atmosphere of elation or expectation in Kid Sweeney's dressing room. The Kid lay stomach down on a table. A towel draped him. The trainer with the hairless hands kneaded his taut, blotched body.

"It was like pissing on a cigarette butt in a terlet," said his manager as he deducted his commission from the purse. He leaned against a dingy wall. His tailored shirt escaped in moist wads from under his vest. He wiped his face with a cloth.

"What's that mean?" The Kid propped on an elbow. His nose had stopped bleeding, thanks to a swabbing with Adrenaline. An application of warm water and spirits of ammonia had lessened the swelling of his eye. Noise from the arena periodically flooded the small room. The main event was underway. "Do I get the shot or what?"

"It don't mean nothing," said the manager sourly. He stuffed a knot of damp bills in the Kid's hand and made for the door. "Drop by tomorrow. I'll tell you what's doing." He had no trouble getting out. No mob of reporters and photographers was waiting to hear his analyses and predictions.

The Kid dressed methodically. He decided against hanging around for a glimpse of the main event. Outside on Eighth Avenue the September night bore a hint of chill. He walked to a nearby blind pig that was frequented by the fight crowd. It was packed, smoky, and booming with disjointed conversation and screeches of laughter.

Standing alone at the end of the bar was Billy Light. He spied the Kid and signaled to him with a raised hand.

"Buy you a drink?" He wore an expensively cut suit. His handsome face was wholly intact. He did not look as if he had just lost a fight.

Kid Sweeney asked for scotch.

"The real stuff," Billy told the bartender, "not that *drek* you buy from the Chinaman." He accepted greetings from a party of stiff-collared, blue-jowled big spenders and animated chorus girls who were making their way to a reserved table. They did not acknowledge Kid Sweeney, much less hail him as the conqueror of Billy Light.

"I'll introduce you to those guys," said Billy. "First I want to tell you something. I've retired."

A look of enlightened skepticism clouded the Kid's battered features. "When'd this happen?" he asked sharply. "Before or after the fight?" A lot of things were adding up. And glowing with symbolic logic.

Billy Light smiled deviously. "I'm in another line of work."

The drinks arrived. Billy paid for them with a ten. The Kid only looked at his glass. Billy did not seem offended.

"Look," said Billy evenly. He tasted his drink. "I knew when this fight was made I had as much chance as an ice cube in hell. Forget the odds they was giving. Who do you think set them? *I* did. I know what it's all about. . . .

"I seen you fight what now? Seven, eight years? I know what you can do. Cute guys like me ain't got a prayer against sluggers like you. Even when I hurt you I knew you wouldn't stay hurt. The reason I hurt you at all was you wasn't looking for me to plant my feet and hit. If I'd kept it up, you'd have clobbered me good. What I'm saying is, I knew I'd get beat, so I figured I'd get beat my way. And do some business." He patted his hip pocket. "The hooples bet on me, I bet a bucketful on you, and I clean up eleven grand. I couldn't have made that much if I'd sold tickets. How much you clear from the win?"

"Two hundred and sixty bucks." The Kid sipped his whiskey; it was the first authentic scotch he had ever tasted; he found the softly burnt flavor of the malt and grain extremely agreeable. He remembered that the loser grossed $100. He chuckled and thought, a man who can't chuckle when he sees how much he hasn't learned is a hoople.

"Closer to two-fifty, really. I owed some change." He drank some more whiskey. "How come you're telling me this?"

"I figured you'd find out anyway. When you don't get the title shot. I don't want you coming after me. A man gets a win and then can't do nothing with it, he gets sore, feels dumb, like he was patting a dime on the head and wishing it would grow up."

Kid Sweeney was warm and loose from the scotch. "You making me an offer."

Billy Light nodded. "There's more action out there than *anybody* can handle. The hooples, I can't tell you, they're crazy for action. Bet on anything that moves." He leaned closer and lowered his voice. "Here's the deal. The tall guy back there"—he indicated the most imposing of the big spenders at the reserved table—"that's Mr. Alvin. He lays off up to twenty-five hundred a day for a book. Above twenty-five hundred, you're on your own. He'll lay off anything big but football. He won't touch football."

"Why not?"

"Can't figure the odds. I mean how do you book teams like Columbia or Duquesne? Them guys are 100 to 1 to win every time they play. The professional teams, forget it."

Kid Sweeney beamed a fourth-dimensional grin. He was a little drunk. "Who needs odds?" He held his glass in front of him. "We'll lay points. Sure, nobody'd bet Colgate to beat Columbia, no matter the odds. "But"—he looked Billy dead in the eye—"what kind of action do you think there'd be if we booked Columbia *ten points* better than Colgate?"

Billy Light's eyes widened. He nodded with the air of a man who has heard the enunciation of an idea that he himself has been trying for a long time to gain access to. "That's it," he cried. "That's the way to do it. Spread the points." Then his enthusiasm waned. "Mr. Alvin wouldn't go for it. He won't touch football."

"Forget Mr. Alvin," said Kid Sweeney; his tone bordered on disdain. "This is new, Billy. *We* can do it."

That autumn they booked every football game they could find bettors for. The bullying uncertainty of the Great Depression was no hindrance. They worked as colleagues, not partners. They assembled and shared extensive, often inferential information on the teams they booked, and hedged each other's bets—balancing the other's books, so to speak. Their "point-spread" system took a few weeks to catch on, so they booked the World Series, offering orthodox odds to their small but growing clientele.

They weren't able to forget Mr. Alvin, but they didn't have to remember him long. As soon as their system was established and popular, Mr. Alvin came to know about it. "I like this point business, Billy, and I want you should run it," he said. "I want a Jewish boy should be known in gambling. Nice for him. Nice for me. A nice 40 percent for me. That's 60 percent for you and your goy. Not bad for a couple of new kids. If it sells like baseball and the horses, we renegotiate. Fair enough?" Mr. Alvin did not collect a nickel of his 40 percent. The day after he informed Billy Light of his intention to take a cut of the McManus-Leitstein point-spread system, he was shot to death by a bootlegging rival.

They celebrated Repeal in Chicago with two hatcheck girls. To their immense satisfaction the Bears upset the Giants to win the professional championship. (The McManus-Leitstein price was the Bears to win by three points, based on a *sotto voce* conversation overheard in the Palmer House lobby that the Giant passer was injured. The other bookies favored the Giants, 3 to 1.)

They continued by train to California for the Rose Bowl and easily sold Columbia as a fourteen-point favorite. The score was Columbia 7, Stanford 0. On January 2, 1934, they boarded an ocean liner, sailed through the Panama Canal, and spent the rest of the winter in Havana. They established themselves in the Hotel Nacional and divided their time among the *jai-alai* frontons, the casinos, and the Oriental Park racetrack. They acquired two Miami blondes and a taste for morro crab at the Crystal Palace and frozen daiquiris at Sloppy Joe's. When they boarded the ship for New York in June for the Baer-Carnera fight, they were wearing white silk suits and straw skimmers, smoking excellent cigars, and each holding in the neighborhood of $300,000.

Mr. McManus glanced again at the other men in the room. He was near the end of the dossier. He was relieved to find that it did not contain everything about him.

"Interesting, no?" said the swarthy man. He seemed unquestionably to be in charge.

Mr. McManus shrugged. He said nothing. He tapped the ash of his cigar.

"Finished?"

Mr. McManus looked back at the dossier. There wasn't much left.

". . . Subject McManus enlisted US Marine Corps 22 March 42 at Fort Lauderdale, Fla., USA. Fact noted because subject was well beyond conscription age. USMC known even then for strenuous physical training scheme. Additionally he volunteered for USMC Raiders, elite assault formation whose training more extensive and strenuous than USMC line units. Participated in Guadalcanal campaign. Later posted to China-Burma-India theater. Duties in CBI unknown. Demobilised 1 June 45 Camp Pendleton, Calif. Conducted American equivalent of football pools for many years. This activity unlawful. Consulted through intermediaries when authorities of state of New York USA established legal wagering on professional and amateur sporting contests. Principal owner of firm that sells 'inside' information of scheduled sporting contests. Principal owner of telephone service 'Dial-a-Score' that offers latest results to sporting enthusiasts. Director of corporation that operates parking-lot concession at number of race courses. Income from these enterprises unknown but believed to be considerable. Enterprises chartered in state of Delaware USA. Subject McManus gravely ill in recent months . . .

". . . Subject Leitstein has reputation as a lawyer (in the American sense; i.e., a lawyer acts simultaneously as barrister and solicitor). No record of attending university or a 'law school.' Never called to a bar. Specializes in negotiations and consultations. Counsel to number of American corporations, notably clothing manufacturers. Does not serve as officer of these corporations. Usually compensated for services to corporate clients with 'finder's fees' or shares in merger, financing, and acquisition transactions. This lowers tax liability. In these transactions he has been known to have power to appoint and dismiss executive officers. Also consulted closely in choice of directors. Subject Leitstein also counsel to number of trade unions. These are unions whose members are employees of clothing manufacturers he represents and of concessionaires at sporting facilities. For example, Subject Leitstein is counsel to corporation that operates parking-lot concessions of which Subject McManus is a director and counsel to trade union whose members are employed by said concession. Note: No record of labor disputes between corporations and labor unions represented by Subject Leitstein. Like Subject

McManus, Subject Leitstein has conducted American equivalent of football pools. (See above.) No military record. Presumably Subject Leitstein exempted from Second War conscription owing to age."

Mr. McManus handed the folder back to the swarthy man. He took a deep, sensual puff on his cigar. He felt vital, almost vigorous. It was something close to the old feeling. Something more than what the digitalis had revived.

He exhaled profusely and then said without a crack in his voice, "What can I do for you hooples?"

"We are here to tell you what you can do—" It was the squat man with the mysterious accent. His face was contorted and burning. He was interrupted by the swarthy man, who shot two fingers into the air and gave him a "shut up!" look.

"One thing at a time, Major," he said and turned back to Mr. McManus. "As I said, we are investors. Investors who, at this time, are looking for a quick return. Very quick. And very large."

"How quick?"

"Before the celebration of Christmas, we would hope."

"Before Christmas?" Mr. McManus sounded doubtful. "Christmas is less than two weeks."

"Yes," replied the swarthy man and added a trifle ceremoniously, as if he were imparting some arcane information, "it is observed somewhat later among the eastern churches. I refer to the western observance.

Mr. McManus shrugged. Then he looked slowly around the room, allowing his gaze to rest a moment on the eyes of each of the other men. He gave the black man and the squat man a somewhat longer look. A mischievous smile animated his face.

"You said a large return." His grin hardened at the edges. He was covering a lot of ground quickly in his mind, including such calculations as: In .445 hands of five-card stud out of 6, your last bet won't be called unless somebody else draws a king or a jack at the top of a bobtail flush. "By large I guess you mean at least double a hundred and fifteen million. Triple maybe? Four times? What?" He looked at them out of the corner of his eye.

Confusion shadowed the swarthy man's face. He glanced quickly at the squat man, who could manage no more than a bewildered expression. Hurriedly the swarthy man gave his two-finger signal. One of the others produced a small loose-leaf notebook. The swarthy man seized it. He hastily thumbed through it. Presently he found what he wanted. He held his index finger on it and looked sternly at Mr. McManus.

"Would you be kind enough to tell us which professional American football team"—he squinted and read verbatim—"had the best point-spread standing?"

He uttered the phrase "point-spread standing" with an interrogatory inflection. Mr. McManus was certain he did not know what he was talking about.

"What year?" Mr. McManus asked casually, stringing him along.

The swarthy man flipped the pages. He motioned with a nod for the man who handed him the notebook. They whispered and looked at the notebook. At length the swarthy man said, "For the regular season between 1969 and 1973."

Mr. McManus inhaled his cigar. "For how much?"

Again the swarthy man looked confused. "I don't understand. What does this mean, 'for how much?'"

Mr. McManus exhaled slowly. "Let's go even money." He took his wallet from his hip pocket. "For old times' sake. As I ain't seen this many hooples in one room since a brassiere salesmen's convention in Atlantic City in 1940." He drew out a sheaf of $100 bills. "Who's playing?"

"Playing?" the swarthy man still looked confused.

"You want to invest? I'm ready to give you some lessons. You hooples can use them, believe me. Let's see if you can afford it."

"Ah. You wish us to wager against the possibility that you cannot answer the question?" The swarthy man sounded confident again.

"What I wish was a pickpocket was in the joint. It would save time." Mr. McManus snuffed his cigar and clucked. "Everybody gets down. A hundred bucks a pop. Everybody plays but Freddie and the babe."

All the others except the black man huddled behind the sofa. They consulted and patted their pockets. At last each was able to hold up $100 in odd combinations. The swarthy man and the squat man—they seemed to be holding most of the money—had to dig further into their own pockets and the attaché case to cover the bet.

"He plays, too." Mr. McManus gestured toward the black man. "Nobody's shy in this game."

"*Ek he nee geld, baas,*" said the black man plaintively. He looked anxiously at the squat man.

The squat man glared at Mr. McManus. He dug into the attaché case. He snatched a handful of bills.

"*Neam dit, dwass!*" he snarled. He flung the money at the black man. It fluttered to the carpet. The black man knelt slowly and retrieved it.

"Everybody covered?" asked Mr. McManus impatiently. The others nodded. "What's the question again?"

"The professional American football team with the best point-spread standing for the regular season between 1969 and 1973," snapped the swarthy man.

"Miami," replied Mr. McManus without a second's hesitation and held out his hand.

The swarthy man consulted the notebook. He nodded curtly to the others. They shuffled across to Mr. McManus and turned over their money.

"Would you mind telling us the percentage?" asked the swarthy man as he placed his stack of fives and tens into Mr. McManus's hand.

"For when? '69 to '73?"

"Of course."

"Double or nothing?"

"What does this mean, 'double or nothing?' "

"Same as before. Everybody ponies up a hundred. Chance to get your money back."

The others, including the squat man, held up their palms. The swarthy man clenched his teeth. He plunged again into the attaché case. The routine of distributing the money was repeated—with the exception that this time the swarthy man handed the black man his money.

"The percentage, please." The swarthy man's heavy lips were stretched thin; the nostrils of his angular nose were wide in suppressed rage.

Mr. McManus leaned back and stretched. He held his winnings in one outstretched hand. It was a trifle difficult because of his arthritic thumb. He did not mind. He found it unusually pleasant to perpetrate a steam job on a roomful of hooples who were going wide with no idea of what they were doing. He took a deep, unimpeded breath.

"Got your eye on the answer?" he asked.

The swarthy man found the appropriate place. He dropped several bills as he thumbed the pages.

"The percentage." Resentment as well as anger hardened his voice. He clearly was not used to being played for a fool. Just as clearly, he was aware that this was happening to him.

Mr. McManus surveyed the room. His gleaming old eyes betrayed no clue that he saw things from the perspective of a realm of incomprehensibly intricate relationships—which in three-dimensional terms meant it was unnatural to let a hoople keep his money.

".668," he said.

The swarthy man looked hard at the notebook and then glanced at Mr. McManus. His eyes were lustrous with consternation and distrust. He looked at the notebook again. Several of the others edged close and peeked over his shoulder.

Mr. McManus relaxed into a bored smile. "Cincinnati's second," he said; his voice was still strong. "For the '69–'73 period. .600 percentage-point–spread standing. 39-26-and-1 won-tied-and-lost record." He wiggled his toes in his slippers and pretended to yawn. "That one's on the house, fellows. Anybody want to play again?" He held out his hand. The "hooples" ambled over and delivered their losses.

The swarthy man came last. Mr. McManus reminded him to pick up the bills he dropped.

"We are very much taken with your extraordinary memory," he said. His resentment and rage had given way to sourness. "It appears every bit as reliable as your reputation for discretion. I—my colleagues and I—are prepared to conclude that your acumen as a speculator is equally reliable."

Mr. McManus studied the wad of bills in his ancient fist. "Like I told you when you started running your trap. I want to know what's doing. You can conclude anything you want, but I don't do business unless I know what's doing. I don't think that's sunk in with you hooples. You should maybe get out your notebook and play some more guess-what. Then you'll maybe get the idea. You can afford it, right? As you got a hundred and fifteen million. But then it ain't all pigeon money, is it?"

The swarthy man looked around impatiently. Abruptly he gestured with two fingers.

The red-haired man jammed the muzzle of his automatic against the nape of Freddie Dee's neck.

"It would be a tragedy, don't you think," said the swarthy man evenly, "for this young man to lose his life because of an *alter trombenik's* stubbornness?"

Mr. McManus's snakelike eyes narrowed. He considered the threat to Freddie and the fact that he had been called an "old four-flusher" in Yiddish. Not Orchard Street Yiddish, either.

At the same instant a rainy afternoon in Burma flashed across his mind. The Shan tribesmen in his section had wanted to decapitate a captured Japanese officer. He had casually given permission "—The more dead Japs the better"—and then hastily, emphatically pointed out that their prisoner could, with some inspiration, locate the positions of the Japanese mortars that were tearing off their arms, legs, feet, and faces. Amid the flaming orange explosions, the Shan tribesmen got the point. So did the Japanese officer—after his head had been shoved several times into the gaping, bloody belly of a dead ammunition mule. By nightfall Sergeant McManus and his guerrillas, armed only with hand grenades and heavy-bladed *dahs*, had slithered through the mud to the top of a westward ridge and slashed and blasted the Japanese mortar batteries out of existence.

Mr. McManus looked straight at Freddie. His blue eyes were as cold as the heart of a hungry whore. "Shoot him," he said monotonously, keeping his gaze level. Freddie gulped and fought back tears. "Shoot the bimbo, too. They don't mean nothing to me. Either one of them."

He turned his icy stare on the swarthy man. "But if you shoot them, you might as well shoot me, too. Because the minute that piece goes off, this joint will be swarming with cops—and if I got one ounce of breath left, I'll finger every one of you God damned hooples. Where will that leave you? With two, maybe three stiffs on your hands and a hundred and fifteen million bucks you ain't got the slightest idea how to *speculate* with."

"A man with your past would hardly be a credible witness for the police," shot back the swarthy man.

"My past!" shouted Mr. McManus. "My past don't mean nothing to the cops. I'm a hero to some of them, for Christ's sake. The kid"—he thrust a finger toward Freddie— "his old man's a retired cop. You got any idea what cops in this town do when a member of a cop's family gets hit? Even a retired cop? They go crazy. They drop everything till they've collared the hoople that was stupid enough to do it."

He puffed his cigar quickly. "Here's how it would look to the cops.

And the DA. A bunch of shady characters bust into the apartment of a semiretired businessman that's recovering from a heart attack. They take out the son of a retired cop that's been generous enough to give the semiretired businessman a hand while he's recuperating. While his family that adores him is waiting on him in Florida so they can celebrate Christmas together. For kicks these same characters bingo the beautiful lady friend of the retired cop's son. The semiretired businessman, too, while they're at it—"

"We have some skill in these matters," interrupted the swarthy man. A faint smile eased his stony expression. "Perhaps—"

"Skill?" Mr. McManus retorted imperviously. "You mean an edge? Look what would happen. Red there"—he indicated the man with the automatic against Freddie's neck— "he does what he's told. Then the cops bust the bunch of you. You get to the precinct and everybody says the shine did it." The black man gave a start. "When the detectives get him alone, he says he didn't do it. He says to himself, 'I'm a long way from home and I ain't taking this rap.' Then he gets confused. He says he takes his orders from Major Espenswhatsit"— the squat man's face drew into a pouchy frown— "and so does Red, most of the time." The red-haired man dropped his automatic an inch or two from Freddie's neck, which Freddie proceeded to rub vigorously with both hands. "Except this time, he tells the bulls, Red took his orders from"—he pointed at the swarthy man— "*you.*"

The swarthy man gestured slowly—with two fingers—to the red-haired man, who slipped his pistol back into its holster.

"*Touché*, sir. I apologize," said the swarthy man, still smiling faintly. "You have given us an adequate lesson. Now, I believe, we are prepared to outline the details of our proposal. There will be no more threats or—"

Mr. McManus raised a hand, the one he was not holding his winnings in. "You don't outline nothing with me. That you do with Nat Leitstein. Then we'll talk it over, Nat and me, and decide if there's any way we can be of service to you hooples. You don't talk to me direct again, ever. You talk to Nat Leitstein. Not me. Understand?"

The swarthy man looked perplexed. He tried to recover. "In that case we must take the son of the retired policeman with us. As a guarantee that you and Mr. Leitstein will begin your collaboration with a sense of urgency."

"You do that," Mr. McManus replied, "and I won't speak to Nat Leitstein again in my life. What I'll do is call the cops. I'll tell them a son of their own has this very second been snatched right under my very flat nose."

"Then we're taking the woman." He made it sound as if this had been understood by everyone from the first.

"Take her," said Mr. McManus a bit wearily.

"Fetch your things." She left and returned wearing knee-length boots with her jeans tucked in and a suede coat with a sheep's wool collar over her sweater. A large bag hung from her shoulder.

They headed for the door. The woman seemed to be leading the way, Mr. McManus observed. The black man brought up the rear. The woman didn't look back at Freddie.

"Hold it," Mr. McManus called out. "You can't go down like that. A half dozen white hooples and a black handyman that my elevator operator or doorman ain't ever laid eyes on. Make up your mind which goes first. And make it up fast."

The white men consulted briefly. The woman leaned against the door and idly lit a cigarette. This time it didn't seem to matter to the squat man. He motioned for the black man to leave first and then closed the door to block the elevator attendant's view.

"Thank you for the advice," said the swarthy man. "How long should we wait to call the lift?"

"The elevator?"

"Yes."

"Couple of minutes. Hey, sweetie. Don't drop ashes on the rug. It'll give lover-boy here more work to do." The woman butted her cigarette in an ashtray on a nearby table. She continued to ignore Freddie.

Presently the squat man said, "I boxed for a time myself. I thought you would be interested to know."

"I wouldn't," replied Mr. McManus.

"Yes. I even sparred with Max Schmeling. In 1938. In Germany. Before his second match with your Kaffir."

"My what?"

"The so-called champion. Joe Louis. It wouldn't have happened in Germany. Not then. Why should Schmeling have to fight this Kaffir again? He had bested him once."

"The second time, Louis put him away in the first round," said Mr. McManus. "Not much of a fight. I was there. Yankee Stadium.

Ringside. Louis floored him twice. Left hook and that combination he had. I think Hitler sent Maxie a telegram telling him how nice it would be for the folks back home if he won."

"Schmeling and I were parachutists together. I was with Schmeling at Crete. Schmeling was as great a soldier as he was a boxer."

"Crete? Who won? Must have been the other side."

"We—Germany—won Crete," said the squat man defiantly.

Mr. McManus noticed that the Schmeling-Crete part of the exchange upset the swarthy man, the woman, and two of the others. Once the swarthy man squinted in anger and seemed about to interrupt. Then he looked at the floor. There was a glimmer of sadness in his eyes.

Why? Mr. McManus wondered. Was it a lie? Was Schmeling not at Crete? Then it dawned on him.

"You hooples can go now," he said. "Remember. Talk to Leitstein. Not to me."

The moment the door closed Mr. McManus turned on Freddie.

"Where'd you find the bimbo?" His voice was harsh, accusatory.

Freddie was weeping, relieved to be alive. "What kind of shit question is that?" he asked between sobs. "You would've let those assholes kill me. You didn't care. All that fast talk was to save your own shriveled ass."

"Shut up. If it wasn't for me, you *would* have a hole in your skull. Drop this crap. Where'd you find the woman?"

"What difference does it make?"

"What difference does it make!" Mr. McManus snorted. "Jesus, they should sell brain tablets. I'd buy you a lifetime supply. Couldn't you see what was going on? She set you up. She—"

"Wait a minute, Mr. McManus." Freddie leaned forward on the sofa and touched his bruised eye. He carefully wiped away his tears with his handkerchief and blew his nose. "I know you don't think I'm real smart. You said so enough. But I'm smarter than that. I don't let no cunt set me up."

"She a hooker?"

Freddie was silent a moment and then said, "No."

"What then? A secretary? A waitress? A hatcheck girl? What?"

"A stew."

"A what?"

"A stewardess. An airline stewardess."

"What airline? A foreign airline? She sounded foreign."

Another pause. Finally Freddie said, "I don't know."

"You pick her up or she pick you up?"

"Well, you know how it is." Freddie rubbed his neck where the muzzle of the red-haired man's automatic had pressed against it. "Guys sitting at the bar, chicks at the bar, they get to talking, coming on, you know—"

"How the hell would I know?" Mr. McManus was exasperated. Then it occurred to him that he would get nothing but more evasiveness if he continued to grill Freddie. He lowered his voice. "Look, kid, something big is riding on this. I don't know exactly what—yet. But something big. You heard the kind of money these hooples are talking. I need all the edge I can get. That's why I need to know everything you can tell me."

Freddie looked at his feet and touched his eye again. "Is that why you said my old man is a retired cop? To get some more edge?"

"Yeah. Sort of."

"Won't they find out he was canned? How come they won't find out he works for you?"

"He wasn't canned. He took early retirement. Lots of cops do it."

"He would've been canned. Ma told me and Jackie before she died. She said he got out just before they brought departmental charges. Who put the fix in? You?"

"I helped. We'll get back to that later. Maybe after you and your pa are speaking again. Right now I got to know how you got tied up with the woman. Where'd you meet her?"

"A joint over to the East Side."

Mr. McManus slowly lit another cigar. "This is important, Freddie. How'd the thing work? Who made the first move? You or the broad?"

Freddie clasped his hands behind his head. He gazed at the ceiling, as if he had been called on to recite at school and was concocting an excuse for not having the answer while simultaneously probing his memory for a shred of it. "Well," he began and sighed, "you know how it is."

Mr. McManus was tempted to interrupt again and say, No, I'm seventy-four years old and I don't know how it is. But he held his tongue and puffed his cigar.

"Lots of chicks in a joint like that. Lots of guys. Don't get me wrong. The place is straight. Anyway, a chick, lots of chicks, ask you for a light, what you do. Or the guys ask the chicks. Works both ways."

Freddie folded his arms and looked down. "To tell you the truth, Mr. McManus, most of the chicks I swing with ain't all that bright. I guess that sounds funny to you, coming from me, but that's the way it goes."

"What about this one?"

"That's what I was going to tell you. This chick comes on like any other chick. Except she's extra beautiful. You saw her. You know what I mean. And when she talks to me, she talks to me like I'm a God damned genius. At first I think she's some kind of screwball. But every time she starts getting over my head, it was like, you know, she could read me. She'd say something like, 'Oh, you know what this philosopher or that genius—guys I never heard of—said about this or that,' and I'd say, 'No way, baby,' and she'd say, 'Great. He was full of shit anyway,' and drag me to the jukebox to play another cut. Pretty soon she ain't having to drag so hard. Or else I'm dragging her and saying some genius she'd mentioned was full of shit, and she's laughing and drinking more beer and everything. Till finally she says we're going to make it, aren't we?"

"Make it?"

"You know. Fuck."

"Why'd you bring her here? Since you didn't know how I'd take it? Why didn't you go to her place?"

"How was I to know you'd be up and around? You ain't been on your feet in three months. Anyway, she said she was in a room with three other stews. So you can see how that was." Freddie glanced about him and added, "I told her I was in town for a while on business. In from California. Chicks dig guys from California. I said I was living in this apartment of this guy that works for me."

"On business?" Mr. McManus chuckled. "You tell her what business you're in?"

"Christ, I ain't that dumb."

Mr. McManus chuckled again. "How'd you get past the doorman? This is supposed to be a high-class joint."

"The overnight guy was on. Not Mike. The other guy. What's-his-name? I slipped him a twenty. The way you do."

Mr. McManus stubbed his cigar. Outside the wind was high and the snow was drifting. He stood up and placed the ashtray on the seat of his chair. "Time for another leak," he said, still chuckling, "and another pill."

He paused before closing the toilet door. "Get Nat Leitstein on the phone." He grinned and then added, "You know where you went wrong, Freddie?"

Freddie shook his head.

"The bit about California."

"What about it?" He sounded indignant. "I'm from California, ain't I?"

"You ain't got a suntan. Every hotshot from California, no matter what time of year it is, has a suntan."

He disappeared into the toilet.

Sixteen floors above Broadway, in a large corner office of an avocado green brick building a few blocks south of Forty-second Street, Nathan Leitstein was perplexed and alarmed.

On the street below, despite the severe snow, workers struggled with garment racks on rollers, maneuvering along the crowded sidewalks and jammed intersections to reach the double-parked and triple-parked trucks waiting to receive their cargo.

He was standing at one of the office's two windows. If the son of a bitch is going to shoot me, he thought, I'd just as leave get it in the back.

The cause of his anxiety was a huge, seedily dressed man leaning against the wall behind his desk.

The man had stationed himself between an expensive wooden filing cabinet—which was empty, because it was a hallmark of Nathan Leitstein's career that he kept no records—and a bookshelf lined with unread books chosen by the interior decorator, who had also chosen the paint, the color-coordinated sofa, carpet, armchairs, and enormous desk and elevated swivel chair. He used the office solely for labor "mediations"; many of his clients were garment manufacturers with offices in the building.

The large man kept one hand in a pocket of his black raincoat. In the other he held a small-caliber pistol with a long barrel. The pistol was aimed at Nathan Leitstein's back.

The man had been in the office when he arrived. The lack of a secretary or other employees, which he did not need, had made the surreptitious entry easy. His first thought was that he was about to be the victim of a petty thief, and he moved to deck the guy. Even at my age, and the weight difference, Billy Light thought, I can take this *schlemiel*. But the man whipped out a pistol, and he drew up short. The pistol had been leveled at him ever since.

"I am not here to rob you," the man had said in awkward English—which was not derived from Italian, as Nathan Leitstein might have expected when he noted the make and style of the gun. "I am here to make certain you receive a special telephone call. I am prepared to remain until the call is completed."

He had protested that the man ought to seek out the person who was supposed to place the call if he wanted to be sure it was made. But the man didn't budge, and Nathan Leitstein took advantage of the interval to reflect on the *meshuggeneh* mishmash that was unfolding.

The retired general who called from Jerusalem the night before—he had been a Sheriff Street playmate before his family emigrated to Israel—undoubtedly was wondering why he had not heard whether "some people" could stuff $115 million in the Commercial and Claims Bank in Basel overnight. Whether the money had been deposited anyway was anybody's guess. For all Nathan Leitstein knew his bank was getting the same treatment he was. The notion struck him as ridiculous. Imagine, he thought, a bunch of hooples barging in with guns and demanding to put money into a bank.

He looked over his shoulder. The man had not moved a fraction and was still holding the gun on him.

He turned around cautiously. "This call, pal. Who's it supposed to be?"

The man hesitated and then said, "You will know if it is the right one."

"What do you mean, the right one? I get lots of calls. I got to know the one you want me to get."

A look of uncertainty came over the man's face.

He saw the man was confused. It was a chance to grab an edge. He grabbed it.

"*Bitte?*" he said plaintively and shrugged, palms extended.

"*Zaier gut,*" the man replied instantaneously. "*Ein alter goy. Zaier krank.* McManus."

"*Dank.*"

The uncertainty on the man's face gave way to twisted anger. He had been tricked and he knew it.

Nathan Leitstein knew it, too. He was careful not to let it show. The pistol was still aimed at him. He knew nothing of the temperament of the man holding it. But he knew more than he did a minute ago. He managed to convey that he did not find the exchange unusual. Just a couple of Jews speaking Yiddish. Happens all the time.

"Is there anything special I should talk about to McManus?"

The anger on the man's face relapsed to confusion. "You must ask him if the arrangement has been made," he said nervously.

"The arrangement? What arrangement?"

"The man McManus. You must ask him. He will know."

"How come?"

"Pardon me?"

"How come?"

"I do not know what means, 'how come' "

"How will McManus know if the arrangement has been made?"

"There have been developments. Now we must speak no more."

He saw that the man had not regained his self-confidence. A man without self-confidence can do a lot of damage with a loaded gun, he reflected. He sought to put the man at ease. "Care for a cigar, pal?"

"I do not smoke. To smoke is bad for the health."

Nathan Leitstein suppressed a smile. A man who would blow me away if I scratched my ass the wrong way tells me smoking is bad for me.

"Mind if I have one?"

"Pardon me?"

"I would like to smoke a cigar. They are here." He pointed to his breast pocket. "If you will permit me, I will remove one—and a match—and light it. Will you permit that?"

The man extended the pistol and sighted Nathan Leitstein's forehead down the barrel. "Have your cigar," he said, "but no deceptions. Is that understood?"

"Understood." He carefully extracted a cigar. "The matches are here." He pointed to his trouser pocket. The man nodded behind the gun barrel.

"You speak very good English, pal," he said as he lit up. "But before McManus calls, I have to tell you that the conversation may be a little difficult to understand."

The man looked puzzled. He lowered the gun when he saw the cigar tip smoldering.

"In our business a lot of people would like to know what we know. So we double-talk. You know, *funfen*." He dropped the Yiddish word casually, as if it were a mere accessory to the explanation; he wanted to make certain the man was not dangerously apprehensive when Kid Sweeney called. "I'm telling you this because there'll probably be a lot of things I say that you won't get. Not to worry. There's no tricks. We talk this way because of that thing." He pointed to the white touch-tone telephone on the desk. "There may be a cheesebox downstairs."

"A cheesebox?"

"A tap."

"Ah, electronic surveillance. This is done by the police?"

"The police maybe. Maybe somebody else. You never know in this business."

He knew the phone wasn't tapped. Charlie Dolan, the ex-cop who once took a dive for him and Mr. McManus on an illegal wiretapping charge, and whom they had set up in the private security business, swept the office for him every week. Dolan knew all about pairs, cables, bridging points, and other telephone equipment that was essential back then to wiretapping; he used their money to bribe the telephone company's chief of security for inside help and provided much useful information; for some time it was an important factor in the McManus-Leitstein "edge." Charlie had kept up with the times and knew about ultra high-frequency waveforms, modulators, and re-creation of signals. But they didn't use him much anymore.

The telephone rang softly.

The man motioned with his pistol. Nathan Leitstein walked behind the desk and sat down in the elevated swivel chair. The man moved to the side of the desk and stared at him as he lifted the receiver.

"Who's sitting?" said the voice on the other end.

"Nobody," replied Nathan Leitstein. He watched the man with the pistol out of the corner of his eye. "Better try Queensborough Park."

"Billy?"

"Yeah, Kid. Good to hear your voice. I got it from a very out-to-lunch source that you been apprised of the skinny on a heavy song and dance. The temperature at my business location is up very high. I think the best way to play it is for you to pitch me the scene and I'll bounce it back to you in singles. You with me?"

"You got company?"

"You took the words right out of my mouth."

"How many?"

Nathan Leitstein inhaled his cigar and tapped the ash in an oversized ceramic ashtray. He looked up at the man with the pistol and pulled a wry face. "I would say an accurate count is ten minus ten plus one. Yeah. I would say that's an accurate count."

"He holding a gun on you?"

"You know how it is, Kid. The maintenance in this building stinks. The rent I pay, not to mention the phone and electric, they should be more considerate. Even a day like this, they shouldn't let the temperature go this high. It's bad for you, a room with temperature like this."

There was a pause and then Mr. McManus said, "Is it a guy the size of a tank in a ratty raincoat? Looks like a stooper at the track only different?"

Nathan Leitstein raised his eyebrows a fraction. "This is a very important client. He's having some difficulty getting a consignment of secondhand toothbrushes out of a bonded warehouse. I wouldn't be surprised if his itinerary includes a visit to a haberdasher."

"He's an Israeli, Billy. He checked me out in the candy store."

"It's for sure he owns stock in the Iroquois Pomegranate Company. I don't recall it was brought to my attention that an official representative of the firm was in the vicinity."

"It didn't seem to matter at the time. It does now." Mr. McManus described his encounter with the intruders; Nathan Leitstein could barely refrain from bursting into laughter at the part about how Mr. McManus had taken their money. "They didn't tell me what they want. I wouldn't let them. It's easy to guess. They want action. But they ain't players. They as much as said they got the hundred and fifteen million. What I don't know is how they want to play it. . . . This hoople with you, it's a cinch he don't know what's doing. Not all of it. I think he's around mostly to lean and stand chicky. What do you think?"

"What makes you sure this is a representative of the Iroquois Pomegranate Company? I admit the idea crossed my mind."

"My guy at the candy store. Leo. He chalked him. The hoople spoke Jewish with a foreign accent. Another thing. These characters at my apartment. It makes sense that some of them are Israelis, right? The others, I got no idea where they come from. They speak a lingo I never heard. One of them is called Major Espensheid. That mean anything to you?"

The huge man's face constricted. He snapped his fingers furiously. Presently he thrust the muzzle of his pistol within inches of Nathan Leitstein's temple.

Nathan Leitstein placed his cigar in the ashtray and lifted his palm slowly to his forehead. "The name does not ring a bell. I will have my secretary set up an introduction. . . . Now the question of the heavy song and dance. My lunched-out authority says you got the dope on it. I don't think the temperature in here is going to drop appreciably if I'm at a loss for words when we're done. So please tell me what's on the menu. Soup du jour to nuts. Can you do that?"

"That close, huh?"

"Kid, I'm talking about a secondhand toothbrush importer who's missed so many lunches he wouldn't know diet salad dressing from Chinese takeout."

"Okay. Here's where we stand. These hooples want action. With that much money we got to have a heavy edge, right? I'll get started on that. I told them to deal with you and leave me alone. This is going to take a lot of moving around. I'll have enough trouble doing that without a bunch of foreign hooples tagging along. I told them to tell you what they want to play. You tell the hoople with you that the characters who came to see me will be in touch. With you. You say you'll be getting the details but you don't know how or when. From what I told you, you figure they'll move when they're ready. That's enough for your hoople to suck on. Meantime, since I got some room to work in, I'll look over the territory. I think they want football. You think?"

"I think."

After a moment Mr. McManus said, "You want me to get you some help? Somebody to take that hoople out?"

"Oh, no, no, no," Nathan Leitstein replied hastily. He glanced at the pistol muzzle verging on his temple. "You do that and the temperature would go out the roof. And I mean quick. If this is a representative of the Iroquois Pomegranate Company, I got an adequate idea of whom I'm dealing with. Thanks, Kid. You been a ton of help. As always. Keep in touch."

He replaced the receiver. He picked up his cigar and puffed it.

The man in the raincoat moved to the front of the desk, his pistol level in front of him. He looked baffled and angry.

"You will now tell me," he said through clenched teeth. "Has the arrangement been made?"

Nathan Leitstein sighed. "The details, they aren't worked out yet. McManus says I'm the one to work them out."

The man frowned. "But the arrangement was to be made with McManus."

"Must have been a change in plans, pal. McManus says the people who discussed it with him agreed to deal with me instead."

The man's frown intensified to a scowl. "I must telephone."

"Be my guest, pal." Nathan Leitstein stood up. It gave the man a start. "Use it all you want," he added quickly, lifting his hands, palms out. "I'm just going to the window. To take the view."

The man stepped behind the desk. He cradled the receiver with his shoulder and punched a number.

The conversation was in Hebrew, of which Nathan Leitstein understood very little. The man shouted a lot. The other party shouted louder. From across the room Nathan Leitstein could hear the voice on the other end. It was a woman. Of necessity the man used a number of non-Hebrew words. Nathan Leitstein noted them all: "subway," "Brooklyn," "Dolan," "dollars," "Espensheid," "Paraguay."

Presently the man slammed the phone down. He ostentatiously shoved his pistol into a holster under his shabby raincoat, as if to advertise that he could easily draw it again.

"You are not to leave this room," he said brusquely. "You will wait here until you receive instructions. Is that understood?"

Nathan Leitstein nodded. He pulled another wry face. Of course he wouldn't leave. He knew what he had to do—which included an immediate call to Kid Sweeney—and he could do it a lot easier from his office than by running all over the city in his Rolls Royce. Which reminded him. He must call the diner down the block and tell his chauffeur he would be longer than he had expected.

The man strode to the door.

"*Shalom,* pal," called Nathan Leitstein.

The huge man looked over his shoulder, sneered, and left.

Nathan Leitstein sank into his swivel chair and lifted his cigar to his mouth. Abruptly he flung it into the enormous ashtray. He clenched his right hand into a fist. If I could've put a couple of punches together, he said bitterly to himself, I could've flattened that big hoople.

He cursed the idea that the expensive lock on his office door could have been picked.

His thoughts shifted to the pistol the man had held on him. A .22 caliber Beretta 76. A target pistol. In vogue the past few years for mob contracts. A client of his in San Diego had been shot to death in a phone booth. In the middle of the night. In a residential neighborhood, no less, where as a matter of prudence he made all his calls. Six times in the back of the head and nobody heard a thing. The reason? The powder packs in the cartridges had been reduced to give the bullets an effective lethal range of less than thirty feet. Practically no noise.

But this hoople was no wise guy. That he was certain of.

He was also certain that whatever else the man did for a living, skillful breaking and entering was one service he provided.

And assassination.

He reached for the phone.

"Whistle me a cab, Mike," said Mr. McManus. He thought of his mother as he handed the doorman a five. Gusts of wind whipped the snow in sheets.

The doorman again protested that Mr. McManus had no business outdoors in such weather. He nevertheless hailed a cab. He did not mention the party of strangers who had left the building a half hour ago.

Mr. McManus felt sure this time that Freddie Dee was too shaken to allow any more "uninvited guests" into the apartment. The question in his mind was whether Freddie would feel confident enough when he returned to open the door at all.

He positioned himself in the cab to allow himself a glance in the rearview mirror. The front and back seats were separated by a Plexiglas partition intended to protect the driver against thieves. Mr. McManus was certain an attempt would be made to follow him, although he spotted no cars pulling away after them as the cab drove south. At Seventy-second Street he ordered the cabbie to turn into Central Park and to keep driving until he was told otherwise.

As the cab headed down the park's West Drive Mr. McManus speculated on the story Nathan Leitstein had told him moments before he left. Clearly this Major Espensheid had a prominent role in whatever was going on. (Despite the reference to Max Schmeling and Crete, Mr. McManus did not think Major Espensheid was a German.

But what was he?) The name "Dolan?" He did not believe Freddie was wired in. Charlie Dolan? Charlie was something of a hoople. Charlie would have to be checked out. How did Paraguay fit in?

He and Nathan Leitstein agreed that the man who gave his orders by pointing with two fingers was *numero uno* among the hooples. Also he was an Israeli. The other hooples, including the black man and the woman, were caddies. Caddies with jobs to do and who knew how to do them. Especially the woman and the red-haired hoople with the automatic. But caddies.

They also agreed that Nathan Leitstein would tell the retired general in Jerusalem that they were available to "invest" the $115 million when it reached the United States.

The cab swung around the park's southern rim and made its way slowly through the heavy snow up the East Drive. Mr. McManus kept watch through the rearview mirror. The snow made it difficult to distinguish the cars behind them, except the other cabs.

Mr. McManus placed a fifty-dollar bill in the sliding tray under the Plexiglas partition in which the cabbie received his fares.

"I want you to hit all the roads in the park," he said. "All of them. Don't worry about how long it takes. If that doesn't cover it, I'll make it another fifty. Okay?"

The cabbie craned for a glimpse of his passenger in the mirror. He reached over his shoulder and retrieved the bill. He looked in the mirror again and nodded. "Thanks," he said tersely.

They crisscrossed and re-crisscrossed the 840-acre park in a bewildering configuration of routes. They did not miss an inch of snow-covered paved road, driving past numerous playgrounds, the rear of the Metropolitan Museum of Art, lakes, ponds, playing fields, the reservoir around which Mr. McManus had done his roadwork as a boxer. Truant children with sleds were on the hilly terrain in droves.

At length Mr. McManus spotted what he was looking for. It turned out to be a car with plates indicating it was rented. It appeared with increasing frequency behind them. At times it was almost on their bumper; then at a discreet distance; sometimes it seemed to disappear. The driver was white. The shotgun passenger was black.

"Where's the worst traffic on the East Side?" Mr. McManus asked.

"By now?" The cabbie scratched his head. They were near the northern tip of the park. The meter registered more than thirty dollars. "Down Fifth Avenue in the Fifties, I guess. Christmas shoppers and all."

"What about the Seventies or Eighties?"

"Madison Avenue and Seventy-ninth Street. Con Ed. Everything's screwed up for blocks. Why?"

"Just wondering." He watched the rearview mirror. The suspicious car was not in sight. "I want you to cut across at the pool there and head back downtown. When you get to the Bethesda Fountain, pull into the parking lot. Got me?"

"The one above the lake?"

"Yeah. But I want you to make the horseshoe. Drive the car around the hill to the exit and then stop." He placed another fifty in the sliding tray. He tapped the partition and pointed to the bill. The cabbie took it and nodded. This time he did not say thanks.

Minutes later they turned into the parking lot. The entrance and exit and a short connecting drive formed a horseshoe around a steep, snow-covered hill; the parking spaces, whose painted lines were obscured by the snow, were at the top of a rise behind them. The cab circled slowly and headed out again.

"Hold it right here," Mr. McManus ordered. The cab came to a dead halt a few feet from the exit. The snow-covered hill made the cab incapable of being seen from the entrance. Mr. McManus squirmed and looked over his shoulder out the back window.

Presently the rented car that had been shadowing them nosed into view from behind the hill. It proceeded tentatively up the rise.

A flight of pigeons alit near a litter basket and pecked for morsels of food.

"Let's go!" shouted Mr. McManus. He shifted and gripped the edge of the seat tightly with both hands.

The startled cabbie floorboarded it. The pigeons scattered. The cab fishtailed onto the slippery park road. It barely missed colliding with a stream of approaching traffic.

"Out at Seventy-second Street!" he shouted again.

Behind them cars skidded, every which way, blocking the parking-lot entrance at pick-up-stick angles. Metal mangled metal in annoying ways. Drivers with fists extended from their windows bellowed curses.

They slipped past the statue of Daniel Webster. Mr. McManus spied the rented car. It was zigzagging along the snow-covered sidewalk adjoining the exit in an effort to get onto the roadway and back into pursuit.

"Up Central Park West," he cried as they left the park. "We'll head for the East Side at Eighty-first Street!" He settled back in his seat. They were only a few blocks from his apartment building. He maintained his vigil in the rearview mirror.

To his amazement he saw the rented car whizzing out of the park. In no time it was tailgating them again.

The traffic on the Eighty-first-Street transverse road was moderate. As they emerged from the park and crossed Fifth Avenue it was almost photographically still.

The cabbie sensed what was going on and managed to put them two cars ahead of their pursuers. He was sensible enough not to ask questions. He perceived that he stood to earn his biggest tip of the year.

The principal cause of the jam was in the middle of the block. There was a large hole in the street. Consolidated Edison workers in blue hard hats loitered around the opening. It was protected by a yellow metal barrier and covered by a tarpaulin.

The cabbie maneuvered around the work site and toward Madison Avenue.

Abruptly a delivery van lurched into the street from a parking space behind them. It was unable to advance in the snowbound traffic. It blocked both eastbound lanes.

At the same instant a gap appeared for a fraction of a second in the traffic ahead of the cab. Room enough for a single car to make a left turn on Madison Avenue.

The gap opened point blank onto a caravan of buses clogged at a stop on the northeast corner.

"Make the turn!" shouted Mr. McManus. The rented car was stuck far up the block.

The cabbie shot the gap. He made it as far as the bus stop and could go no farther.

"I'm getting out here," said Mr. McManus. "Keep the change. And thanks."

"Have a good day," said the cabbie as the door slammed.

The buses rumbled and snorted at the stop. Each was packed with parcel-laden shoppers. People elbowed and shoved to board at the front and struggled with their burdens as they alit from the side door.

Mr. McManus edged up to the side door of a Number 3. He pulled his muffler to his dewlap. He held his hat on with his free gloved hand against the hostile wind.

Like a devilish schoolboy he waited until an overweight woman was helped down the steps by a young man. Before the man released the swinging double door, Mr. McManus gripped the passenger bar inside and pulled himself aboard.

The driver spotted it instantaneously in the convex mirror above the door. "Hey, you! Buddy! Mister! *Off!*"

Mr. McManus was gasping. But he knew he would last. Sneaking onto a bus foreboded no danger to his health. He dug into his trouser pocket and withdrew several coins. He softly nudged a young woman who was grasping the same aisle pole and asked her to deliver his change to the driver.

He explained that he boarded irregularly because he had recently suffered a heart seizure and feared he would experience a relapse if he were forced to endure the long boarding line. He added that he would appreciate it if the woman would ask a passenger to give him a seat.

"He has his fare, driver!" the young woman shouted. "Here it is!" She held his change aloft. "He isn't feeling well. Would someone give him a seat, please? And would you pass the man's fare to the front? Thank you." She looked reproachfully at a man about her own age who had looked up from a book. "Please let the man sit down."

A resentful look came over the man's face. It meant: Why should I give this old bastard my seat? I paid my fare.

Mr. McManus got his seat. He shifted and looked out the window at the entangled crosstown traffic.

A compact, red-haired man was dodging his way toward the bus stop. It was the man who had accosted him in his lobby and held the automatic on Freddie. In seconds he disappeared around the back of the bus.

More turmoil. This time at the front. It was accompanied by loud, harsh complaining and scornful comments on the state of the city's public transportation.

"Can't you read, mister?" It was the bus driver again. "What? Does anybody understand what this guy is saying? Look, sport. It says exact change. Everybody else pays exact change. What are you? Some kind of prima donna?"

The crowd shifted and a small space opened. Mr. McManus could see the driver duck under the stainless steel bar that guarded his seat to deal with the difficult passenger.

"I have only a twenty-dollar note!" It was the red-haired man. He was on the top step. "Take it! It will buy dozens of bloody tickets! I *must* board this bus, you sod!"

With that the driver, a well-fed man with a talent for rudeness, shot out a ferocious stiff-arm. The heel of his palm caught the red-haired man flush in the chest.

Mr. McManus couldn't see it—the crowd had closed off his view—but the blow sent the man sprawling backward into the slushy gutter. A last-second effort to retain his balance prevented him from cracking his spine on the curbstone.

"Merry Christmas, asshole," the driver growled.

This was greeted with equal portions of applause and protest.

What Mr. McManus was able to see as the bus pulled away was a policeman at the driver's window of the rented car. He was writing a ticket. The black man in the passenger's seat was gesturing frantically in the direction of the bus stop, where the red-haired man was hauling himself up from the slush.

The bus lumbered up Madison Avenue and turned west on 110th Street. After a dozen or so stops, enough passengers had disembarked to allow everyone a seat. By the time they turned up Manhattan Avenue all the other riders except Mr. McManus were black. They made their way onto St. Nicholas Avenue. They were in Harlem.

They crossed 126th Street. Mr. McManus recalled that Father Divine had maintained his "Kingdom" down the block. He had admired Father Divine. Father Divine was one of the earliest believers in the McManus-Leitstein point-spread system. The district attorney and the Internal Revenue Service spent a lot of time trying to find out how "God" financed his string of grocery stores, farms, missions, and gasoline stations. They put a good deal of heat in particular on an "angel" going under the name of Magnificent Consolation—who kept quiet as a nun. Maggie and the other angels had put their names on the legal papers, but Father Divine personally ran the whole operation.

"You know," Father Divine told him after winning $35,000 in a single weekend, "the faithful say I got the world in a jug and the stopper in my hand. I'm pretty sure about the jug, but I don't know about the stopper. I believe you and Billy got that. What y'all dealing on Texas Christian and Texas?"

A few blocks above 140th Street, Mr. McManus got off. The snow was blowing hard. Considering his experience and where he was, he looked on the snow as a blessing. Less opportunity for some desperate black to yield to temptation and jump a dapper old white man. An old white man who knew the risks of walking alone uptown with close to $2,000 in small bills on him.

He reached the corner of a short block. It was a cul-de-sac, a pocket of affluence within crawling distance of frigid misery. A snowplow had cleared the streets. The sidewalks had been shoveled and salted.

The address he wanted was several doors up. One of the huge, renovated brownstones that lined the block.

As he approached he saw a Rolls Royce. It was a Phantom, like Billy Light's except it was maroon instead of black. A black man was behind the wheel.

Descending the front steps was another black man. He was large, bearded, unsmiling, and wearing an ankle-length mink benny. Mr. McManus recognized him immediately, despite the biting wind that made his eyes water.

Snakehips Davis. All-pro the last eight years on a losing team. At least 1,500 yards a season since he came up. More than 2,000 twice. A slasher, a bulldozer. Nickname hung on him by a smart-ass sportswriter and irrelevant to his running style. Worth nearly a million a year in salary alone. Also a brooder, a loner, Ted Williams type. On the field total confidence, total concentration. Infatuated with challenge. Bitched when he wasn't allowed to run against stacked defenses. Denied having said he wanted to play one game before he hung it up in which the offense consisted only of him and a center to snap the ball.

One of Snakehips's most impressive performances, in Mr. McManus's opinion, had been off the field. It had been before the legislative committee that drafted the law legalizing sports gambling in the state of New York. The hearings had been televised, and Snakehips had overwhelmed them. It was a rare moment. Snakehips had never before sided with the club owners.

"We in football do not want favors from the government," Snakehips had pronounced. "Especially the *favor* of having ourselves licensed. We want to continue to do what we've been doing for nearly sixty years. We want to continue to do the football fans of this country a favor. We want to continue to give them quality professional football games."

In the end—as Mr. McManus had had it at 3 to 1—legalization was sanctioned. Professional football became a government-regulated industry. Like horse racing. As Snakehips had noted, licensing was particularly nettlesome. Everyone—players, coaches, trainers, scouts, public relations men, team doctors, even the owners—had to be licensed. And they were incensed.

There were threats of canceling the season, then bitter speeches at postseason banquets predicting that the day was not far off when this unhappy set of regulations would be imposed on colleges, high schools, and the sandlots. And on other sports. What would Jim Thorpe have thought? What would George Halas have thought? What would Big Daddy Lipscombe have thought? When the outrage quietened to an ornery roar, it became clear that the state and the teams would make a lot of money. The Off-Track Betting Corporation, which operated the system, cut the teams in for 2½ percent of the total handle. In the first year each team made an additional $5 million. Now, in New York alone, they were earning more from their OTB cut than they were from gate receipts and television combined. Season tickets were going for $20 a copy.

None of which mattered at all to Mr. McManus. They hadn't tried to license *him*. Or any bookmaker. Which meant not a hell of a lot had changed.

He watched the large black man slide into the back seat. Under other circumstances Mr. McManus might have introduced himself to Hips. Congratulated him on his game yesterday. Wished him luck next Sunday, the last game of the season, expressed confidence that he would get the 74 yards he needed to break 1,500 again. He had done it innumerable times with athletes with a view toward getting a response such as, "I'll be in there all the way if my ankle holds up," or, "The doc don't know if my arm'll be a hundred percent." It helped the edge.

In this case he passed up the opportunity.

He slowly mounted the steps and pressed the buzzer. A small, dark woman with forbidding eyes opened the door.

"The name's McManus. I'm here to see Madam Excella." He gently insinuated himself past her into the vestibule.

The woman recovered. She stepped quickly behind a desk at the foot of the staircase. A metal-on-Lucite strip on the desk identified her as the receptionist.

She seated herself. "Madam Excella sees no one without an appointment," she said coldly in a Caribbean accent. "I'm *sure* that *you* don't have an appointment."

There was an adjoining parlor. It was dominated by a gigantic Christmas tree with twinkling lights. Mr. McManus trudged inside. He sat down in a wing-back chair. A gas heater glowed in the fireplace. He removed his shoes and socks and propped his bare feet before the heat.

"You *don't* have an appointment," the woman snapped from her desk. "I'm giving you exactly thirty seconds to get out. Or I'm calling the police. Did you hear me? I'm calling the police!"

Mr. McManus leaned across the arm of the chair. "You get upstairs," he said maliciously over his shoulder, "or wherever Madam Excella is. You tell her I want to see her. *Now!*"

The woman shot up from her chair. She shoved one hand against her hip and glared at him. She tossed her head and spun around. She cast a last, caustic look over her shoulder and stalked up the stairs. She tried to flounce but her hips were too narrow to bring it off.

Moments later another female voice could be heard three floors above. It boomed.

"And you let him in? I *told* you, girl! It ain't *ever* supposed to be no white men in *my* house! What do you mean, you *couldn't* get him out? You come with me! I'll *show* you how to get the motherfucker out!"

There was noise on the staircase. The women were coming down.

"And you just *opened* the door?"

"The doorbell rang."

"Where is he?"

"In the parlor."

"In the *parlor?*"

They were nearly to the ground floor.

"Yes, ma'am. In the big chair."

In the *big chair?* Who told him he could sit down? *You?*"

"No, ma'am." There was a clear note of intimidation in the other woman's voice.

"It's some things they can't teach you in books! You about to see one of them!"

The owner of the scolding voice was within a few feet of the parlor doorway.

"All right, motherfucker! You got in easy, but you going out the hard way! So—"

The voice fell silent.

The tall, walnut-colored woman with long, narrow eyes and a thin nose stood in the door. A flowing, orange gown covered her daintily fleshy body. She wore an emerald green turban. Her eyes had been angry and threatening when she appeared. Now they were moist and filled with pain. Worry wrinkled her broad forehead.

"Mac?" Her voice was plaintive.

"Hello, Lula." He smiled thinly over his shoulder. "Thanks for coming down." He was still holding his bare feet before the gas heater.

The woman was only a year or two younger than Mr. McManus. She walked tentatively to where he was sitting and slowly knelt beside him. She took one of his weathered hands and pressed it against her cheek.

"I thought you was dead," she said in a near whisper. "Why didn't you let me know?" Her tone made it clear she didn't expect an answer.

The receptionist was still at the door. Presently she returned to her desk. She sat down and rested her chin on her hand. She wore a mystified look.

"What happened?" Lula asked softly.

Mr. McManus told her. At length he said, "This is my first day on my feet." Then he lifted her chin with his other hand and looked at her. He smiled broadly—the first time he had smiled like that in months. "It's a shame, Lula. Not a chance in hell of us slanting it today."

She pulled back a trifle, still holding his hand against her face. "It's all you ever thought a nigger woman was good for. Getting her legs spread." She chuckled and kissed his fingers. "That ain't what you got in mind, is it? Not in the shape you in?"

"No."

"I kind of wish it was." She sounded wistful. "You know, I didn't have no idea a white boy knew how to do it. How long we know each other? Going on fifty years? I didn't have no idea. Did I ever tell you that?"

"You used to tell me all the time. The first time was the night I took Poodle Grant at the Star Casino. You were still at the Kit Kat. That was the first time."

A remote look glazed her narrow eyes. "I did? I did, didn't I? It comes back to me now. My memory ain't what it used to be."

"How about your dreams?"

She straightened up. "I can still count the spokes on Ezekiel's Wheel." She nodded craftily in the direction of the receptionist.

"She's ignorant," she said quietly. "I want her to stay that way. Let's go up to my consulting room."

"I can't. I'd never make a full flight of stairs."

She smiled apologetically and then called out, "Pauline, put on your coat and all, honey. Get some money so you can take a cab. I want you to go over to Amsterdam Avenue and get me some books over to the little store. I want the new *Erasmus Authentic Aztec Secrets*. Don't let him sell you the last year's one. And *Sister Polly's Policy Players Dream Book*. And the new *Moon Book*, if he's got it. Don't let him sell you *Sister Rosemary*. Sister Rosemary says play 106 if you dream about taking a trip. What kind of foolishness is that?"

The receptionist had slipped on her coat and was zipping her boots.

"When you get done over to the little store, go to that place at 103rd and First and see what they got for the Puerto Ricans. Get them in English unless you want to have to read to me."

The receptionist let herself out and locked the door. Lula sighed and heaved herself to her feet. She went to the heavy oak door and turned several other locks. "That girl's my student. Says she wants to learn my gift. I think she believes it's a system. I told her from the start I'm the seventh daughter of a seventh daughter's seventh daughter. You can't teach *that*. It ain't the same as a seventh son, but it ain't no system. She's from Panama. Helps me when I'm advising people that can't speak English. Puerto Ricans and Cubans. Puerto Ricans, mostly. What she don't seem to know is how to lock the door right."

She walked back into the parlor.

"Action?" She seated herself in a smaller chair opposite Mr. McManus.

He grunted with a nod.

"Had to be." She laughed and shook her head. "Man has a heart attack and what does he do first thing they let him out of the bed? *Gamble!* And it damn near a blizzard outside. Don't give a thought to the best nigger trim he ever had"— she smiled as broadly as he had— "or how she might feel about it. No, sir. He thinks about gambling."

Mr. McManus was growing weary again. He studied his toes. The nails were yellow and cracked. He was finding it difficult to focus his thoughts. He divided 279,936, first by 3 and then by 2. It was an exercise he used to regain his concentration.

"What's the book on Hips?" he asked absently.

Her eyebrows furrowed a trifle. Her mouth turned down slightly at the corners, betraying doubt.

"He's fine," she said after a moment; her tone was a fraction noncommittal, hesitant with caution. "Everybody's proud of Melvin. Community loves him."

Her voice turned declamatory. "He ain't happy about having to pee in a jar after every game. None of them is. Says it makes him feel like an animal. He ain't no racehorse, you know. Melvin don't touch no kind of dope. Everybody knows it. Why should he have to pee in a jar just to show the *National Football League* he ain't had no dope? He don't like it, either, that some *state official*—just exactly like the one at the track—can look at his little tv and make them run a play over again if he don't think the referee got it right the first time. And licensing. That ain't right. Melvin says it's a lot of colored boys don't get to play on account of some little thing they done a long time ago and can't get licensed. Like he said on tv."

Mr. McManus shrugged. Probably a lot of white boys, too, he thought, but deemed it unwise to raise the point. He knew of old that Lula moralized or took a stand on principle only when she wished to stall or to be evasive. At the moment, he decided, she was being evasive. He couldn't understand why.

"Name a price, Lula. Give me a setup. Any way you want to play it."

The doubt on the old woman's face burst into fretful astonishment. "What do you mean, name a price?" Her voice rose, edging toward angry despair, as if she sensed that a stone were about to fall and shatter the trust and intimacy they had cemented over half a century. "You know *my* price. Five thousand to listen. Seven if you hit. It ain't been no change in that."

He understood. "That ain't the point," he said kindly. He understood he had made her believe he was toying with her dignity, and it made her feel cheap. "This ain't like anything we've played before. This time you can name it. This is a big fat one. Bigger and fatter than we've ever seen."

"How big and fat you talking about?" She still sounded doubtful. "Two million? Five million? We ain't ever broke five million in one pop."

"More than that?"

"How much more?"

"A *lot* more."

She scrutinized him. He was a Cancer and she was an Aquarius. That had lurked in her mind from the first. Cancers and Aquariuses weren't supposed to get along. They had always gotten along, to say the least. Even though he was radical and fruitful and she was fixed and barren. She had concluded long ago that he had a lot of Leo. That had made the difference.

"You mean a percentage or just a higher fixed rate?" The defensiveness was gone from her voice.

"I mean however you want it. So long as there's some left over for the rest of us."

"Who's the rest of us? Somebody besides you and Billy?"

"Yeah."

"Who?"

"I don't have it figured out. Foreigners. That's all I know."

"Italian?"

"No. Some Israelis are fronting it. The others, I don't know. They speak funny English-English. They may be fronting, too. I'll know in plenty of time."

"Them Jews are slick. Got to watch them."

"This ain't a Seventh Avenue crowd."

She smiled, not quite affectionately, but it was clear that her trust in him had been restored. "Hips got a sore big toe," she said evenly. "Left foot. Be fine on Sunday. Too early on the dreams. I told him we'd check them out Friday and Saturday. Sunday, too, if he still don't feel right."

"Why don't he feel right?"

"Been dreaming about rats crawling all over him."

"So?"

"Ah, shit, Mac. Everybody knows that. Dreaming about rats crawling on you means somebody trying to do you in."

Colonel Garovsky ate the other half of his buttered onion roll. He waited for the cup of black, sugarless instant coffee, prepared with a heating element, to cool. It wouldn't take long. The room was gray and raw. The only warmth came from a small electric heater a few feet away.

The room was on the second story of a historic mansion in the Jamaica section of Queens. The mansion was an officially designated landmark and served as a museum. It had been built in Colonial times and was situated in a spacious park. It was closed to visitors for repairs, but funds for renovation had dried up. Thus the mansion was empty except for Colonel Garovsky.

He was eating at a desk cluttered with papers and notebooks filled with handwritten information on the mansion's architectural consequence. Colonel Garovsky was an architectural historian and held a post in the Ministry of Development and Housing in Jerusalem. He was also an occasional university lecturer. He had gained access to the mansion by requesting permission to conduct research for a paper to be delivered at an international congress.

Actually, the information on the papers and in the notebooks had been assembled in advance and written by an Israeli intelligence operative whose talents included forgery. The most astute graphologist could not have detected that the modern Hebrew characters had not come from Colonel Garovsky's own hand. Every day or two he rearranged the papers and notebooks to give the appearance that he was engaged in research—in case someone should raise doubts that he was something other than an architectural historian.

He glanced at his watch. Late, he thought, but not unduly, considering the weather. He arose and walked to the window. He noticed that the drifting snow had collected to the depth of a foot at the base of the lamppost beyond the covered front porch.

Presently the outline of a tall man in a black raincoat emerged in the distance. The man was making his way across the park as if it were a Lake Kinneret beach on a clear day in April. Lake Kinneret. He would see it as soon as he returned. He would visit his daughter at her kibbutz below the Golan Heights. Only now he must not think of it as Lake Kinneret. He must think of it as the Americans did—as the Sea of Galilee.

He heard a key in the door beneath and then footsteps on the 250-year-old stairs. The stairs fascinated him. In some respects he regarded them as superior to the stairs in his father's house in Cape Province. His father's limestone-walled house was almost as old as this one.

Captain Zanin appeared in the room. He was taller than Colonel Garovsky, who was regarded as a tall man. Both were swarthy and had fresh haircuts.

They greeted each other traditionally in Hebrew.

Colonel Garovsky gestured with two fingers. He indicated a chair near the electric heater.

Captain Zanin declined with a heavy shake of his head. Colonel Garovsky understood why without being told. Captain Zanin did not want to go through the process of reacclimatizing his body to the cold.

Captain Zanin was sullen. Colonel Garovsky knew the reason. This was Captain Zanin's first nonmilitary clandestine operation, and a ticklish phase had gone off badly. Had this been his, Colonel Garovsky's, first undercover mission and something of the sort had occurred at the outset, he, too, might have been sullen. But he was an experienced hand and at least twenty years older than Captain Zanin. He no longer grew dejected when events failed to conform to advance planning.

"I should be withdrawn from the operation," Captain Zanin said abruptly in Hebrew. He reached into his raincoat pocket and dug out two hard-boiled eggs. He offered one to Colonel Garovsky.

"Please, no," replied Colonel Garovsky, also in Hebrew. "I have had my breakfast. American rolls, American butter, American coffee. They are not the same. How are American hard-boiled eggs?"

Captain Zanin was too unhappy to appreciate Colonel Garovsky's attempt to put him at ease. "The man, Leitstein," he said bitterly, "he deceived me. I was helpless to stop it. I compromised my role. I forced Ayala to tell me things about the operation that I should not know. I *forced* her to tell me. I have destroyed compartmentalization. I should be sent home, Yakov. Get someone here who does not forget how to speak English the moment he hears a word of Yiddish."

Colonel Garovsky smiled tolerantly. "I was with Ayala when you called. It was all right." He sipped his coffee and placed the cup back on the desk. "You should have seen the charade she performed for McManus. She was magnificent." He paused again and looked closely at Captain Zanin, who remained cheerless. He knew he had to reassure the young officer. He blew on his hands and changed directions. "Perhaps we have compartmentalized too much. It is an occupational hazard. No permanent damage was done. Many things cannot be foreseen in an extraordinarily specialized operation. For example, I did not foresee when I arose today that before noon I would have lost more than a thousand American dollars to an old man who, at first sight, should be in a cemetery."

Captain Zanin's eyes widened. He stopped peeling his hard-boiled egg. "I do not understand."

Colonel Garovsky described the encounter with Mr. McManus and how he had taken their money.

"So we were all tricked a bit," he said at last and laughed. "Do you know, I read everything available on gambling to prepare for this operation. What happens? The American expression, so I read, is that I was 'taken to cleaners.'"

"What does that mean?"

"A gambler's phrase. The old man outwitted us. We were 'tap city.' Another phrase. We did not have taxi fare when we left McManus's apartment. Ayala had to pay. Luckily, McManus did not insist that she gamble."

Captain Zanin stalked to the window. He stared at the snow-swept park and then, after taking a number of deep breaths, slowly turned around. He tossed his hard-boiled egg into a wastebasket. "Dolan is on the verge of collapse," he said in a tone that made it clear he was not fully aware of the reasons. "I have had to lie to him, insult him, deprive him."

"Who is Dolan?" Colonel Garovsky had deliberately avoided learning the identity of the assassin whom Captain Zanin had in play. As a matter of compartmentalization. He had his role. The others had theirs. He made a mental note that Ayala had said that the McManus valet also was named Dolan.

Captain Zanin shook his head several times. Then he explained Jackie Dolan. It took some time. At length he said, "He may no longer be reliable."

"Why not?"

"I told him that today would be the last time."

"You told him *what?*"

"I did it in haste. He refused to leave his lodging until I assured him that today was the last time. Afterward, I told him there would be another contact. I don't know whether I can depend on him again. For the special assignment, that is."

"Why not?" Colonel Garovsky frowned. "I understood he is proficient with explosives. Is this not so?"

"He is proficient, yes. But I am convinced he has lost heart for the job."

"What do you propose?"

"That one of us take the assignment."

"One of us?" Colonel Garovsky studied his huge hands. "Do you mean another member of the team?"

"An Israeli member, yes. I have no faith in the South Africans."

Colonel Garovsky sipped his coffee. He himself now had serious questions about Captain Zanin's suitability. But it was too late to replace him. The joint organization had taken months to establish. The operation was underway. The morning distinctly had not been a success, but it was only the first step. The schedule was intact. He meant to keep it that way.

"Eli," he began slowly, "allow me to explain about this Dolan. Then I will tell you a few other things. Dolan was selected for one reason—from our point of view he is expendable. I would guess that is Major Espensheid's view also, since he put a member of his Defense Force under a foreign command. Our policy—more accurately, our precept—is that no Israeli soldier is, out of hand, expendable. Do you see my point."

"I suppose so."

"Let me be more explicit. The state of Israel cannot afford to expose itself to any extreme embarrassment in this city. Particularly in light of the main thrust of the operation. My knowledge of the New York City police tells me that a criminal as notorious as the 'elephant gun killer' will find it very difficult to remain at large forever. Our subterfuges—misleading descriptions and the rest—will be penetrated sooner or later. It would be disastrous for us if this popular maniac turned out to be a member of Israel's armed forces. By the same token it would be disastrous if an Israeli were implicated in a catastrophe that conceivably could claim dozens, perhaps hundreds, of innocent American lives. Now do you see?"

"Yes," Captain Zanin replied tentatively.

"Our purpose here is not to murder unsuspecting young men," Colonel Garovsky went on, his tone now emphatic, "or for that matter to explode *plastique* in a crowded public place. Those things are operational necessities . . . like putting refugees to flight before an armored action. We proposed them, the South Africans agreed to them, and they supplied your Dolan. Our obligation is to use him. To divert attention from the operation itself. I believe we have succeeded so far. Do you agree?"

Captain Zanin nodded.

There was silence. Both men looked a moment at the gloomy morning. Then they looked back at each other. Presently Colonel Garovsky set down his coffee cup and said dryly, "You realize, of course, that a number of other diversions were proposed. Violence was the last choice—absolutely the very last choice—especially as the operation was to be directed against New York. After all, the state of

Israel adheres to every decent and humane standard of international conduct. We are not comfortable laying ourselves open to the possibility of being caught behaving like criminals."

He paused a moment to let this sink in and then continued, "At first we imagined we could resort to something rather conventional, such as fabricating a scandal for a politician, ideally a politician with an interest in law enforcement. That was rejected. There is currently no politician in this state whose public disgrace would be sufficiently disruptive for our purposes. More subtly, we contemplated acquiring a bank in New York and driving it to the verge of insolvency—risky loans, you know, capricious securities trading and investment, heavy borrowing of short-term money, erratic speculation in foreign-exchange trading, and so on—the object being to threaten the state with severe economic damage. That, too, was rejected. It would have taken a number of years to accomplish, and we don't have that much time. Also it would have left us vulnerable to exposure. Imagine the repercussions if it were discovered that the state of Israel had put bank depositors in danger of financial ruin. The legal consequences alone convinced us to abandon *that* idea. So we decided to lay on something rather simple. Operationally simple, that is. Simplicity is best for short-term operational diversions, if one is attentive to all the details. You see, the shock value of your 'Finger of God' action not only engages the resources of the police—the police, by the way, do not directly monitor activities of the sort we will be engaged in—but it also creates a climate of emotional confusion. In a climate of emotional confusion almost any intelligence operation, if it is planned thoroughly, is guaranteed to succeed."

He picked up his coffee cup and drained it and added in a somewhat ironic voice, "This is logically a task for the Ministry of Finance. Rapid growth of investments and so on. Not at all a mission that an intelligence service is accustomed to. Or adept at. One would have thought that Finance, with all their connections, could have found an easier way. Apparently, they decided that men who are accomplished at formulating budgets, even inflationary ones, and making speeches to the United Jewish Appeal, should be spared this sort of thing. That's why we have it."

"May I ask a question?"

"Yes," said Colonel Garovsky. "I don't guarantee an answer."

"I gathered from Ayala that this has very much to do with wagering. The mission, that is. Is that right?"

"Yes."

"To win money?" Captain Zanin looked puzzled. His ignorance of gambling was almost total.

"Money, yes," Colonel Garovsky replied evenly, "and the casino as well."

He made his two-fingered gesture. They exchanged the traditional farewell. Captain Zanin left.

Colonel Garovsky watched from the window as Captain Zanin made his way across the park through the gusting snow. He was peeling his other hard-boiled egg.

4

The same snowstorm was in the course of converting Washington to an arctic lump. The skyline was obscured and the streets and avenues were deprived of shadows and a sense of depth. Traffic was stifled. The wind was viciously cold; it snapped at the garments of pedestrians and filled their eyes with tears. The only spot in which the bleakness seemed less than encompassing was Lafayette Park, across the street from the White House, where an animated party of young men and women gulped from a jug of cheap wine as they constructed a shoulder-high phallus out of snow.

Several blocks away, a few doors south of Scott Circle, a huge, grizzled man with hooded eyes sat on the defendant's side of a desk in a lawyer's office. He wore a wrinkled wool suit and listened, without a sign of emotion apart from gnawing his fingernails, to a series of legal steps that would dispossess him of his last penny on earth.

"I have subpoena power, Mr. Coombes," the lawyer said resentfully. His name was Adley and he wore the wild-eyed look of a man determined never to be taken advantage of again in his life. "I can make it easy or I can make it rough. It's up to you."

The lawyer knew from the stack of buff files on his desk that the man in front of him was past sixty. What he did not know was that age had not mellowed the man's disorderly temper. Had he known it, he probably would have taken care to tone down the impatient menace in his voice; the rumpled man had disfigured more men than one who had made the mistake of trying to intimidate him.

This pitiless morning, however, Coombes was distracted. Although he did not drink, he was like a recently dried-out alcoholic; his movements were sluggish and his expression was duller than usual. One reason was the lawyer himself. Coombes was certain he knew Adley from somewhere. Was it Burma? Iran? Had he been on one of the nonoperational staffs? Coombes couldn't remember, but Adley was definitely familiar.

Another reason was that he simply wanted to get it over with.

"What do I have to do?" Coombes said at last. He sounded vague. He was resigned today. To everything.

He was thoroughly and suffocatingly in debt. For months he had ignored his creditors, not all of whom he could call to mind. Now he wanted a final accounting, so to speak. He needed desperately to shed the sense of helplessness and sentimentality that had engulfed him since the death of his wife. She had taken a long time to die, and Coombes, who had scarcely been able to pay his bills before, fell irrecoverably behind. He had shut the mounting medical expenses out of his mind. Not out of love, but out of a furious desire for his wife to survive. (Her feeling for him could have best been described as tolerance, and Coombes required lots of that.) As her condition worsened he frantically sought new sources of funds, the way a commander of a besieged position in enemy territory sends out messages urgently at midnight for reinforcements and ammunition. When finally the doctor told him it was over, he felt only the disgust of defeat. It was as if he had dug in for a last stand, ready to give no quarter, and then been ordered to surrender. What he wanted now was to rid himself of shame. To sign the armistice. To consent to the reparations agreement. He wanted the mop-up troops—that was how he regarded the bill collectors who were hounding him—to withdraw beyond the truce line and cease fattening themselves on his despair.

"Do you have any other income?" the lawyer asked in a shrill voice. "Anything besides your pension? Any stocks or bonds? Any real estate? Anything in your wife's estate coming to you other than that insurance policy that named you as beneficiary?"

"What do I have to do?" Coombes repeated gruffly, sinking his teeth into a cuticle. He was no longer absorbed by his uncertain memory of Adley. In fact he was beginning to loathe the man, as if Adley were a small, destructive insect. He had nothing left, and he knew Adley knew it. When his wife's hospitalization plan ran out, he had sold his house in his ordinary Virginia suburb in an effort to pay for the extensive surgery. Then Adley, as agent for all his other creditors, had frozen his meager bank account, attached his salary (this had resulted in his dismissal as a used-car salesman; the owner of the lot in Maryland said that salesmen who couldn't pay their bills were poor employees; he implied that they would be tempted to cheat and possibly steal from the till), and had placed liens against his pension and the amount still owed him from the life insurance policy. What else does the son of a bitch want? he wondered.

"I want you to place your signature on these assignments," Adley said and pushed a sheaf of legal documents in front of Coombes. They obliged him to relinquish his remaining income and assets to pay off, as far as possible, a lengthy list of bank and finance-company loans.

"Where do I sign?"

"On the last page of each." He offered a ball-point pen.

Coombes shot out a thick hand and seized it. He rapidly scrawled his name on the papers, roughly shoving each one aside as he moved on to the next. He noted indifferently that in the process he had signed away his eight-year-old car. At length he finished and stood up.

"Thank you, very much," said Adley; there was a clear note of smugness in his voice. He examined the documents quickly. "I appreciate your cooperation. Better this way for everybody concerned." He straightened the papers. "By the way, I wonder if you would clear something up for me. In your loan applications and so forth you listed your government employer as the Department of Agriculture, but nobody at Agriculture has ever heard of you, and your pension is authorized by the Defense Department. Why is that?"

Coombes reached into his pocket and withdrew his car keys. "My car—your car now—is parked a couple of blocks from here. You might have some trouble starting it in this weather. I had to jump the battery this morning. It was hell getting somebody to stop."

He dangled the keys a moment for the lawyer to see and then let them fall to the floor in front of the desk.

A pained look came over Adley's face, giving him the appearance of a hunting dog that had allowed its quarry to escape. "But where is it?" he cried. "It might be papered with tickets before I find it!"

"Anything's possible."

Adley leapt to his feet and started for the front of the desk. Coombes raised his hand sharply and the lawyer stopped in his tracks.

"Don't go for those keys until I'm out of here," Coombes snarled. "If you do, I'll kick your teeth down your God damned throat."

Adley began to tremble. "Are you threatening me?" he whined.

"Yes."

Adley sank back into his chair. Coombes grabbed his hat and threadbare overcoat from a rack and then walked to the door. He waited a moment and then, with a massive heave, slammed it shut behind him.

Moments later, Coombes stood behind the shatterproof glass doors at the building entrance and watched the blowing snow. A Christmas tree blinked in the lobby behind him. He chewed a fingernail and took a deep breath. He was by nature incapable of exhilaration, but he was satisfied. His disgrace had been absolved. He had achieved the result that he came here for. To Coombes that justified the incontestable fact that he was flat broke and without job or prospects.

The men and women who passed through the doors and stamped snow from their shoes before boarding the elevators might have assumed that Coombes's expression conveyed the glow of success. They couldn't have been more wrong. Coombes had spent more than thirty years as an intelligence officer. He had long ago given up the conceit that triumph equals success and failure is the same as defeat. His profession heeded one commandment: Results vindicate everything.

At no time in his life had Coombes accomplished or expected anything other than results. Growing up in an isolated New England town, he was recognized as a large, rather slow lineman on an undistinguished high school football team. This recognition procured him a scholarship at a small nearby college, where he kept to himself and attained membership in the great fraternity of C-minus; he was rescued from anonymity on the football field by learning to cover short distances in a hurry and by exploiting a native aptitude for concealed violence; the team lost a good deal more games than it won, but at least once each autumn Saturday an opposing player was borne unconscious from the stadium, the victim of an undetected Coombes blow.

Upon graduating he had no luck finding a job and hit the road. He supported himself for several years as a zoo keeper in St. Louis, a nightclub bouncer in Detroit, a movie stuntman in Hollywood, and a dock-walloper in Boston.

The day after Pearl Harbor he enlisted in the marines. He received a commission on the strength of his college diploma and volunteered for the parachute battalion.

Pain and death soon became commonplace to him. The paratroops joined the Raider Battalion on Guadalcanal; they were the numb, thirsty defenders of Bloody Ridge; at one point Coombes was one of only sixty men maintaining a slippery hold on the crest; the fighting lasted deep into the night; it was cruel and confused; Coombes's platoon beat back charge after charge by the Japanese, while American naval fire from offshore pulverized the grassy slopes in the darkness; he radioed in vain that the barrage was killing as many marines as the enemy.

A few weeks later he was transferred to an OSS unit in Burma. The unit was led by a Raider major known only as Headlight. Coombes was given command of a section of Shan partisans.

The only other white man in the section was a Raider sergeant who was a number of years older than most of the other men who had joined at the outset of the war. To Coombes's relief the sergeant kept his own counsel in the slashing rain and oozing mud. Coombes knew nothing of the man except that he had once been a prizefighter and played an astonishing game of poker—and that he was prudently ruthless in combat.

After the war Coombes served for a time as an advisor to Chiang Kai-shek's Nationalist army. He fled back to Burma when Mao Tse-tung's peasants overran China, and he took part in a secret campaign organized by the new-fledged American intelligence service against the Burmese communists. Then, after nine years in Asia, he returned to the States.

He narrowly avoided dismissal for disobeying orders during the coup d'état in Iran. He was kept on but marked down as unsuitable for promotion and assigned to one of Special Operation Group's action teams that worked under Agriculture Department cover. He was suspended for an alleged security breach in an operation code-named Cricket, reinstated at a lower grade and put behind a desk in the Domestic Operations Division, and finally forced to retire at less than full pension when a new, reform-minded director was appointed.

It was a dreary business. Coombes had not wanted or looked forward to many things, but he had anticipated, with a measure of conviction, that he would be kept in harness until the mandatory retirement age. He wanted to be allowed to serve out his career as a token that, taken as a whole, his service had been valuable and the stains on his record were simply the battle scars of intelligence work. Now he knew. He wasn't up to the new standard. He blamed himself for not perceiving that the newer, younger men had to have age-wounded veterans such as he on whom to lever their ambitions. He wondered if they possessed their elders' primal resolution to survive. He had made no attempt to curb his resentment. He was a seasoned loser, but he certainly was not a good one.

He thrust his hands into his overcoat pockets and felt two or three coins, less than a dollar in change. He wondered how he would get back in this snowstorm to his untidy rented house in Maryland. It crossed his mind that he might well have to walk.

At once, a large, shiny car pulled up outside. Coombes turned away and then turned back suddenly. The driver leaned over and rolled down the window on the passenger's side. He had a muscular, lined face and iron gray hair trimmed just so. He smiled broadly and motioned for Coombes to hurry and get in. It was Headlight.

"Don't ask me how I knew where to find you," Headlight said breezily in a well-bred drawl. His smile settled down to an amused grin. Coombes muttered something and looked straight ahead.

Headlight slowly circled the block. The heavy snow obliged him to steer as if he were piloting an oversparred sailboat in a cross sea. Presently he pulled into a parking garage near a hotel that offered a lavish breakfast.

"This is my treat. I hope you haven't eaten yet," Headlight said amiably after the maitre d' had seated them. It was after ten o'clock.

He looked younger than Coombes even though he was a year or two older. His fashionable blazer, dark turtleneck, and gray slacks emphasized the wear and tear of Coombes's attire. He took out a gold case and lit one of the English cigarettes he preferred. "I tried to call, but all I got was a recording. Your phone seems to be out of order."

"It's been disconnected," Coombes said bitterly. He waited until the coffee had been poured and then added, "How did you know where I was?"

Headlight cupped his hands around his cigarette and inhaled evenly; it was a habit carried over from years in tropical rain forests, in remote neighborhoods in Europe, and on the decks of small, fast ships. His fingers were narrow and manicured. "It was the damnedest coincidence. My wife and Adley's wife are in the same ceramics class." His voice had an air of practiced modesty.

"What does that have to do with it?" Coombes persisted, biting a bit of loose skin on his thumb. "How does a woman who doesn't know me from page eight in the Blue Book just happen to mention my name? To your wife?"

Headlight carefully sipped his coffee and gave Coombes a searching look over the rim of his cup. His eyes shone with a glint of compassion, which Coombes did not believe for an instant was genuine. "It seems that Mrs. Adley likes to talk a lot about things she hears at home," he replied apologetically. "It seems that Adley likes to talk a lot to Mrs. Adley about his law practice."

"Law practice?" Coombes put in heatedly. "Adley is nothing but a glorified bill collector." He turned and glared at the empty table next to them.

Headlight shrugged. "Adley told his wife that he was taking action against a man who owed more money than any other retired government employee he had ever come across. A man named Coombes. That's what she told my wife, anyway." He butted his cigarette. "My wife knew I was trying to get in touch with you. . . . I called the used-car place, by the way. They said you weren't with them anymore."

Coombes abruptly turned back and faced Headlight. "Where do I know Adley from? Wasn't he one of the direct-hire people after the war? He looks about our age."

"Adley? To tell you the truth I've never met the man. Or his wife, either, for that matter. As far as I know he's exactly what you say he is. A glorified bill collector."

"I'm sure I've seen him before."

"What does he look like?"

"On the short side. A little overweight. Saucer eyed. Expensive haircuts that don't turn out right. Chip on his shoulder. Acts like he got pushed around when he was a kid and it's still on his mind."

Headlight shook his head slowly. "He doesn't sound familiar." Then his grin vanished. "If he had worked for us"—his tone sharpened a trifle—"I would remember him."

There was no doubt of that. Headlight had been a singularly discerning deputy director of operations. His attention to shades and subtleties had been astonishingly undivided. He remained congenial, but gradually he became almost solely preoccupied with the natural history of his officers and their agents; the longer he stayed in the job, the more assiduously did he acquire details of their most frivolous habits and distinctions. He was like an aquarium curator in a seafood restaurant who had been served dogfish instead of the filet of sole he ordered; he did not care that both fish tasted the same to him as long as he could detect the difference in texture in a fraction of a second.

In time he came to be regarded as a refined gossip box, a purveyor of dirty jokes who succeeded in staying in good taste. When an operation was under discussion, he might rule out the participation of a certain officer with a comment such as, "I know it was his idea, but have you seen his supplementary medical workup? This thing is going to take a fair amount of socializing, and he's having trouble holding his liquor. Do you know why? Because his girlfriend walked out on him and he's scared to death his wife will find out he had one." Or, if he concluded that an agent was ill chosen, he might say, "Read what the Romanian ambassador says about her. Her father was a member of the Iron Guard and she has the same inclinations. That scar on her cheek makes her too conspicuous. In any event she's too old for a crowd of Italian anarchists, and I've found out she spends an average of seven hours a week at her dressmaker." Toward the end the station chiefs complained—among themselves—that he was obsessed with trivia and was making decisions that were properly the business of the men in the field.

With the advent of the new regime the charge was circulated that Headlight and the rest of the old guard relied too much on their wits and not enough on modern technology. The new men also had different notions about right and wrong. Acts of the past, which Headlight and the others had contrived out of perceived necessity if not in virtue, were brought to light and judged to be the work of Satan. Repentance and resignations were demanded.

Headlight departed with more publicity than he wanted. He was annoyed that the newspapers got his real name one-third correct. But he remained in character, sardonically convivial. If he felt insulted or humiliated—or penitent—he did not show it. He maintained his contacts and managed to stay on sociable terms with the new director. He opened a consulting business and had no trouble finding clients, principally manufacturing firms with overseas branches. Former colleagues guessed that he dealt in industrial espionage.

Coombes did not pursue the question of Adley. He was more curious about Headlight's hospitality, behind which he suspected at least a slightly dishonorable motive. There had been a time when he trusted Headlight without reservation; in the early stages of his advancement through the hierarchy Headlight had been true to Coombes and the others who had been his companions-in-arms in Burma; by observable degrees, however, his old loyalty became ambiguous; more than once he had exploited his friendship with Coombes, to his benefit and at Coombes's expense, until finally his every move was perfidious to some extent in Coombes's eyes. In fact Coombes had been profoundly uneasy when Headlight appeared at his wife's funeral.

They ordered breakfast. Headlight urged Coombes to have whatever and as much as he liked from the extensive menu. "You understand this is on me," he said.

That had been Coombes's impression all along. He decided that this was an underhanded plea for assistance and not a graceless manifestation of a magnanimous spirit.

"I need some experienced help," Headlight continued. His grin was back. "You remember McManus, don't you?"

"No."

"Of course you do. He was with us in Burma. Older than most enlisted men. Known as 'Pop,' I believe. Had a reputation as a gambler."

Coombes's mind wandered briefly back through time. "A feather merchant." he said at length, nodding reflectively, "but tough as hell. He said he was at Guadalcanal, too, at the Ridge. I don't remember him if he was. Then again, I don't remember anybody who was at the Ridge. . . . What about him?"

"Some people want him to answer a couple of questions."

Coombes said nothing.

Headlight knitted his brow. His grin vanished again. He glanced furtively from side to side and leaned forward on his elbows. "I have a contract," he said dramatically. "I may have to mount an operation."

Coombes only frowned.

Headlight stroked his cheek thoughtfully. "I'll show you the summary later. It's in my car. What it amounts to is this. National Security Agency monitored a series of open telephone calls over the past forty-eight hours. They involved discussions about the movement of a huge sum of money to this country. To New York, to be precise. Tomorrow."

"What has that got to do with McManus?" Coombes felt himself being drawn in. Had he trusted Headlight, he would not have resisted. "Or me, for Christ's sake?"

"McManus lives in New York." Headlight paused as the breakfast was served. When the waiter had gone, he resumed. "He's been very sick lately, by the way. The point about him is, he's part owner of a bank in Switzerland that was approached about the money. The other owner, a man named Leitstein, was approached, too. I won't go into details about him; they're in the summary. Oh. Another thing about McManus and Leitstein. They've been in the rackets nearly all their lives."

"Who made the calls?"

"They came from Jerusalem. But it's not that simple. For several months some very well-researched questions have been asked here in Washington about McManus and Leitstein. Law-enforcement questions by and large. Nobody noticed until a man at Alcohol, Tobacco, and Firearms—the man worked for us in Angola, incidentally—until he got the same question about McManus that he'd gotten about Leitstein two weeks earlier. He did some checking and found out that damned near *everybody* had been getting questions about them. The questions themselves were remarkable as hell. They were based on extremely complete information about McManus and Leitstein."

"What's so interesting about them? Are they gun dealers?"

"In every case the people asking the questions were Israelis."

Coombes was mystified. His expression showed it.

"Israelis," Headlight repeated. He sounded impatient. "The Mossad."

Coombes continued to look perplexed. He found nothing unusual in the knowledge that the Israeli secret service was openly gathering information in Washington; Mossad operatives enjoyed virtually limitless freedom to ask questions—and expect answers—in their relationship with American intelligence and investigative agencies. He shrugged and took another bite of his eggs Benedict.

"Luckily," Headlight went on, impervious, "the man at ATF took his suspicions to Counter Intelligence instead of the FBI or somebody else at Treasury. Luckier still, the director did *not* give Counter Intelligence carte blanche to follow up." Coombes failed to see what "luck" had to do with it but did not interrupt. "It so happened that, at the time, the economic people in National Estimates were analyzing balance-of-payment deficits for Jerusalem and Pretoria."

"So what?"

"Over the past six months South Africa has been moving money into Israel. A good portion ostensibly was earmarked to pay for a dozen or so joint ventures. Military research, agricultural development, and so on. A public corporation was established in Jerusalem to receive the money. A communiqué said Israel and South Africa would contribute on a fifty-fifty basis, but as individual projects were announced, anybody could see that at least 70 percent was coming from South Africa. What's more, the results of an audit completed ten days ago showed that the corporation had more than five times as much money as it had projects to spend it on. And all but a few million of it in dollars."

"*Dollars?*" A look of astonishment spread across Coombes's face.

"It turns out that South Africa has been very busy. The government itself has been buying dollars like mad. From international reserves mostly. At commercial banks in Hong Kong, Kuwait, Grand Cayman. All over. At the spot rate. But that's just a drop in the bucket. The South African private sector has been doing most of the buying. The catch is, the government has allowed these business types to export piles of South African currency to finance the purchases in violation of their own currency laws."

"I still don't see the point."

Headlight clasped his hands under his chin and narrowed his eyes. "Israel doesn't have currency restrictions anymore. The audit showed that the public corporation in Jerusalem has cash on hand to the tune of one hundred and fifteen million dollars. That's exactly the amount the caller from Jerusalem said he wants to bring to New York tomorrow by way of McManus's and Leitstein's Swiss bank."

"Why are they collecting dollars?" Coombes asked and cast his eyes at the table. He hated discussing things he didn't understand, such as international monetary practices. "Why don't they buy something worth a damn with their money?"

Headlight smiled indulgently. "That's what I'm being paid to find out."

"Why you?" Coombes sounded dubious. At the same time his training asserted itself. He had heard an intriguing bit of private information and would not be satisfied until he had heard more.

"On the face of it," Headlight replied, "our national security isn't affected. There's nothing illegal, per se, about bringing dollars into the country."

He paused and lit another cigarette from his gold case.

"But the whole thing has rainy day written all over it. For one thing the South African money. South Africa is this close to a civil war, and it's shipping its dollar reserves to Israel—which has never been a bedrock of financial stability. Nothing is happening to the money, either. It's sitting in the bank on Yehuda Halevy Street in Tel Aviv and not drawing a cent of interest."

The waiter appeared, poured more coffee, and departed.

"Naturally, the analysts want to see how the money and McManus are connected. If they really are, of course. The trouble is, we can't approach Mossad or the South Africans." Headlight exhaled a breath of smoke. His habit of saying "we," as if he still had proprietary rights as one of his country's professional conspirators, annoyed Coombes; had the man not understood that he was bounced just the same as the rest of us? "As you know, Mossad puts a hundred-foot wall around every operation they run. We've never actually penetrated a Mossad job. We find out what they're up to only when they ask us for help. If you ask Mossad what they're doing, they peel off into a convoluted contingency action and freeze you out altogether."

Headlight took his napkin from his lap and laid it neatly beside his plate. "The South Africans are the same, given a few differences in style. Bureau of State Security shares a little here and there, mostly African stuff south of the Sahara, but they're damned closemouthed about their operations. Time was, we could simply plead we were fellow white men and BOSS would welcome us as rich members of the same family. Spoiled, to their way of thinking, but rich. Now they think we're hypocrites on the race question. They take the attitude that if we couldn't be trusted to keep our blacks in their place, why should we be trusted to help them maintain policies that keep *their* blacks in their place."

They were the only remaining breakfast customers. Men and women in dun-colored uniforms set the other tables for lunch. Their waiter slouched near the cash register.

Coombes put his palm to his face; the stubble was rough; he often did a haphazard job of shaving. "Is Counter Intelligence running its own operation against Mossad? Or BOSS?" He would not have dared ask such a question in the old days; it would have been a breach of discipline. It did not seem to matter now; he was retired and could ask questions when he felt like it.

Headlight gave the impression that he was offended by the mention of Counter Intelligence; he believed that the department had become worthless, perhaps even a liability, under the new director. He raised an eyebrow. "I said I have a contract." His drawl was less noticeable, and he sounded a bit like a schoolmaster. "I also said there's no obvious threat to national security. I'm driving at something. Do you see what it is?"

"Of course I see," Coombes replied acidly; he bit harshly at a fingernail.

"Well?"

"What I haven't seen is how much you're paying."

Headlight stubbed his cigarette irritably. "All right. Two hundred dollars a day plus itemized expenses. Ten-day maximum. No bonuses, no benefits."

"Support?"

"Limited but adequate. It's a way of keeping the operation on a manageable scale. There'll be immunity, but only for routine surveillance. No firearms, no electronic stuff, no surreptitious entries."

Coombes thought hard. He needed the money, God knows. He guessed that Headlight more than likely was galled by the terms that he had put on the table; they had the ring of second-class about them, and Headlight hated going second-class. Finally, he asked, "How much in advance?"

Headlight's face fell a fraction. "Frankly, this isn't the deal I wanted," he said with an obvious sense of shame, "but it was available and I took it. I prefer to work outside the country. But"—he sighed deeply and shook his head—"Counter Intelligence is in no shape to take this on. Even the director admits it. The law-enforcement people are out of the question, of course." He slumped back in his chair. "Look. Times have changed. We aren't case officers, anymore, or planners, or anything else official. I'm a hired hand, like an oil-company sheikh. (Neither man was aware that the comparison was out of date.) For all intents and purposes, I'm an agent. I've been recruited—literally, if you want to look at it that way—and I'm trying to recruit you."

"How much in advance?" Coombes said again and added forlornly, "for Christ's sake."

"Nothing," replied Headlight morosely. Coombes shook his head vigorously and tried to interrupt, but Headlight continued, softening his voice, "I have an operational allowance. I'll give you five thousand now against expenses. Itemized expenses. There are some credit cards and a driver's permit; they're part of the support I mentioned; don't be inhibited with the credit cards; they don't count against expenses. The cover is a military police unit; I have an ID card for you; it's in my office; I'll give it to you when we sign the papers. I've had a special line installed; it's secure; it will back up your cover when you call. By the way, I'll pay your next three months' rent and get your phone service restored. That's the best I can do, I'm afraid. How does it sound? Is it good enough?"

Coombes nodded. "I suppose I'm going to New York?"

"Yes."

"I'm not in the best shape. Will I have time for a workout?"

"I'm afraid not. I want you to leave today. Take the train. No planes in this weather. Find McManus. I have his address. Be careful how you approach him. Keep in mind about Mossad. They asked some damned knowledgeable questions about him and Leitstein."

"What if I run up against Mossad? If they're operational, I mean? Mossad plays pretty dirty with operational security."

"Don't do anything. Just report it. There's a reporting schedule. A contingency for a countermove is in the works. In case. Report to me and I'll take it from there. You're too old to play footsie with Mossad or BOSS. . . . Let's go. You can read the summary on the way to my office."

New York City's Lower East Side was white and silent. Not far from Chatham Square, on the fringe of Chinatown, Mr. McManus told the cab to stop. He got out and quickly looked about. He guessed he had succeeded in eluding his trackers.

Moving as fast as he could in the snow and biting wind, he made his way to a low, solitary building that stood near an abutment of the Manhattan Bridge; vacant lots on either side, strewn with shattered masonry, resembled miniature alpine ranges.

The building was gray and smudged; the snow made its outline seem medieval. Mr. McManus held his muffler to his throat and peered down at the basement door; it was flanked by two heavily barred, shuttered windows. He cautiously descended the stone steps, iced over now, and tiptoed over a litter of broken bottles and tin cans. He rapped with the handle of his umbrella.

There were shuffling footsteps and the clank of several locks. The door opened an inch or so on a thick chain. A flicker of light could be seen through the crack. A blinking, birdlike eye appeared. "What in hell you want here?" demanded a female voice; it was laden with terror and ancient, Balkan rage.

"To come in out of this weather." His voice was trembling again.

The door slammed shut. The chain slipped free. The shuffling feet retreated, loose slippers flapping.

Mr. McManus let himself in and bolted the door behind him.

The small, square room was murky and rank; jerky shadows were thrown against the walls by a single candle; it was deadly cold and reeked with revolting smells—decayed food, rancid cosmetics, human excretions. From floor to ceiling, in ungainly piles and bulging willy-nilly from greasy, puckered shopping bags, were old newspapers, odd bundles of wood, lampshade skeletons, bits of string, fragments of crockery, assorted filthy clothing, broken clocks.

He paused to allow his eyes to adjust to the poor light. "Where can I sit?" he asked after a moment.

"Not yet sitting," said the old woman. "Is impolite." She was at the far end of the room, seated in an armchair whose stuffing sprouted about her elbows. She made a fluttery gesture. "Come here. Is long time, I think. Very long time. I am missing visits of my clever son."

Mr. McManus breathed deeply, shuddered a trifle at the odor, and then trudged forward. "How are you, Ma?"

She surveyed him craftily. Her cheeks were thick with rouge; she wore a variety of things, ranging from a heavy blanket held together with lengths of wire to a pin-striped jacket whose frayed sleeves tumbled onto her spotted hands. Her features were sharp, hinting of reserves of strength in an obviously frail body. Her dark eyes were set apart, and they were clear and wild.

"Is stupid question. *You* are feeling no good, yes? Here. I am giving you place to sit."

He tried to protest but she interrupted. "Courtesy, please. Is poor taste to argue with your mother. Sit down." She arose with remarkable agility and helped him into the chair. "Is no refreshments. No *kajmak*. Nothing," she shouted, shoving aside a mound of junk and freeing a rickety crate. "A thousand pardons. Is too cold for me to panhandle in street." She sat down and pulled a pipe from her rags; she lit it with a broom straw held to the candle. "I am having no money, naturally. Of course, I am not expecting you. Is so long since you are here in old neighborhood. Why you feel no good?"

Mr. McManus leaned back and closed his eyes. "Heart attack," he mumbled. "I tried to let you know. Nobody could find you."

"Irish blood," she said, sucking the pipe, "is weak. Is bad luck to go through life with Irish blood. I am wishing for you pure, thick Montenegrin blood, but was not God's will. May God curse the Irish peoples. How is your Irish wife?"

The challenge rang in his ears. On another day, had he been stronger, he might have accepted it and done combat with her, despite his conviction that, in this matter at least, virtue and innocence were entirely on her side.

He had never shrunk from his mother as she slid from eccentricity to periodic—and aggressively independent—insanity; but his wife had, and he had tolerated it.

His mother had not seen his wife or children for more than thirty years. Affairs came to a crisis after the war. He had tried to ignore it as his wife complained bitterly about the bizarre woman who showed up unannounced with shopping bags of trash, talking to herself.

One day, his wife turned her away. "I won't have that dirty woman in my home!" she screamed that evening in tearful despair. "She's crazy, she embarrasses me and the kids, and she scares *everybody*. It might be different if she could speak English. The priest says she ought to be in an institution. I think you ought to send her back to Yugoslavia."

Mr. McManus knocked her down with the back of his hand and shouted that his mother could visit him and his children any time she felt like it. But the damage was done. The old woman scorned his entreaties to return. From then on she received him in her basement room (it was the only home in America she had ever known; she had moved in as a penniless, pregnant immigrant and had given birth to her only child in a bed that was still there, buried now under the rubbish) and turned down all his offers of money. Her only request of him was that he protect her from attempts to have her confined. He complied.

Until his heart attack, he visited her once a month. Often he found her squatting in a doorway, sorting her scraps of garbage. She always recognized him, no matter what intensity her madness, and invited him to her room for *kajmak*, a traditional Montenegrin cheese she usually managed to have on hand.

He looked at her blankly and set his jaw. "Leave that off for now, Ma. I ain't in shape for it."

She smiled benignly. "Yes. Is not time to speak of *her*. I am seeing that." Her eyes glittered. "Is time to speak of you. You are hearing wings of death, no?"

"It was close," he said, relieved that she was not determined to press the matter of his wife. "I guess I'll make it. Look at you. You're more than a hundred."

"Yes. I am living forever. No Irish blood. Even in Pike Street, so far from Montenegro, I am living forever. Strange place for niece of King Nicholas to live. Even forever. Of course Cetinje was *very* strange place for Montenegrin girl to find *Irish* lover." Her expression became curiously coy. "Am I telling you before that your father is Liverpool Irish?"

"Yes, Ma."

"Yes. Commercial attaché in British legation. Was beautiful man. Red haired. I am never before seeing man with red hair. Was playing the *gusle* in bay window of coffee house. *Gusle* with snake carved on neck. Gorgeous music. Very unusual. I am thinking only Montenegrin man plays *gusle* like that." She puffed her pipe and swayed slowly from side to side. "We love, but we are foolish. He is getting child on me—you—but before bishop is saying vows, McManus, your unworthy father, is drowning in Lake Scutari. Irish lout." She stopped swaying. "I am with child. I am having no husband. I am afraid. I am running away, no?"

Mr. McManus said nothing. He knew it was pointless to interrupt. She would reminisce—fantasize?—until she tired of it. He wondered whether she would say she fled Montenegro because her father threatened to kill her or because she feared that the king would hang her up by her thumbs.

"Yes. I am running away. Montenegrin girl, even niece of king, must have husband if she is with child. Irish husband will do, but *must* have husband. Well. What to do? Uncle is barbarian. Is shooting me with pistol if he knows. Father is barbarian. Is hanging me by my thumbs to punish disgrace. Was tradition. I am taking small sum of gold and sailing from Kotor to Bari. On midnight ship. I am not wanting to draw attention. I am dressing like Irish peasant. Top of morning."

She paused and reached under her tattered pin-striped jacket and scratched vigorously. Presently she was relieved and said quietly, "You are not barbarian. Am not knowing what you are. You are fighting with fists because of uncouth Irish blood. Montenegrin man, he laugh, he sing, he go to die. Is killing Mohammedans and Catholics. With pistol. Is loving death and pain and honor. Montenegrin man is barbarian, but is *never* fighting for money. You are not barbarian. . . . Is a mystery to your Montenegrin mother." She touched her temple with her forefinger. "You are still making the bets?"

"Maybe. If I can get a lock on the price. I'll have to have a heavy edge—as much skinny as I can get outside the pipeline."

The old woman brightened. Her skin was the color of a tallow candle under her rouge. "You are wanting the life pulses, yes? For the edge?"

"Yeah, Ma."

"Racehorse or human being?"

"A football player. Snakehips Davis."

"Snakes Hip? Is baptized Snakes Hip?"

"It's a nickname."

"Ah. A nickname. You are using nickname when you box for the nickels and dimes and I rub your body. Was what?"

"Kid Sweeney."

"Yes. A silly Irish name. Why you are not calling yourself Prince Danilo? Very noble. Prince Danilo is Montenegrin hero. Is killing every fool who leaves church of Christ to worship Mohammed."

"Not much interest on West Sixty-sixth Street in Yugoslavian princes. At least there wasn't in my day."

"Better having Irish nickname. Fighting like baboon with fists is no disgrace to Irishman."

She rummaged in a heap of trash and retrieved a clutch of yellowed sheets of paper. They were covered with handwritten charts and calculations. She dug into a jacket pocket and withdrew a pencil stub.

"Hold candle closer. Thank you. Please, date of birth for Snakes Hip."

Mr. McManus told her Snakehips's birth date.

She scribbled furiously on her lap for several minutes, muttering and humming. At length she turned the pages around for him to see.

"The football? Is playing Sunday, yes?"

Mr. McManus nodded.

She glanced at him briefly with her blinking, birdlike stare and then continued, "Looking at top of paper. Noticing three lines. First line. Body pulse. On Sunday, Snakes Hip is having positive body pulse. Is having strength of two, three men. Also is wanting woman. Or maybe man or young boy. Whatever. Is having much strength and much lust."

"He has a sore toe. Will he be going full steam on Sunday?"

"If toe is sore, Snakes Hip is not concerned. But"—she tapped the page with her pencil stub—"noticing the second line. The soul pulse. Is negative. On Sunday Snakes Hip is sad, maybe angry. Is like child. Is not cooperating."

"What about his brain?"

"Noticing third line. Mind pulse. Terrible. On Sunday Snakes Hip is having severe mind pulse. Not thinking straight. Forgetting to lock door. Difficulty making change. Not deciding which hat to wear."

"So how does it read?"

She tossed the yellowed pages back onto the pile of rubbish and relit her pipe. "On Sunday Snakes Hip is powerful man. But is sulking. And—important!—is thinking like stumblebum who drinks the hair tonic."

"Can I count on him? For the edge, I mean?"

"No. But do not be upset. Is only numbers on a piece of paper. A passing thing. Montenegrin kings such as my uncle the barbarian want the people to learn to read and do the sums. Buy printing press and make the books. Thousands of them. Then comes the trouble. Do the books help? Ha. The printing press, he is melted down and turned into bullets to shoot at the smelly Turks."

Mr. McManus rose to go. He needed warmth and more rest.

"Taking care with your health," said his mother. "Man with Irish blood is tasty morsel for the germs."

He closed the door and listened as the locks turned behind him. He computed Snakehips's biorhythms in his formula and tentatively decided that New Orleans-Philadelphia might be interesting. Two lousy teams going nowhere . . . either one could be the underdog . . . underdogs always win that kind of game. Definitely interesting.

The snow was still heavy but the hostility had gone out of the wind. Mr. McManus stepped into a nearby Chinese restaurant; it was operated by a man who had recently made a lot of money betting against his brother-in-law on whether the last digit of license plate numbers on Doyers Street during a two-hour interval would come up more often odd than even.

Mr. McManus spoke to the owner and made his way to the phone booth and called a cab. The owner, a perpetually cheerful man, saw no point to telling Mr. McManus that a large black man who spoke with an unusual accent had been in asking questions about him.

Major Espensheid sat down on the bed and removed his shoes, aligning them meticulously as if for inspection. Then he lay down and folded his thick arms across his chest. He did not relax, however, and his stocky body heaved as he pondered the interview with Special Branch Detective Sergeant Mazibuko.

"For a time the situation was out of hand, my boss," the tall Zulu policeman had said in Afrikaans after apologizing profusely for calling on the white major at his hotel. He was now wearing a suit. "The old man McManus tried to escape our surveillance. He took advantage of the snow. But I consulted the research document and traced him without much difficulty."

"You did this on your own authority?" Major Espensheid had been stunned when he answered the door and found Sergeant Mazibuko standing there. He had always had difficulty recognizing individual Africans; Sergeant Mazibuko's height had further disconcerted him. In his confusion he had admitted the black man—and poured him a cup of tea! Such an occurrence had no place in his divinely decreed, static universe of lawless authority and unappealable obedience; it simply was not done.

"Yes, my boss."

"Without instructions? Lieutenant Van Hooff was in charge . . ."

"Lieutenant Van Hooff was in an awkward spot, my boss. There was a mishap and he soiled his clothes. Sopping wet and freezing, he was. I thought it best to move ahead. The old man was shaking free of us."

"Where did he go?" Major Espensheid took a seat but did not offer one to Sergeant Mazibuko. He was offended that Sergeant Mazibuko had undertaken an independent course of action—and brought it off successfully; it flew in the face of his belief that Bantu policemen performed effectively only under the strict guidance of white superiors.

"To the black quarter," Sergeant Mazibuko said; the words came out with a clicking sound. "To Harlem. He called at the woman's house."

Major Espensheid frowned. "He visited his old sheila? The Kaffir fortune-teller?"

"Yes, my boss," Sergeant Mazibuko replied, glancing for a place to set his teacup.

"Well? Let's have it. Don't be shy, boy."

"Another visitor was departing as McManus arrived. It was Davis. Unquestionably. I consulted the photographs."

"Davis? The footballer?"

"Yes, my boss."

Major Espensheid brightened. His scalp prickled under his close-cropped, gray hair, and he rubbed his hands vigorously. Suddenly he felt on top of things again. Something like this was what he had been waiting for, a development that would allow him to take total control of the operation out of the hands of the Jews.

"The old woman," he said, "she's something of a *sangoma*, isn't she? Davis pays her to peer into his future, and she tosses the bones to keep the wizards away from him during a match. That's it, isn't it?"

He grinned crookedly as he noticed what he took to be a glimmer of fright in Sergeant Mazibuko's eyes. Nothing like talk of the bones to put the wind up a Kaffir, he thought.

"I don't suppose McManus paid any other calls, considering tbe poor state of his health."

"One other call, my boss. A small flat in the waterfront district. To pay respects to his mother, I presume."

Major Espensheid shrugged and wondered how anyone could live in this vile city, with its blasphemous absence of *basic* racial separation and its repulsive weather. Thcn he set his jaw.

"Listen carefully, Sergeant," he said, switching to English for no apparent reason. "This visit of Davis's to the old woman. No one's to hear of that. No one. None of your little mivvies, in fact no other Kaffirs at all, and especially not our friends the Jewboys. Is that clear?"

"Yes, my boss."

"What did I say?"

"I'm to keep mum in front of the Jewboys."

"Very good . . . Now. I've a task for you. A special task. You're to put Davis under surveillance. You're to watch him until I give the order for a stand-easy. It will mean a journey to Philadelphia, of course. A car will be ready for you, and you'll be given money for food and lodging. Don't be afraid of being on your own. Keep in mind that Davis is a Kaffir like you. He thinks the same as you do about most things. That should make him easy to follow. I'm right, aren't I?"

"Yes, my boss."

"Of course I am. Put your cup on the table there. Another thing. Not a word about your having tea here."

As the door closed behind Sergeant Mazibuko, Major Espensheid picked up the telephone and dialed. He recalled with a mixture of envy and regret that it was the Israelis' idea to include a black in the operation; a black will come in very handy in New York, Garovsky had said.

"Van Hooff? Major Espensheid here."

"Yes, Major."

There was a pause and then Major Espensheid blurted out angrily, "Mazibuko reported to me!" His fist tightened around the receiver. "He reported *here*. To my *room*."

"Oh, lord, sir, I'm sorry. I had no idea. I—"

"It's unacceptable, Lieutenant, letting a Kaffir run about on his own. Unacceptable. Mazibuko's a good copper, for a Kaffir, but he *must* have supervision. See that he's kept on a tighter rein in the future."

Lieutenant Van Hooff acknowledged the rebuke and at once launched into an elaborate account of the auto chase and of his violent encounter with the bus driver. He managed to convey that whatever might have gone wrong was the fault of Sergeant Mazibuko.

"Yes, yes," Major Espensheid broke in at length; he had regained his composure. "A Kaffir rarely works well with white men. They're not up to our standard. In any event you won't be bothered with him for a while. I've found some Kaffir work for him."

Both men laughed. Then he continued, "Get hold of the Jews. Tell them we want to use Dolan for a bit. Tell them we think he needs to spend some time with his countrymen."

"He's assigned to Zanin, sir."

Major Espensheid's pouchy face constricted. "I know he's assigned to Zanin, but, damn it, man, he's Uitmoormag. I'm his commanding officer. Point that out if the Jews get cheeky. Do anything that's necessary, but see to it that Dolan's available. . . ."

The Metroliner crept northward toward New York. Coombes stared from the window of a "No Smoking" car and watched the snow sweep the countryside in seething sheets.

Before boarding he had traveled by taxi to his cluttered suburban house. The front walk was hazardous; his only attempt to deal with the ice had been to sprinkle sand on it. He collected a few extra shirts and changes of underwear and stuffed them into a time-worn valise, along with his shaving things, a shoulder holster, a box of cartridges, and a square-stocked Colt Cobra revolver; the Colt was a relic of his Burma service.

At Union station he looked up Adley's home telephone and called from a phone booth. A female voice answered.

"I want to speak to Mrs. Adley."

"Mrs. Adley?"

"Yes. This is Mr. Walker at Potomac Savings and Loan. Who am I speaking to?"

"The maid."

"May I speak to Mrs. Adley?"

"Ain't no Mrs. Adley here. Attorney Adley ain't married."

Coombes slammed the phone onto the hook. Why had Headlight lied about Adley? he wondered in disgust. What else had he lied about? Was Headlight using him as a "pilot fish?"

He was on the point of walking out of the station, and throwing the contract he had signed in Headlight's face, when he remembered the money. Immediately he realized that, once again, at Headlight's urging, he was taking a risk whose dimensions Headlight had obscured. He detested the realization because he knew that his only choice was to go ahead.

For the money. For the God damned money.

5

Darkness and deepening snow.

Nathan Leitstein emerged from the subway at Sheridan Square. Seventh Avenue was hushed, a frozen river sunk in shadow, ancient, sinister, and disastrous; the neon lights seemed shrouded in gauze. Rough, dirty ice encrusted the sidewalks.

The tricky footing impeded his progress, but he had no difficulty finding the restaurant; it was a five-minute walk from the subway station, near the confluence of a number of narrow, dimly lit streets; it occupied the ground floor of one of those odd-shaped buildings that establish the character of the western portion of Greenwich Village; it was new. The oval plate-glass window next to the entrance was fogged.

He huddled a moment in a doorway across the street. He looked sharply first in one direction, then the other. The cold, borne on a destructive wind, was heavy and hard as bone; it threatened his hat and loosened the mucus in his nose. He had thought it wiser to arrive on foot than in his Rolls-Royce; more opportunity to look around unobserved, to see who might be loitering outside in spite of the weather. There seemed to be no one. He had instructed his driver to call for him at nine. It was eight now. He crossed over and stepped inside.

The Cafe Dromio was not Nathan Leitstein's sort of place. Joints like this open on a handful of pawn tickets, he said to himself as he blew his nose, and fold before the waiters get a week's pay; like nightclubs during Prohibition. It was crowded and loud and resolutely informal. There was no coatroom and reservations were not accepted. The decor was framed reproductions of French music-hall posters and imitation Tiffany lamps. A jukebox blared popular music.

The bar, presided over by three mesomorphic young men with beards and unbuttoned shirts, took up one side of a low-ceilinged passage. Men and women, mostly young and attired in fashionably plain denim or corduroy, competed for seats and laughed self-consciously. Domestic white wine was the prevailing drink.

He pushed past the shifting bodies and gesturing arms to the brink of the dining room and edged himself into the front rank of a half dozen couples waiting to be seated; they stood with folded arms and anxious faces, fearful that somebody would get a table ahead of them.

At once he was greeted by the maitre d', a reedy young man with a watery smile and a clipboard cradled in one arm.

"Leitstein," he muttered, struggling out of his overcoat; it was soggy with snow.

The maitre d' consulted his clipboard. Then he said in a gulpy midwestern voice, "There aren't any tables for one right now, sir. If you'll give me your name, you can have a cocktail and I'll—"

"Leitstein," he repeated a trifle irritably; for a fraction of a second he longed for the saturnine formality of Lou Siegel's. "A party's expecting me . . . for a meet—"

He handed the young man a five—which was received with a quizzical expression; this etiquette was unknown to headwaiters at the Cafe Dromio; it was also unknown to the people behind him; they surmised resentfully that this sleek little man was getting preferential treatment; probably in show business, they grumbled, or politics.

The maitre d' blushed and fumbled with the money. He gazed again at his list. Nathan Leitstein peered around his shoulder.

"What's the party's name, sir?"

"I don't know. They said they're expecting me."

"What's the name again?"

"I just told you. I don't know."

"Your name, sir, I mean?"

"Leitstein."

He ran his finger down the page. "I have a Lightstone," he said with a sigh. "Could that be it?"

"Maybe. Who gave you it?"

The maitre d' nervously surveyed the room. It was a paneled cavern of small tables and drooping daisies in old mustard jars. Presently he made a startled noise and jabbed the air with his finger. "There they are," he cried, pointing to a table near the kitchen. "We're so busy tonight, it slipped my mind."

"What's the party's name?"

"They didn't give one. They said they were expecting you."

"Tell them I'm here."

"They asked me to send you straight back. Enjoy your dinner."

He shrugged and walked to the table.

The others stared at him. Their eyes were livid with indignation.

He made his way cautiously. Activity in the room was galvanic. Waitresses struggled under trays of food to avoid collision with busboys weighed down with dirty dishes. He spied a blackboard fastened partway up one wall; it was the menu: omelets, fish, salads garnished with bean sprouts, at modest prices. Three to one, they're out of half the things listed, he thought.

At length he found them. There were three men and a woman, each sipping club soda; they studied the blackboard with indifference and indecision. A fidgety waitress stood by. One of the men, tall, muscular, with skin of a color approaching copper, rose and extended his hand.

"Mr. Leitstein?" He gripped his hand and looked closely into his face. He was older than the others and had wiry, gray hair. "Yes, of course. It took a moment to recognize you. You look older than your photographs. They were taken some time back, I suppose. Delighted you could join us. Won't you have a seat? We're about to order."

He gestured with two fingers to an extra place.

"Take your time, pal. I ate already." He pulled up a chair, draped his overcoat over the back, and sat down. "Get me a drink," he said to the waitress. "Armagnac, a double, straight up." He lit a cigar and shivered involuntarily. The woman extravagantly fanned away the smoke. "Freeze your ass off, this weather. Something new for you people, I guess."

There was difficulty ordering dinner. The menu specified listed dishes only, no substitutes. They insisted on variations and squabbled with the waitress and changed their minds several times. At length they decided, and the waitress, who had been impatiently tapping her pad, stalked away.

"That was most disagreeable," the man said when calm returned, "and most inappropriate. Quarreling with employees is bad form. I apologize. But they shouldn't be so rigid about the cuisine. . . .

"Ah. I am neglecting my duties as a host," he went on; his tone was cordial. "I am Mr. Katz. May I present my associates, Mr. Cohen and Mr. Goldberg"—the other men, equally lean and dark, bowed slightly—"and my secretary, Miss Levine." The woman only looked at him over her club soda. She was a blonde with cool eyes and high cheekbones.

Nathan Leitstein glanced slowly from face to face. A number of facetious associations, drawn from early talking pictures, crossed his mind. "Katz" and "Miss Levine" he recognized immediately; Kid Sweeney had described them faithfully. Katz was the hoople who had gone on the hook in the Kid's apartment. Miss Levine was the patootie who had hustled Dolan's kid. "Cohen" and "Goldberg," who knew?

Are these guys kidding? he thought, even in New York, a Katz, a Cohen, a Goldberg, and a Levine—and nobody else—at the *same* table?

"*Shalom*," he said and puffed his cigar.

Miss Levine again fanned away the smoke. Cohen and Goldberg remained expressionless.

Katz scowled. Then he put his hands together and touched his chin. "Let's get down to business, Mr. Leitstein, if you don't mind," he said somewhat irascibly. "We wasted quite a bit of time with your colleague McManus. We don't intend to waste any more. You have something we need. We have something you want."

The waitress brought his brandy. He tilted the balloon and sniffed it and took a sip. He had first tasted Armagnac in Havana before the war. There had been a bar where they knew he was an ex-fighter; he stopped in whenever it was raining and the track was sloppy at Oriental Park. One of the regulars, whose name he never caught, was a big, loud American with a mustache and a sunburn; the guy got a load on every afternoon and talked about boxing and whores—Kansas City whores, not Havana whores. Everybody seemed engrossed by the guy's monologues; everybody except Nathan Leitstein, who disregarded noisy drunks; and the fact that even one customer wasn't paying attention to him drove the guy to talk at the top of his lungs. One day the guy cornered him at the bar and mumbled in his face that it would be a noble and glorious thing if they stepped outside and found out who had the best left hook. Without looking up, he placed his thick-knuckled left hand on the bar, palm down so the guy could see, and said quietly, "Thanks, pal, but amateurs don't always get up healthy from left hooks." The guy looked as if he were about to say, this isn't the way it was supposed to happen; then his face constricted in pain like a sudden toothache and he walked unsteadily out. The bartender, who had been watching, poured him a drink from a round, flat bottle. "*Algo especial*, Señor Leitstein," he said with a modest smile of relief, "*Armagnac. Salud*," and added, shaking his head, "*Ernesto es un buche y pluma*." He never saw the guy again.

He took another sip and considered Katz's gambit. He guessed that Katz and the others had heard that their $115 million would not be welcome at the Commercial and Claims Bank. He thought of his return call to Jerusalem; the retired general had been called out of the country, he was told, and could not be reached; he had left the message with the woman who answered.

"Okay, pal. Let's start with what I got that you need."

Katz straightened up. He placed his hands on the table. The gesture was deliberate, as if he had rehearsed it. "We are not birds of passage," he began, relaxing a fraction, "but we have confidence in the possibilities of speculation. Also we have a bit of venture capital. Regrettably, our skills leave something to be desired, to say nothing of our instincts." He permitted himself a wintry smile. "We are conservative by nature, so we are extremely reluctant to make dogmatic statements on the outcome of uncertain events—and we are not disposed to throw our lot in with a single possibility. That is why we have come to you. We need your experience and your advice. And a degree of your participation. Indirect participation, that is. You know our terms, do you not?"

Kid Sweeney had warned him that this hoople was full of prunes, but he had not expected this. "Experience? What do you mean, experience? A few things I've learned that I'd rather not know? What the hell good is that?"

Katz looked astonished. Then he turned away and stared across the room.

It was Miss Levine who finally spoke.

"We understand you've been quite successful at sports betting." she said with a strange smile. "We would like you to enlighten us on the fine points."

"You been misinformed. I don't bet. I look at what's moving and what's standing still and squeeze the line. Nothing tricky about it."

"Then you're one of those persons who gives odds on various sporting events, and so forth?"

"Not gives, sweetie, sells."

Miss Levine raised an eyebrow and lit a cigarette. Nathan Leitstein was startled; he had guessed she loathed smoking.

Another silence. Katz leaned over and whispered in the ear of Cohen, who looked at the ceiling as he listened and then whispered back. After a moment Katz said, "If you do not bet, and if you do not take bets, then how do you—"

"I keep in touch with people who bet. And people who take bets—for a commission. How the hell do you think books make money? They try to even things out so they got more losers than winners."

"But your experience—"

"I got no experience. Maybe I'll get some one day when I got nothing else. What I got is a habit of not thinking I know too much." He swallowed more brandy. "I got no advice, either. That, I'll give when I'm too old to get into trouble. I ain't that old, yet, no matter what you might've heard. So why don't you stop beating your chops and get to the point?"

Katz looked puzzled. He glanced at his companions. They looked puzzled, too. "You do know what we're willing to pay, don't you?"

"Yeah. A good dollar. Do you mind telling me what you're buying?"

"Might we discuss your participation? An indispensable condition would be our right to reserve your services until a week from today."

"If you're thinking of my bank, forget it. That's out."

Katz smiled wryly. "First things first, Mr. Leitstein. Banks are convenient but not essential nowadays. Let's speak frankly, shall we?"

"It would be a relief."

"What we need is not complicated. Detailed to the point of some drudgery, perhaps, but not complicated. Certainly not as complicated as McManus seemed to believe. We are flexible. Also we are discreet, and we expect those whom we engage as middlemen and what-not to act as discreetly as we do. Is that understood?"

"I can put two and two together and keep my mouth shut."

"Excellent. Then I take it you are amenable to an arrangement?"

He tasted his brandy. "What arrangement is that, pal?"

Katz exhaled an angry sigh. He clenched his teeth and rolled his eyes toward the ceiling. "What is it?" he rasped. "Why the *shtuss*? Why the insults? Why all the questions? First McManus. Now you. McManus I can understand. He's sick and out of sorts. But you? You're the picture of health—you suffer only from hemorrhoids—and you're even more impossible than he is." Abruptly his mouth turned down at the corners. "And we thought we could make business with a Jew. . . . *Vos tut zich*?"

"Is that why you sent that ham-and-egg pistolero to my office?" he shot back. "Because you thought you could make business with a Jew?"

Katz glared at him.

Nathan Leitstein sniffed his brandy, tossed it off, and motioned to the waitress for a refill. He placed his hands on his knees and leaned forward. "You can make business with me, pal," he said evenly, "but forget trying to call the shots. You ain't ready for it. A man gets sandbagged the way you did should realize that."

Katz thrust out his chin. "McManus only wanted to show us that he is clever. He did not want to make business."

"The word is you tried to flash a buster on McManus and he put you on the *schneid*. You want a tip? That ain't the way to make business."

"How do *you* propose to make business, Mr. Leitstein?" It was Miss Levine again. She looked slightly bored. Her head was inclined a degree. A forefinger rested against her cheek, just below the corner of her eye.

The waitress set his drink on the table. "I hear you got a nice stack of chips," he continued; he ignored the woman and spoke directly to Katz, "and you sound like you want to tap the table. But you got a problem, right? You got no idea what the cards mean."

Katz's glare softened. He looked at the others. His expression invited comment. They shrugged. He looked back across the table and nodded tentatively.

"First, I got to know what kind of action you want, and, second, how big a shot you want to take."

"We wish to bet on your professional football," Katz replied immediately.

"This Sunday?"

"Yes."

"For how much?"

Katz was silent a moment. Then he said, "Sixty million American dollars. Cash."

Nathan Leitstein sipped his brandy. He had trouble swallowing. He was gravely perplexed. He hoped it didn't show. Where the hell's the other $55 million? he wondered and gulped. Why did they tell Lemmer $115 million, and who's getting the rest of it?

"You do not look well, Mr. Leitstein," said Miss Levine. She was studying her manicure. "Perhaps alcohol does not agree with you. Many men do not need it. We *do* hope you can make business for such a piddling sum."

He cleared his throat. "I heard a higher figure," he said. "It's no problem, the cheaper amount. It's just that I heard a higher figure. I done some planning using a higher figure."

"*Planning?*" Katz put in.

The other two men braced themselves in their seats.

"We ain't talking a bag of seashells, pal. You got to plan ahead, you want to take a shot like this. You got to find the books that'll lay off heavy. You got to work out the pay and collect. You got to—"

"The planning is our province," Katz interrupted. "We, too, have been busy, and we are capable. We have conducted a trial run, so to speak. This afternoon we were able to visit 197 bank branches in all districts and purchase one-dollar money orders in each branch. This we accomplished in less than two hours. I'm sure we would have done better had the weather not hindered us."

"The four of you did this?"

Katz smiled. "We will not be just four. Does that reassure you?"

"What the hell does buying money orders have to do with taking a shot?"

His smile vanished. "No more planning," he snapped. "It is not your concern."

The dinner arrived. The table was too small. Goldberg got a greasy sleeve when he reached for his club soda and Miss Levine simultaneously put out her knife for the butter. They spoke only to each other, sparingly and in Hebrew. At one point Katz and Miss Levine exchanged glances; Miss Levine ran her tongue across her upper lip, and Katz's expression was briefly wolfish.

Nathan Leitstein nursed his brandy and puffed his cigar and watched. In his career he had found that seemingly coincidental phenomena were often crucial to the edge; such as, a liquor bottle sticking out of a golf bag (to convince a sucker he is playing against a lush); or a college basketball player in a $300 suit; or a horse race in which all the best bets finish out of the money—or the fact that Miss Levine was Katz's pound cake.

None of which helped to explain Katz's astonishing ultimatum. What the hell had the hoople meant, no more planning? Was it for nothing that he had been on the telephone all afternoon—to the West Coast, to Las Vegas and Reno, to Chicago, Philadelphia, and Boston—activating a network of bookies to write the unparalleled volume of action he had assumed he and Kid Sweeney would be steering? What was this crap about God damned money orders? Was Katz floating another dutch? He didn't think so. What he had heard so far sounded like the Three Stooges filling out their income tax.

The dishes were cleared away. Katz again put his fingers together in a peak. "I apologize for the rudeness, Mr. Leitstein," he began graciously. "It was unintentional. When I said no more planning, I meant that inquiries at this time would be indiscreet."

"Who's making inquiries?" He deliberately sounded indignant. "All I done was make a few calls. Discreet calls. You tell me you want action. Football. This weekend. You can't walk into a cash-and-carry joint Sunday morning and say, 'My name is Katz. Leitstein called and said I'd be dropping by. Give me the Dolphins sixty million times.' You see you can't do that, don't you? Like I told you, you want to give the guys this much work, you got to give them time to get ready for it."

"What Mr. Katz is saying," said Miss Levine, "is that the kind of planning you have indicated isn't necessary for our purposes."

"Jesus Christ!" He drew up his shoulders and threw out his palms. "Where do you hooples get off, telling me you can't deal with me? I'm telling you, I can't deal with you!"

Katz frowned. "But you agreed to an arrangement."

"I said I was open to one. I ain't heard one yet."

"You know the commissions we will pay?"

"I told you I did. Seven hundred and fifty grand to the bank, right? And two-fifty apiece to me and McManus?"

"Yes."

"So? Nobody puts out that kind of dough for experience and advice. What the hell do you want?"

"Your services," said Miss Levine. She lit another cigarette and exhaled through her nose.

"What services? From what I heard that's exactly what you don't want."

"We want to purchase your services," said Katz; his tone remained polite, "yours and your colleague McManus's. We want you—and McManus—to calculate for us"—he lowered his voice—"an upset. A long-shot upset."

Nathan Leitstein was quiet a moment. Then he said, "That's all?"

Katz's eyes blazed. "Don't test our patience, Leitstein," he said sharply. "When we engage someone like you"—he pointed with two fingers; the "you" was spoken with a clear note of distaste—"we *will* have what we pay for. Is that clear? When we say we want a long-shot upset, and you say we will have it, then we damned well *will* have a long-shot upset. If we do not have it, you will not find our next rendezvous at all amusing. Do we understand each other?"

He emitted a drawn-out sigh. "Skip the Bill Daley act, pal. You still got a long way to go. Let's get this straight right off the bat. Nobody in the world knows from a sure thing. Firecrackers and fuck-ups, yeah, but no duck soup. I can figure a spread for you, and I can tell you a hundred ways to play it. Chalk, reverse, over-under, you name it. But the way your wheels are spinning, you'll be sixty million balloons in the tub with nothing in your hand but your putz. . . . That's assuming I track you on this double-clocked overlay you got your heart set on."

"Would you explain, please?" said Miss Levine. She carefully butted her cigarette.

"Yeah, sweetie, I'll explain, I'll explain like you been dying all night to hear. Like you got no way of hearing from anybody else." Then he looked directly at Katz. "And you know it. So no more of this muscle crap."

Katz nodded.

"To start with, no single book would take that kind of action. Couldn't afford it. Couldn't take the chance of leaving himself wide open. For the sake of argument, though, let's say you seen the light and find more than one book and don't get it all down at one throw.

"Also for the sake of argument, let's say you go with Philadelphia-New Orleans. Philadelphia is eight and seven on the year and out of the running, but they got Snakehips Davis plus tough defense, and they won all but two on the road. New Orleans is definitely a dog, lost fourteen games—but only three or four by much. Game's in New Orleans, and Philadelphia goes off as a ten-point favorite.

"You're taking the short, right? New Orleans? So you give it a little gas, play it a little at a time with each book. They ain't fresh off the boat, the books, so they see what's cooking. Plus they want to stay out of the middle. What happens? They move the line.

"At which point the law of gravity takes over—except in reverse. The points on the bottom go up. You slip in a little more, and then New Orleans is, say, minus five. You rev it again, and they're even money. Then you pile it on, and the line starts to shimmy, and before you know it, New Orleans is, say, a three-point *favorite*." He puffed his cigar. "It could happen."

"New Orleans will then win by three points?" Miss Levine asked incredulously.

"It don't matter. This is a maybe-maybe not. I'm giving you the lowdown on how it works."

Katz drummed his fingers on the table. "It is true, is it not, that Philadelphia is still the better team? And more than likely to win after all? Possibly by ten points?"

"What do you care who wins? You ain't rooting for nobody. You want to pull the spread. That's what it's all about. Shake the line early, aim for the middle, and get the spread you want, not the one the books want you to have.

"That's why you need me—to watch the line when it's moving and tell you where the soft spots are and how hard to hit them." He swirled his brandy in a wide arc and then sipped it. "Catch the line when it's moving, pal. That's how you cash the big tickets."

The others stared at him.

At length Katz asked, "What is the middle?"

"Like a box at the track. Except instead of betting three horses one-two-three six different ways in three different races, you bet one game—early and heavy on the underdog to lower the spread, then put the family heirlooms on the favorite; you win either way, maybe both."

"We can do this?"

"Depends you know what's doing. Ain't worth a whore's hello if you don't."

"You will guarantee it?"

"You want a guarantee, put your money in a savings account."

The check was placed on the table, face up. They bickered over it, forgetting what each had eaten and glancing at the blackboard to confirm the prices.

"When you have determined what I must pay, please tell me," said Miss Levine.

"Mr. Leitstein had two items from the bar," said Goldberg, who had taken charge of the arithmetic.

Nathan Leitstein bent forward from his chair and seized the check. He fished a $100 bill from his wallet and signaled the waitress. "It's on me," he said with a grunt and turned to Katz. "The Vegas line came in for the big guys at noon today. Only the big guys get first look. They bet noon on the dot. Five minutes later the line starts moving, and by one o'clock it's on the board. What I'm saying is, next Sunday's line is on the board now. Normally a hoople would be insane to take a heavy shot after it's on the board"—he polished off his brandy—"but you ain't taking no garden-variety heavy shot."

Katz stroked his chin. Presently he said, "We most certainly will be betting. However, for reasons of our own, we cannot tell you definitely at this point whether we will be betting tomorrow."

"Are you one of the big guys, Mr. Leitstein?" Miss Levine broke in. Her mouth was turned up in a knowing smile.

"Depends. You know how it is."

Katz shot her a hard glance and continued, "If our position sounds inconsistent, or even muddleheaded, I'm sorry. In any event, by noon tomorrow the commission will have been delivered to your bank. How should we arrange to pay your fee? And McManus's, of course?"

"Hold it, pal. We ain't decided what you're paying for."

"For your marksmanship," said Katz. "We are paying for your ability to—how did you put it?—to hit the soft spots."

Nathan Leitstein pulled a face. "And get my putz in a crack if you screw up and take a bath? Not a chance. Here's what we'll do. You let me know when you're ready to get on the sheet, and I'll tell you how to play it. If you score, *then* me and McManus'll take the fee and you can put the other dough in the bank. Agreed?"

"Agreed."

"When's the money going to be available?"

"We'll contact you tomorrow."

"When? Give me a time so I can be by the phone."

"We'll call your office at ten. Is that convenient?"

"Great. Any chance there'll be more? More than the sixty mil?"

"Why?"

"If it's sixty million, you play it one way. If it's sixty-one, seventy-one, you play it another. See what I mean?"

"Thank you for the dinner, Mr. Leitstein."

They rose and trooped away single file. Katz and Miss Levine fell into an animated argument as they passed through the bar.

Nathan Leitstein left a few minutes later. He did not bother with the change from the hundred. There was a sassiness in his step. He was happy he had gotten what he wanted. His Rolls-Royce was waiting.

The snow was gusting violently. The streets were ghostly.

"Get out of this neighborhood," he told his driver. The Armagnac was still on his breath. It tasted wonderful. He decided against another cigar. "Pull up at the first phone you come to."

At the same time Special Branch Detective Sergeant Mazibuko sat fingering his watch in the narrow lobby of the St. Regis Hotel. He wondered how soon he would be thrown out.

The place was thronged with businessmen. They were stranded in the city by the snowstorm. Some laughed and said they were ready to sleep on the floor. Others were grim and quiet. The reception desk was under siege by a dense, jittery mob. "If you don't have a reservation, please step aside," said a haggard clerk.

Sergeant Mazibuko saw not a single other black face.

At first he had thought the hotel was whites-only. That had put him on edge. He had never taken a seat in a white hotel. Already the bell captain had given him a nasty look.

He hoped they wouldn't order him to leave before Snakehips Davis came back downstairs. He was uncertain how much more of this vicious weather he could take.

Today was the first time he had seen snow. In the morning it had fascinated him. By nightfall it had become a thick, white, painful burden.

Opposite him several men pulled up chairs. They began a rubber of bridge. Each man glanced at him a moment, then paid him no more attention.

Sergeant Mazibuko noticed their clothes; they were obviously off the peg but they fit nicely. He shifted a fraction. He tested the fit of his own suit; it, too, was off the peg, from Payne Bros.; it did not fit nicely. Far from it. It was as if his large, powerfully built body had changed shape in the course of the day. His jacket seemed smaller than when he had put it on. His pockets seemed to have filled up on their own. He felt lonely and very countrified.

Involuntarily, he reached inside his jacket. He withdrew his passport and gazed at it. The photograph was close enough: narrow face in late middle age, arched-up mouth, prominent nose. The pages were watermarked and stamped with a back-dated forged visa. It described him as a diplomat. It looked remarkably like his well-fingered passbook.

He had carried his passbook since he was sixteen. His passbook was the document of his existence. He had been tapped on the shoulder many times by white policemen. Automatically he produced his passbook before showing his Special Branch identity card. Without his passbook he was just an illegal Bantu certain to be "endorsed out" on the next bus to his tribal homeland, Special Branch or not.

He slipped the passport back into his pocket.

He rejected the idea of going for a drink. Where in this hotel could he relax? He decided against telephoning Major Espensheid. He had nothing to report. He touched his watch again. It was a stainless steel Rado Diastar. He had had it only a few months. It was quite expensive. A Pakistani general dealer had pressed it on him. The man's brother had been detained under the Suppression of Communism Act. "A token of my respect, Sergeant," the Pakistani had murmured; the back room of his cluttered store reeked of curry, "my respect for a man who will keep in mind that my brother and I share no political views."

The card players were chatting about the previous day's football matches. They talked mainly about the play of one of the local sides.

Sergeant Mazibuko had himself watched the local match on the television. He had grown bored after a few minutes. He was indifferent to football. To him it was a flamboyant ritual, not an expression of life itself. He had continued to watch because of the advertisements. One of them called attention to an insurance company. "Life is full of complications," the voice said.

The slogan intrigued Sergeant Mazibuko. He loved puzzles; sorting out complications. Crosswords were his passion. He had trained himself to look for what he did not expect. He had been in CID before transferring to the Branch. On his first CID job he had found the clue that made the prosecution's case. A murder. The victim was a wife; her headless body was found in a shallow grave near a secluded spot where she rendezvoused with her lover. The prime suspect was the lover; he had found the woman's car at the site of their trysts. The husband had been away on business; he admitted bitter, sometimes hostile relations with his wife, but he furnished receipts to show that he had sold his gun collection a week before the tragedy. Controversy abounded. How long had the woman been dead? Was she dead or alive when her head was cut off? Where was the head? Sergeant Mazibuko was questioning the Bantu servants about the woman's comings and goings when he spotted a hole in a bookcase. It had been covered with a child's crayon. He dug into the wood with a knife and found a .38 caliber slug—which had been fired from one of the guns the husband had sold. The head turned up in a river, a bullet hole clean through it. The husband soon confessed to shooting the woman in the temple on the servants' day off, chopped off her head with a cane blade, cleaning and selling all his firearms, burying the woman that night at the place where he knew she met the suspect, disposing of the head, walking home, and leaving town the next day. A white detective got credit for breaking the case.

When he transferred to the Branch, he divided his time between surveillance and liaison with a small network of informers. They kept him abreast of security law violations among the nonwhite population. He quickly established in his mind a distinction between subversion and infraction. It was a nice point, and it would not have set well with his white superiors had they been aware of it, but he stuck to it scrupulously. He wouldn't hesitate to run in a fellow Zulu suspected of instructing schoolboys in the use of explosives. But he weighed what he called the "illusion factor" when he heard that a banned person, especially a woman, had been seen chatting with her neighbor.

At home, in Durban, Sergeant Mazibuko relished solo surveillance jobs. He worked best alone. Solo jobs let him organize his attention and execute his techniques free of official or social second-guessing. That was at home. Here, in frozen New York, his rules of thumb did not apply. Shadowing another black man in New York was *not* the same as shadowing a black man in Durban. In Durban you had one advantage you could count on no matter what. There were "white zones" and "nonwhite zones." In Durban you knew where blacks would *not* go. In New York they seemed to go any place they jolly well pleased.

That was certainly true of Snakehips Davis.

He had picked up Davis's trail in the early afternoon. For a time it appeared that Davis had launched on a tour of the city. Sergeant Mazibuko checked the research document; Davis was a man of habit; he followed the same routine during his Monday trips to New York: midmorning conference with Madam Excella; a brief visit with his sister in the Bronx; lunch with his business partners at a fancy restaurant; an hour or so at a studio to film a television commercial; consultations at his lawyer's; and then the drive back to Philadelphia.

Several times Sergeant Mazibuko feared he had lost Davis's maroon limousine. The snow and his unfamiliarity with the city made driving tedious. Each time he found that Davis was proceeding true to form to his next appointment. Unexpectedly he broke his pattern when he left the lawyer. He had turned back at the Lincoln Tunnel and come to this hotel. This white hotel.

Sergeant Mazibuko was annoyed. Had Davis turned up for the night? Would he attempt the journey later? He tried to telephone Davis's room. The switchboard told him no one by that name was registered. He concluded that the chauffeur had engaged the room. The chauffeur's name was not in the research document.

He looked at his watch. The Pakistani had told him it kept time to the half second. He had been in the hotel nearly an hour. He shuddered to think he might have to pass the night standing outside in the snow.

Across the way a waiter served drinks to the card players. The management had grasped the opportunities of the snowstorm and extended its bar service—at room-service prices—to the lobby.

"You springing, Ed?" asked one of them.

"Eddie baby cleaned up on the Jets," said another.

"You bet OTB, didn't you, Ed? How much was the tax bite?"

It was a chief complaint against New York's Off-Track Betting Corporation that the state took a hefty share in taxes of every winning football bet. The policy kept the bookies in business.

"I should have gone for the Jets big," said Ed, shaking his head as he paid for the drinks. "Fuck the taxes. I should have mortgaged my house. I'd own OTB . . . and the God damned state."

Ed stood up and stretched. He was a bulgy man with lank, blond hair. He lit a cigarette.

"You see who's here?" he said.

"Who?"

"Snakehips Davis."

The other card players half rose and craned their necks.

"Where?"

"Not *here*. He checked in about an hour ago. They were talking about him at the desk. He's in the hotel."

"Wish I'd seen him. Get his autograph. Give it to my kid for Christmas. It'd knock him out."

"They pay these colored guys too much," said Ed.

"The guy gains more yardage than any other back in the league. Christ."

"He doesn't gain it. They *let* him gain it."

"You really believe that, Ed?"

"Hell, yes . . . Philadelphia could buy a new team for what they pay that nigger."

Sergeant Mazibuko listened closely. Then, unobtrusively, he stepped forward. "Excuse me, sir. I could not help overhearing your conversation. I am a visitor from Lesotho and—"

"Lesotho?" Ed grinned stupidly. "What the hell is that?"

"It is in Africa, sir. It was once called Basutoland. Perhaps—"

"Prosciutto Land?" Ed continued to grin. His cigarette had burned down to the filter. He looked for some place to put it out.

Sergeant Mazibuko wanted to take this man into a corner and go to work on him. With his fingers, not his fists. He had never struck a white man. This seemed a good time to start. Instead he decided to render the man innocuous. He whisked the man's cigarette from his hand and butted it in a nearby ashtray.

"That an old custom back in the jungle?" Ed said and gawked. The others ignored him. Their eyes were fixed on the black man.

"I am an admirer of American football," said Sergeant Mazibuko, smiling humbly, "although I know very little of it. I, too, saw Davis arrive. An impressive man. There was someone with him. His chauffeur, I believe. Is he a footballer also?"

The others looked puzzled. Ed scratched his head.

"Oh," Ed said at length, "I know who you mean. Colored guy. Played for L.A. Quit when they wouldn't pay him what he wanted. Signed with Philadelphia. Got hurt. What's his name?"

More silence. Then one of the others snapped his fingers. "Ernie Parks. That's the guy. Good linebacker before he got hurt. I didn't know he was Snakehips's chauffeur."

"These colored guys don't know how to hang on to their money."

"Thank you very much, gentlemen," Sergeant Mazibuko said with a bow and retired to his chair. A bit of progress, he thought; not much, but better than nothing. He touched his watch.

A few minutes later he went to the house phone. He asked for the room of Mr. Ernie Parks.

"Look lively, Dolan," snapped Lieutenant Van Hooff. His close-cropped red hair was sprinkled with snow. "You're Uitmoormag again. For the moment, anyway. . . . We've laid on a show of our own."

Jackie struggled with his clothes. The cold was brutal in the squalid apartment. He was slightly dazed with sleep and alcohol. He had paused to pinch a swollen blemish on his cheek.

"You're sure, sir, that this is on track with Captain Zanin?" he asked for the third time. His voice was edged with doubt. "I'm under his orders and—"

"Yes, yes, you long streak of piss." Lieutenant Van Hooff surveyed the room. The liquor bottle, the jumble of cartons, the littered clothing, the filthy mattress. It had taken him several moments to recognize that this was the billet of a South African soldier. "Do you imagine I'd be here if it wasn't. Forget Zanin for a bit, will you? This is a composite operation. Zanin hasn't the final word on everything." He grinned crookedly and added, "Zanin tends to get rather tiresome, doesn't he?"

The question was so unexpected that Jackie simply said, "Yes, sir."

Actually, Lieutenant Van Hooff had been startled by the eagerness with which the Israelis accepted his proposal to visit Jackie; they were usually stubborn about planning changes. "Of course you should see him, Piet," Colonel Garovsky had said when he returned from telephoning for the address. "We should have thought of it ourselves. Probably just what he needs. Zanin says he's a bit windy. What do you think, Ayala?" Fancy that, he had thought, Garovsky and the blonde sharing a flat on a bloody operation; elegant place, too; trust the Jews to put themselves up cozy; the blonde just shrugs and puffs her cigarette; she thinks she looks like a film star; not that she isn't a juicy bit of goods; insolent bitch. "Ayala and I must be running along. Dinner engagement in Greenwich Village. The bohemian quarter, you know."

Jackie had been equally startled to find Lieutenant Van Hooff at the door shaking the snow from the shoulders of his overcoat. Lieutenant Van Hooff was Uitmoormag's intelligence officer; like Major Espensheid, he had something to do with Special Branch and the Bureau of State Security. Ordinarily he was distant and curt. Jackie had seen him affable only once; during the Rhodesia campaign; at sundown one day he entertained Jackie's stick with his Jew routine: "Leessen, Cleesstianss. Ve luff ze Kaffirss, but chu musst remoof zeir foresskinss. Pleess be careful viz ze knackerss. A Kaffir vithout a foresskin iss no pleassure to a Chewiss vuman if he hass no knackerss."

Jackie pulled on his parka and stomped to attention. "Sir—"

Lieutenant Van Hooff gazed at him with distaste. "Fetch the weapon, Dolan."

"The H&H, sir?"

"Oh, for God's sake. Do you have another weapon?"

"No, sir."

"Well?"

"Sir!"

Jackie spun on his heel and walked stiffly to the kitchen. He returned carrying the enormous rifle at port-arms.

Lieutenant Van Hooff gave an order. Jackie brought the rifle to his side.

"Ammunition?"

"How many rounds should I take, sir?"

"How many do you usually take?"

"One, sir."

"Then one it is."

Jackie leaned the rifle against a wall. He took a cartridge from a tray next to the arbor press and dropped it in his pocket. He picked up the rifle and looked around the desolate room. There was a desperate glint in his eye, as if he had forgotten something.

"Stop mucking about, Dolan. We've no time to waste."

Jackie snapped back to attention.

"We going to Queens, sir?"

"No, Manhattan. Why?"

"Captain Zanin sends me to Queens to pick up a car."

"Oh damn Zanin. This is *our* show."

"Will I be out long, sir? It's snowing like a fuck."

"I don't know." Lieutenant Van Hooff opened the door. His small, square face lit up with malice. "All I can tell you is that we expect to have a little bit of very traditional fun."

Sergeant Mazibuko found the room easily. It was high up in the hotel at the end of a shadowy corridor embellished with dull, gilt plasterwork and lamps in brackets. Loud, emotionless music emanated from inside. He touched his watch and then knocked. When the door opened it disclosed a view of a television set tuned to a football game and a large chair around which were strewn glossy magazines displaying photographs of nude women.

The door was opened by a towering black man in stockinged feet. He blinked dully. His jaw was slack. A tiny clot of spittle clung to the corner of his mouth.

The music blasted into the corridor. It was broken at intervals by voices and applause from the television.

"My name is Mazibuko. I've an appointment with Mr. Davis."

The man gazed impassively. "Uh uh," he said. He was young. His voice was thick. Although muscular, he conveyed the impression of shyness and destructibility. "Hips ain't seeing nobody." He started to close the door.

"I telephoned from the lobby. You must be Mr. Parks. You said Mr. Davis would receive me . . . Mazibuko."

The man shook his head in a series of snaps. He blinked rapidly several times. Suddenly his eyes became alert. His jaw drew firm. He licked away the spittle. He smiled and extended his hand. "Hips!" he shouted crisply over his shoulder. "It's the dude that called! Mazibolo! The African dude!"

"Tell him I'll be out in a minute!" a voice called above the gale of music. It came from the bedroom. "Give him something to drink and tell him to sit down!"

The man admitted Sergeant Mazibuko and closed the door. The room was very warm. The ceiling was high. He gestured to a serving cart. There were bottles of white wine in an ice bucket and stemmed glasses. "Help yourself. I want to catch some more of the game. Second half's just starting." He eased himself into the chair in front of the television. He gave the magazines a careless kick. Within moments his eyes closed. His head lolled against his shoulder.

Sergeant Mazibuko ignored the wine. He couldn't ignore the music. He sat down on the sofa. It was solid, but ample and soft. He couldn't remember sitting on anything else so comfortable. He tried to think a move ahead. The music, blaring from a radio, prevented it. Ordinarily he liked loud, insistent music. But this had no instinctive impulses, no tension. It was comfortable, like this sofa—and disconcerting, like this hotel. The musicians must be white, he thought.

He wondered about the man who opened the door. Was he addicted to narcotics? He had read this was a common failing of blacks in America. If so, it seemed highly indiscreet for someone of Davis's stature to allow such a man to serve him personally.

"How you?" a voice soared over the music; it was sharp and distinct. It was Davis.

He was athletically heavy and bearded. His expression was gloomy and forbidding. He wore a fresh polyantha rose in the lapel of his stylish three-piece suit.

"I was dictating some letters." He limped slightly as he crossed the room. "Sorry to keep you waiting, Mr., ah—"

"Mazibuko."

He shook Sergeant Mazibuko's hand with a firm, almost painful grip. Then he turned and walked over to the unconscious figure of Parks.

"Straighten up, Boop," he said quietly. "Can't be sliding off now." He shook him gently. "Boop, straighten up. Time for your medicine."

Parks bristled awake, as if he had experienced a dream leap. "Where they at?" he mumbled.

"Right here. You want some water?"

"Uh uh."

Parks took a green-and-white capsule from Davis's hand. He popped it into his mouth and gulped. Then he doubled his legs against his chest and rested his chin on his knees. Soon he was absorbed in the television.

"He got dinged," said Davis matter-of-factly. "Right now, he ain't wrapped too tight, but he'll be okay." He turned off the music, poured himself a glass of wine, and took a seat next to Sergeant Mazibuko. He propped his left foot on the coffee table.

"Pardon me?"

"Dinged. Thumped in the head. You didn't hear about it? Exhibition game in Florida. In a coma damned near a month . . . Hey, Boop, turn that down a little bit." Parks leaned over and twisted a knob. The noise faded. "He's on this medicine and getting some kind of therapy. Best therapy so far is driving. He says he can't stay awake and pay attention for more than five minutes if he ain't driving. Medicine works some, but driving's best . . . What was it you wanted to see me about, Mr., ah—"

"Mazibuko." He sat up and clasped his hands to give himself an official air. "I bring you salutations from Chief Mangosuthu Gatsha Buthelezi, chief councillor of the Legislative Assembly of KwaZulu, homeland of the Zulu nation. Chief Buthelezi has applauded each new phase of your extraordinary career. He takes heart, as does every Zulu man and woman, that black people everywhere can turn to you as a symbol of steadfastness and pride in a troubled world. He sees your achievements as a beacon of hope, particularly in these perilous times, when our country is beset by turmoil and our people seek to uphold their dignity and traditions."

Davis listened carefully. His expression remained unpleasant. He was vainer than most men—but he was doubtful. Twelve years as a national celebrity had taught him to beware of flattery; too often it was accompanied by requests for contributions, either in coin or service. At length he said coldly, "What is your title, Mr. Makibozo?"

"I am Chief Buthelezi's advisor for foreign affairs. It is an unofficial appointment." Sergeant Mazibuko smiled as he watched to see how this lie would be received.

Davis's expression remained dubious. He tried to keep abreast of African developments, but it was difficult. All those tribes, all those countries with new names—whose old names he couldn't be sure of half the time. "You connected with the UN?"

"No, sir. As I said, my duties are unofficial. I carry no portfolio. I undertake assignments for Chief Buthelezi outside normal diplomatic channels. I am—how do you call it?—a trouble man."

"A troubleshooter?"

"Precisely. It is often politically unwise for official representatives to address themselves to sensitive situations."

Davis stirred uncomfortably. He rotated his heavy shoulders a fraction, suggesting menace. Over the years he had fostered an image of disagreeable self-confidence; he used it to turn ordinary conversations with strangers into confrontations, he believed it intimidated them. This African didn't seem intimidated. Davis was perplexed. "What's so sensitive about bringing me greetings from"—the mask slipped slightly—"Chief . . . ah—"

"Chief Buthelezi. Nothing whatsoever, Mr. Davis, let me assure you. It is a most pleasant task. It so happens that I am in your country on other business. Chief Buthelezi gave me this additional assignment. I must say I welcomed it."

Davis glanced around the room. His eyes rested a moment on the television screen. An important play was in progress. Then he turned to Sergeant Mazibuko. "Well, thank the chief for me," he said; his tone indicated he was ending the interview. "Wish him the best of luck in the struggle. Tell him I might get to Africa sometime soon. If I do, I'll look him up. Always glad to wish good luck to a brother."

"Yes," said Sergeant Mazibuko. He broadened his smile. He touched his watch. He had concluded that it would be simpler to insinuate himself into Davis's company than to continue his surveillance from a distance. He did not intend for Davis to slip away now. "Brotherhood. That is another of my assignments. I am to invite you to share the *isibongo* of the Buthelezi clan."

"The what?"

"The *isibongo*." Sergeant Mazibuko knew only fragments of tribal lore. He was confident Davis would not detect his inventions. "Among Zulus, each clan has a common ancestral name, an *isibongo*. The *isibongo* of the Buthelezi clan is"—he paused awkwardly "—Buthelezi. Chief Buthelezi is deeply honored to offer you the kinship of his clan."

"You mean be a blood brother? I'm already an honorary Ashanti. They even gave me an honorary ancestor. A rock python. I wouldn't let them make me a blood brother, though. They said I'd have to be circumcised and get my front teeth busted out."

"Zulus and the Ashanti have very little in common," said Sergeant Mazibuko; his voice was reassuring; he continued to smile, "apart from a warrior tradition and having fought the British—unsuccessfully. No, Zulu custom includes no mutilation."

"What would I have to do?"

"Share some milk with me."

"Milk?" A skeptical look came over Davis's face. "You mean there ain't no mumbo-jum—" He thrust out his chin and cleared his throat. "Is there a ritual?"

"Sharing the milk is the ritual."

"That's all?"

"It pledges you to brotherhood. It also demands that you not marry a woman of the clan . . . on pain of death," he added dramatically.

Davis laughed. "I'll damned sure remember that. Hey, Boop, call room service. Tell them to send up a glass of milk. I'm going to be a Zulu."

Parks slowly rose and went to the telephone. A short time later a uniformed attendant appeared with a glass of milk on a tray. The man was white. Sergeant Mazibuko was astounded. Davis tipped him five dollars and he departed.

"What now?" Davis was standing. He shifted to keep his weight off his left foot.

"We share the glass," said Sergeant Mazibuko, getting to his feet. "I must take the first sip."

"How about Boop? Can he do it, too?"

Sergeant Mazibuko scowled. "Chief Buthelezi did not mention Mr. Parks. I'm not certain—"

"Aw, come on. Boop'll appreciate it."

"As you wish."

"Get over here, Boop. Mr. Makibozo's going to make us Zulus."

Parks trudged across the room. He looked bewildered. Sergeant Mazibuko sipped the milk and passed the glass to Parks, who sipped it and passed it on to Davis. Parks returned to the television and mumbled something about the inferior play of one of the teams.

"You must drink it all without lowering the glass," Sergeant Mazibuko said solemnly. "That is the etiquette."

Davis obeyed.

"Peace be upon your house. You are now one with your ancestors and your brothers and sisters, the eternal amaButhelezi. Your name is Davis. Your *isibongo* is Buthelezi."

Sergeant Mazibuko took the empty glass and set it on the coffee table. "Now we must have some wine. To celebrate your new life."

Davis refilled his own and poured another and handed it to Sergeant Mazibuko. They touched glasses. Davis looked at the carpet and sighed. Abruptly he looked up. "This is kind of embarrassing, Mr. Makibozo. I feel like a damned fool. I don't even know where you're from."

"The land washed by the Tugela River," said Sergeant Mazibuko. He took a sip. There's really nothing much the matter with California wine, he said to himself. "It is called KwaZulu. You must consider it your ancestral home."

"Where is it? Where in Africa, I mean?"

"KwaZulu is the homeland of the Zulu nation . . . in the Republic of South Africa."

"*South Africa!*" Davis's eyes bulged. He sat down heavily on the sofa. "God Almighty, man! Did you see the news tonight? The top's popping off that God damned place! Those white motherfuckers are bombing kids! *Kids!* Motherfuckers bombed a God damned school with a helicopter!"

Sergeant Mazibuko's face was expressionless. He had not seen the news. "Where was the bombing?" he asked evenly. "Near Thekini?"

"Where?"

"Excuse me. I meant Durban. Thekini is the Zulu name. I live at a township near there. Umlazi."

For a fleeting moment he thought of the four-room house where he lived as a lodger with a sawmill worker and his wife and five children. The house had no running water, no plumbing, and no electricity. He slept under a blanket next to the coal stove and kept his possessions in a packing crate that was covered with a swatch of fabric during the day to serve as a table; atop it sat a headless porcelain cat, a gift from one of the children. He decided against mentioning to Davis that, having no wife or other family of his own, he had no legal right to live in Umlazi.

"I don't remember the *name*," Davis said impatiently. "The brothers were standing up, though. Fighting like it didn't make no difference to them, like they got to die sometime, so they just as well die now. I guess they're just finally tired of putting up with all that shit, huh?"

"Young men are often enamored of minor tactics without regard to strategy," replied Sergeant Mazibuko complacently; he sat down next to Davis. "Your Philadelphia football side. They review an opponent's strength and methods before a match, do they not?"

Davis inclined his head. His lips were pursed. His nose was upturned as if he had detected a fetid odor. He tried to convey that he found Sergeant Mazibuko's comment bereft of social sensibility. He succeeded only in appearing supercilious. After a moment he said, "I didn't get the idea they were thinking about tactics or strategy or anything else. Looked to me like they knew one thing. They knew it was time to kiss the natural-born baby good-bye. Like they had been shoved one time too many and wasn't going to be shoved one foot further." He rotated his shoulders again; his voice had taken on a fruity, bullying quality. "Looked to me like they could have turned the whole thing around if *somebody*—some of their go-slow brothers, for instance—if somebody had come in behind their shit. *Most* black folks believe it would be a good idea if some of those black countries just said fuck it and saddled up and rolled in and—"

"Ah, no, Mr. Davis." The interruption was polite but determined; Sergeant Mazibuko sounded as if he were warning a white motorist who had ignored a one-way-street sign. "That would only bring the pain of someone else's heel on our necks. A black heel hurts just as much as a white heel." He thought of the job he had done recently on a Xhosa swankie called Fast Talk; Fast Talk had sold a tub of poisoned *skokiaan* on pay night; fifty cents a swig from a calabash; twenty Zulus, all of them fathers, had died; Sergeant Mazibuko had kicked Fast Talk's head until the blood trickled from his ears; before he lapsed into a coma and died Fast Talk had revealed that the stuff was supplied by the white manager of a food-processing plant; the white man was awaiting trial for violation of the liquor laws; Fast Talk's death was listed as a suicide. "One day we shall have our country," he continued, "and we shall have it in one piece and as rich as it is today. But first we must flow quietly into the bases of real power in South Africa. We must flow into the South African Police, into the Defense Force, into those places where you are as indispensable to the white man as the mine boy or the sweep boy."

"Oh, shit, man, those brothers ain't flowing quietly. They mean business. I can tell you that, and I ain't even there. All you have to do is look at television."

"Those young fools"—his voice rose; he was unaccustomed to expressing opinions on current affairs—"they mean for the world to see clenched-fist salutes and slogans and a building here and there set afire by the odd bottle of petrol. And, of course, huge numbers of themselves shot to death or hanged. They've been put up to it by white men, you may be sure of it, and I'll tell you why. It's suicidal, and suicide is a white man's habit."

Davis leaned over and snatched a newspaper from a table at the end of the sofa. He stabbed the front page with his finger. "Did *he* commit suicide?" he demanded.

There was a photograph of a black man. He was smiling and wearing eyeglasses. The accompanying article was datelined Johannesburg. It described the man as a lawyer. He had defended a number of persons arrested for sabotage and subversion. He had also made speeches roughly chiding the police. The point of the article was that the man died in police detention. The police said he hanged himself in his cell. With his socks.

"I'll tell you this," Davis went on heatedly. "Ain't a *black* man in *this* country believes he committed suicide. He was murdered by the motherfucking police! Are you going to tell *me* he wasn't?"

"Certainly not," replied Sergeant Mazibuko; the wine had relaxed him; his voice was tinged with light sarcasm; it was a tone he rarely used. "I would no more tell you that than I would tell you to spread your picnic in baboon country. The man in the photo there, he knew the danger of baboons. Everyone in South Africa knows. Vicious beasts, baboons are, when they're hungry. They are always hungry. They don't care whether your picnic is cucumber sandwiches or tinned tongue. They will eat it all. They will eat you, too, starting with your throat, if you protest or try to humor them. It's only noise to them. They become frightened. Baboons kill when they become frightened. Perhaps they murder. But—if a man knows baboons, and he spreads his picnic within view of a baboon troop, and the baboons kill him, he has committed suicide just as surely as if he had—"

"—got himself arrested for trying to see to it that some black kids got a fair trial?"

"Exactly. He knew what hungry baboons are like. Possibly his judgment failed him. It sometimes happens to men who pass the time petitioning for writs and citing rules of evidence. Hungry baboons want meat. It is foolish to think they will be pacified with writs and rules. This man was well educated. He should have thought of that. . . . Of course, he was not a Zulu."

"You mean to tell me that you don't give a damn that your own people are getting the shit beat out of them just because they're asking for some simple-ass human dignity?"

"I regret to say that I do not. To care about that at this point is a dreamy notion, like a fair trial. The whites are too well armed. This is an expression of anger, not the revolt the whites think it is. It's a case of a pack of desperate boys throwing stones and lighting fires. Besides, if the whites thought for an instant that they would lose, they would destroy the whole country rather than turn it over to us."

Davis thrust out his chin. "I still say you ought to ask some of those black countries for help. You couldn't lose anything. You sure as hell wouldn't be any worse off than you are now."

"Who do you suggest? Angola? Mozambique? Zimbabwe? To us they are merely outsiders. Enemies, if you like, who know how rich South Africa is and would dearly love to have her. But they did not make South Africa rich. We did. As I said, we shall have our country one day. When that day comes, we do not intend to share her with someone who claims to have given us our . . . freedom."

"What would you say if the United States went in and cleaned the damned thing up once and for all?"

"I think the United States would then have more gold than the Pope," Sergeant Mazibuko replied with a laconic smile, "and the Zulu would still have his jug of beer and his Methodist hymnal." He drained his glass. "Ah, we have fallen to disputing politics. An absurd digression. Let us not mention the subject again. We must be festive. After all, only once in his life does a man receive his *isibongo* and join the communion of his ancestors. More wine, Mr. Davis, if you please."

Davis looked as if he were about to pursue the matter regardless and then changed his mind. He poured more wine. They touched glasses again.

"You have assumed a magnificent heritage tonight, Mr. Davis."

Davis's stern look eased a bit. "You tell the chief I'm damned proud to be a Zulu."

"Yes. Are you acquainted with the history of the Zulu nation?"

Davis shook his head.

"We honor our ancestors and our chiefs, but we revere one man. King Tjhaka. He was completely ruthless, Mr. Davis, but he was a man of vision. From a small clan he forged a nation and an empire.

Tjhaka understood military power. Zulus were not merely a people under Tjhaka, we were an army. Even today, when a Zulu boy attains his strength, we say he has joined his regiment."

"Did I join my regiment when we drank that milk?"

"Your membership is retroactive," Sergeant Mazibuko said after a moment.

"What do I have to do? For my regiment, I mean?"

"You must wage battle with your talents. I would say you can best do that on the rugby pitch."

"On the what?"

"The rugby pitch. The football field, I believe it is called in America."

Davis nodded as if he had heard a full recognition of his worth. A warm glow replaced his stern look. He turned to his visitor. "Tell me, Mr. Makibozo, what do you do back home? Just wait for the chief to give you your orders?"

Sergeant Mazibuko wasn't ready for this. He touched his watch. "I am attached to the department of community affairs," he began, "but my work keeps me in Durban a good deal of the time. And, of course, Umlazi . . ."

"Spend much time on the reservation?"

"As much as possible." He sighed. He was relieved that Davis had not pursued the question of his livelihood. "But, you see, I have made my *makoweng*, my move to the city, and I am out of touch with rural life." In fact he had not visited his family *kraal* in the slopes above the Nsuze River in more than twenty years. "Rural custom has many aspects. One of them is that younger sons observe the prerogatives of primogeniture. I am the youngest in my family, and there has been no death of a male kinsman or collateral in my lifetime. If I lived in the *kraal*, I would one day have to assume responsibility for all the wives of my father, my uncles, and my brothers. That is a flaming lot of old women, Mr. Davis. My father has six brothers, of whom he is the youngest. I have six brothers, of whom I am the youngest. I've lost track of the wives, not to mention—"

"Wait a minute!" Davis broke in excitedly. He waved a hand back and forth. "You mean to tell me you're the seventh son of a seventh son?"

"That is so. Birth control is still largely unknown among—"

"You hear that, Boop? My blood brother is a seventh son! We got to take him to see Lula!"

Parks, whose head had again fallen against his shoulder, grunted noncommittally.

Davis turned back to Sergeant Mazibuko. "You should have told me when you came in."

"Pardon me?"

"You should have told me you're a seventh son."

"Why should I tell you that?"

"Why? Aw, man, don't give me that. What I want to know is how it feels."

"How it feels?"

"To be a seventh son of a seventh son. You know, to have second sight."

A look of astonishment spread across Sergeant Mazibuko's face and then receded. "Ah, yes," he said, smiling tolerantly, "the seventh son of a seventh son. A superstition. The Europeans invented it, I think. I've never known whether they took it seriously. Something to do with crystal gazing, isn't it?"

"You don't think you've got the gift?"

"To see the shape of tomorrow? Or next week? I doubt it." It was more than a doubt. It was a conviction. In his last year at mission school he had run afoul of the schoolmaster, an Anglican clergyman. He was sixteen. The clergyman had caned him for failing to smile during his recitation. He sought out the local *sangoma* for help. The *sangoma* sold him a needle fashioned from a splinter of zebra hoof; he was to scratch his slate with it before he recited and the white man would not lay a hand on him, whether he smiled or not. Next day, he scratched his slate and recited stone faced—and received ten of the best. That afternoon he found the *sangoma* tossing the bones for a man concerned about the future of his millet crop. Creeping up from behind, he swung his arm in a low, powerful arc. The needle caught the *sangoma* square in the seat of the pants. The *sangoma* screamed in pain. Before sundown, Sergeant Mazibuko had set out for the city. "My experience has been," he added, "that tomorrow is nothing more than yesterday seen through another window. Best to take good care of today and leave tomorrow to itself, don't you think?"

Davis was not listening. Already he was setting things in motion. "Boop, call downstairs and tell them to bring the car around. I wonder if I ought to call Lula and tell her we're coming. Better not. She might say it's too late and tell me to stay off my foot."

Parks came to life at the mention of driving. He switched off the television and went to the telephone.

Davis squirmed into his ankle-length mink benny. He was absorbed in contemplation of the phenomenal. He tapped one forefinger against the other as he listed his sanctions and prohibitions. "If you dream about clear water, that's good luck. Digging a hole after dark is bad luck. So is a bird flying in the house. A tree struck by lightning—" Suddenly he hobbled into the bedroom and returned with a small leather pouch which he stuffed inside his coat. "Devil's snuff and graveyard dirt," he said. "Somebody works a root on you, you got to have devil's snuff and graveyard dirt or you can forget it."

Parks moved to the door. He was alert, even jaunty, at the prospect of getting behind the wheel of Davis's Rolls-Royce.

"Excuse me," said Sergeant Mazibuko. He bowed slightly. "May I telephone? Some associates are expecting me. I must tell them to go about their plans."

"You dial nine for outside."

"Thank you." He glanced at his watch as he waited for his number to answer; a long time since he had reported; oh, well, it couldn't be helped. A voice came on the line. Sergeant Mazibuko spoke rapidly in Afrikaans, paused, spoke again, and hung up.

"What was that you were speaking?" Davis asked. "Zulu?"

"One of the dialects."

They left the room.

The refugees from the storm now overflowed the hotel. A siege mentality had overtaken them. There were more than a thousand of them—in the lobby, the bar, and the lounge, they stood, sat, and leaned. They had had a good deal to drink, and their earlier lightheartedness had given way to torpid resignation. Suddenly a current of intensity revived them. It stemmed from a commotion at the elevators.

"That's Snakehips Davis!" went up the cry.

Parks led the way, breasting the crowd, Davis was close behind, his collar pulled high around his neck. Sergeant Mazibuko struggled to stay at Davis's heels.

The crowd closed in. One of them was Ed, the card player, who was now very drunk. Dozens of scraps of paper and ball-point pens were thrust forward for autographs. Davis signed each with an indecipherable streak of ink and pushed a step closer to the revolving

door. He noticed someone at his shoulder. It was a white woman, a
brunette with a firm, slim body; she was holding a glass; she looked a
bit unsteady.

"Hips!" she exclaimed; she smiled invitingly. "Of all places to run
into you." Her eyes were slightly out of focus. "Got any plans for the
blizzard?"

Davis looked at her closely. Then he smiled back. "Baby, am I glad
to see you," he said. He took her hand and kissed her lightly. "Boop,
you and Mr. Makibozo meet me in the car. Nobody but me talks to
this woman." The crowd parted as he led the woman some distance
away. He put his arms around her, spoke quietly to her for several
moments, then kissed her again and left the hotel. Still smiling, the
woman made her wobbly way back to the bar.

"Who was the trim?" Parks asked over his shoulder as Davis slid
into the back seat next to Sergeant Mazibuko.

"I got no idea," Davis replied. He flecked snow from his mink coat.
"Never saw her before in my life. She said we made it once in L.A.
and how good it was and how she was ready for more. Right then.
Middle of the night. In the morning. You name it. Poor bitch."

"What'd you tell her?"

"What'd I tell her? I told her we might hit Charlie O's. I said I'd
catch up with her later on. We ain't going near Charlie O's."

"What you going to do? You ain't going to stay too long at Lula's,
are you?"

"Depends on how long she wants to talk to Mr. Makibozo. Then
we'll hit a few joints. P.J.'s, the Flash. Chase some crack. How about
it, Mr. Makibozo? You in the mood to chase some crack?"

"Are you often approached by women in that way?" asked Sergeant
Mazibuko. He sounded incredulous. "In public, I mean, by white
women?"

"White women, black women, oriental women. It's mostly white
chicks do shit like that, not caring who's looking or anything. Hey, it
made her feel good, I guess. Nothing wrong with making a chick feel
good, right, Boop?"

"Not long as they don't be hanging around all the time." Parks
slowly turned up Sixth Avenue. In no way did he resemble the
drooling, lethargic man who had greeted Sergeant Mazibuko. He
slipped a cassette into a tape deck and music—the same kind of loud,
overrefined music that was playing in Davis's hotel room—flooded
the car.

"Maybe we'll chase some crack, maybe we won't." Davis turned and looked out the window. "This is our town, ain't it, Boop? Even under ten feet of snow, it's our town. . . . You spend much time in New York, Mr. Makibozo?"

"This is my first visit."

"Oh, yeah? Let me tell you something. Sooner or later, everybody who wants something, something big, comes to New York. Henry Ford wants to sell a new car, he comes to New York and hires an advertising agency. Hollywood Jews want to make a movie, they come to New York for the money—it don't matter that the money probably belongs to the A-rabs. I want to make a deal to endorse deodorant, I come to New York."

They turned east on Fifty-ninth Street, proceeded to Madison Avenue, and turned uptown.

"I'm a winner in Philadelphia," Davis continued after telling Parks to lower the volume of the music, "but New York is where I cash in. Ain't no place in the world lets a winner cash in like New York. In New York you can be a winner a long time after you quit playing. In Philadelphia you a plaque in the wall the minute you hang it up. You got to keep your stuff tight, though. Raggedy stuff don't go down, not in New York. In some places you can do something, and if the people you hang with like it, you feel like you won something. You ain't won shit, but you feel like you did. In New York they let you know right off the bat. You can't keep a fat head for long in New York."

"Why do you play for the Philadelphia side?" asked Sergeant Mazibuko. He noticed that they were passing the intersection where Mr. McManus tried to elude him. "Why not play for one of the New York sides?"

Davis was silent a moment. Then he said with a small, satisfied laugh, "There are plenty of big fish in little ponds. They get bonuses and long-term contracts and single hotel rooms. I'm a whale in a bathtub. I get anything I want.

They turned west on 110th Street along the northern border of Central Park and then up St. Nicholas Avenue. Even in the dark and the blinding snow Sergeant Mazibuko recognized the route. North of 140th Street they turned, and a block or two later they turned again. They were in the cul-de-sac where Madam Excella lived.

Parks halted the car in front of the brownstone. The house was dark except for the blinking Christmas tree. The snow was blowing wildly.

The headlights beamed on another car facing them on the same side of the narrow street. It was not more than twenty feet away. It was idling with its lights off. Exhaust and vapor boiled from beneath it. Sergeant Mazibuko squinted and saw a figure in a ski mask behind the wheel.

"Boop, you go ring the doorbell," said Davis. "You know, it really might be too late. Lula's an old woman. I know she's dying to meet a seventh son, but . . ."

Sergeant Mazibuko saw the driver's door of the other car swing open. He nervously fingered his watch.

"Aw, hell, Hips. If it's going to make her mad, I don't want her cussing at me."

The figure in the other car stepped out into the snow. It was unmistakably a man.

"Go on, Boop. Give me a break."

At that moment Sergeant Mazibuko saw the figure bring a rifle to his shoulder and rest it atop the open door. The rifle appeared to be very heavy. It was aimed at the limousine.

"Everyone down!" he shouted. He dove to the floor and tugged violently at Davis's mink coat.

Davis tried to pull himself free. Instead he tumbled on top of Sergeant Mazibuko. "What the fuck's got into you?" he screamed.

"Down, Mr. Parks! Please, get down!" Sergeant Mazibuko cried as he struggled to keep Davis below the seat.

Parks opened his door a fraction. The interior light went on. Snow and frigid air swept into the car. He shifted and looked into the back seat. "What the hell y'all going down—"

There was a blast of bewildering force. The windshield shattered. Parks's skull exploded. Blood, flesh, and fragments of bone spattered the upholstery. The impact hurled him against the seat as if he had been struck by a colossal fist. Then he slumped forward against the steering column. The horn wailed.

"Out of the car, Mr. Davis! Quickly!" shouted Sergeant Mazibuko. "And, for God's sake, stay low!"

Davis scrambled into the snow. He rose and bolted for the house. Then he fell to the sidewalk. He writhed a second and squirmed into a sitting position. He groaned and gripped his injured toe.

Parks's body toppled from the car. The horn went silent.

Sergeant Mazibuko rolled out and flattened himself in the snow beyond the curb-side rear fender. He heard the door of the other car slam shut. An instant later he saw the car speed past and make a reckless turn out of the cul-de-sac.

He shot a glance at Davis, who had pulled himself to the top of the icy stoop and was straining to press the buzzer. He drew himself into a crouch and peered through the snow at the lifeless Parks sprawled half in and half out of the limousine.

The words of Mr. McManus appeared suddenly across his mind—". . . *the cops bust the bunch of you. You get to the precinct and everybody says the shine did it. . . .*"

He rapidly totaled up his alternatives. To stay where he was meant he would be subjected to questions by the police that he couldn't begin to answer. To flee meant he would be on his own—on foot—until he could reach his rented car, which was God knows how far away.

He hated this alien city and its malevolent weather. It was no place for a Zulu.

He looked at his watch but could not make out the time, sighed, and broke from his crouch. He set off at a trot. It took an immense effort in the deep snow. He reached the end of the cul-de-sac and rounded the corner.

Jackie Dolan was close to hysterics. He guided the car as well as he could with one hand. With the other he massaged his tender right shoulder.

Fright and frustration tore at his mind. The H&H. Should he get rid of the H&H? He knew he had broken the pattern, wasting a nigger, in a neighborhood where there were no witnesses. Or were there? Somebody had jumped out of that fucking limousine. At least one of them was a nigger, he was sure of that. Who was the other one? Another nigger? Had they seen him? Had they seen the license plate? If the cops stopped him and found the H&H, he was fucked. Oh, Jesus.

He was someplace in the Bronx. He wasn't sure where. The streets were unfamiliar. The signs were obscured by the snow. He had left Broadway near the George Washington Bridge and driven onto the Cross Bronx Expressway. He had turned off when he saw a flashing light—it was an amber light atop a snowplow—and he had been turning first right, then left ever since through the maze of small streets.

Jackie wiped the fog from the windshield. Another flashing light.

He shook in a spasm of fear. Abruptly he turned, not realizing it was only a fire engine. He drove another few blocks and . . . another flashing light! *Oh, God!* He moaned and felt a dampness between his legs.

He turned again, desperately fighting a compulsion to floorboard it. His damp shirt clung to the middle of his back. He lost all notion of time. His lower lip quivered. He forgot his shoulder a moment and clawed at his acne.

He spied the ski mask on the seat. Furiously he rolled down the window and flung it out. The stream of cold air cleared his mind. He tried to come up with a reason for Lieutenant Van Hooff's ordering this operation. Besides taking out a nigger, that is. It made no sense. It occurred to him that there was no contingency for getting rid of the car. He supposed he would simply have to ditch it. That left the H&H. Just how the hell was he supposed to get that fucking cannon back to Brooklyn? On the fucking subway? Oh, shit. For an instant he entertained a qualified respect for Captain Zanin. Captain Zanin was an arrogant, chicken-shit Jew, but he knew how to put together an operation. He shivered and rolled up the window. He wished the car had a radio. He wanted to know what the hell was going on.

Suddenly, without quite being aware of it, Jackie knew where he was. He was on Sedgewick Avenue, near the old neighborhood, near the place where he grew up. Cannon Heights, where they lived until his old man retired from the department. He exhaled a deep, long breath. He felt elated. He was enveloped by a sense of safety. Cannon Heights. The old neighborhood. Jesus. He believed he would have a drink. Yes, he believed he would.

His worries about the car and the H&H vanished as he double-parked the car in the middle of a block near Fort Independence Park. Nobody'll care in this snow, he said to himself, least of all the cops. Cops know Cannon Heights. It's Irish. They're Irish, most of them, like me. They get worried about the car, the worst they'll do is stick their head in the tavern and ask whose car it is and ask me to move it—when I've finished my drink, of course. And they won't say a word about the H&H, you can bet on it, even if they see it.

He locked the car. His crotch grew intensely cold where he had wet himself. Only the discomfort bothered him. He knew that half the customers inside had the same problem for one reason or another.

The Cork House was wedged between a funeral home and a

doorway that gave onto stairs leading to a Knights of Columbus hall. It was a long, wood-paneled room with a high ceiling festooned with meager Christmas decorations. A cut-glass mirror behind the wooden bar reflected bottles and glasses lined up in front of it. A half dozen men, all in caps and worn tweed coats, propped their feet on the brass rail and stared into their pints.

Jackie took a five-dollar bill from his wallet. It was the only money to his name. Lieutenant Van Hooff had given it to him. He laid it on the bar.

The bartender was a short, bald man with a baggy face. He was on the telephone. "There's someone ringing for you, Mr. Mahon," he called out. "She doesn't say who she is. Are you here?"

A patron looked up from his glass and shook his head.

The bartender replaced the receiver and stepped up to Jackie.

"Good evening, sir. What might it be?"

"A Paddy and a beer."

"Certainly, sir. A ball o' malt and a jar."

The bartender drew a glass of beer and set it on the bar. Then he poured a shot of Irish whisky.

"All the best, sir."

"How's business, Dermot?" said Jackie, downing the shot.

The bartender scrutinized him. "Are we acquainted, sir?"

Jackie swallowed some beer and smiled. "You poured me my first legal drink, Dermot. My old man brought me here more than twenty years ago. Charlie Dolan."

"Charlie Dolan!" The bartender clapped his thighs. "Oh, oh, oh! You're Charlie Dolan's boy! Charlie Dolan the policeman! Let me look at you! Charlie Dolan's boy! I'd have never dreamed! Charlie Dolan's boy! Now you had a brother, didn't you? And which are you?"

"Jackie."

"Jackie. Ah, yes. To be sure. And your brother was—"

"—Freddie."

"Freddie. To be sure. Freddie. And your lovely mother?"

"She passed away."

"God rest her soul. Now what brings you back to the old neighborhood, Jackie Dolan?"

"I'm in town for a few days. Christmas and that. In from California. Me and Freddie got a business out there."

"A business in California, now do you? Pay well, does it?"

"Fair enough. Times being what they are."

"The times. The times." The bartender took Jackie's five, rang the cash register, and returned his change. "The times are hard and evil. Not atall like you knew them as a boy. Do you know I had to turn off the radio on account of the news. The news, mind. It was upsetting the boys. That 'elephant gun' character again."

Jackie's eyes widened.

"You know of him, of course. But do you know he's murdered again. And one of his own kind this time. A darky going by the name of Parks. And the radio says it wasn't Parks he was after atall but another darky, the football player, Davis. Of course, it could well have been Parks he wanted. How's the radio to know? I'll have to wait 'til I get back to me quarters to find out. The boys'll hear no more news. News never hurt a living man, I says. They're afraid the black eejit may at this very moment be wading through the blizzard, making for the Bronx, intent on murdering innocent Irishmen. If he gets here in the face of this, then I says maybe God wants the lot of us dead. . . . Another, sir?"

Panic set in as the bartender spoke.

"Got to be getting along, Dermot," Jackie said, feeling his hand shake.

"My regards to your father and a Merry Christmas," said the bartender as Jackie hurried out. "A fine man, Charlie Dolan."

An office adjoining the reception room at the emergency entrance of Roosevelt Hospital. Scuffed tile floors, the smell of isopropyl, and an overhead fluorescent light that buzzed.

Detective Lieutenant Burns and Detective Second Grade Tedesco were waiting and hoping for their moment amid the ruins of the day.

Burns slumped in a chair behind the desk. He burped and glanced at the wall clock. Two A.M. His stomach throbbed. He cursed the pastry and the greasy sandwiches. He also cursed the day he agreed to command the Special Homicide Unit. He wondered whether he would ever clear this God damned thing.

Tedesco was on the phone. He sat on the edge of the desk. He cradled the receiver between his shoulder and neck. He grunted appropriately as he jotted in his notebook with a scratchy ball-point pen.

They had been on the fly all day. It started with the snow. The report came from the borough commander's office. Male, Caucasian, early twenties, shot from moving vehicle, Central Park West between 80-something and 80-something Street. Burns and the rest of the unit scrambled to the scene.

There had been plenty of witnesses. There always were. They gave vague, clashing accounts.

Then it was back to their second-floor room in a midtown precinct. The detectives typed their "fives" and dropped them on Burns's desk. He was reading them when the hospital called. The victim had regained consciousness. He could be questioned. Burns and two other detectives drove over as quickly as they could in the slashing snow. When they got there the doctor said they would have to wait.

Burns rubbed his eyes. He burped again. He knew better than to hope. He had been a cop too long. It was just a feeling he had. For one thing, the nut had hit in daylight. The first time in daylight. He wanted to reread the "fives" to see whether any of the witnesses . . . there was something about one of the witnesses. What was it? He took out his notebook. He wrote himself a reminder to check on one of the witnesses. A woman? The one who called Tedesco the last time?

Tedesco replaced the receiver. His face was drawn. "That was Smitty from the Fifth Zone. He's honchoing the Ernie Parks thing." He spoke precisely. He did not take his eyes from his notebook. "He said they dug a .375 mag slug from the back seat of Davis's limo."

"So what?" Burns held his queasy stomach.

"He says it looks homemade."

"*Homemade?*" Burns bolted from his chair and began pacing the room. He paused and thrust his hand into his pocket. He retrieved a misshapen lump of lead. It was a .375 magnum slug. It weighed a little more than half an ounce. Ballistics tests concluded that it was discharged from a handcrafted cartridge. It was taken from the body of the first victim of the "Finger of God." He studied it a moment and shoved it back in his pocket.

"Smitty says it looks like the others," Tedesco said. "You know, just eyeballing it. He says they won't know for sure until they've tested it."

"How the hell does Smitty know what they look like?"

"You showed them to him that night, remember?"

"Oh."

"That ain't all. Smitty says Davis told them there was an African with them and the African seemed to know what was going on and pulled Davis out of the line of fire."

"What else?"

"This African said he was a South African diplomat of some kind. From some place in South Africa that Davis had never heard of. That's according to Smitty."

"A black South African diplomat? That's bullshit."

"And they got a witness."

"A *witness?* You mean they got somebody besides Davis? In this God damned weather? Who?"

"A Mrs. Meyers. She gave them a description. Looks like our boy."

"Where is she?" said Burns. He seized his overcoat.

"She called the Three-O about forty-five minutes ago. Said she lives on the block. She left a number. Smitty said one of his guys would canvass her in the morning. She ain't going anywhere. Not what it's doing out."

"Let me see it. The number."

Tedesco held up his notebook. Burns thrust his nose within an inch of the page. He shook his head and clucked.

"That's no Harlem number," he said. He tossed his overcoat on the chair. It slid to the floor.

Tedesco looked at his notebook and said nothing.

Burns was pacing again. He rubbed his stomach. He stopped, snapped his fingers as if he were about to say something and then thought better, and then resumed pacing. Abruptly he stopped again.

"I'm going to dial that number," he said. "Get over here close so you can hear."

"What do you want me to do that for?"

"Just do what I tell you, for Christ's sake."

Burns punched the number on the touch-tone phone. Tedesco crowded close until they were nearly cheek to cheek. "You need to brush your fucking teeth," Burns said in a stage whisper.

"Yes," said a woman's voice. She had a European accent.

"Mrs. Meyers?"

"Who?"

"Mrs. Meyers."

"Who's calling please?"

"This is Sergeant Moran, Thirtieth Precinct. Sorry to disturb you again. I need to check your address. For Lieutenant Schmidt. What's it again?"

"I gave all the information to the officer. I spoke to him by telephone. I agreed to receive his investigators in the morning."

Tedesco pulled away. His eyes were wide. Silently he framed the words, "It's her! It's her!"

"Would you be kind enough to confirm the address for me?"

Tedesco leaned close again.

"The lieutenant *has* the information. I will be more than happy to assist him with his inquiries *in the morning*.

Click.

"What now?" Tedesco said excitedly. "We get the unit out and start canvassing that block? Jesus, canvassing in Harlem on a night like this."

Burns burped and quickly punched another number. "This is Burns. Give me Schmidt . . . I don't give a damn if he's getting a Chinese blow job. Get him on the phone." He closed his eyes and sighed through clenched teeth. "Yeah, good, Smitty . . . Okay, okay. God damn it, will you shut the fuck up and listen . . . If you'll pipe down, I'll tell you for Christ's sake . . . Good. I'll see you get a commendation. Now, look. Get to Davis and tell him to keep his mouth shut. Especially about this African. No talking to the media or anything. This African may be a break for us. One of my guys will talk to Davis, okay? Good. Nothing about this witness, either, this Mrs. Meyers. Tedesco made her—she's our thing. What do you mean, how? We called that number, that's how. And that slug you found. Keep that under your hat. One of my guys'll be up there tonight and get the thing. We'll get the test results. I'll fix it with the ME . . . I'll fix it with the chief, too, Smitty. I won't leave you standing on your prick . . . I got no idea . . . You, too."

After several unfruitful attempts he reached the assistant medical examiner. He asked him to give an inaccurate report on the autopsy of Parks. It would throw a monkey wrench in the investigation, he said, if the assistant ME released details indicating that Parks's death resembled the "elephant gun" murders. After an acrimonious exchange about ethics and politics, the pathologist agreed.

Then Burns called his home in Rockland County and told his wife he would not be home. The snowstorm, he said gloomily as he contemplated spending the night on a cot in his office.

The office door opened. Another detective stuck his head in. "The kid died," he said.

Burns was not surprised. He told the detective to close the door. He outlined the information from Lieutenant Schmidt. "Take the car and go up to the Three-O and get the bullet and take it downtown and call me after they've run it through."

The detective left.

Tedesco slipped on his overcoat. He looked bewildered. "Put this together for me, will you, boss?"

Burns rose slowly and put on his own coat. "I'll tell you at Leahy's. You can do with a drink, can't you? I'm buying."

They left the office. Burns conferred with a uniformed sergeant about transportation of the body to the morgue and about getting a lift in a patrol car. Then he told a mob of reporters, photographers, and television cameramen that the police were still searching for clues to the identity of the "Finger of God." He was thankful that none of them asked whether Ernie Parks might have been a victim of the same killer.

The patrol car dropped them at a bar several blocks away. The place was popular with off-duty policemen. It was a neighborhood tavern. It was virtually empty. "I would've closed up hours ago, but how can I get home in this mess?" said the bartender. He was a thin man with a high forehead who lived in New Jersey.

They ordered scotch.

"You know the saying in this job," said Burns. "Get off your ass and knock on doors. We done that, right, and we got exactly what we asked, right? No more, no less."

"I don't follow you," said Tedesco.

"Look at what we got. We got a stack of paper this high and names and—"

"Hey, Lieutenant," said the bartender as he poured the drinks. "Guess who's here? Charlie Dolan."

"Who's Charlie Dolan?" asked Tedesco.

Burns shrugged. "He was my partner twenty years ago. Went in the tank for some gamblers. Beat the rap on some kind of fix and took early retirement. He's a bail bondsman or private investigator, something like that. Not a bad cop. Average. Didn't know how to keep his nose clean or his ass covered."

A huge man with a puffy face stepped from behind a partition at the end of the bar. He was overweight, but his clothes were smartly spruce. He cut an impressive figure at Communion breakfasts. A kid on the street would have immediately "made" him as a detective.

"Hey, Charlie," the bartender said to the man, "look who walked in out of the snow. Your old partner."

Charlie Dolan's face lit up. "Burnsy!" he cried and made his way to where Burns and Tedesco were huddled over their drinks.

They shook hands. Burns introduced Dolan to Tedesco. He did not mention that Dolan had two sons who were about Tedesco's age. Dolan offered to buy the next round.

"I seen your name in the paper, Burnsy," said Dolan. He slouched against the bar. "Seen you on television, too. You look good. Lot of the young guys, they get work in television, the movies and that. Card-carrying actors, some of them. Maybe you should have them look you over, Burnsy. They might have something for an older guy."

"How's by you, Charlie?"

"Getting by. You know how it is. A little of this. A little of that. Hey, Burnsy, what's the deal? You getting anywhere with this 'elephant gun' clown?"

"Maybe," Burns replied diffidently. "Tonight maybe we got a break. I don't know. We'll see." He sipped his scotch. It tasted funny on account of his stomach. He turned to Tedesco. "What I mean is, I think we been getting our chain pulled. In fact I'm sure of it. By some of these God damned witnesses. All of them, maybe. I don't know."

"You mean somebody besides this Meyers broad?" said Tedesco. "Or whatever her name is?"

"What I mean is, if this nut hits again, the first thing we do is grab every fucking body that comes running up and says they seen it." Burns sighed and rubbed the back of his neck. He paid no attention to Dolan. Dolan was an ex-cop. He might have stepped in the shit once, but he was still an ex-cop. That meant he used to be a cop. And *that* meant, as far as Lieutenant Burns was concerned, that he could listen to any theories he had. "We grab them," he went on, "and we bring them in and we check them out. All the way out."

Tedesco shrugged. "We had a lot of flakes call since this started. She sounded like another flake, this Meyers."

"For Christ's sake." Burns set his glass down with a bang. "You heard the broad on the phone. The same one that called the time before this, right? From an address on First Avenue? That's what you said on the way over here."

"I think she's a flake."

Burns snorted in disgust. He burped and stroked his belly. He turned to Dolan. "It's like this, Charlie," he said. He was thankful Dolan was there. They had been through a lot together. You have a right to try out some off-the-wall theories on a man who was your partner for two years in the Bronx. "Every time this nut hits, we got witnesses by the carload. The usual shit. Ten, twelve people say they seen it all. Some of them got it all fucked up, or are just lying for the hell of it, but enough of them say the same thing until we got a pattern. We canvass and recanvass and what happens? We're meeting ourselves coming around the corner. The truth is, we ain't got an idea who this nut is. Or where he is. Or what the hell's wrong with him . . ."

"It's just a lunatic nigger, that's what I heard," said Dolan.

". . . and the reason we ain't got an idea," Burns continued; he turned back to Tedesco, "is because these fucking witnesses ain't real witnesses. They're some kind of God damned smoke screen."

Tedesco shrugged again. He wondered how long Burns intended to stay here going on with his absurd suppositions.

"That broad, Meyers," said Burns, "how come you recognized her voice?"

"I told you. She's the one that called last time."

"What's she look like?"

"Good-looking. European, I guess. Could be Italian, but I don't think so. Blond. Too fair."

"You got to be dark to be Italian?"

"No, but she looks more French or something. She ain't Neapolitano, I'll tell you that."

"How do you know what she looks like?"

"Oh, Christ. It's the same broad that was at Lexington Avenue and—" Tedesco stood up straight. He carefully placed his glass on the bar. "This makes the third time she's been around," he said in quiet amazement.

Burns leaned close to him. "And this Harlem thing ain't even a 'Finger of God' hit"— he signaled the bartender for a refill— "is it?" He smiled slowly.

"He take somebody out in Harlem?" asked Charlie Dolan. He paid for Burns's second drink and motioned to the bartender to pour another for him and Tedesco.

"Somebody took a shot at Snakehips Davis," Burns said. He considered what Tedesco had just said. He was no longer dealing with an off-the-wall theory. He had a hypothesis which had undergone a considerable amount of verification. There may even be some facts. Charlie Dolan could no longer be privy to his thinking. "His bodyguard or driver or whatever he was caught it. A nigger killing. Nothing to it."

"Snakehips Davis," Dolan said and whistled. "That's a hell of a note."

Burns nodded to Tedesco. "We'll split a cab. I got to see if I can find a hotel room. Take care, Charlie. Thanks for the drink."

"Take care, Burnsy. Don't lean too hard on them witnesses. Charm them. Like we used to do in the Bronx."

By a stroke of luck they managed to find a cab. The driver attempted to overcharge them. Burns gruffly told him they were policemen. The driver said the ride was free. Burns regretted having let Dolan hear him think out loud. Dolan might be dumb enough to shoot off his mouth to a reporter.

"What we're going to do," he said to Tedesco," is to go through every 'five' we've got if it takes all night. We're going to forget Mr. Elephant Gun and start looking for witnesses that've been at the scene more than once. And we're going to look like hell for this African. When we find any one of them, the African or the Meyers broad or whoever, God help them."

⑥

By daybreak the blizzard was total and unyielding. The wind blew as if to leave no doubt of the depth of nature's meanness. There was no other sound but the wind. The cold gnawed and scraped. A person rash enough to step outside could see nothing, living or otherwise, more than five feet away.

Snowplows pushed and shoved and broke down. Abandoned cars were embedded in drifts that arched fifteen feet in the air. Subway service was spotty. Commuter trains were buried in the suburbs. Food and fuel deliveries were canceled. Shops, schools, and offices did not attempt to open. The airports forbade takeoffs and landings.

In Major Espensheid's hotel the temperature was near freezing. The heating system had collapsed. Electric heaters had been distributed but were ineffectual.

In the major's room the mood was resentment and tension.

"You've crossed lines, Major," said Colonel Garovsky, abruptly shifting from English to Afrikaans; his tone was harsh; he pointed with two gloved fingers for emphasis. "You've ignored compartmentalization . . . in the stupidest way imaginable."

He shivered and sank his ears into the fur collar of his car coat.

"Leave off this smug talk about compartmentalization," snapped Major Espensheid after a moment. A heavy woolen muffler was wound twice around his thick neck. His shoulders were bent. His hands were plunged into his overcoat pockets. "As of today there is no more compartmentalization. As of today this is a composite operation. The composite operation it was planned to be."

They had been engaged in accusation and cross-accusation since Colonel Garovsky arrived. That had been some time before. Major Espensheid was offended that Colonel Garovsky spoke Afrikaans; a Jew had no business speaking Afrikaans, even if he had been born in South Africa. Oh, he knew the contributions of the Jews, Barnato and Marks and Beit, the money men, and now nuclear power and arms and the like. The trouble was, the path from one Jew to another was an easy one. They were aloof bastards, like the bloody English, and slim in their dealings with Boers, too clever by half. Major Espensheid despised the Jews and the English in equal parts, and he was positive that both of them would side with the Kaffirs if given the opportunity. Their loyalties lay in places other than South Africa, and you could be sure that only a Brit would tell you that Jesus was a non-European, and, legally speaking, he would have been a prohibited immigrant in the Republic of South Africa. He wondered whether Colonel Garovsky would say that. Probably. Jews never understood the point.

"My God, man!" retorted Colonel Garovsky. "What does it take to make you see the stupidity of this? This is a very delicate operation. Timing is everything. We've difficulties enough with this snowstorm. We do not need unilateral actions whose results can't be predicted. Or whose side effects can't be contained."

Major Espensheid thrust out his chin. His pudgy face glowed in the bitter cold. "Listen to me, Garovsky," he said; his breathing was heavy with rage. "If we had brought this off, if we'd actually slotted this Kaffir, you'd be congratulating us instead of fuming like a maiden auntie. Not that we need your congratulations. You may be sure of that. Or your indignation."

Colonel Garovsky emitted a hollow laugh. "Why on earth should we congratulate for something as mindless as trying to kill this footballer Davis?"

Major Espensheid's nostrils flared. He looked as if he were about to shout. Then he smiled crookedly. "You don't play much football in Israel, do you, Colonel?" he said with a note of bitterness; he recalled the time that Israel suspended its sports relations with South Africa so the Israeli team would be allowed to compete in the Olympics in

Moscow; the Jews had rather dance with the bloody communists than compete against the Springboks; imagine, he thought, the Russians, of all people, say we oppress the Kaffirs, and the Jews, who've been known to tread on a wog or two, take the part of the bloody Russians. "I think it would be accurate," he went on, "to say you don't know a great deal about football, wouldn't you?"

Colonel Garovsky looked bewildered. "Not much interest in rugby, no, not in Israel. Soccer is our national game, I suppose. Why?"

"Because," Major Espensheid replied sharply, "we know a very great deal about football in South Africa. Football isn't just a recreation for us. It's a passion. I've had a great deal of experience with it, personal experience. I was a Springbok fly-half, you know, before the war, after I gave up boxing. You may have heard about my triple-dummy and try against . . . My point is, I know the game inside and out. And this much is certain. If a remarkable player is absent at the time of a match, his side's chances are greatly reduced. It's all rot, a missing hero being an inspiration to his mates. I trust I make myself clear. Had Davis been unavailable, the Philadelphia side would not stand a chance against the New Orleans side on Sunday."

"We plan to place our wager on Philadelphia," Colonel Garovsky said evenly. He explained the point-spread system—as Nathan Leitstein had explained it to him the night before. It took the better part of an hour. He was careful to omit that the more money is bet, the more the point spread fluctuates; he also omitted other interesting possibilities raised by Nathan Leitstein. At length he said, "That is why we must have Davis as healthy as possible."

"But with Davis out of the way," Major Espensheid protested, "we could have put our money on New Orleans. We would have won easily. I'm certain of it."

Colonel Garovsky folded his arms. "That simply isn't how the thing is done," he said curtly and then shoved his hands against his hips. "Now listen to me carefully, Major," he went on, "listen to me very carefully. Mossad—I should say the state of Israel—is taking virtually all the risks in this operation. We have, unofficially, what amounts to a free hand in this city, because this city is extremely hospitable to Israel. Imagine, if you can, BOSS conducting this operation. It's out of the question. Why, a South African can hardly show his face here. If he does, he is wise to keep his nationality a close secret. An Israeli, on the other hand, is just another Jew in a Jewish city. That, my dear

Major, is why Mossad will retain control of planning and execution and BOSS will confine itself to surveillance and support. Do we understand each other?"

"Do you take us for fools, Colonel?" Major Espensheid snorted. He clapped his hands and then thrust them back into the pockets of his overcoat. "South Africa is supplying 60 percent of the money for this operation. Sixty percent! That's more than sixty million dollars! Think of that when you speak of risks. When the thing is done, your people will share the earnings and benefits equally, but it is South Africa that has supplied the money. We're paying for this operation, so please don't try and dictate our role in it!"

Colonel Garovsky knew he must regain control of the confrontation. A memory flashed in his brain . . . summer, 1945. Italy, near Milan. He was a lieutenant in the Sixth South African Armored Division. The division was to parade with units of the Palestinian Brigade of the British Army. There was talk of a mutiny in his squadron. "Nothing personal, sir," said his sergeant. The sergeant was English-speaking and a volunteer, as were all the other men in the squadron. "It's a question of how it will look back home. The men aren't Nazis or anything. Fought Jerry like madmen, they did, as you well know, sir. It's well, they want no trouble with the Cape Dutch after demob. It's South Africa we're going back to, isn't it, sir, not England or the States." The lieutenant, content but weary from spending the night in a brothel, thought the matter over and then said, "If the men don't want to parade with the Palestinians, so be it. I'm not about to turn them out under armed guard. Messy situation, though. Messy. Tell those who won't parade to report to hospital. We mustn't, however, overlook a general deterioration of discipline. Someone has to carry the keg. As senior NCO you're it, Sergeant. Have the corporal prepare the papers." The sergeant braced and hurriedly told the lieutenant that *all* the men would be ready for the parade at the advertised hour. They were. The American general commented on the smartness of the South Africans. . . . Colonel Garovsky stroked his chin. "Your black? What's his name. Have you any idea where he is now?"

"Mazibuko. Van Hooff and his men are trying to run him to earth. They'll succeed. Don't concern yourself with Mazibuko."

"If the police nab him first, what then, Major?"

Major Espensheid bit his lip. He glared a moment at Colonel Garovsky and then looked away.

"It will be a balls-up if he falls into the hands of the police," Colonel Garovsky persisted. "You know, of course, that Ayala telephoned an eye-witness report."

"Of course I know," Major Espensheid replied irritably. "I followed it on the wireless. I'm in the picture. Completely in the picture."

"It was the best we could do. We probably could have laid on something more convincing if we'd had advance notice. At the moment it's still a loose end. Very untidy . . . Mazibuko."

Major Espensheid frowned. "Mazibuko is our concern. Van Hooff will find him."

"And then what?"

"He'll kill him, of course."

"Unavoidable, I suppose," said Colonel Garovsky. "As you said, he's your concern, not ours." He felt the hair tingle on his arms. He took a deep breath and then said through clenched teeth, "Where is Dolan?"

"Dolan?"

"Yes, damn it! Your Uitmoor troopie! Your sharpshooter! The 'Finger of God!'" Colonel Garovsky was pointing with two fingers. "Dolan may be compromised by now, too. He can't be located. Zanin looked in and said he wasn't there. That was two hours after your so-called action took place."

Major Espensheid narrowed his eyes.

"Let me make this as plain as I can, Major. We need Dolan. Both of us." He paused to let this sink in and then went on, in English, "Mossad has the scheme in play. Dolan is essential to its success. The operation can't afford any further distractions. A fat lot of good our fifty kilos of explosives will do us if we don't have Dolan." He raised his hands in a conciliatory gesture and softened his voice. "I haven't the vaguest notion about explosives. Have you?"

Major Espensheid shook his head. "No, not the vaguest," he replied in English." His eyes blinked nervously.

"Well," Colonel Garovsky continued in a pleasant tone, "I suppose Van Hooff must get onto Dolan, too. When he finds him, you and I must make certain that Zanin keeps him under lock and key." He glanced about and then lowered his voice. "We've moved up the timetable. We're bringing it in today."

"The money?"

"Yes."

"In this weather?" A look of astonishment spread across Major Espensheid's sunburned face. "That's insane. Surely you don't mean a landing in New York."

"Yes. The weather will work in our favor, actually."

Major Espensheid walked slowly to a chair next to the electric heater. He paused a moment and then sat down. "Wouldn't it be advisable," he began tentatively, "to divert the flight, put it down some place nearby, and then transport the money here? It would take longer, but think of the safety element. If they land in, say, Boston, we could be sure of their getting here in one piece. Attempting to put down here, in this mess, well, I'm afraid we're risking our cargo—a bloody lot of someone else's money. Colonel—as well as a hundred and fifty South African and Israeli lives. A bit steep, don't you think?"

"It has to be," Colonel Garovsky said. He clasped his hands behind his back. "The weather isn't going to lift in time. If we wait any longer, the operation will be valueless. We'd just be gambling like the sheikhs do at Monte. No, it has to be today, and it has to be in New York. You see, if we brought it in someplace else, there's no telling when it would reach New York by ground transport. It could very well become lost in that glacier out there. A hundred and fifteen million dollars on deposit until the spring thaw.

"The fact of the matter is, we have no choice but to bring it here. Weather apart, we must land at Kennedy. It's the only East Coast airport that allows us—El Al, that is—full control of our airline program. We insisted on it some years ago for security reasons. To make sure the Arabs don't sabotage our aircraft or bomb our terminal or get aboard one of our jets and hijack it. The Port Authority were quite receptive to our request. They thought it reasonable enough, given the activities of the Arabs at the time. Consequently, El Al got permission to recruit its own mechanics, its own ground crews, and so forth. On occasion El Al people have ridden the fire trucks and ambulances on the runway when an El Al plane lands with engine trouble. It usually happens when trouble is suspected aboard the aircraft and one of the prearranged emergency codes is garbled. Of course, the mechanics and what have you must abide by regulations—customs, safety standards, union rules, that sort of thing—and, of course, they do. They will today, the difference being that today they will be members of the Mossad."

"You mean to say your people are trained in the ground operations of an international airline?"

Colonel Garovsky smiled. "They're trained well enough. After all, they aren't the ones with the problem, are they? Their only concern will be unloading the money."

"This is fascinating, Colonel. Do you mind telling me where on board the money is stored?"

"Everywhere—I mean that literally—except the cargo hold. It will be taken off while the passengers are claiming their luggage in the usual tourist way. As soon as it's unloaded it will be taken to a safe house."

"Ingenious. Ingenious. Where is this safe house?"

"In a remote section of the city. You may inspect it anytime you like, Major. Anytime you are in a mood to cope with this weather."

Major Espensheid laughed. "I expect there will be plenty of time for that." He wore a knowing look. "Thank you for sharing this information with me. I think our cooperation will be greatly improved in the future. It's the nature of intelligence work, I'm afraid, to be secretive and suspicious—and jealous of one's ability to make things work on one's own." He nodded with self-satisfaction. "There will be no more independent actions. At any rate not by our side." He emphasized the "our."

"Thank you, Major."

"By the way, Colonel. Your pilot. The El Al chap. Is he good?"

"Very good. One of the best, in fact. He's called Harian. Perhaps you've heard the name. No? He perfected the high-low-high technique for evading SAM-6 missiles. You know the one I mean. The pilot comes in low directly against the launcher, then pops up immediately behind it and dive-bombs the mobile radar unit. Somehow he breaks away low again and drops flares—in case the SAM battery gets off a shot. The missiles are heat-seeking, you see, and the flares confuse them. A tricky maneuver, the high-low-high. I'm sure Harian has devised something equally devilish for this snowstorm."

They shook hands. In the corridor Colonel Garovsky found a shivering crowd at the elevator. A man from the hotel said it was out of order. Service was expected back at any moment.

Colonel Garovsky rotated his neck against his fur collar. The sensation was pleasurable. He thought of going back to Major Espensheid's room and telling him he ought to move to a decent hotel, someplace with a bit of luxury to it. The man would be less likely to create more difficulties if he were comfortable. He decided against it. A Boer, he reflected, thinks he can't do his duty if he's comfortable.

There had been a time when he feared that his own father was falling prey to the same monotonous habits. It was during the empty months that followed the death of his mother. Why, he asked as gently as possible, should a Jew from Romania enjoy no more of life than a Dutch Reformed dominie? Was work everything—even if the only real work was seeing to it that your Kaffirs kept their backs bent—just because the Boers thought it was?

Sammy Garovsky laughed. He was sitting with his son in the ample *stoep* that ran the length of his Cape Dutch house. It was January 1940. The house overlooked the vineyards. The summer sun was low.

"Not work, Jack," he said in Yiddish, "land. Don't tell me the land belongs to the Kaffirs. It may have been theirs once. Not in my time. I bought this farm, every morgen of it, from a land agent in Paarl. It was no small thing, either, for a Jew who'd never seen another Jew's name on a land register. A Jew was up against it in Romania, let me tell you. He couldn't acquire property or vote or live where he chose. I've heard life's sweetened a bit there since I left. How sweet can life get for a Jew in Romania in twenty-three years?"

"Not very," said his son. "Tatarescu has struck a deal with the Iron Guard. It was on the wireless."

Since the death of his mother, Jack Garovsky had journeyed often from Cape Town, where he was an architect's apprentice, to his father's farm. He was bewildered by his father's lack of interest in matters beyond the boundaries of his property—or in other women.

"Why do you *mutche* me?" his father said irritably. "What you really mean is another wife, isn't it? Well, I don't want another wife. Your mother was a good woman, but a wife's no help running a farm. Liz cooks my meals. If I want a woman, I'll take her, the Immorality Act be damned. Do I *mutche* you to get married? If I were a good Jew, I would tell you what Rabbi Bierman told *my* father. 'Reb Garovsky, your Shimshon is nineteen. You must see Lowitz the matchmaker and have him make a *shiddach* for your son. He will fetch a good dowry. A man who is unmarried after twenty is cursed by God Himself, living without joy or blessing.' But I'm not a good Jew. I hope you never will be either. It's enough just to be a Jew. Why do you think I've never observed Holy Days, or worried about what I ate, or given you a *Bar Mitzvah?* Because I am not a *tzaddik*. I know exactly one prayer, Rabbi Akiva's. 'Don't help us, Lord, and don't spoil it for us.'"

"Why do you speak Yiddish to me?"

"Why? So you'll remember you're a Jew. But not a good Jew. If I wanted you to be a good Jew, at least I'd have had you circumcised."

Jack Garovsky gazed into the sunset. The grapes were blood red in the slanting light. At length he said, "The Boers are agitating, you know. They've revived 'Hoggenheimer.' I saw one of the cartoons on a notice board. They've formed something called the *Ossewa Brandwag*. The Ox-Wagon Sentinel. Their program is a muddle. Basically, they say Hitler is right. They want him to 'liberate' South Africa from the English and the Jews."

"What do you expect?" his father said. "The Boers have hated the Brits for seventy years, at least. Probably a lot longer. When someone has made war against you, you always have a reason to hate them. Of course they hate Jews, too. For one reason. We're not Boers. I wouldn't look to the Brits for much support, though, just because the Boers get mouthy and say they want rid of both of us. The Brits hate Jews as much as the Boers do, only they're usually more polite about it. The Brits like to think of themselves as firm but fair. You won't catch a Brit mistreating a Kaffir. He gets a Boer to do it for him."

"But Britain has declared war on Germany."

"You don't suppose they did it for the good of the Jews, do you?"

"At least they've done it. The Boers want the Union to stay out of it altogether."

"Why shouldn't they? The Germans took the Boers' part when the English attacked them. That was before the turn of the century, but a Boer's memory is long. . . . What are you getting at, Jack? Are you itching to have a go at the Germans? What's the point? Look at all this around us. There's space. There's isolation. Let England fight the Germans if they must. A war in Europe, what's it got to do with us?"

The son looked at the floor. "I can't explain it. Not all of it. It seems the thing to do, that's all. I suppose it's because I remembered I'm a Jew. It doesn't often cross your mind in Cape Town, you know. Or it didn't until recently."

"Until you saw old 'Hoggenheimer,' you mean? Do they still draw him fat? With a cigar and diamond rings and a top hat? Yes, I suppose they do. Hoggenheimer wouldn't be Hoggenheimer if he looked like John Gilbert, would he?"

Jack Garovsky glared at his father. Sammy Garovsky felt it and realized he had gone too far. He broke into a smile. "A Jewish soldier," he said. "My, my. That will be a novelty. I imagine you will cut a dashing figure when you're tricked out. When do you leave?"

"Next month," his son replied. His glared softened. He was not the kind of man who forgets that there is a great deal of his father in himself. "I think I can get a commission. Will you come to Cape Town? There are the wine tastings if you get bored with military splendor."

"Why should I go to Cape Town? How many times must I tell you? I enjoy my life? I love my farm. The wine I make, *nyeh*. But plum brandy, that I enjoy. It was plum brandy that got me out of Romania. I was drinking masses of the stuff—I had already cut off my curls and was wearing *goyish* clothes—and I was the disgrace of the *shtetl*. One day I was *shikker* in the back of my pony cart. The beast pulled me all the way to Constanta. When I sobered up, I looked at the Black Sea and thought, 'If I'm not for myself, who is?' The next morning I signed on a four-masted Danish barque bound for Foochow. . . . Liz! Bring us some plum brandy! Liz is the only Kaffir I know who understands Yiddish. My father used to say that a Jew who enjoys himself is asking for trouble. Don't believe a word of it."

Six months later Jack Garovsky completed infantry training at Gil Gil in Kenya. Then came a year of heat and cold against the Italians in the waterless Chalbi and the Dorze highlands of Ethiopia. After the fall of Addis Ababa he was commissioned and posted to tanks. Then it was off to western Egypt, where he was introduced to the clanky art of armored warfare.

In Egypt he found another enemy as fierce as the Germans: the desert. He had to fight for breath as the stifling *khamsin* swept onto the Eighth Army from the Sahara. It blotted out the sun and blasted them with tons of powdery sand. Everyone had dysentery. One night, returning to his "bivy" from his eleventh bowel seizure in two hours, he got lost in the featureless landscape. It was dawn before he made his way back to his tank.

His mail caught up with him in early October. There were two letters.

The first read:

Dear Jack:
I have the most amazing news. I've married again. Her name is Annie and she's forty years younger than I and she's an English *shiksa*. I found her in

Cape Town. She came here for a rest from Dar es Salaam. It seems her father is some sort of colonial wallah there. She wanted to get away from the troop ships and found the Cape busier with them than Dar. So rather than get messed about by another lot of soldiers, she took up with a lecherous old Jew who lives on a farm. She absolutely forbids me to discuss the war, and to make sure I don't she keeps me indoors a lot and does the most incredible things. I had no idea young women were so imaginative. Why didn't you tell me? Do Jewish girls do these things, too?

I might as well admit that I was more or less forced into it. There were two considerations. First, Liz turned me down cold. I threatened to whip her unless she consented, but she stood fast—and now I think she's a bit jealous because she is very cheeky with Annie. The other thing was an old auntie, woman my age, with whom Annie was lodging. The woman cried scandal when Annie invited me to tea and had to be given a nerve potion when she found us in bed together next morning. I expected social attitudes to be a bit looser in the Union with a war on. I was saved by a riot. The local Hitler crowd and some service chaps on leave were going at it with chains and knuckledusters and they couldn't spare a constable to charge me under the Immorality Act. We drove to Paarl—on auntie's petrol card—and found a Methodist parson to pronounce us.

The war is doing wonders for the wine trade.

Your father,
S. Garovsky.

He laughed and marveled that the letter had gotten past the censors. Then he opened the second letter.

Dear Lieutenant Garovsky:

I hardly know how to begin this letter as we have not been introduced. Your father and I were married on 16th July and I regret to inform you that this union lasted only until 31st July as your father passed away on that date. You will be pleased to know that he died at peace with his Hebrew heritage. He was in his bed, content under the roof of his house and protected from the winter afternoon, at the time he was summoned by the Creator. I was unable to arrange a Hebrew service, but the minister who read our vows drove up from Paarl and gave him a proper Christian burial. I hope this meets with your approval.

May I say that your father was one of the most understanding and high-minded men I've ever known. He spoke often of his happiness as a young man in Paris although he was glad to have put all that behind him. Mr. Garovsky was proud that he was able to rear you in the Hebrew tradition and he also was gratified that you took it upon yourself to serve your king in this time of peril. We discussed the war often and tried as best we could to keep up with your part in it.

I have taken the liberty of hiring an overseer until you decide on the future of the farm. Your father gave me to believe that he would have preferred to live for a time someplace other than the countryside. I think he had lost some of his enthusiasm for farming and the wine trade.

It has been necessary for me to make some changes in the staff. I have replaced the cook, Liz, with another native. I chose one of the young pickers. The sentiment nowadays is that men, if they are taught properly, make the best cooks. I hope this meets with your approval.

Your father's affairs were not in order when he passed away. He left no will. I hope the army will allow you to come to the Cape as soon as possible to attend to this matter.

Yours etc.,
Ann Stapleford Garovsky

Leave was out of the question. The Eighth Army was preparing for a fall offensive into Libya against the Afrika Korps. Lieutenant Garovsky recited what fragments he knew from the prayer for the dead. He dashed off a note to—to whom? his stepmother?—instructing her to make no further changes in the operation of the farm.

It was raining the morning the offensive began. Five days later Lieutenant Garovsky's squadron, attached to a British formation, drove to the top of a hundred-foot-high ridge that guarded the approaches to Tobruk. Resistance was surprisingly light. The place was Sidi Rezegh. Rommel wanted it back.

The counterattack was biting and howling. The German tanks rampaged with a purpose, scattering their shells. They came on without warning. The defenders scrambled wildly. Sidi Rezegh was a confusion of searing flashes and crushing roars. "Get mounted!" Lieutenant Garovsky screamed to his crew. It was too late. A German shell smashed into the tracks of his Valentine tank. The tank buckled to the ridge floor. Lieutenant Garovsky was flattened by an irresistible weight on his head and back. He drifted into unconsciousness almost immediately.

When he came to, he was aware of very little except a dull ache all over and the sensation that his right hand was on fire. He was in a field-dressing station. "You've a concussion," said a doctor, squinting through tired eyes. "Nothing to worry about. Your hand's another matter. Oh, you won't lose it, of course. But I don't know when you'll be able to bend those two fingers." Lieutenant Garovsky asked about the battle. "Fifth Brigade no longer exists," said the doctor wearily. "We were Jerry's prisoner for a time, but the Germans moved on as soon as they'd overrun us. They're obviously trying to break through to Egypt. The situation's not clear. Half the wounded in here are Germans."

With infinite slowness the Afrika Korps was thrown back, then defeated. Lieutenant Garovsky took a spot of leave. He returned to the Cape. His father's widow had departed. He satisfied himself that the overseer was keeping the farm reasonably solvent. Then he joined the division that landed in Italy in the spring of 1944.

Italy seemed to be a vast sea of mud in which every identifiable thing was charred or crushed. The Germans were on the run. They fled Rome, blew the bridges in Florence, and fled there, too, and then, one day, they gave up. Everywhere Lieutenant Garovsky looked there were German corpses. Their white faces glared at him through masks of dried blood. "Driver, advance," he ordered from the belly of his Crusader tank.

One warm afternoon, not far from Lake Como, he watched a small horse-drawn cart as it made its way from a rail siding. The cart was jammed with people. They were feeble and tattered, men and women of all ages, unknotted, it seemed to him, from the roots of time. The sight did not move him but simply made him curious about their destination. Where could they be going? What could they possibly do when they got there?"

"Palestine," said a refugee worker, a man with one arm. "Eretz Israel."

Lieutenant Garovsky shook his head and thought, the poor bastards, they'd turn around on the spot if they knew what was in store for them; Palestine was as dismal as Mediterranean Africa, by all accounts. What stuck in his mind was the way the people in the carts stirred at the words "Eretz Israel."

"Where are they from?"

"Romania, most of them," replied the refugee worker.

Lieutenant Garovsky's eyes widened. "My father was born in Romania!" he exclaimed. "I say, are any of them Jews?"

The refugee worker looked at him warily. He studied his pips and insignias. "South African," he muttered and nodded. At length he said, "They're all Jews."

"May I speak to them?" Lieutenant Garovsky asked excitedly. "Do they speak Yiddish?"

The refugee worker nodded again and shrugged.

He ran down the narrow road and grasped the top rail of the cart. The faces of the people inside were shrunken and without expression.

"Are any of you from a *shtetl* near Evidiu? he shouted in Yiddish. "Perhaps it's Ovidiu! A small place not far from Constanta!"

The blank faces did not respond. The cart bumped and jostled. The scarecrow figures seemed to need something more than questions from a mere mortal to elicit a response.

"Is anyone here called Garovsky?" There was a pleading note in his voice. "My father's name was Garovsky. Shimshon Garovsky."

After a moment a female voice said, "His name is Garovsky." He looked from face to face. None of the lips seemed to have moved.

"Which one?"

"Him." The voice belonged to a woman with a broken nose. It was the only part of her that seemed the feature of a human being. She slowly turned her head to a man next to her whose eyes were closed. "He does not speak. He has no manhood." She nudged the man. "Garovsky?" she said. The man did not move. "See. He does not speak. He might be dead."

"What happened to you?"

The blank silence returned.

Lieutenant Garovsky loosened his grip on the rail. The cart rumbled slowly down the road and out of sight. He trudged back to the rail siding.

"What happened to them?"

The refugee worker said nothing.

"Why are they going to Palestine?" he demanded. "Why are they leaving Romania?"

"I take it you're a Jew," the refugee worker snapped. "I haven't run across many *goyim* who speak Yiddish."

"Of course I'm a Jew."

"Then surely you know another Jew or two in the British army. Find one of them and ask him. He's sure to know."

"Damn it!" he shouted. "What the hell's the mystery? Why are these people leaving Romania?"

The refugee worker glanced from side to side. No one else was about. He gripped the stump of his arm and said in a low voice, "They haven't been in Romania for some time. . . . They've been in Poland."

"Why Poland?"

The refugee worker glared at him. "Where have you been since 1941?" he asked hotly. "In a cellar?"

Lieutenant Garovsky pointed at the refugee worker with the two fingers he still had difficulty bending. "Fighting the bloody Germans," he growled, "that's where I've been. And the bloody Italians. All over Africa and all over bloody Italy. From Ethiopia to this bloody spot. On foot and in tanks. So do you mind not giving me a load of slosh when I ask you a simple question. I have no scruples whatsoever about beating the bloody breakfast out of a one-armed cripple!"

The refugee worker looked pensive. "Did you say tanks?"

"I bloody well did!"

"Do you mind giving me your name and an address where you can be reached after demobilization?" He produced a small notebook and a pen.

Lieutenant Garovsky scribbled furiously and then thrust the notebook back into the refugee worker's hand. "Now," he said, "unless you tell me at once why those people are leaving Romania, I'll have you arrested. For espionage."

The refugee worker sighed. Then in a voice so composed that it bordered on callousness he told him about Brzeznica and Oswiecim ("The complex was called *Konzentrationslager Auschwitz*. Rhymes with *auswischen*. 'To wipe out,' you know. The gassings were done a mile or so away. Area called Birkenau.") and Treblinka and Maidanek and Belsec and Chelmno and Sibibor and the rest of the camps where the SS had erected the apparatus for the "final solution" of Europe's "Jewish question."

Lieutenant Garovsky sat down cross-legged on a patch of grass. "I don't believe it," he said forlornly. He stared at the empty, open rail car from which the cartload of refugees had pulled away. "There are thousands of displaced persons . . . All over Italy . . . I've seen them . . . Everywhere . . . It's war . . . Homes get bombed . . . All kinds of shortages . . . People go wherever they think there's food. . . ."

"These are going to Palestine," said the refugee worker. "It isn't a matter for them of simply being hungry. No one wants them. They just aren't Romanians anymore. England won't take them. America won't. No. They're going to Eretz Israel. If they can get through the British blockade."

"British blockade?"

"They don't want more Jews in Palestine. Afraid it will upset the

Arabs. Of course it will upset them. It's a hard choice for the British, I suppose, having to decide between Jews in Palestine, who want to bring in more Jews, and the Arabs, who can plainly see they stand to be pushed aside. We intend to make the choice even harder."

"What do you mean?"

"I must be getting along," said the refugee worker. "By the way, if anyone asks, would you be kind enough to keep dark about what you've seen? You see, I actually could be arrested. The British don't like us *mazikim* hauling Jews through their sector. Shalom." He waved with his remaining hand.

The man from the hotel returned from the telephone. "They're still working on the elevator," he said. "If any of you are in a big hurry, you can use the service elevator. If you'll follow me, please." Colonel Garovsky and the others shuffled off behind him down the corridor.

Three months later Jack Garovsky was out of uniform and back in the Cape. He longed for his father. His father, he realized now that he was dead, was the only man he'd ever admired without a taste of jealousy or regret. He obtained a commission to write a monograph on the architecture of his father's house. He knew what he wanted to write. Something that conveyed how impressed he was by the way the Boers had expanded the styles of their forefathers in Holland to match the massiveness of the land they had conquered. He couldn't concentrate. His mind was gripped by images of terror. The carnage at Sidi Rezegh. The mud and death in Italy. The most persistent image was the man in the refugee cart. The man who had "lost his manhood." The man named Garovsky.

Finally he shelved the project. He wrote the architectural society that the farm demanded all his attention and began spending weeks at a time in pursuit of an actress in a tame little repertory theater in Cape Town. Her name was Helen. She was emotional and turbulent. But as the months wore on she became merely a battlefield on whose body he fought his gathering demons. Finally he announced he was returning to his farm. Helen was wounded. "Now you're going," she said bitterly. "Why didn't you do it sooner? Before we started going about in public. Everyone's seen us, you know. Oh, I can hear them now—if they speak to me at all. 'Where's your fancy Jew, Helen?' Get out."

Early in 1947 he received an odd notice in the mail. In rather urgent language he was asked to attend an interview with a group of men whose names he recognized as prominent Cape Town Jews. He accepted and was ushered by one of the prominent Jews into another room. Seated behind a desk was a man with one arm, who bade him take a chair.

"Weren't you doing refugee work a year or two back," he asked. "In Italy?"

"Possibly," the man said; he thumbed impatiently through a sheaf of papers; he steadied them with the stump of his missing arm. "Ah, here we are. Garovsky, Jacob." He peered intently a moment at the paper and then looked up. "I remember you. In fact this is my own chit. You're the chap who was amazed that Hitler tried to slaughter all the Jews." He tossed the paper aside. "My name is Pinchas Werner."

"Do you mind if we speak Yiddish? It's been a long time and I don't often have the opportunity."

"Very well," Werner said, switching from English. "My reason for being here is straightforward. I'm recruiting men with military experience for service in Eretz Israel. Still the Palestine mandate for the moment, but that's changing fast. I'll take anyone who'll sign on, but, frankly, I'm looking for Jews. As you know the British are doing all they can to stop us in our tracks. They spout legality this and legality that, but the fact is they're arresting us in droves on pretexts, hanging any Jew they suspect of being a so-called leader—"

"I've followed it in the newspapers. The SABC carries it," Jack Garovsky interrupted. He leaned back and studied the man across the desk. "May I ask you a question? On whose behalf are you, as you put it, recruiting Jews with military experience? Whom do you propose to fight? The British? You know, don't you, that I'm a citizen of the Union of South Africa and a member of the British Commonwealth? During the war I was a member of His Majesty's Forces."

"So was I. So was the Arab Legion," Werner retorted. "My little jaunt was in Syria. Cost me my arm. That's hardly the point. You don't suppose Palestinian Jews fought the Germans for Britain's benefit, do you? We fought the Germans for *our* benefit. It wasn't the first time we've consorted with the enemy for our own purposes. My God, I was in Vienna myself in 1938, bargaining face-to-face with Heydrich to let Jews out of Austria. I told him that the more Jews there were in Palestine, the worse time the British would have with the Arabs."

"Then it's the British you plan to fight?"

"If we have to. May I answer your other question? I represent a point of view as much as anything else," he said, in what seemed to be a well-practiced speech, "that being the creation of a Jewish state in Palestine. We're in the course of an international program of gathering not only Jews with military backgrounds, but also—"

"Ah, you're a Zionist."

"Naturally."

"Some sort of Jewish communist, aren't you?"

Werner laughed and clapped his palm against his forehead. "I didn't know anyone actually believed that. Of course we aren't communists. Zionism aims to get all the Diaspora Jews back to Palestine. Nothing political about that, is there? Except that we want them to come back and form a nation."

"Do you mean you're going to convoke another Great Sanhedrin or whatever it's called and install a lot of rabbis and lay down the law and so forth?"

"Good God, no," Werner shouted. "You astound me, Garovsky." He briefly consulted a paper and then continued, "Do you recall a man at that rail siding in Italy, fellow named Garovsky? He'd been castrated."

Jack Garovsky felt the hair bristle on the back of his neck. He nodded slowly.

"Well, do you know where that man is?" he went on. His voice rasped. "He's in a grave on Cyprus. Died in a detention camp. A *British* detention camp. Already he'd been behind Nazi wire for three years at Wolzek. That was after two years behind the wall in Warsaw—where he was sent from Romania to make Europe a clean place for the Germans! When you last saw him, he had a chance for a measure of kindness, perhaps even some peace in what little mind he had left. He was going to Eretz Israel! The Promised Land! . . . He got as far as Cyprus. The British intercepted his ship five hours after it left La Spezia and interned him. He didn't last two weeks." Werner rubbed his eyes. "That's what Zionism means, Garovsky, survival. Not the Great Sanhedrin, not kosher salami, not rounding up a tenth man for a *minyan*. It means survival. Do you understand?"

Jack Garovsky was silent a moment. Then he said, "The wireless says the British are trying to deal evenhandedly with Jews and Arabs. If you get your Jewish state, do you imagine the Arabs are going to march off quietly into the desert. The SABC man said yesterday—"

"That's the British wireless. Look. To be perfectly frank, I'm only concerned with Jews. I should think you'd be able to grasp that, living here. The Boers are concerned only with the Boers, aren't they? They see themselves as a Chosen People. We do, too, of course. Sooner or later—depending on the circumstances—Chosen People move to the head of the queue."

"That's a bit oversimplified, isn't it?"

"Is it? I was in Jo'burg two days ago. Your Nationalist Party is gearing up for a general election next year. Have you read their program? It sounds like Berlin, 1933, all over again. They even have a cartoon that Julius Streicher would approve of. 'Hoggenheimer,' I believe it's called. Of course the Boers aren't out for the Jews, primarily, or even the English-speaking types, are they? The ones they want to push around are the Kaffirs. Not exterminate them, God knows—who else would do the work here?—just keep them in their place."

"Is that what the Jewish state has in mind for the Arabs?"

"What the Jewish state has in mind is a Jewish state. A Jewish state can't very well be run by Arabs, can it, any more than a Boer State can be run by Kaffirs? The Arabs will have to survive the best they know how. We will survive any way we can. But, by God, we *will* survive, the British and the Arabs be damned. . . . What do you say, Garovsky? I may be able to find a tank for you."

Jack Garovsky was wondering what his father would say to all this when he heard his own voice. "Where will you get a tank?"

"You're aboard then?"

"Yes," he replied after taking a deep breath. He was about to say he didn't know much about being a Jew when he realized it would mean more lecturing from Werner. Werner was a teachy sort, he decided, but he found his hopeful manner and fine, slippery mind appealing. Werner and his father and a bottle of plum brandy. That would have been a show.

Werner grinned broadly. "One of our people is in Pretoria at the moment. Purchasing arms. General Smuts says he's sympathetic to us. He's also sympathetic to the British." He stood up and began awkwardly raking his papers into a satchel. "Even if he agrees to sell us a tank, we have to convince him to let us take it to Palestine."

Jack Garovsky sailed for Palestine as soon as he had placed his farm in the hands of a trustee. He traveled on a tourist visa. He didn't want to be turned back as a forbidden immigrant. He landed at Haifa. The other passengers praised the landscape. Whitewashed buildings on hills surrounding a bay. He shrugged. It was hard to be impressed by other scenery if you had ever sailed into the Cape at Table Bay. Hulks of other ships lay beached nearby, relics of illegal immigrations. British soldiers stood guard.

He retrieved his single piece of luggage and went to a coffee house in the Arab quarter near the docks. A taxi driver appeared at his table. The man had a tattoo of blue numbers inside his left forearm. Jack Garovsky looked at him with a start.

"When I eat, they can all go to hell," the driver said in Yiddish.

Jack Garovsky continued to stare at him, shocked. Then he gave the countersign. "What a sober man has on his mind, a drunkard has on his tongue."

The same dialogue took place simultaneously at a dozen other tables. He recognized most of the faces. They had been fellow passengers who joined the ship at Marseilles. They departed without paying for their coffee. The proprietor cursed them.

In the taxi Jack Garovsky said, "Excuse me. Are you called Garovsky by any chance?"

"My name is Garonsky. Why do you ask?"

"I thought you were someone I saw a couple of years ago. In Italy. Somone from Romania."

"I am from Romania. Have we met?"

"I think I saw you near Lake Como."

"Ah, near Lake Como. I was recovering from typhus. Nasty thing, typhus. The SS infected me with it deliberately."

"There was a woman at the rail siding. She said you were . . . you had been . . ."

"You know her, too? Mrs. Mandel? Very mischievous, she was. She said Mr. Kaplan was not a Jew. Kaplan not a Jew? Hah. She said *I* had lost my *baitsim*. Such talk. Didn't like Palestine. She went to America."

They drove north to a village in the "finger of Galilee," a panhandle between the Syrian and Lebanese borders at the head of the Hula Valley. It was a Jewish village. The taxi deposited him at a long, low building. The fare was enormous. A number of young men kicked a soccer ball. An equal number of young women suntanned on a strip of grass.

A barrel-chested man burst through the front door. "Hah! You must be Pinchas's South African," he shouted and clapped him on the back.

"I am Piotr. I command this Haganah unit. We shall call you Yakov. Come, everyone, come. Greet Yakov. He has made his *aliyah*." Everyone rushed over. The soccer players hugged him. The sunbathers kissed him. Everyone questioned him at once in Hebrew. He replied in Yiddish that he did not speak Hebrew. So they spoke in Yiddish.

"When will the UN vote on partition?"

"Did you bring any good books?"

"Will Elizabeth marry Mountbatten?"

"Have you seen *Gone With The Wind?*"

"Are you married?"

After a time he was able to speak to Piotr alone. "I don't mean to put a damper on the fun," he said after kicking the soccer ball a considerable distance, "but I must ask you something. Who are we fighting?"

Piotr doubled over with laughter. "Fighting? Fighting?" he gasped for breath. "Why, no one at the moment."

"What about the British? Werner said—"

"Yakov, Yakov, will you relax? We are Haganah, not Irgun. We aren't fighting anyone. Certainly we aren't going to fight the British. What would we fight them with? Do you know what arms we have? Two Enfield revolvers and forty-six rounds of ammunition. There's an antipersonnel mine buried on an unused track a mile or two from here. No one knows exactly where. Don't be impatient. The Irgun will finish the British—even if they are all hanged in the process. Then Haganah will fight."

He knitted his eyebrows. "The Arabs?"

"Of course the Arabs. The talk is everywhere. Even the moderate Arabs say why should Palestine become full of Jews because of sinfulness in Europe. A silly thought. How many Jews have sinned in Europe? It's *narrishkeit*. Oil is a sin in Europe, maybe, but not Jews."

"What if there's no partition and the British don't leave?"

"The British are leaving, partition or not. Six months, a year at most. We know. When the British aren't arresting us, they tell us things. Unofficially, of course—we tap their telephones. When the British leave, then the fun begins."

"Fun? You must be mad."

"What have the Arabs got? I'll tell you. The Arab Legion. Nothing more. The Arab Legion is good, damned good. They can do much damage, but not enough to cancel us out. They're shock troops, and shock troops can't mop up against people whose feet are planted. Our feet are planted. We will turn the tables when the Arabs bring up their reserves. The *fellahin*. Wretched people. Hopeless peasants since the dawn of time. Blink your eyes, break wind, the *fellahin* flutter away like leaves in a sandstorm. I am twenty-nine years old and I have seen the Arabs strike hard two times against the Jews. Two times! In 1929 at Hebron—a slaughter, the fools hugged their Torahs and wouldn't fight back—and 1936 when the Mufti obtained weapons for the *fellahin* from the Germans. The Irgun stopped them."

"But there are so many of them and so few of . . . us."

"The *fellahin* are like your natives in South Africa. They have been taught to cringe by the *effendis*. Tonight you will reconnoiter with Shuna. She will show you."

"Who is Shuna?"

Piotr pointed to one of the sunbathers. "That is Shuna. She knows everything about reconnaissance. *Everything*."

At sundown he and Shuna set out on foot in the direction of Lebanon. There was a hint of chill in the air. He wore khakis. Shuna wore blue shorts and a denim shirt. In a holster around her waist was one of the Enfield revolvers.

"I hope you're in condition," Shuna said in English. She was slender and firm and had short, dark hair. Her face was heartshaped and inclined to pout. "We've several miles to cover. If you tire, say so. I'll leave you to rest and collect you on the way back."

"I'm all right. I had expected some training, though."

"This is training," she said a trifle waspishly. "Do you know how to use the Enfield?"

"Yes. I carried one in the war."

"Ah, you were an officer. I don't think British officers know how to use them effectively. I saw a Guards captain fire at an Irgunist at a distance of no more than ten feet. The Irgunist was no older than I. He had blown up a lorry. The officer missed him completely."

"Even an officer needs practice."

"You didn't suppose you'd be allowed to shoot at targets, did you? With no more ammunition than we have? Besides, the British would hear it and give us a headache."

"No, I suppose not," he said. He felt a blister forming inside one of his heavy, high-top shoes. "Tell me. Why wasn't the briefing more explicit?"

"Piotr was very explicit. He said reconnaissance and improvisation. How much more can you be told?"

"What does he mean, improvisation?"

Shuna halted and stood with her legs apart, hands on hips. "This is a different kind of war," she snapped. "That's why I, a farm girl, am showing you, an officer, how to fight it. You might as well forget about textbook tactics and tanks and air support. We don't have those. We do have an advantage, though—for the moment, at least. The Arabs are terrified of us. To be effective at terror you have to im-pro-vise. So please don't question the briefing."

They moved on. It was dark now. He wondered what had provoked her. Nervousness? Resentment? He decided against further discussion. Some time later Shuna raised her hand. "This is the frontier," she said, making no effort to keep her voice down.

Before them stretched a dry plain. The moon was behind a curtain of clouds. No feature of the landscape was apparent. "Syria is that way. Mount Hermon is ahead," Shuna said.

Presently they saw a glow behind a low mound. "Just a shepherd," said Shuna. They rounded the hillock and came upon a goat-hair tent before which squatted a robed man at the edge of a fire. He appeared to be old. Yakov Garovsky thought it was merely a picturesque scene in the darkness when all at once Shuna began to shout in Arabic.

The shepherd shouted back and scrambled toward his tent.

He didn't make it. Shuna was on him, kicking his legs out from under him and pounding his head with the butt of the revolver. The shepherd groaned and then sat down, holding his head. The goats bleated.

In swift jerks Shuna pulled down the tent. On the floor was an ancient muzzle-loading rifle. She picked it up and removed the firing cap. Then she raised it over her head and crashed it against the ground. The stock broke in half. The goats frisked away.

Her face was lit by the glow of the fire. Her expression was grim. She shouted again at the shepherd and spat on him. She motioned that it was time for them to start back to Palestine.

As they recrossed the frontier she stopped. "How do you feel?" she asked.

"Some pain in my feet. Nothing more."

"Any questions?"

He wished it weren't so dark. He wanted to see her face. "Would you explain what that was about?" he said at last.

"Yes. To create instability. The Arabs in this sector will be unstable for at least a week, maybe two. That old goatherd will spread the word of what happened to him. But he will lie. He has no choice but to say that he was set upon by twenty heavily armed Jews. How else can he explain the loss of his rifle? He cannot say a Jewish woman did this to him. He would be ridiculed. It works like this. We sent out four patrols tonight. If they all had the luck we had, the Arabs will think our unit has a strength of eighty, all with rifles." She allowed herself a small laugh. "In addition to the eighteen of us who sat down to dinner and our two pistols."

"Are you serious?"

"It bought time," she said. "Time is what we need until we are able to arm ourselves. Then we can have a real war. A war for more territory. At the moment the Arabs do not realize that they must take *themselves* seriously if they are going to try and push us into the sea . . . I could have shot him, you know. It would have been pointless. The Arabs would have thought another Arab did it. This way there is someone to scream it was the work of the bloodthirsty Jews." She glanced around. "Let's go. I know a spot near here."

He said nothing and followed. He was limping slightly from his blister.

Suddenly the clouds blew past. The moon was bright and stark. Their shadows were vivid. They came to a stand of cercis shrub. Shuna kicked away a stone and knelt down and smoothed the dirt with her hand. "This isn't the place," she said, "but it will do." She stood up and quickly removed her shirt and shorts. She wore no underclothes.

"Are you sure this is safe?" he said with a gulp; this was obviously, incomprehensibly ridiculous. "I mean, that old man might have—"

"Of course it's safe."

She lowered herself to the ground and stretched out on her back. Her body was supremely good of its kind: full thighs, tapered calves, slim ankles; full breasts that didn't sprawl; dark bush accentuated by a suntan line. "I have a French letter," she said. "You must use it. I can't become pregnant. Don't remove your shoes. If you have trouble becoming erect, I will help you."

He had no trouble. He stripped—except for his shoes—and took the condom from her and slipped it on. He knelt between her arched legs. She lifted herself to meet him. He advanced tentatively, a centimeter at most, testing the terrain, as it were. He found her moist and receptive. He plunged—and they merged.

His knees ground painfully into the crunchy soil. His stay in Palestine was starting off either well or badly, depending on how you viewed the world. He had arrived ready to look the enemy in the face. British, Arab, they were one and the same. Bring them on. All of them. A Jew does the job in the Holy Land. We're tough as hell in our own backyard. Can it really matter in a moment like this that the chair of Elijah was empty? Is seed that passes through a prepuce evil seed? There are any number of ways to beat a sword into a plow-share. Even a sword that does not bear the seal of God. Ah, yes, this is a different kind of war.

Shuna slowed their movement to a fragile sway. "You are very large, Yakov," she whispered. "Yes, very large. It hurts a bit. I must adjust. There. Go ahead."

To take his mind off his knees he thought of a passage of music, a delectable imitation of natural sounds, the gush of essential unctuous fluids pouring through bushels of flax, anointing his soreness . . . It didn't work. The earth here was not so kind. He tried to remember if there had been a opportunity like this at Sidi Rezegh. He didn't think so. If there had been, he would remember. You don't forget it when you've suffered shredded knees at the instigation of a pumping female body. He was on the verge of stopping, unfulfilled, when Shuna grasped his neck and began to move with a motion that was no longer solely her own.

Her arms locked around him. He felt her hardened nipples against his chest. Their bodies were waxed with sweat and sand. Their pelvises rocked in cadence, sometimes slowly, sometimes at reckless speeds. He concentrated on the oil flooding through the flax, bathing his lacerated flesh. I may not be circumcised, but in some ways I am a good Jew. I know how to wait. This girl is a good Jew. What is she waiting for?

Shuna, for her part, was a child of hope and waited for nothing. She had learned a great deal in a short time, and she galloped through fire, consuming the universe. "Oh, Yakov!" she shrieked, fighting away his hand as he tried to muffle her for security reasons. It was a sound of violence and joy, a warning to all foes that they approached at their own risk. She was oblivious, burning, pillaging, reducing empires to rubble. *"Zisser Gottenyu!"* She pulled his face to hers and sucked his tongue, thrusting her belly toward heaven—and pulling him inexorably, riotously toward sun storms and sorrow and the fat of the land. . . .

Abruptly she stopped. She pushed him away. "Now from the rear." she said before he could protest. Her voice was full of bubbles. "You may remove the French letter." She turned around on all-fours. "One moment," she said over her shoulder. She reached behind and transferred her juices from one orifice to the other. "For lubrication. You are very large, Yakov."

There they were in the moonlight, two silent hills, vibrations spreading in all directions from the seismic focus. Wasn't the orthodox thinking nowadays that an earthquake doesn't originate at a single point, but along a line? He entered and found the source of the tremors. It was a cave, which had seen its share of sunlight. He drove forward, engaging both vertical and horizontal components. She uttered a piercing, shuddering cry of pleasure—or was it pain? He couldn't be sure. He made no attempt to silence her this time. "The climaxes! Oh, my God!" she screamed. "They don't end, Yakov! They don't end!"

This was a happy cave, nothing Stygian about it, and he was determined to see whether its channel was continuous or intermittent. It's tame enough so far. Perhaps it's wilder farther on. Enough of external considerations, like bleeding knees. In a calisthenic motion he kicked one leg, then the other, in front of him and collapsed to the ground with Shuna seated on him. He felt the dirt against his back and in his hair. She sat harder and his body rose and fell and at once he was at the mercy of ravenous subterranean creatures. They had teeth of moss and they gnawed with the convulsive insistence of scavengers, nosing and struggling, lacking all notion of their capacity. He pleaded with them to retreat beyond the crest of the thrust fault, to take into consideration that a little corruption is only human, but they gobbled without letup. Outside the earth's crust there was another voice. It, too, pleaded, beseeching him in one of the common languages of history, to slow down. What could he say? He was in flight, striving unceremoniously to contain the great amplitude of the world. The earth, sun, and moon were practically in the same straight line. He was under attack underground. His cells and nerve endings were being seized upon and appropriated greedily. He was falling apart in a partial vacuum. Resistance was futile. Surrender was in order. Let the beasts have their banquet. Let them ply their tongues, their lips, or the like until . . . they sucked him . . . dry.

He put his arm around her waist and tried to kiss her back, but she pulled free and hopped up. "We're behind schedule," she said, slipping into her shorts and shirt. "I did not think we would be so long. Do you always take this long?"

"Well, the longer it lasts, the better—"

"I didn't know it could last so long. I have known men for only two years. I think I was wrong in my choices. They were all boys from the camps. I was trying to be compassionate. They have much difficulty with sex. Only Micha seemed to enjoy it, but he was fretful. He could not decide whether to accept pleasure."

"Where is Micha? Back in the village?"

"Micha is dead. A tractor fell on him. He knew nothing of machinery. He was angry with me when it happened. He was not thinking about the tractor. He wanted all the adventure of pleasure, and when I gave myself, he became angry. I think it was because I liked the adventure, too. Micha wanted to hurt me, and when it didn't hurt, he was angry. Do you care that you do not hurt me?"

"No."

"I didn't think so. You know, Yakov, you have been in Palestine not a full day, and already you act as if you were a *chalutz*. No one would guess you had not been here for many years. Are all Jews in South Africa like you?"

"To tell you the truth I don't know many Jews in South Africa."

"Do you have a metier? What did you do before you came to Eretz Israel to help us fight? Before you made your *aliyah*?"

"I was—I am—an architecturalist."

"What is that?"

"I write papers on architecture. I give advice now and then on how to preserve old buildings. When someone asks, I tell them how to build new buildings that preserve the old styles."

"That's a useful talent. We will need you to tell us what kind of buildings we need when we get our country. Let's go. You must sleep under my blanket with me tonight. We will ask Piotr if we may patrol together from now on. Tomorrow you will begin your Hebrew instruction. An architecturalist in Eretz Israel must know Hebrew."

In no time Yakov Garovsky learned Hebrew. He fended off suggestions that he be circumcised. He was too old, he argued, and, after all, hadn't Moses neglected the circumcision of his own son in violation of God's covenant with Abraham? There *are* exceptions, he maintained.

The United Nations voted to partition Palestine into Jewish and Arab sectors, the British departed, the state of Israel was established, and the Arabs declared war on the Jews.

He and Shuna were married in a bunker at her kibbutz in Galilee. The services of a matchmaker were not required. Shuna was pregnant. They had run out of French letters. Half the guests were armed. They had ducked in from their battle posts. Three other couples were married the same night for purposes of economy. The rabbi was frightened and rude. They sipped the wine from Coca-Cola bottles and smashed them against a British-made shell casing.

The marriage did not flourish. Neither he nor Shuna was prepared to let those pieces of themselves die that must wither away if they were to settle down as man and wife. They valued adventure more than commitment to each other. They feared that their libidinous wildness would be driven into a hole by familiarity and responsibility. He was in bed with another woman in less than a month; an arms-buying mission to Czechoslovakia; the woman had attended his wedding and was fluent in Slovak. After the birth of the child Shuna, too, fled domesticity. She entrusted the infant girl to the care of the kibbutz and went to work for the Ministry of Agriculture and took one lover after another. They attempted to reconcile, but their hearts weren't in it. Their friends put it down to the pressures of war.

The war wasn't the simple scrap Piotr had predicted, but it wasn't Sidi Rezegh, either. It turned on the question of which side was prepared to reap the dragon's teeth. The usual yardsticks for gauging the outcome of armed conflicts—who has the most men, who has the best weapons—did not apply. The Jews had no tanks or airplanes, and the Arabs had both. Ignoring quantitative conclusions, the Jews said they would not be moved, and they weren't. Because he held a South African passport, Yakov Garovsky was assigned to the Haganah's intelligence service. He spent most of his time abroad. He bought arms for Israel and subverted the delivery of arms to the Arabs. He set up espionage networks and planned assassinations of Arab commanders and disseminated enormous lies about Israeli military strength. He spent a good deal of time in the company of American intelligence men. "One Jewish soldier is better than twelve Arabs if he has the proper weapons," went his line to the Americans. "The Arabs might become good workers one day if they let us train them, but they'll never be fighters. They don't like noise." He was amazed that no one challenged his assertion that only the Arabs wanted war. He thought it was apparent that Israel wanted it, too; that war was the way that Israel intended to establish herself as the absolute ruler of her homeland. Wasn't it clear, he thought, that war was in our hearts; that we had to expunge our lonely shame; that we had to humiliate the Arabs in payment for our having been humiliated by the Germans; that we had to restore our honor and vindicate our name by drawing our swords as brave men.

He accepted the dangers and, being a selfish man, exploited them; a man who risks his life is entitled to special consideration. He quickly gained a reputation as an efficient, daring operative—whose brusqueness in later years often gave way to pomposity. By the time he moved over to Mossad he had become a meticulous planner who involved himself in the most niggling details of his operations. He brought off his share of showy coups, and he expected gratitude and rewards. He also exhibited a gift for getting his way in matters in which less self-affirming men would have yielded to custom, caution, or compromise.

As the years passed he gained a great deal of experience in combatting Arab guerrillas intent on regaining at least some of their territory in Palestine. The experience proved exportable. In time he was spending first weeks, then months at a stretch with South African military units. He advised them on counterinsurgency tactics against black saboteurs. Frequently he joined them in field operations. He was too honest to overlook the irony, but he experienced no discomfort over the fact that many of his South African colleagues had spent the war jailed by the British as Nazi agents. The Boers can teach us a thing or two about fighting terrorists, he told the Mossad—and himself—and they want to buy our arms. He found that his feelings for South Africa were strictly nostalgic, connected solely with his father. He sometimes visited his father's house in the Cape to admire the architecture.

The service elevator lurched to a halt. The operator had difficulty aligning it with the main-floor landing. Incidents of this kind had occurred with regularity during their descent. The frozen passengers were unrestrained in their expressions of dissatisfaction with the hotel.

Colonel Garovsky pushed his way into the lobby and went directly to a bank of pay telephones. He glanced about him. He could identify no South African operatives among the haggard guests.

"Ayala, get to Zanin immediately on the safe phone," he said when a sleepy woman's voice answered. He spoke rapidly in Hebrew. "Tell him we're taking over the disruptive action. I want him to lay on a scheme. Tell him to include a contingency for doing it himself. Also tell him to put his squad out and find Dolan."

"What happened?"

"I'll tell you when I get back to the flat. The short of it is Dolan's vanished. What about the flares?"

"They haven't found any so far."

"What? You mean none of these war-surplus shops has ordinary aircraft signal flares?"

"The shops aren't open yet. Yakov. It's only half-past nine. They probably won't open today at all. The snow."

"Is a burglary laid on?"

"Out of the question. We've done no research. We had weeks for Leitstein's office. We know nothing of these shops. What we have are fireworks."

"*Fireworks?*"

"The spectacular variety. The sort they use for outdoor galas. We bought them in Chinatown. Apparently they were stolen from a consignment to be used for a New Year's Eve celebration in Central Park. But really, Yakov, are they necessary?"

"Can they be seen in a blizzard? Well enough for an airplane to see them?"

"What does it matter? Kennedy is a modern airport. Radar and all sorts of electronic gadgets. It seems a bit pointless, our trying to guide a jetliner in with flares or fireworks. We might as well stand in the snow and snap our fingers and hope he hears us. You do think Shlomo is a good pilot, don't you?"

Colonel Garovsky paused and then said, "Shlomo Harian is an excellent pilot." He sounded defensive; he thought he detected a touch of ridicule in Ayala's tone. "But he's never been called on to land 350,000 pounds of metal in weather like this. At night, yet."

"I believe pilots understand how to do these things."

"I'll decide later. Meantime get back to the police. Tell them you want to amend your report. Tell them you saw a second man running from Davis's car."

"Why should I tell them that?"

"Because there was a second man. A black. That constable of Espensheid's. I'll give you the details later."

"The police called back. They called after you'd gone. Wanted my address."

"Damn. Well, call them back, anyway. It's the only thing to do. We have to be as consistent as we can. . . . Shall we have breakfast?"

He could hear Ayala lighting a cigarette. He wondered how she could smoke those things first thing in the morning.

"You must make love to me first," she said, exhaling smoke.

"Must I?"

"Yes. You left me in the middle of the night. I don't like that."

"Do you think I like it? Espensheid is impossible. Typical Boer."

"Are you still cross that I twitted Leitstein?"

"No."

"You said your daughter is only a year or two younger than I and she would have behaved better."

"Don't remind me of what I said last night."

"Will you let me bet some of the money?"

"I told you it isn't in the planning. I must think about it."

"Will you rush directly to the flat and make love to me?"

"Yes. I will pretend there is no blizzard and rush directly to the flat."

"And make love to me? The way we did in Tokyo?"

"You complained that it hurt."

"I think I'm ready now."

He rang off. He was grinning wolfishly.

Nine eyes were on Sergeant Mazibuko. He warmed his hands over a fire in the basement of an abandoned building on West 116th Street. The fire came from rubbish in a fuel drum set on concrete blocks. The eyes were in the faces of five other black men. They were not dressed for the weather and looked as if they would never have the means to do so. Their eyes were tired and fixed on the fire. Their faces were young and scarred.

With small half-turns and muttered asides they inched toward Sergeant Mazibuko.

"Time for breakfast, ain't it, Egg?" said one of them. He stared at the fire. His question had the ring of a signal.

"Going to have to take up a collection," said Egg, the one-eyed man. His blind eye was a blob of viscous yellow, like a runny fried egg. "Reckon my man here got enough change to go around?"

Sergeant Mazibuko shifted his weight slightly. He had had a sense of menace from the moment an hour ago when he kicked aside a litter of snow-covered planks and ducked into the building. A trail of smoke had attracted him. He had passed the night in doorways and under staircases. He had not dared enter one of the coffee shops or other establishments he found open during the course of the night. He had never been so cold. He feared that some of his joints might be damaged.

When he stepped up to the fire, he had been careless. He had allowed his watch to show from under his sleeve as he extended his hands for warmth. The other homeless men had seen it at once.

He glanced from face to face; these men are *tsotsis*, but there are times when a man must put himself in the company of *tsotsis*. Who'll make the play? he wondered.

"What you holding, man?" said Egg. He was rail thin. His one-eyed gaze was leveled at Sergeant Mazibuko.

The four other men shuffled a fraction in Sergeant Mazibuko's direction. Gray light filtered in. There was no other sound but the wind outside.

Abruptly Egg stepped back from the fire. With a whiplike motion he drew a knife from his pocket. He snapped it open and held it with forefinger and thumb three-quarters up the blade.

"I said, what you holding, man?" His tone was sneering anger. "Empty your pockets! Now! And put that motherfucking watch down right *here!*" He pointed to a spot at his feet.

Sergeant Mazibuko touched his watch. He seemed involved in unbuckling it from his wrist. Then his right arm shot out. He seized the man nearest him by his flimsy windbreaker. He jerked the man toward him and pounded him in the solar plexus with the heel of his hand. He spun the man around and gripped his collar and the seat of his pants and bent him double. Then he drove the man's head full force against the fuel drum.

The fuel drum overturned. Burning paper, pieces of wood, and scraps of roofing material scattered over the basement floor. Sergeant Mazibuko flung the man aside.

The others formed a ragged flank to one side of Egg. They armed themselves with fragments of glass and masonry. Then they began to circle, as if they hoped to stampede Sergeant Mazibuko into Egg's knife.

"You dumb ass!" shouted Egg; the anger in his voice had given way to twitching anxiety. "I'm going to cut you now! You dumb ass! Oh, I'm going to cut *you!*"

Sergeant Mazibuko stormed forward.

Egg took a half step back. Then he held his ground. He swung the knife in a wide, crossing pattern.

Sergeant Mazibuko stopped. He made a yoke with his hands, one thumb atop the other, and stuck them in front of him.

Egg feinted. Then he lunged, bringing the knife up from his knees.

His wrist was blocked by Sergeant Mazibuko's yoke. Sergeant Mazibuko spun, drawing Egg's wrist to the level of his shoulder. Detaching one hand, he levered Egg's elbow toward the ceiling.

Egg's shoulder came apart. He screamed in agony. His knife clattered on the floor. He dropped to his knees, holding his shoulder. Then he toppled on his face.

Sergeant Mazibuko kicked his legs apart and stepped between them. He looked at the others. His face was expressionless. He kicked as hard as he could. His shoe caught Egg in the groin and lifted him off the floor. Dust sprayed from under him as he came down. Egg groaned and lost consciousness.

The others flinched.

Sergeant Mazibuko dragged the other unconscious man to his feet. Standing behind him, he fastened one hand viselike on the man's left ear; the other hand, fingers stiff, he drove beneath the man's rib cage. The man cried out.

"It will be worse, much bloody worse," Sergeant Mazibuko growled, "unless you speak frankly."

"I can't hardly breathe!" The man struggled to free himself. Sergeant Mazibuko applied pressure and the struggling ended. He kneed the man in the tail bone for good measure. "God Almighty, man, what do you want? God Almighty!"

"The bloke on the floor there. What's his name?"

"His name's Egg! God damn, man, you about to pull my fucking ribs out!"

"What are his other names?"

"How the shit do I know? His name's Egg! Damn, man!"

Sergeant Mazibuko glared at the others. "What's his name?"

"Egg!" they replied in unison.

Sergeant Mazibuko shook the man violently. He heard something crack. The man moaned. "Is he known to the police?"

"Yeah," the man gasped. "Egg done time."

"And you?"

"Me, too."

Sergeant Mazibuko glared again at the others. They nodded vigorously. At the same time they dropped their pieces of glass and masonry.

He shoved the man to the floor. The man did not move. Sergeant Mazibuko, was satisfied. These men would not speak to the police— about him, about the injured men on the floor, about the attempted assault with the knife, about anything at all. He backed out the basement door and disappeared into the snow.

Jackie Dolan stumbled into the Brooklyn apartment. He was sopping wet and weary beyond hope. He found the bottle of rye, knocked back two slugs, and wept.

It had taken him six hours to reach the apartment. The last four miles he had made on foot. At times he had nearly given up and dropped into the snow.

The alcohol warmed him but did not calm his trembling hands. His courage had oozed out, sneaked off. He was, as they said in Uitmoormag, "too scared to say boo to a goose." Oh, God, the Jew would have his ass, not to mention the lieutenant and Major Espensheid.

He had gotten rid of the H&H!

It had been the only thing to do, he told himself bitterly. If they had been in my shoes, they would've done the same God damned thing. He had stopped on the Manhattan Bridge and heaved it into the East River. The snow had been blinding. There had been no other traffic. No one had seen him. He was certain of it. A short time later he had ditched the car. He had rammed it into a snowbank a few blocks east of the Flatbush Avenue Extension. The Puerto Ricans will strip it the minute they find it, he had figured.

He snuffled and dried his eyes and scratched a pimple. The cold penetrated to his bones. He changed clothes as quickly as he could. The new ones smelled as awful as the ones he had taken off.

His hands were steadier now. He felt hungry. He trudged into the kitchen. The bag of hamburgers that Captain Zanin had brought the day before was on the drainboard. Jackie opened the bag and sniffed. They smelled all right. Too cold in this fucking place for anything to spoil, he said to himself. There must be some way to heat them up.

He was about to attempt to light the oven—he knew nothing of kitchens; his mother, and later his wife, had cooked every meal he had ever eaten at home—when he noticed a sheet of paper covering something on the table. He slowly put down the bag and picked up the sheet. It was a message composed of words and letters snipped from newspapers and glued on an odd angles.

"Put this into operational order," it said. "Take care with the attachments."

Under the paper was a device resembling an alarm clock. Beside it were two blades, a heavy spring, and a roll of masking tape. There was also a slender cylinder with what appeared to be a small nail protruding from one end. Jackie recognized it. It was a primer for setting off an explosive charge.

Major Espensheid was trying to rekindle his sense of humor. The operation had gotten a straddle of him. He admitted it. He was tired of speaking English, tired of Jews, tired of the cold.

He knew he was not a quick man to anger. He could be a demanding officer, ruthless if he had to be, but he also was a kindly, leisurely gentleman, even something of a fatalist. What was it about Garovsky that had enraged him—apart from the fact that Garovsky was a Jew? He supposed it was because he was accustomed to exercising power, breathing it with his whole body, and Garovsky, somehow, had managed to invade his domain. In the future he would keep that in mind about Garovsky. Garovsky acted in ways like a Brit who's late for luncheon at his club and apologizes—to himself—by worrying about the deportment of the younger members in the billiard room.

At length he regained his perspective. He thought of having served tea to the Kaffir sergeant. How damned funny, he thought. Mazibuko would have to go, of course, operational necessity, but it *was* funny. It would make a good story, the kind he was good at telling. He had a reputation for squeezing the last drop out of an absurdly incongruous situation. He also had good manners and dignity. That was what would make the story so funny. A good Boer like himself, who under no circumstances could be imagined to make a gesture of equality to a Kaffir, had actually served tea to one. Yes, it would make a good story.

He picked up the telephone and dialed. Tomorrow was the Day of the Covenant. He hadn't been away from home on the Day of the

Covenant since the war—except for the year he had been interned by the British. There would have to be a celebration. Nothing elaborate, just himself and Van Hooff. They were "brothers" in the *Broederbond*. He was many years the senior *broeder,* of course. There could be no *braaivleis,* and the American version of barbecue was unfit for consideration even as a token, but Van Hooff should be able to locate a bottle of Nederburg. He was gladdened by the idea.

His number answered.

"Would you be so kind as to connect me with Mr. Charles Dolan?" he said cordially.

"You want to know what I don't like about it?" said Mr. McManus. His voice was strong and caustic. He had arisen early for the second straight day. Only one digitalis tablet since he got up. "I'll tell you what I don't like. I don't like it that somebody takes a shot at Snakehips Davis in front of Lula's house. I don't like it that a black hoople that watched me take a piss is with him when it happens. A black hoople that turns out to be an African. I don't like it that Charlie Dolan pulls a vanishing act."

"How do you know it was the same one, this African?" asked Nathan Leitstein. "Place is full of Africans. Exchange students, the UN, the clubs."

They were seated across from each other in Mr. McManus's apartment. Each puffed a cigar. They had finished a late lunch an hour ago. Corned-beef sandwiches and celery tonic from a neighborhood delicatessen. The delivery boy had arrived in an apron and a short-sleeved shirt. He had explained that the owner always sent him on deliveries without his coat. So he wouldn't waste time getting back. Freddie Dee was in another room watching television.

"I told you," Mr. McManus said impatiently. His eyes gleamed under his white eyebrows. "Lula got a read on him from Davis. It was the same guy."

"How come the cops didn't say nothing about an African?" Nathan Leitstein was glum. He had spent the morning waiting in vain for "Katz" to telephone. He had serious doubts that Katz and his friends had all that money or that they really meant to bet on a football game. He had angrily expressed this to Mr. McManus. "I heard it on the radio. They didn't say nothing about no African."

"If we knew where Charlie was, we could find out why they didn't say nothing about it, couldn't we?" Mr. McManus retorted. His mind was elsewhere. He was trying to project the coordinates of Katz's floater in a way that allowed for a generous angle of dip. He was also thinking of his flight to Florida that Freddie had arranged that morning. He calculated the probable winnings if he gave each of his grandchildren twenty dollars and took them to the track as a Christmas present.

"The problem with Katz and them other hooples," Mr. McManus went on, "is they ain't letting us see the daylight. I mean, if they was horseplayers, they'd be around horseplayers, right? We'd know who's winning, who's losing, who owes a grand to his bookie by noon tomorrow, who's doing bad checks, who's taking from the cookie jar, who's scared shitless his wife'll find out a shylock's after him. We'd know that kind of stuff, right? If just one of them was making faces at gin rummy or, even better, if they was trying to put in a fix, we could get a read on them." He took a long puff on his cigar and stared a moment out the window at the relentless snow. "But these hooples are coming from nowhere. It's like if you was to walk into the archdiocese and say, 'Your Eminence, I want to head up this charity or that building drive, and I guarantee I'll triple what you took in last year, and all I want is 10 percent. By the way I know you been banging Sister Philomena, and I ain't a Catholic, and somebody's got it in for Father Anthony, and I'll get back to you.' See what I mean? It don't hang together, even the part Charlie could help with. So why don't we put these hooples on the back of the stove? If they got the dough, and they want to get down, they'll be in touch. What do you think?"

Nathan Leitstein walked to the sideboard and poured himself a brandy. "Ah, what the hell," he said, returning to his chair. "Charlie takes a powder, who cares? The hoople's useless. It burns my ass, though, that this Katz or whoever he is drops out. That would have been a sweet click, Kid, any way you cut it. . . . I wonder what happened to the other fifty-five million. . . ."

Mr. McManus cocked his head. "When was the last time you seen him, Charlie?"

Nathan Leitstein shrugged. "Two weeks ago. A month, maybe. The day he done the phone. Why?"

"Nothing probably. It's just that thing you said about the dame, the one that said 'Dolan' over the phone when that big hoople was in your office."

Freddie Dee walked in. He announced that he was ordering a pizza and asked whether they needed anything. They shook their heads.

"What about him?" asked Nathan Leitstein, nodding toward the door as Freddie closed it behind him. Freddie's eye was still swollen. "Why don't you ask him where his old man is?"

"I asked him already. He ain't seen Charlie in five years. If he'd seen him yesterday, he couldn't remember where it was."

"Don't he have another kid, Charlie? Older, I think he is. Used to be ugly as hell. Maybe he would know, the other kid."

"He joined the Foreign Legion or some fucking thing. Forget him. He's dumber than Freddie." He exhaled a gust of smoke and continued. "What was on Charlie's mind last time you saw him?"

"Nothing much. The usual. Asked me a lot about the old days. A great one for the old days, Charlie, like there was something to them except what you made out of them." He sniffed his brandy deeply and then took a sip. "You know what he asked me, Charlie? We're sitting around after he's done with the phone and he says, 'How come Mac joined the Marines?'"

A grin spread over Mr. McManus's face. He held his cigar in front of him like a prop. "What'd you tell him?" he asked dryly.

"Are you kidding? I told him zilch." Nathan Leitstein peered over the rim of his brandy. He decided to shed his gloom and enjoy himself. He knew how to pitch a line—in the manner of an interlocutor working with an end man. "I don't answer a question like that, especially from a hoople like Dolan. I told him you was in Florida and the war started and you must've felt like it was your duty. That's what you done, right, joined up on account of it was your duty?"

"You sure that's all you told him?"

"Sure I'm sure. What was I going to say? That joining the Marines must be a load of laughs for a guy that's thirty-five, thirty-six years old?"

Mr. McManus tapped his cigar in an ashtray. "It ain't funny to me," he said with mock annoyance. He knew the routine. "Look. I own property in Florida. I'm known down there. The wife's known. How would it look if it got out that there's an old murder warrant on me in Broward County?"

"You was using another name, right? Besides, they never got the real goods on you, did they?"

"God damn it, think how it'd look if it got out. A respectable retired businessman mixed up in some rinky-dink card-game killing."

"What was the name of the place?" Nathan Leitstein put his hand over his mouth. He didn't want to laugh out loud too soon. It would spoil the routine.

"The Green Lantern." Mr. McManus stretched a fraction. He eyed Billy Light with a crafty look. "The Story of the Green Lantern" was one of the few things that Kid Sweeney would reminisce about, and Billy knew it. "Joints like it all over down south back then. Roadhouses, they called them. Slot machines and a bunch of drunks up front and a card game in the back. Out in a God damned swamp."

"You clean them out or what?"

"I took out a couple of hundred in cash. Not bad for a Florida swamp in 1942. Plus a stack of personal checks I knew was bad, and all kinds of other paper. One guy signs over his drug store so he can stay in. Three or four sign over their houses. I'm even holding half interest in a Confederate cannon. In all everybody but me is down ten grand or so—on paper. They figure they can't win big by betting small, so they keep pouring it on hoping to turn the corner.

"About three in the morning this hoople next to me is in the hole up to his hat. He's tried everything, cold decks, the works. Even had a shill with him who cut the cards funny. I'm working alone. Well, it's his deal. He takes one card up, a deuce, and folds and I take the pot with a pair of eights, nothing down. I rake it in, cash, paper, everything, don't bother to count it. It's lying there on the table.

"The hoople leaves the room and comes back pulling on a pint of rye and popping off about something being fishy in the game. He should know, right? The hoople walks out again and leaves the door open. Somebody gets up to close it and then, all of a sudden, the place goes dark. And bam! Must've been a shotgun. A character across the table gets it. Before he hits the deck I hear, 'That Yankee shot Monroe!' Christ, bottles are breaking, the table flips over, people are crawling around feeling for money off the floor, four or five of them are yelling that Italian name I was using. I'm on my knees looking for a way out. I grab a chair and throw it through the window—just a screen, too hot to have the joint closed up—and I follow it to the ground. The sheriff's already been around to collect, so I figure I got some time, and I take off. I'm all night in the swamp, fighting off the bugs and trying to find the highway in the dark.

"About daylight I'm walking in the bushes next to this road and what do I see? A God damned chain gang. First I think I'll just walk right by them. Then I see that something's going on. One of the prisoners is bitching about how his feet hurt. The guy don't have on but one shoe and he's hopping around on one foot—which wasn't easy on account of his legs is chained together at the ankles. The screw tells the guy to shut up and get back to pulling weeds. But the guy keeps on bitching—there's these little thorns all over; they call them sandspurs—and he's hopping this way and that. Well, the screw walks down the line. He stops in front of the guy and don't say anything. He just looks at him with this shit-eating grin. The guy's holding his bare foot and trying to keep his balance. Out of nowhere the screw cracks the guy across the jaw with the butt of his shotgun. The guy keels over in the ditch. Out cold. The other prisoners don't even look up. I duck back in the bushes. For all I know the screw works for the sheriff.

"Another two, three hours, I'm in Fort Lauderdale. Just a dry place in the swamp back then. I'm holding fifty, sixty bucks. I figure I'll catch a bus to Miami and hop the boat to Havana. Guy at the bus station says no bus 'til noon. Hitchhiking is out, and I think, oh, Christ, it won't take the hooples forever to round up a posse. I walk out, looking this way and that, trying to think what to do next, and I already seen what it's like to do time down there. Next door is a Marine recruiter. Busted-up type working out of a trailer. I feel him out for particulars and then I ask him how soon can I sign up. He says he can put me on a train to boot camp in twenty minutes. I raise my hand and he walks me to the train. There's a crap game in the head. I took out six bills and sent it to the wife when we got to New Orleans. In no time I'm up a grand. I sent it to Lula. She boxed it on the Belmont. The horse was Shut Out, remember?

"Ten days later I'm in California. My head's shaved and I'm running my ass off. Worse than any road work I ever done. I looked like an onion. One day the shore patrol grabs this punk in my outfit. Southern kid who's into my slush fund for nearly fifty bucks. The word is he killed a guy back home. The DI pulls us out and says, 'The Marine Corps is not a hiding place for scum.' I kiss the fifty bucks good-bye. I also figure I ain't deep enough in the Marine Corps, so I ask a few questions about a hush-hush bunch called the Raiders. Nobody knows nothing about them except they're doing things nobody knows nothing about. Just what I'm looking for."

Nathan Leitstein howled and poured himself another brandy. "You was over there someplace funny, right? Where was it?"

Before Mr. McManus could answer, Freddie Dee summoned him to the telephone. He rose slowly and left the room. Several minutes later he reappeared. He looked stunned. He eased himself back into his chair.

"You all right, Kid?" Nathan Leitstein hurried to his feet. There was alarm in his voice.

"Yeah," said Mr. McManus. He motioned for Nathan Leitstein to sit down. "Nothing to worry about. I don't need a pill or anything." He thought of lighting another cigar and decided against it. "A guy wants to see me. Says it's important."

"Is it?"

Mr. McManus shook his head. "Who knows?" In a fraction of an instant he divided the number of ways he could have received that phone call by the number of calls he could have received that day. The answer was astronomical. The odds against it were even greater. Abruptly he clapped his knees and stood up. "I need a lift. Can you drop me at Leo's?"

"Now?"

"Yeah. Let's go."

Nathan Leitstein's driver made good time, considering the depth of the snow, which was approaching two feet. Nathan Leitstein was annoyed by the mystery of the telephone call and was not really put at ease by Mr. McManus's promise to let him know what it was all about as soon as he found out himself.

Mr. McManus stepped into the candy store. He nodded to Leo and took a seat at the counter next to a bulky man in a well-worn overcoat. The man was bent over a cup of coffee.

"This the best place to talk?" Coombes asked gruffly. He did not offer to shake hands. He tugged at his grizzled chin and then bit a fingernail.

Mr. McManus looked up and down the counter with only a slight movement of his head. The only other customer was a deranged but harmless man who lived in a nearby furnished room, a familiar face in the neighborhood. He was very much aware of Coombes's presence. The man radiated a sense of awkwardness and calamity.

"Good as any," he said casually. He lit a cigar and looked at Coombes out of the corner of his eye. Looks like he's on the skids, he thought. Then he noticed the bulge under Coombes's left arm. "Unless you want a drink. There's a tavern down the block."

"No," he said. He stared at his coffee cup.

They sat, poised in silence. Whatever Mr. McManus had expected, this was not it. His memory of Coombes was of a taciturn, rather

sloppy Marine officer who took the direct approach to everything—
planning, reconnaissance, giving orders, killing. But that was in
Burma thirty-five years ago. Age was supposed to polish a man's
rough spots, give him a comfortable perspective. Coombes looked as
if he had been born with bitter memories. Apart from being
thirty-five years older—and here in Leo's candy store—Coombes
appeared not to have changed a bit. He assumed that Coombes's
clothes were at least ten years old.

"What brings you to New York on a day like this?" Mr. McManus
asked at last. He motioned to the candy-store owner to refill
Coombes's cup.

Coombes's hooded eyes were red rimmed from lack of sleep. The
snow had stalled the Metroliner north of Philadelphia. Immediately
the train had grown as cold as the bleak countryside. It had arrived at
Pennsylvania Station at noon, sixteen hours late. Coombes had
shivered the entire journey.

"Can the small talk, Mac," he said. "I'm not good at it. It's a waste
of time." He turned and looked directly at Mr. McManus. His face
was immobile. "The apartment building you live in. It's staked out.
Any idea why?"

Mr. McManus studied his cigar. He decided that Coombes hadn't
changed all that much. "I got an idea or two," he said. "Maybe we can
both get a better idea if you tell me how come it interests you."

Coombes shot a glance at the candy-store owner. Then he looked at
the quiet lunatic and then back at Mr. McManus. "Who the hell are
they?" he said in a low snarl.

Mr. McManus signaled for a cup of tea. He pushed his hat back on
his head and unbuttoned his overcoat. "Hold it," he said. He slowly
stroked his cheek and noticed he had missed a spot shaving. "Let's
take a couple of minutes and get caught up. We ain't seen each other
since the war, right? Rangoon, right? I don't know what you been
doing. You look like you won some, lost some. I don't know. I
bounced around a lot, a little of this, a little of that, and I'll tell you
something. A lot of things ain't the same when you take a second look.
Let me tell you what I mean. A guy walks in here and says he's got a
dozen color tv's for a hundred bucks, I figure he knows what he's
doing but it don't cross my mind he's talking about Gimbel's
basement. On the other hand the guy could be talking about a fire
sale or maybe he works for a finance company. Just because it's a little
abnormal don't mean across the board that the tv's are hot. If I'm

going to take advantage of this bargain, I'm going to take a second look, right?" He glanced at Coombes for a reaction. He saw none. "Some hooples are hanging around outside my house—in weather like this—I figure it's their business. Or look at it another way. If it *is* my business, well, I'm warm and dry and they ain't and I know my business better than they do." He took a tiny puff on his cigar. "Which brings us to you. You said on the phone you come up from Washington, right? What for? You made it clear this ain't no trip to look up an old war buddy. You don't seem like the kind of guy who likes to cut touches for old times' sake. What the hell gives?"

Coombes said nothing. He chewed on a fingernail.

The candy-store owner set Mr. McManus's tea before him. "Look at it this way," Mr. McManus went on. He placed the teabag on the saucer and blew on the tea to cool it. "I'm out here in the snow, the likes of which ain't been seen in years. A guy I was with in the Marines shows up and what does he do? Does he ask how're the wife and kids? Does he ask how's business? Does he even say it's been a long time and how's by you? No. He says do I know why some hooples are hanging around outside in the snow. Now I ask you. If you was in my place, how would you take that?"

Coombes avoided Mr. McManus's eyes. He hated the fact that he was on the shelf. His instinct was to seize this little guy by the throat and throttle the information out of him. It was an approach he was notorious for. It had landed him in the soup on countless occasions. He checked himself. If he caused trouble now, the kind of trouble he was inclined to cause, he would land in jail—and rot there, because Headlight would disown him in a wink—and his hopes of getting his money would end with a crash. At length he tried again. "Are you telling me you don't know who those people are?"

Mr. McManus sipped his tea. "Let me ask you a question," he said, replacing his cup. "Are you a cop?"

Coombes drew a deep breath and released it gradually. It was a technique he had learned in Burma for keeping his temper. "No," he said hoarsely, "I'm not a cop. I used to work for the government. I don't work for the government anymore. I've got a per diem contract with another man who used to work for the government. In fact this man is working for the government again himself." He spun halfway around on his stool. His sleeve brushed his coffee cup and picked up another stain. "This man who's paying my way has some damned interesting information," he continued; he bared his teeth as he spoke. "This man says some people who work for *other* governments have been asking a lot of questions about you. You and your partner Leitstein. They were careful, itemized questions. What I'm being paid to find out is what these people want from you. A good place to start is with the people who're watching your house."

Mr. McManus raised an eyebrow. "These foreigners. Are they legit?"

"What do you mean?"

"Is what they're up to legal?"

"How the hell do I know?" Coombes replied heatedly. "That's what I'm asking you, for Christ's sake."

"And what I want to know is why you're asking me."

"Because the sons of bitches have your house staked out."

Mr. McManus gazed at the ceiling. He might have been wrong about Coombes, he thought; Coombes might not be the superfluous man he appears to be; all his choices lately seem to have been negative ones, but you never know. Then he looked back at Coombes and said, "What do you know about me?"

"More than I care to," Coombes replied indifferently. "I'm retired."

"For instance."

"Nothing that's very hard to find out."

"Like what?"

"Like the fact that the boys turned over $300,000 in cash last month through your Swiss bank. Things like that."

"What else?"

"You get big fees for helping heavy hitters figure out how to win and you don't report the fees as income . . . and you nearly died of a heart attack a while back."

Mr. McManus frowned. "You prove any of this in court?" he asked sharply. He did not regard Coombes's information as something that was not very hard to find out. "Besides my heart attack, I mean?"

Coombes bit hard at a fingernail. "I'm not a God damned cop." He heard his voice rise and immediately lowered it. "I'm not trying to prove anything in court. I'm trying to find out why Israel and South Africa are bringing a boxcarful of money here today"—he paused and blew on his hands—"money that spent the night in your bank."

Mr. McManus's frown deepened. His eyes gleamed. Abruptly he raised his palm. "Hold it. Hold everything. Let's straighten this shit out right now. Somebody's got their wires crossed. Nobody's bringing no money here from my bank. Nobody. Not today. Not tomorrow. Not yesterday. Never. At no time. No Israel. No South Africa. Nobody. Understand?"

"Leitstein told a guy in Jerusalem he'd think it over. The deal was, you and Leitstein would get fancy commissions. Two-hundred and fifty thousand dollars each, more or less."

Mr. McManus set his cigar on the edge of the counter and propped on his elbows. How the hell does Coombes know about that? he wondered. Lemmer? Not Lemmer. Lemmer would have warned him if somebody had been asking questions. Billy? Not Billy. Not this time. Then how? Well, somehow, Coombes had found out at least that much, and the thing to do now was to feed him a little more and see whether it would satisfy him. "Okay," he said with a sigh, "you might as well know what's doing." He picked up his cigar and puffed it. "There was a proposal. That's all it was. A proposal, a bloop. You know, the kind of thing that looks so good you got to ask what's on the inside that makes it tick. We asked and we couldn't find out. So we decided to stay away from the whole thing. We told the guy to blow it out his nose."

He made a quick mental note. The other foreign hooples. Major Espenwhatsit and Red and the dame and the black guy were South Africans.

"The people outside your apartment," Coombes said, "you think they want you to change your mind?"

"They from Israel and South Africa?"

"I wouldn't be surprised. They aren't tourists."

"Who are they?"

"Mossad and BOSS, more than likely."

Mr. McManus looked bewildered. "What's that?"

"Intelligence services. Mossad is Israeli. BOSS is South African." Coombes opened and closed his massive fist. His hands ached from the cold. "When they want something, they usually find a way to get it. Mossad, especially. BOSS, yes and no. To tell you the truth, if I know anything about them, they don't give a damn that your bank turned them down. If they want to get that money here, they'll find a way to do it. . . . If they want something from you, they'll find a way to get that, too. Do you understand what the hell I'm talking about?"

"Sounds like a bunch of spies."

"It's a God damned operation, and you're going to get hurt if you don't watch your step."

"Is it legal?"

"Oh, for Christ's sake."

Mr. McManus was tempted for a fraction of a second to tell Coombes about the confrontation in his apartment; the chase through the park; Billy Light's dinner with "Katz," "Miss Levine," and the other two hooples; the African who was with Snakehips Davis when Ernie Parks was murdered. Then he thought of what Coombes had said. *If they want to get that money here, they'll find a way to do it.* He smiled faintly and puffed his cigar. He and Billy Light had fretted for nothing.

He studied Coombes for a moment. He wondered if he was a man of his own making. If he wasn't, what was he? A war-horse who couldn't help getting involved with things he had nothing to do with and whose main talent was for being dangerous? Or was Coombes not anything at all, just an advertisement for what had happened to him, a big lunk doing a ridiculous job?

"You need anything?" he asked finally. "Place to stay or anything? I got plenty of room."

Coombes stared at him. His eyes shown with resentment. Mr. McManus asked the candy-store owner to telephone for a taxi.

"Tell you what," said Mr. McManus. He began buttoning his overcoat. "I'll keep my ears open. I hear a lot of things in my business. Give me a number where I can reach you. I hear anything about Israelis or South Africans that might help you, I'll give you a call. Okay? I got to get home now. Time for some rest. Doctor's orders."

Coombes clenched his teeth. Then he nodded and scrawled a telephone number on a scrap of paper. The numerals were large and ill formed, like a child's. "By the way," he said as he handed it to Mr. McManus, "did you know that the day you enlisted, a murder warrant was issued in Florida for a guy named Battaglia. A shooting in a place called the Green Lantern. The victim was one Monroe Quinn. Some of the people who saw it are still around. The description of Battaglia fits you to a tee, the way you looked back then."

Mr. McManus was startled. He looked up and down the counter. "So what?" he said harshly. "So fucking what? The day I enlisted was nearly forty years ago. They got statutes of limitation, even in Florida."

"This warrant came from a grand jury. It'll stay in effect until another grand jury takes the trouble to get rid of it. That's not likely to happen. You know how grand juries are."

"What the hell are you trying to do, Coombes?" Mr. McManus snapped.

An odd look came over Coombes's face; not a smile, but a look of satisfaction. "I'll tell you what I'm trying to do. I'm trying to find what you and a few hundred million dollars have to do with each other. I'm trying to do it so nobody gets hurt who's just standing in the way. But to tell you the truth, I don't care as long as I find out. That's what I'm getting paid for."

It was not accurate, as Colonel Garovsky had said, that Shlomo Harian perfected the high-low-high dive-bombing technique. However, in the 1973 war he was one of its most adept practitioners. He had lost count of the sorties he had flown against the SAM-6 missile batteries southwest of Damascus. He attributed his success to a secret—he thought of it as a superior habit—he had never shared with his fellow Israeli Air Force pilots; he rarely looked beyond the canopy of his Phantom F-4E fighter bomber and had only glimpsed patches of the Syrian countryside. He flew almost solely by the instruments.

That was what he was doing now. Flying by the instruments. El Al Flight 7 was on a northeasterly course over the Atlantic Ocean. It was one hundred and sixty miles from John F. Kennedy International Airport. The flight was a charter. The one hundred and thirty-three passengers were Mossad and BOSS agents carrying tourist visas stamped on forged passports. Harian had not taken his eyes off the instruments since they took off from Bermuda. In fact he had rarely diverted his gaze from the seven hundred or so lights, gauges, knobs, dials, and switches since the Boeing 707 left Tel Aviv for Asunción, Paraguay, three days ago, even though the plane had been on automatic pilot for most of the journey.

"No break in the weather," said the first officer in Hebrew. He had just received the latest data from Kennedy Tower. "Even if it lifts a bit, it's so unstable it could thicken up again in an instant."

Harian nodded slightly. He glanced at the radar scope. At the upper margin was an arc of greenish white. It was the outer fringe of the blizzard. The arc was growing larger by the second.

"There's going to be an awful rumpus when we get down," the first officer went on. He placed his headset aside and scanned the western horizon. The sun was dazzling above the massive clouds. "If we get down, that is. The authorities will demand our heads for coming in when they've declared the airport closed."

"A technicality," said Harian. He did not lift his eyes from the instrument panel. "There will be a forfeiture. A suspension, perhaps. Nothing more."

He hoped this would satisfy the first officer. He knew the hazards. He disliked chatting. Only the instruments interested him when he was on the flight deck. Most pilots found this kind of flying intolerably boring. Not Harian. He was fascinated by electronic gadgetry. He did not see the instruments merely as indispensable aids to modern aviation. To him they were the essence of flying. He often thought he would have been very unhappy as a pilot in the early days of aviation technology. Not nearly enough instruments.

"What do you suppose Yakov was thinking?" asked the first officer. "Wanting to shoot off a batch of Roman candles and the like?"

"He wanted to be helpful, I suppose."

The first officer was quiet a moment. Then he said, "Yakov doesn't know anything about flying, does he?"

"No."

The first officer began to think of minimal visual references, downburst cells, and approach-light bars. He shuddered and sighed. "This is my first Mossad mission," he said. There was a note of strain in his voice. "Have you done much work for Mossad?"

"When I'm told to," said Harian. He glanced again at the radar screen. Then he donned his headset.

A short time later the single air-traffic controller on duty in the Kennedy tower was in a state of alarm. Moments earlier he had been enjoying a cup of coffee and sighing with relief that his wife had been able in the blizzard to find a carton of milk for their infant son. There hadn't been much for him to do during his shift. Nothing was taking off. New York Center was diverting all inbound stuff. Now this. He hurriedly signaled the watch chief.

"You told him our status, didn't you?" shouted the watch chief as he bustled into the tower.

"Hell, yes!"

"Is he in the precip?"

"Not yet."

"Where is he?"

The controller keyed his microphone. "El Al 7, this is Kennedy Tower. Squawk indent, please."

The controller and the watch chief stared at their radar screen. There were more than a dozen blips on it. Each represented an airplane awaiting instructions. One of the blips doubled in size. It was El Al 7.

"Repeat it to him," the watch chief said sourly.

The controller nodded. "El Al 7, this is Kennedy Tower." He spoke in a monotone that masked his heightening nervousness. "We are diverting all flights until further notice. Please switch frequency to New York Center. We have zero ceiling. Visibility less than a half mile if that. Heavy blowing snow. Surface winds 300 to 325 degrees at 25 knots, gusting to 40. Advise intentions."

They exchanged glances. If the ceiling and visibility don't scare him off, they thought, the crosswind will.

"Kennedy Tower, this is El Al 7," crackled the reply. "Please say your surface condition."

The two men stared at each other. Then the controller said into his microphone, "We have only one runway partially cleared—22 left. It's covered with rough ice and accumulating wet snow. Braking poor to nil for a 707."

"Roger, Kennedy Tower. El Al 7 would like to land."

The watch chief's mouth dropped open. He shook his head in despair. This is all I need, he thought. He looked out the tower window. It was prematurely dark. He could see nothing but his face reflected in the glass. Beyond was an impenetrable gray blur. He shrugged his shoulders in resignation.

The controller's forehead was beaded. He rotated his neck in an effort to relax. What the hell, he thought. It's up to you, Captain. "El Al 7, this is Kennedy Tower," he said. "You're clear to land on 22 left. I'll give you final wind checks on final approach. Do you want emergency equipment standby?"

"Affirmative."

Colonel Garovsky listened in the El Al operations center. His face was constricted. Damn it, he said to himself, why did I let Ayala talk me out of those flares? Why? He resisted the urge to kick the water cooler.

* * *

In the cockpits of the other planes in the holding pattern there was profound astonishment at the El Al transmission.

"Ride 'em, cowboy," said one on the air.

"Let it snow, let it snow, let it snow," sang another.

Thirty miles from Runway 22 Left, El Al 7 was bucking wildly.

"Seat belts, no smoking, engine de-icing," said the first officer, completing the final flight-deck check.

Shlomo Harian switched on the intercom. "The landing might be somewhat uncomfortable," he announced in Hebrew. "If there is a need for emergency procedures, I will tell you. Otherwise stay in your seats." He repeated the announcement in English for the South Africans.

The first officer had a heavy, leather binder on his lap. He had difficulty holding it steady. It was open to the "approach plate" for Kennedy. He quickly scanned the diagram for approach altitude, proper course headings, and the amount of time that would elapse after they passed the electronic "outer marker" until they reached the runway.

"Want to look at it?" he asked. His eyes were wide and his throat was tight.

Harian shook his head. His eyes were fastened on the instruments. He knew the Kennedy approach plate by heart. He had memorized it during dozens of practice landings at Sirkin Flying School near Tel Aviv. He regretted he had not practiced in snow. Odd, he thought. Mossad usually foresees that kind of thing.

The sky roared with the hollow blasts of the blizzard. Sometimes the plane pitched. Sometimes it wobbled from side to side. Sometimes it seemed to stand absolutely still and shudder all over, then barrel like a bobsled down the Cresta and up again with abandon into the storm. Sometimes it would charge like a salmon butting its way upstream. Sometimes it would plunge into a weightless cavity.

Fifteen miles to go. Harian adjusted the heading and fought to hold El Al 7 on course. He glanced at the flight director, an instrument that told him, among other things, that the plane was level with the horizon.

The radio came alive. "El Al 7, you're clear to descend to 2,000 feet."

"Roger, Kennedy Tower. El Al 7 clear to 2,000."

The descent was underway. The weather raced and churned. The plane soared and then dipped sharply, trembling and creaking. Harian noticed the altimeter. He was fifty feet too low. He grasped the control stick and tugged it back and held it there.

Five more miles.

In silence the first officer stared at the approach plate. He had the look of a man who had suddenly realized, too late, that he had made a big mistake. He felt a scream gurgling in his throat. He heard himself moan. He had been in an earthquake in Turkey once. It was nothing like this.

A purple light flashed on the instrument panel.

"El Al 7, this is Kennedy Tower. You're over the outer marker. Clear to 1,400 feet."

"Roger, Kennedy Tower. El Al 7 clear to 1,400 feet," Harian replied and forced the plane downward. He checked the altimeter. The plane was at the altitude it was supposed to be. Then he said to the first officer, "Flaps down, landing gear down."

The jetliner shook and bounced as though it were being pummeled by a giant animal. Harian knew he was seconds away from the point where his experience—and good sense—would tell him to pull back the control stick and fly away from potential disaster. Tonight he would ignore his experience and try to put his good sense to use in the face of folly. Tonight he had to put this plane on the ground. Pulling up was out of the question.

An amber light flashed.

"Kennedy Tower, this is El Al 7. We're over the inner marker."

"El Al 7, this is Kennedy Tower. You're clear to land 22 Left. Emergency equipment standing by. Wind is now steady 300 degrees at 30 knots."

Five hundred more feet. Not a single landmark was visible. Only dense, swirling snow. Grains of ice rattled against the windshield.

"Flash strobes," said Harian. The first officer flipped a switch.

Glaring lights blazed on the wings and nose. For the first time Harian peered over the instrument panel. Squinting through the snow, he spotted what he took to be the end of the runway. He looked back at the instruments. He had lost some airspeed. A marginal difficulty, he decided.

The first officer thought otherwise. "Pull up!" he screamed.

Harian lowered the nose. He had both hands on the control stick. The plane touched down within the first 200 feet of the runway.

The landing was hard. The ground came up with a kick.

The tower had been wrong about the wind. It was not steady. It was whistling violently across their landing path. Harian battled to keep the plane from drifting off the runway.

Shrieks and moans arose in the rear of the plane.

"We're going to break up!" shouted the first officer.

Harian applied forward pressure on the wheel. That ought to pin us down, he said to himself.

The tail began to settle. The first officer sighed and rubbed his eyes with both hands.

They were traveling nearly a hundred miles an hour.

Suddenly Harian realized he did not have control. The plane was like a headstrong horse. The wheels were unable to grip the icy surface!

He held his breath. He released his grip a trifle on the control stick. Nature was in charge now.

The plane veered in the convulsive wind. It skidded toward a snowbank. Harian feared that the landing gear would collapse.

He thought of a crash landing he had made in 1973. A SAM-6 missile had exploded near his Phantom. The landing gear was blown away. He came in on his belly. Once he set it down, the Phantom took its own course.

Abruptly the wind shifted with a ferocious snap. For a fraction of a second the plane was jolted dead still. Then it swerved away from the snowbank and shot on down the runway.

Harian cut the throttles and raised the spoilers on the wings. He cautiously applied the footbrakes. . . .

By slow, painful degrees El Al 7 staggered to a halt. The ice crunched under the tires. The plane rocked slightly in the wind.

The passengers cheered.

A Mossad agent in the uniform of a stewardess opened the flight-deck door. "Some of the South Africans were sick. It was to be expected, of course," she said and stepped out.

Harian leaned forward and looked about. He had heard of an area at the South Pole that was known as the home of the blizzard. We could be there, he thought. At once he saw the faint flicker of a flashing light. It was atop one of the standby crash trucks. He called the tower. "This is El Al 7. I don't believe my ship is in condition to make it to the gate."

"Roger, El Al 7. We have you on ground radar. Towing equipment is on the way."

The first officer reached into his flight bag. He produced a pharmaceutical cylinder. "Tranquilizer?" he asked.

"I don't use them," Harian said.

A towing vehicle backed up to the nose wheel. Several men in parkas went to work attaching a movable arm to the axle.

One of the men seemed to be a supernumerary. He walked away from the others and stood a few feet from the plane in the fuzzy glow of the landing lights. He pushed back the hood of his parka and grinned broadly.

It was Colonel Garovsky. He gave a thumbs-up sign.

From the flight deck Harian smiled and returned the sign.

Mr. Foster, the Federal Aviation Administration representative, strode into the customs area. He was the FAA's number-two man at Kennedy. The number one had taken the day off because of the storm. Mr. Foster was smoking a pipe. The watch chief was at his side.

"Which one's the cowboy?" the watch chief asked one of the customs officials. His voice was raspy.

"The short one," said the customs official. He pointed to two men in pilots' uniforms among the throng of El Al passengers awaiting their luggage. "Name's Harian."

Mr. Foster and the watch chief marched forward.

"Captain Harian?" said Mr. Foster, extending his hand and introducing himself. He was several inches taller than the pilot. "The watch chief here tells me you did a hell of a job bringing your aircraft in." He sounded amiable. "Was there some mix-up? We broadcast that the facility was closed."

"The passengers are on a package tour. Many of them are eager to get to their hotels. They seemed to have developed intestinal complaints. We visited Paraguay, you see."

"That's very thoughtful," Mr. Foster replied. He snatched his pipe from his mouth. "So God damned thoughtful, in fact, that I'm putting you on the beach as of right now at this facility. I expect your chief pilot will have something to say about it, too." He clamped his pipe between his teeth and sucked it inconclusively. "I'm putting your name on the wire tonight. You guys can be a menace to yourselves if you want to, but not to other people—and not at this facility. If I had my way, you'd never put another aircraft down at this facility again. Ever. You'll be facing a hearing, mister, I guarantee you that."

* * *

At the passenger-exit ramp a cleaning crew went about its business in the cabin of El Al 7. Security men with UZI 9mm submachine guns slung from their shoulders stood guard at the door.

A pair of Port Authority patrolmen watched indifferently for a few minutes and then moved on. They found nothing intriguing about an El Al plane under armed guard. They saw it all the time. They thought the El Al people overdid it when it came to security.

Systematically the crew removed all the blue seat backs and cushions and passenger pillows and loaded them onto flatbed trolleys, which were rolled to an elevator and lowered to a storage room in the El Al terminal. Next they unloaded dozens of bulging fifty-gallon garbage bags from the toilets, the galleys, and the baggage racks.

The storage room was icy cold. A door to the outside was open. The wind had a cutting edge. It scattered wisps of powdery snow across the floor. Workers, all Mossad operatives in coveralls, pushed the cushions, pillows, and garbage bags through the door and loaded them onto five unmarked vans backed up to the building.

Colonel Garovsky supervised them. He gave occasional directions, pointing with two fingers. Presently he was joined by Shlomo Harian.

"A muddle with the authorities?" Colonel Garovsky asked.

"A technicality," replied Harian. His tone was neutral. "There will be a forfeiture. A suspension, perhaps. Nothing more." He watched the work a moment and then said, "You don't plan an inventory now, do you?"

"No," said Colonel Garovsky. "We'll do that when we have it in a secure place. Can't have the Boers asking to count it too soon. They could be very difficult if they found out that only a little more than half of it is here." He instructed one of the Mossad men to be careful with a garbage bag and then turned back to Harian. His face wrinkled into a scowl. "Did I understand correctly that only seventeen of them were affected? I don't believe it."

"It's true," Harian said. "South Africans must have very stout stomachs."

Colonel Garovsky shook his head. "We had hoped it would put at least half of them in hospital. At least half."

"Eleven of them were unable to continue from Asunción," Harian said. "Six others left the flight at Bermuda. Perhaps the preparation was not strong enough."

"Not strong enough?" He looked reproachfully at Harian. "It was strong enough to send a Bedouin scampering to the toilet for a week. Perhaps it was not administered in sufficient quantities. That was your responsibility, Shlomo."

"It was sufficient," Harian countered. His voice was even. He had a reputation of being hard to intimidate. "The servants at the hotel delivered only the bottled water that they were paid to deliver. The problem was the strength of the dosage. Or the natural resistance of the South Africans."

"This means we must spend more time throwing the Boers off the track," Colonel Garovsky said crossly. "I trust you're aware of that."

"I'm more than aware of it," Harian said a trifle sharply. "These additional people caused me trouble, too. They caused me to have to land a plane that was perilously overloaded. In a blizzard. I trust you're aware of *that*. American dollars, taken one or two at the time, are not very heavy. Sixty million of them are like lead."

Colonel Garovsky rubbed his gloved hands together. He smiled at Harian. "You did a splendid job, Shlomo. I apologize for this quarrel. I seem to be apologizing a lot lately. Run along. Ayala has a car waiting out front. You are in for a long drive. The snow is quite unbelievable. *Shalom*."

Harian pulled a face and shook his head. "*Shalom*," he said and left the storage room.

The loading was completed. Two men with UZIs climbed into the back of each van and faced the rear. Each of the passenger-seat riders also carried one of the light automatic weapons.

Colonel Garovsky took his seat in the lead van. He set his UZI across his lap.

They made their way through a gate. There was no guard. It was the snow. Colonel Garovsky gazed ahead. Snow. Nothing but snow. He estimated it would take them at least five hours to cover seven miles.

7

"Mr. McManus?" the voice said cordially on the telephone. "Good morning. My name is Katz. I had the pleasure of dining the evening before last with your associate, Mr. Leitstein. I apologize for calling so early, but my business is rather urgent."

Mr. McManus smacked his lips several times and switched on the bedside lamp. He blinked and tried to make himself comfortable with the receiver. He had difficulty holding it. His thumbs were stiff. He looked at the alarm clock. Five o'clock in the morning . . . Katz? Who the hell is Katz? Oh, Katz . . .

"What's the idea, calling this time of night?" he snapped. "I'm supposed to be recuperating, for Christ's sake. Need my rest." He squirmed and got himself to rights with the phone. "You got a thick skull or something? I told you not to talk to me direct. I told you to talk to Nat Leitstein. What the—"

"I talked with Mr. Leitstein. In fact we had a rather detailed discussion. Unfortunately it was not the kind of discussion I had hoped for. Mr. Leitstein posed a good many hypothetical situations. I got the impression that Mr. Leitstein doubts our seriousness."

"So I heard. I also heard you ain't learned how to talk straight. Why the hell didn't you get back to Leitstein yesterday? He hung around all morning waiting for your call. You decided you want to lay it on the line, you get back to Leitstein. I need my—"

"That is precisely what we want to do. Lay it on the line. I said my business is urgent. However, we have reservations about Mr. Leitstein. I needn't go into them. We're trying to recover our manners. Let us say that we are uncomfortable with him. Or should I say we have misgivings about his assumptions."

Talk about assumptions, thought Mr. McManus. This hoople would assume he was entitled to a basket of breadsticks if he ordered one meatball. He raised his body a fraction and tugged at his pajamas, which were wrenching his crotch.

"Look, Katz—or whatever your name is. You got a pair of balls, I give you that, calling up in the middle of the night and saying you had the pleasure of dining with Nat Leitstein, talking like I ain't got a clue you was the hoople that busted into my apartment. Either that, or you're so dumb you ain't figured I know what you hooples're up to. So why don't you drop the crap and say what's on your mind?"

"Now?"

"Hell, yes, now. It's your troubles we're talking about, not mine."

"I thought I might visit your flat."

"Oh, yeah? That's rich. You thought I'd let you in my apartment? After what you done? You must be dumber than I thought. What's wrong with you? You didn't lose enough money the first time?"

"I meant that I would prefer not to discuss this on the telephone."

"Why not? On account of you ain't figured out how to pull a gun over the phone?"

"The details are rather delicate."

Mr. McManus was silent a moment. This was what he had been waiting for—and expecting. The guy had a way of putting it, he thought; he sounds like an embezzler on his way to see the DA. Then he said, "Tell you what. You be here in two hours. Seven on the dot. Just show up like you was a normal human being. Here's the hook. You come alone. And don't pack heat. That means no guns. Got me? In the meantime you call off these hooples that are standing chicky across the street. They stick out like a neon sign, plus they must be freezing. You must be nuts, making them guys stay out like that in the snow. So call them off."

"Very well . . . I appreciate this, Mr. McManus."

"Remember. Just you. None of them other hooples. And no iron. There's a cop coops in my lobby this time of day. You pull any funny stuff, he'll be up here so fast it'll make your head swim. With lots of help."

Mr. McManus replaced the receiver. He went to the bathroom,

urinated somewhat painfully, and then roused Freddie Dee.

"There's a hammer somewhere in the kitchen," he said. "I want you to have it in your hand when this hoople shows up. I want you to make sure he sees it when you open the door."

"You want me to hit him?" Freddie asked, putting on his clothes.

"For Christ's sake, the guy's coming to talk business. What good is he if his head's busted? No, I don't want you to hit him. I want you to let him see he can get hit if he fucks around. You know who he is?"

"Who?"

"It's the tall hoople," Mr. McManus said, "the one that done all the talking the other day. The one that was trying to flash busters on me."

"I don't think there's much to him," said Freddie, looking at himself in the mirror; he touched the purple bruise under his eye. "Not if it's just him."

"Don't try him. At least not just for the hell of it. If he fucks around, okay, but not just for the hell of it . . . You know what else about him?"

"What?"

"Him and the bimbo that set you up, they're a number."

Freddie shrugged and looked bashfully at the floor. "So what?"

"I need some edge with this hoople. How many times you hump her? It'll throw the hoople off if I zing him a couple of times about it. She do any perverted stuff, rim job or anything?"

Freddie didn't answer.

"Come on, for Christ's sake. Did she?"

Freddie made a face, still looking at the floor. "No," he said finally.

"No what?"

"No, she didn't do none of that stuff."

"What was it? Just a straight hump?"

Freddie sighed and then looked at the ceiling. "I didn't get any," he mumbled.

"What do you mean, you didn't get any? You had her in bed all night, didn't you?"

Freddie rubbed the back of his neck and blinked several times. "When we got here," he said abjectly, "she wouldn't let me. Said she'd had too much to drink. Said she needed some sleep and we'd do it when we woke up. Next thing I knew, the doorbell was ringing and, well . . ."

Mr. McManus cackled. "And you didn't even dip your lizard. Jesus Christ."

Promptly at seven o'clock the doorman called. He said a Mr. Katz was there to see Mr. McManus. Send him up, said Freddie, who stationed himself, hammer in hand, at the door.

Mr. McManus sipped a cup of tea and looked out the living room window. The snow lay hard on the city. It was not falling at the moment, but the sky was gray and threatening. Tunnels had been shoveled through the drifts along the sidewalk, like rat-runs in a white no-man's land. The trees in Central Park stood like odd, crystal ornaments. He could spot none of the stakeout men who had alarmed Coombes.

He set the teacup aside and took several short, measured breaths. He felt happy for the third straight morning. He was upright, he had shaved and dressed himself . . . he smoothed the front of his jacket and adjusted his tie. Some people might get used to the idea of dying, he reflected. Not me. Not as long as . . .

Freddie opened the door. There stood Colonel Garovsky. He walked down the long corridor to the living room, smiling confidently. Freddie conspicuously tapped the head of the hammer against his palm. Colonel Garovsky did not appear intimidated. Freddie trailed him into the room.

Colonel Garovsky peeled off his overcoat and held open the front of his jacket. "You see, I'm unarmed," he said. He ungripped his lapels and pointed at himself with two fingers. "As we agreed."

"Sit down, Katz," said Mr. McManus. He motioned to a straight-back chair. He sat down on a sofa and told Freddie to make him another cup of tea. He did not offer a cup to "Katz."

"All right," he said. "What's doing?"

"I wonder if I might have a cup of tea. I'm afraid I haven't—"

"No."

Colonel Garovsky shrugged. "Very well. Let me apologize again for the—"

"What's doing?"

Colonel Garovsky sighed and tried to make himself at ease in the narrow chair. His self-assurance was not as solid as when he arrived. "We don't have the confidence in Leitstein we had anticipated," he said shortly. "It's a question of discretion. Leitstein made a number of inquiries. He tried to assure us there was nothing—"

"Look, Katz. You said you had something urgent to talk about. How you don't like the way Nat Leitstein parts his hair don't sound very urgent to me. I'm giving you one more chance. If I don't like what I hear, there's the door."

Colonel Garovsky clasped his hands and touched his chin. "We propose to make business with you," he began, "and avoid Leitstein altogether. Our terms are attractive, I think. We will pay you an additional two hundred and fifty thousand dollars for your services."

There was a silence as he looked quizzically at Mr. McManus.

"On top of the two-fifty you already mentioned?"

"Of course."

"An even half a mil?"

"Yes. A half million dollars."

Freddie delivered the tea. Mr. McManus told him to get the hammer and come back in the living room and have a seat and keep his mouth shut.

"Okay," Mr. McManus said. "I heard the payoff. What's doing?"

"Do you accept the terms?"

"How the hell can I accept the terms if I don't know what I'm getting paid for. For all I know you want to pay me all this dough to go a round with a contender. My brain ain't that mushy. Not yet. Like I told you, I know what's doing or I don't make deals."

Colonel Garovsky leaned forward and placed his hands on his thighs. He glanced at Freddie and then back at Mr. McManus. His expression said he would rather not talk in front of Freddie.

"Don't worry about him," said Mr. McManus. "He ain't interested in but one thing. Swinging that hammer if I give him the nod."

Colonel Garovsky appeared to think this over. "In that case I suppose it's all right," he said, trying to conceal his growing unease. "Here is our proposal." His voice bore a trace of hesitation. "We wish to bet on a professional football game. This Sunday. It is the last game of the current season, I believe. We have available a rather large sum with which to—"

"Sixty million, right?"

"That is correct."

"The first figure I heard was a hundred and fifteen million. How come it's cheaper now?"

"Well, actually"—Colonel Garovsky could stand it no longer; he stood up and leaned with his elbow on the mantelpiece; Freddie started from his seat; Mr. McManus gestured for him to take it easy—"you see, there are sixty million dollars at the moment. At a few hours notice the balance can be available if necessary—if you and I are able to come to an understanding."

"Get to the point, Katz." Mr. McManus set his teacup on a table at the end of the sofa.

"Yes, well, the point is—our point is—we would like to bet the first sum, the sixty million dollars, in such a way that we would win." He stared a moment at Mr. McManus and then added, "and we would like to bet the fifty-five million dollars, the money that is not available, in such a way that we would . . . lose."

Mr. McManus carefully bit the end off a cigar and lit it gradually. He thought of the hundred dollars that Freddie had wanted to borrow from him late the previous afternoon. Freddie had said he had hot tips on four horses running in the last race at a California track. The book who had tipped Freddie was an old-timer who wrote a small sheet up in Cannon Heights. Mr. McManus knew him to be reliable; he had quoted prices of 5–1, 7–1, 4–1, and 6–1. Freddie had wanted to play $25 on each horse to win. Mr. McManus gave him $640 and told him to bet $170 on the first horse, $120 on the second, $210 on the third, and $140 on the fourth. "You'll come out two hundred ahead minus the vig if any of them win," he told Freddie. "A bill for you . . . and a bill for me for figuring it out for you." He was right. One of them finished first and Freddie shook his head as he anticipated a visit to the old neighborhood to collect a total of $840, minus the vig and what he owed Mr. McManus.

"You told Leitstein you didn't want to lay it with the books." Mr. McManus exhaled a wisp of smoke. "Why not?"

Colonel Garovsky stood up straight and folded his arms. "We believe it would be indiscreet," he said; his tone was vague. "Enormous sums of money attract attention. We don't want to attract attention . . . for attention's sake."

"Don't kid yourself, Katz. You go into action with a hundred and fifteen big balloons, you going to attract attention."

Colonel Garovsky slowly stroked his chin. "We do not want to place our bets in the manner of ordinary extravagant gamblers," he said seriously. "Quite the reverse. What we have in mind—or, should I say, what we intend—is to place our bets through your Off-Track Betting Corporation."

Mr. McManus pulled a face and studied his cigar from several angles. He glanced at Colonel Garovsky and then back at his cigar.

He had heard a lot of cockamamie ideas in his life. Eating contests, flatpole sitting, diving twenty feet into a bathtub. A train derailed once somewhere over a river out West. The picture was on the front of the *Graphic*—a freight car dangling from a trestle with the number 382 on it showing as big as day. Everybody, but everybody, played that number somehow. The number three horse for $8 in the second race. Twenty-eight dollars on this, that, or the other fighter in the third round. Thirty-two dollars on the eight ball in the side pocket . . .

"Let me get this straight," Mr. McManus said at length. "You want to bet sixty million dollars at OTB to win, right? And you want to bet fifty-five million dollars to *lose?* You want to lose at OTB, too?"

"That would suit our purposes, yes."

Quickly Mr. McManus computed the payoff. He shook his head. "Forget it, Katz. You'd get stiffed. Even with the fifty-five mil you say you want to dump, the state'd never be able to pay off what you'd be owed. Christ, they'd have to hock everything from the railroads to the governor's salary to cash your tickets. That ain't counting all the other winners. Forget it. OTB ain't set up to handle that kind of action. You'd break them in half, you take out sixty million at one pop."

"I thought that might be the case. I don't quite understand why. Would you explain?"

"Look. Say a book is writing a Giants-Jets game and he gets more action than he can handle on the Giants. What does he do? He finds another book and lays off an equal amount on the Jets. Or if he sees a steam job coming, he'll play around with the line. If he gets a case of the horrors, he might call me and say would I call Carmine and fix up a *very* big layoff. For OTB it's a different bowl of chop suey. OTB is wide open—they can't lay off action, on account of there ain't but one OTB, and the law says they can't take a game off the board, on account of every hoople holding a ticket, winners and losers both, would sue their ass off. The only thing OTB can do is move the line—and if they get a heavy shot like this, the only thing they can do is pray like hell they don't get hung up."

"Leitstein mentioned something about 'catching the middle.' What would be the effect of that?"

Mr. McManus butted his cigar. "What you're asking, it'd mean you'd cash all your tickets except them you're throwing in the toilet on purpose. You'd collect the bets you made to close up the price plus what you'd bet coming back the other way. The effect? Who knows? Probably a lot of politicians making a lot of calls trying to find out how come their limousines are going up for sale."

Colonel Garovsky smiled smugly. "Might I conclude that we have a deal?"

"Not yet. I know what you want. I still don't know what's doing. Like I told you, I don't—"

The smile disappeared. "Our reasons are our own. You are being well paid. You are getting an extra quarter of a million dollars in cash. That is money that would have gone to Leitstein, except we decided it would be more prudent to make business with you. You know what we want. The other . . . considerations . . . are none of your concern."

Freddie was on his feet, brandishing the hammer. "You want me to hit him?" he said with a scowl.

In a barely noticeable motion Colonel Garovsky shifted his weight and drew his left forearm to his body. He made a fist, the knuckle of his middle finger protruding. Mr. McManus saw it and guessed Freddie wouldn't have a prayer of landing a blow and would probably get torn apart if he tried.

"Not now," he said somewhat wearily and motioned for Freddie to sit down. "If Katz here comes down off his high horse, not at all." Then he turned to Colonel Garovsky. "Let me give you a couple, so you'll get an idea why I got to know what's doing. I done a little checking on you, Katz. On you and the other hooples that was in here the other day acting like gorillas. What I heard is, you're from overseas, Israel I think it is, and your sidekicks, Espenwhatsit and them, are from Africa someplace."

Colonel Garovsky placed his hands on his hips and looked angrily at Mr. McManus. "How do you know that I'm—"

Mr. McManus raised his hand. "Don't get your nose out of joint," he said. "I'm just trying to figure the angles. What else I heard is, you hooples are running a—what the hell is it? Oh, yeah, some kind of fancy-shmancy sandbag. Now I don't give a damn if you're running a cotton-candy machine on the boardwalk. It's your business and you can run it any way you want to. But if you want me in on it, you got to give me more than this high-priced runaround. A lot more, as you want to cut out Nat Leitstein, who ain't no dummy and'll figure that he's getting squeezed out. What I'm saying to you, Katz, is I don't think this thing is twenty-four carat kosher—which don't exactly bother me, except that it leaves me with this: Is it legal?"

Colonel Garovsky relaxed a trifle and inclined his head. "Let me ask you a question," he said, leaning again on the mantelpiece. "Is it legal to bet on football games at the Off-Track Betting Corporation? Of course it's legal. That's what we want to do. Bet on a football game. So where have I not fully informed you of our intentions?"

"It's legal to play blackjack in Vegas, but they'll bounce you on your ear, they catch you counting cards."

"Pardon me?"

"You ain't told me why you want to lose fifty-five million bucks."

Colonel Garovsky sat down on the narrow chair. "If I'm mistaken, the sacrifice of a certain amount of money might be required, might it not? To, ah, what's the phrase, make the line move to our advantage?"

Mr. McManus nodded.

"Then why can't we use it for that purpose? To make the line move?"

"You pull the line with that kind of dough, you can skip rope with it."

"Is that a disadvantage?"

"Not for you it ain't. They'll be going bazoo at OTB. . . . You still ain't told me why you want to play it at OTB and why you want to lose all that money."

Colonel Garovsky sighed and looked pensive. "I'm afraid I can't tell you that."

There was a silence. Then Mr. McManus said, "You heard what I said, didn't you? You hit big, OTB'll stiff you. You'll have to go to court or declare war or something, you want to get paid."

"Would you be as concerned," Colonel Garovsky said, "if we had proposed to bet in the orthodox way? That is, even if we had decided to go on the market, so to speak, with illegal bookmakers?"

Mr. McManus shrugged and chuckled. "It's your dough, Katz. Who am I to suggest to you lovely people you shouldn't get down with a bush-league setup? You want to throw away fifty-five million dollars, you want to bet a ton on something you'll never collect a dime on, who am I to stop you?"

"Do we have a deal?"

"How do you want to play it?"

"We want to bet on one game. Both winning and losing bets."

"Why one game?"

Colonel Garovsky smiled. "It's our money. I believe it's our privilege to bet on one game if we prefer. I'm right, aren't I?"

"You're a hoople, but you can bet any way you want to."

"Thank you. We would like you to inform us as soon as possible of a schedule of when we should begin betting. I believe time is an important consideration. I will telephone at one o'clock this afternoon if that is convenient. I will expect you to tell me which game we are to bet on and in what fashion we are to place our bets."

"What units are you using?"

"Pardon me?"

"Units. How much you getting down at a pop? Also what denominations you using? How many runners you got?"

"We will have seventy-five people to place the winning bets and fifty-eight to place the losing ones. Naturally they will do it in a way that will not attract attention to any particular individual. The currency is largely ten-dollar and twenty-dollar bills, all used. A hundred thousand or so in fifties. We will rely on you to instruct us on when and how much to bet. We will be able to operate efficiently in spite of the snow. I will give you two telephone numbers—one for the winning bets, the other for the losing ones. At no time should the business of the one be discussed on the telephone with the other. Is that clear?"

"It's your money."

Colonel Garovsky stood up. "How should we pay your fee?"

"I'll let you know when you tell me you're ready to get down. When will the money be available?"

"The instant you tell us which game we should bet and how to go about betting on it."

Mr. McManus nodded with a grunt.

"I appreciate your cooperation. Please, not a word of this to Leitstein. I think things will work much more smoothly with him off the scene. I'll call at one. Your man there needn't bother to see me to the door. I would be forced to take his mallet away from him. He would probably get hurt. I can find my way out."

Colonel Garovsky slipped on his overcoat and left.

Freddie's face twisted in anger. He was about to say something when Mr. McManus said, "Look by my bed. There's a piece of paper with a number on it. Call and ask for a guy by the name of Coombes."

Freddie expelled his breath through clenched teeth and trudged toward Mr. McManus's bedroom. Abruptly Mr. McManus called to him, "Wait a minute. Forget that. Don't call Coombes. Get Nat Leitstein on the phone."

A few minutes later, Freddie shouted from beyond the living room, "Mr. Leitstein ain't there."

"Where'd you call?"

"I tried New Jersey, I tried 1407, and I tried the apartment."

"Keep trying. He's probably hung up in the snow."

Major Espensheid and Nathan Leitstein shook hands.

"I can't emphasize too strongly the need for absolute discretion in the matter," said Major Espensheid. "That means, of course, no future discussions of any sort with the Israelis or with your Mr. McManus. I think we're entitled to that stipulation, don't you? Given the amount of your commission?"

"I think you covered all the ground, pal," said Nathan Leitstein, opening the door of the hotel room. The room was painfully cold.

"Until five o'clock then," said Major Espensheid. "I'll telephone promptly at five."

He closed the door and walked to the window and looked out for a moment. The snow was again blowing hard. It eddied and whirled and rattled the windowpanes. Despite the lack of heat in the hotel he did not feel really uncomfortable. He was on top of the job again. He had seen through a thing or two, and he had acted. Leitstein, for example. That was an inspired idea. Pretoria had agreed.

Leitstein was an uncommonly sound fellow, he decided, for a Jew. Not at all like the Jews at home; why, the man was a boxer, and he seemed agreeable enough. Certainly not like Garovsky and the rest of the Israelis. Leitstein was cheeky, like all Jews everywhere, but not like the lawyers and shopkeepers and clothes makers back home. No, Leitstein wasn't at all like the Jews back home. Of course the man was being well paid. Very well paid.

A short time later Lieutenant Van Hooff arrived. He was carrying a bottle of wine.

"I wasn't able to find a Nederburg, sir," he said. He placed the bottle and a cheap corkscrew on a table and stood before the electric heater. "This is from California. I'm told it's comparable to one of the Cape drys."

"It's to be expected," said Major Espensheid in Afrikaans. "New York is an extremely narrow city. It's absurd, the shops' not selling

South African wines as a way of making political statements. He uncorked the bottle and filled two glasses he got from the bathroom.

Holding their glasses in gloved hands, they toasted the Day of the Covenant. Major Espensheid remarked that what they were up to in America could be likened to a defensive tactic used by the *Trekkers* when they fought off Dingane's Zulus in 1838.

"Have no doubt of it," he added, "the Jews have proved just as treacherous as the Kaffirs. That bloody Garovsky underestimates us to the point of insult."

"How do you mean, sir?" said Lieutenant Van Hooff. He was rather impressed with the wine. He would order another bottle of it at their luncheon. He was also relieved; he had feared that Major Espensheid would raise a fuss and protest that Afrikaaners should drink only South African wine on the Day of the Covenant.

"You don't suppose it was just a bit of bad luck, do you, that only our people took ill in Paraguay?"

"Well, frankly, sir, I hadn't—"

"Of course you hadn't. Why should you? Why should any of us? We've listened so long to all that slim talk from the Jews that we've stopped listening to ourselves. What was it that fellow said in Jerusalem? 'When Western civilization falls, a new period of history will see Israel and South Africa emerge into the forefront of the nations of the future.' That's what he said, wasn't it? Well, the thinking has been modified somewhat, at least for the purposes of this operation."

Lieutenant Van Hooff looked puzzled.

"There's been a shift in emphasis, to put it mildly," Major Espensheid went on. "A great deal is at stake. The short of it is, we aren't going to let the Jews share the results of an operation that we can, at this stage, run successfully ourselves."

"I'm afraid I don't quite understand, sir."

"Let me put you in the picture," said Major Espensheid. He then enumerated the original goals of the "composite operation." It took some time. "Of course we needed the Jews," he said at length. "They have the connections in New York and we don't. On our own we've done a number of things like it in the past. On a much smaller scale, of course. The idea then—as it is now—was to gain a significant foothold here that would give us some sort of leverage in America's South Africa policy."

"Like the attempt to purchase that newspaper in Washington?"

Major Espensheid's expression grew stern. Lieutenant Van Hooff had touched a tender spot. The newspaper-buying episode had exploded in BOSS's face. It had been one aspect of an operation to brighten South Africa's image in America. Then some politicians in Pretoria got into the thing and started spending lavishly all over the globe, and the English-language press got hold of it and spread the filthy news that solid, patriotic Afrikaaners had been in such places as Las Vegas in the company of unsavory women and the money they spent was all from the public treasury and . . .

"Yes," said Major Espensheid with a note of distaste. "That and conducting tours for American congressmen in South Africa, occasionally buying their votes outright the way the Jews do, sending speakers about to friendly audiences, mainly in the southern states. Finally we realized that we needed something more substantial, more dependable than public relations—which, by the way, some of us realized years ago was getting us nowhere. Now, of course, we haven't any choice. The Griquas and the Kaffirs have sent up the balloon."

"What will it get us, sir, having a lot of tote tickets that can't be paid off?"

Major Espensheid sipped some wine and giggled slyly. "The goal of the composite operation," he said, "was for us and the Jews to appear Monday morning and present our tickets for cashing. The Off-Track Betting establishment would be unable to pay and the entire business would be turned over to the diplomats—who would then inform the officials of this state that we, South Africa and the Jews, would cancel the debt in exchange for concrete political aid. Namely, we would demand that the governor propose a program, changes in the banking laws and the like, that would suit our purposes. We would demand that this state's members of Congress propose legislation that would, on every count, be favorable to South Africa and Israel. This would apply to questions dealing with economics, trade, military purchases, social matters like so-called human rights, things of that sort, and any number of other things as well. . . . That was the composite operation. Now, as a result of simple arithmetic, we have an operation of our own."

"Simple arithmetic?"

"Very simple. I'm embarrassed it didn't occur to me sooner. You see, the Jews couldn't possibly have brought all the currency in on a single 707. It isn't physically possible. The most they could have brought is a bit more than half. Perhaps two-thirds, taking into account that seventeen of our chaps weren't aboard."

A stunned look spread over Lieutenant Van Hooff's square face. "The bloody swine," he said hotly. "What are they doing with the rest of it?"

"Stealing it. At any rate that's what they think they're doing with it. I've demanded an accounting. I'll know this afternoon exactly how much money is here. As it turns out it's a bit of Jew greed that plays directly into our hands. You see, our move now is to play along with the Jews until the money is distributed and then to act independently. Garovsky will tell our chaps how the bets are to be placed, but as soon as they're clear of him, we'll give other instructions."

"Do you understand gambling, sir?"

"I'm receiving expert advice. Chap named Leitstein. A Jew, but quite brainy in his way. He's in the research document. An associate of McManus. He was recommended by an agent we're using. He's receiving an enormous sum, enormous, but it will be worth it. When the thing's done, we may not own the state of New York, but we will have the Jews in exactly the position we want them, which is much the same thing."

"How do you mean?"

"We shall simply tell them that unless they do a number of things we want, we intend to expose them. We'll expose the little gambling scheme they concocted without our knowledge. We'll expose all these killings that Zanin arranged. Don't forget, all these counterfeit witnesses are Garovsky's people, too. And we shall threaten public legal action in the matter of several million dollars of our money still in their possession. What we'll insist on to keep quiet about all this is that Israel defy the UN arms program and develop weaponry for us. We'll insist that Israel not only take our part on all international questions, but that they actively promote the interests of South Africa. Above all, we'll insist that Israel endorse apartheid without reservation."

"Will they do it?"

"They will. If there is one thing that Israel can't afford, it's a major scandal in New York. Half their support in the world is here. More than half. Of course we shall pass the word to the Jews at home and in Britain that we expect their cooperation in persuading their American cousins. I think a Jew in South Africa understands straight talk, don't you?"

Lieutenant Van Hooff nodded complacently.

"Now," said Major Espensheid, "we should be getting along to the restaurant. We can order more wine if we feel like it. Catch me up on our Kaffir policeman. Any leads on him?"

"Nothing yet. I'm taking over the tracking operation myself today. When I was in CID, I found it extraordinarily easy to locate Kaffirs."

"It's different here, you realize."

"Yes, but a Kaffir is a Kaffir anywhere. Mazibuko may be mad for crosswords, but he's still a Kaffir. That's what will make the job a cinch. He's still a Kaffir."

"Do you know his first name, by the way?"

"I'm afraid not, sir."

"Neither do I. Odd, most Kaffirs, I've never known their last names. . . . What of Dolan?"

"I spoke with Zanin. He has him in tow. I have a spot of bad news on that count, sir. Dolan lost your rifle. Apparently he lost his nerve and chucked it in the river."

Major Espensheid's red face grew tight. "My H&H?" His clipped Transvaaler voice was thick with pain. "Dolan chucked my H&H in a river?" His shoulders sagged as he spoke. "He can't have done that. . . . My father gave me that rifle. . . . It's been in my family for more than sixty years. . . . It was supposed to have gone to my grandson."

After an appropriate period of respectful silence Lieutenant Van Hooff suggested they go to their luncheon. After all it was the Day of the Covenant and two *broeders* would enjoy observing it together.

"We don't want to take Dolan home with us if we don't have to," Major Espensheid said quietly as they walked down the corridor."

In the lobby they turned up their collars against the weather.

Detective Second Grade Tedesco maneuvered his way inelegantly into the Special Homicide Task Force office on the second floor of a midtown precinct. Snow clung to his overcoat and his hair. The other detectives were at their desks, which were wedged anywhere they would fit in the low-ceilinged room. The desks were littered with paper and coffee containers. The detectives, seated or standing at an astonishing variety of angles, talked on the telephone or labored over typewriters. Tedesco was carrying a long, narrow parcel wrapped in brown paper.

"Got it?" called Detective Lieutenant Burns from his own disordered desk at the read of the office.

"Got it," answered Tedesco. He swept aside a stack of dust-laden manila folders on the top of a filing cabinet and began to unwrap the parcel.

Burns and the other detectives dropped what they were doing and edged close to him. Paper and string flew in all directions. Then Tedesco held it up triumphantly.

"Jesus, it *is* an elephant gun."

"The thing would blow the wall down."

"You got to respect a gun like that."

"My brother-in-law would—"

"What kind is it?" asked Burns.

"A .375 magnum Holland and Holland," said Tedesco; he spoke with the air of a man proud of his mastery of the exotica of armory, "made in England in 1912. It's built on an old FN Mauser action. New stock. Made by E.C. Bishop and Sons. Don't worry about those rust spots. They'll come off in no time. This baby is good as new."

Burns took the rifle and examined it. Heavy son of a bitch, he thought, heavier than the Garand he carried during the war; a really solid piece, though. He laid it back on the filing cabinet.

"For those of you didn't get the word," he said with a burp, "we got this thing with an assist from the fire department. A fireboat working that pier fire in Brooklyn Heights found it sticking out of a chunk of ice in the river. Ballistics cleaned it up. They fired it. Right, Tedesco?"

"Yeah. Kicked like a mule. It was worse when they fired it from a bench. Anyway, they got a guy to build them some cartridges and they fired them. Same curve, same bore. It's the same weapon, all right. The one our boy's been playing with."

Each detective in turn picked it up, aimed it, and worked the bolt.

Burns walked back to his desk and sat down. "The rifle," he said loudly, "we ain't getting anywhere oohing and ahing over it. What we need is the idiot that's been shooting it. Anybody but Tedesco got anything else on these witnesses?"

The other detectives shook their heads and muttered no. Burns ordered six men to leave for Brooklyn and lower Manhattan and start asking questions in the neighborhoods at both ends of the Manhattan and Brooklyn bridges. He knew they were highly unlikely to come up with anything, but he had no choice but to go through the motions. You find a murder weapon at a certain location, you canvass the area. That's police work. At this point he would do anything to clear this case.

The "Meyers broad" continued to puzzle him. She'd called again on the Ernie Parks thing. The third time she'd called. She said she'd seen a second man running from Davis's car. The call had come to another precinct and evaded the electronic tracing equipment that Lieutenant Schmidt had requisitioned at his insistence.

Burns picked up a stapled sheaf of badly typed pages. Each one was filled with names, addresses, and telephone numbers. They were the witnesses to the "Finger of God" murders. Beside each name was an "X," signifying that, as far as could be established, not one of them had given a true name, address, or phone number. He idly flipped the pages. He came to the end and started over. His face was growing blank with weariness; he had spent the past two nights on a cot that was folded against the wall behind him. Abruptly he stopped turning the pages.

"Tedesco," he said with a growl, "come over here."

Tedesco looked around, paused half a beat to make sure the lieutenant really wanted him, and then walked over.

"Take a close look at this and tell me what you see." Burns shoved the list at him across the desk.

Tedesco fiddled a moment with the knot of his tie and then looked at the list. He ran his eyes down each page, item by item, and flipped to the next. He had typed the thing. With two fingers. It was the part he hated about being a detective. The typing.

"Yeah, I know," he said as he finished. "A big, fat zero."

"I know the zero part," Burns said testily. His cheeks ballooned with a burp. "Look again."

Tedesco raised his eyebrows and then hastily rethumbed through the pages. "Looks the same as before," he said without interest. "Nothing."

Burns leaned over the desk and seized the list. "Look at the addresses, God damn it," he snapped. "Three-fourths of them are midtown hotels. Look at this"—he turned the page around and held it up—"One . . . eight . . . thirteen. Thirteen in the fucking Waldorf.

And not one of them gives the right phone number. Take this one, this Fackenheim. He's staying at the Waldorf, right? Where's he a witness? Washington Heights, for Christ's sake."

"He could've been visiting relatives."

"And this one"—Burns stabbed the page with his finger—"Weiner. Staying at the Americana. Wrong phone number. Nobody by that name registered in the Americana on that date. He's a witness for the one at Canal and the Bowery."

"Maybe he was having late Chinese, Weiner."

"Where?"

"How the hell do I know? One of them all-night joints."

Burns tossed the sheaf of papers on his desk. "It could be," he said bitterly, "that every cop in this unit is a mental deficient. It could be he said he lived on Amber Street, Brooklyn. It could be, but there's no way in hell we could get *every* one of them wrong. . . . Don't it hit you as God damned weird that that many witnesses give hotels as addresses? I mean, nearly every fucking witness is from out of town. No wonder New York gets a bad rep. People come here and what do they see? A crazy on the loose with that bazooka there. And he looks the same to every one of them. Jesus Christ. I been a cop a long time and I never seen this many witnesses from out of town. . . . Another thing. Look at the names. All but ten or twelve are Jewish. The rest are Protestant. Not colored Protestant, either. Not one colored, not one Puerto Rican—this Seixas ain't Puerto Rican; that's a Jewish name—no Italians, no Polacks, no micks."

"So what? What's so strange about Jewish witnesses?"

"Who're all from out of town and staying at hotels—where nobody's ever heard of them? Christ, not a single neighborhood type. Not a single fucking one." Burns rubbed his forehead with a rough, jerky motion. "This African don't check out, either. We called the South African consulate. Naturally, they don't have any blacks on their staff. Davis said his name's Makibozo. A lie, probably. The consulate's going to check passports and get back to us. And the Meyers broad, she—"

"We canvassed that block in Harlem," Tedesco interrupted. "No Meyers. No whites lived on that block for years. We seen Davis, too. At the old woman's. You know how they're getting him back to Philadelphia? Putting him on a Coast Guard cutter. The guy owns the Eagles, what's his name, he's going to reimburse the government."

Burns sat down and patted his stomach. He forgot what he was going to say. He leaned back and said casually, "You know what Davis was doing up there? In Harlem?"

"Going to see that old woman for something. He goes up there all the time. She reads his mind or some fucking thing. It was in the papers."

"That's what I'm going to tell you," said Burns. "The old woman. Her name ain't Viola Holton like they had in the paper. It's Lula something. A singer at the Yeah Man in the old days. She used to be the old lady of a white guy that was a tough little featherweight named Kid Sweeney. That was years ago. I seen him fight at the Garden, Kid Sweeney. Took a classy guy named Billy Light in four rounds. Some fight. I was just a kid."

"What happened to him, Kid Sweeney?"

"I don't know. Quit fighting. Probably dead. Him and Billy Light both. I mean, that was 1933."

Tedesco shrugged and walked away. As he reached his desk he turned around and called, "Hey, Lieutenant, you want to get down for this Sunday at OTB?"

Burns screwed up his mouth. "Maybe," he said. "I ain't seen the line. What looks good?"

"Zimmerman in the Post, he's got Philadelphia by ten over New Orleans."

"Ten points?"

"Might be good. Oh, I didn't tell you. Davis was limping around. Sore foot. Toe or something. If he's gimpy, Davis, Philadelphia might have it tough covering ten points."

Burns took out his wallet. "Here's a sawbuck. Get me New Orleans if they're still giving ten points."

"If this Katz don't need me," said Nathan Leitstein, "I don't need him." He gazed out the window of his office in the Garment Center. "It's screwy, anyway. The whole thing."

"For Christ's sake," said Mr. McManus; he shifted impatiently in one of the armchairs. "How many times do I have to tell you? The two-hundred and fifty grand is yours. Katz is just trying to run a number."

"Katz wants me out, I'm out—and fuck him."

"You ain't out. I told you. Katz is playing cute. The dough's there. Good as in your sock."

"Katz don't want me in."

"The hell with Katz. I got the thing locked up."

"It sounds like he's looking for a free ride, Katz," said Nathan Leitstein. He turned around slowly. He avoided Mr. McManus's eyes. "I say we call it off. Talk about flashing our ass, what if it got out we dumped fifty-five big ones? We'd have to close up shop. Who'd pay a wooden nickel this time next week? I mean, we got a certain reputation. What'd it be worth, word got around we sent somebody in the tub like that? At OTB yet?"

"It's Katz's money. Where does it say we can't tell a hoople how to lose dough? If he meets our price? Besides, he'll win a ton, anyhow. What the hell's wrong with you?"

Nathan Leitstein walked behind his desk and sat down in his

elevated swivel chair. He toyed a moment with a letter opener and then lit a cigar. "Maybe," he said at length, "but I don't like Philadelphia-New Orleans." He sounded vague. "If we're going to do it—and this don't mean I'm in—let's go with somebody else. San Diego-Houston, maybe, or—"

"What're you, kidding?" Mr. McManus put in and frowned. "They're playing for a wild card. And this is Thursday, for Christ's sake. You know where they're playing?"

Nathan Leitstein snorted. "San Diego, and—"

"And San Diego's plus four and a half."

"I seen the line."

"San Diego by four and a half God damned points," Mr. McManus repeated hotly.

"I said I seen the line."

"Don't it tell you something?"

"It tells me the spread'll shrink. It tells me San Diego but not by four and a half."

Mr. McManus tapped his foot on the carpet. "How come it don't tell you Houston?" he asked irritably. "How come it don't tell you that 77 percent of the time the visiting team'll kick a spread that's three and a half to six and a half? That's what it's been telling you for the last forty-five years."

Nathan Leitstein studied the ash on his cigar. "Well, if we hit it and move the line, we close it up, right?"

"Are you nuts? We hit that line with sixty million bucks, it'll jump like you put a match to it. The spread'll be so wide nobody can cover it. That four and a half points is real. You pull the line, all you'll get is pick-'em."

"So? If it's pick-'em, it's still San Diego, right? Tell the hooples to shake the line 'til it's even money. Then they got . . . What's it you get when it's pick-'em?"

"A seven-to-two shot. But it can't be pick-'em, San Diego-Houston. Jesus, are you insane? Didn't you hear what I told you. Katz *wants* to get burned. Why, I don't know. He's a secret degenerate, maybe. But the thing'll get fucked up beyond recognition, they drop a wad on a short that's four and a half under away from home. How the hell are they going to lose if the short comes on?"

"Tell them to buckshot San Diego if they're worried they ain't going to lose enough." Nathan Leitstein looked at the ceiling. "Who the hell cares? The whole thing stinks."

Mr. McManus was bewildered. On Monday Billy Light was hot as hell for this. Now, unaccountably, he was indifferent almost to the point of rejection—and sloppiness. Why was he suggesting something as reckless as San Diego-Houston? They had differed before, but never on the principles which served as the groundwork for their system. It was as if Billy were saying: This ain't a football game. It's a drawing for a door prize on Bingo night. Forget the probabilities. Forget the alternatives. We'll bet we pull the winning stub and then we'll bet we don't pull it. We got as much chance of pulling a winner as a loser, right? Which he might have expected from Billy in another lifetime. Before they both understood that the Law of Insufficient Reason did not apply when you're equalizing a sporting contest for betting purposes.

"You think it stinks, I'll let you out," Mr. McManus said nonchalantly. "But I'll tell you what. I'll take Houston and the points for two hundred and fifty grand. Won't cost you a thing. It's like a double-or-nothing, except I'm starting out even and you're starting out two-fifty up. You on?"

Nathan Leitstein stared at him a moment. "Are you serious?" he asked.

"Why not?"

"It's a lousy bet."

"What do you mean?"

"Jesus Christ. San Diego is an overlay. Two'll get you three they get knocked off at home on a close spread."

Mr. McManus clenched his teeth. His brow furrowed. He felt his breath come in heaves as his anger rose. "If you don't want it," he said acidly, "why the hell are you trying to promote it onto me?"

"I don't get you," Nathan Leitstein said. His tone was ingenuous.

"What the hell do you mean, you don't get me?" Mr. McManus shouted. "I'm the guy you used to call from the bowling alley in Hoboken, remember? I win three in a row, lose two, and win a couple more, remember? So don't give me this I-don't-get-you shit. You get me fine. I don't get *you*, is what I don't get." Mr. McManus sucked his teeth a moment and then added, "How come you was out of touch all day yesterday?"

"I told you. I had business in Jersey."

"With Solly from the Teamsters?"

"Yeah. With Solly from the Teamsters."

"About the parking lot thing in Phoenix, right?"

"So what?"

"I'll tell you so what. You ain't spoke to Solly since last Friday. Solly's on the phone to *me* last night asking for his dough. His note's due tomorrow. He says you told him you'd fix it yesterday but he ain't heard from you and would I talk to his guy. So I talked to him and told him it was all right 'til next week. *But you ain't spoke to Solly!*

"Also I call the service and ask Sid for the breakdown on Philadelphia-New Orleans and Sid says, 'Oh, Jeez, Mr. McManus, I'm running out the door. I can call you later if you want, but I already give the updated stuff to Mr. Leitstein. He asked for everything, power ratings, injuries, the lines, everything.' I says you must've took the laundry list and Sid says, 'Nah, just Philadelphia-New Orleans.' Now, here we are and you're telling me, San Diego-Houston. What the hell's doing?"

Nathan Leitstein clamped his cigar between his teeth and stalked back to the window. He clasped his hands behind his back and stared at the snow. Then he spun around and plucked the cigar from his mouth. "I'll tell you what's doing," he snarled, jutting his chin. "You might be dead by Sunday. You might be dead in five minutes. That's what's doing!"

"What the hell's that supposed to mean, I might be dead by Sunday? You ain't exactly driving down a one-way street yourself."

"I mean you're sick. God damned sick. You got no business running around in this weather. You got a condition, for Christ's sake. A condition."

"You didn't think I had no condition when you called me at five o'clock Monday morning."

"That was Monday. You been going downhill. I seen it. I mean, you're having trouble—"

"Having trouble doing what?"

"Getting around, paying attention, staying awake."

"Did I have trouble this morning? Did I walk out of my building—on my own, no cane or nothing, jump right into your car—or didn't I? Did I make the calls. Did I run around town like a whirling dervish? Did I put together an edge on Philadelphia-New Orleans? Did I?"

"You got a condition. You're what, seventy-four years old?"

"You ain't a day younger, God damn it."

"If you was in my place, wouldn't you try to take some of the work off a guy's been under the weather? A guy you known since—"

"You call talking like this taking some of the work off? San Diego-Houston, Jesus. You think I'm some kind of moron?"

Nathan Leitstein walked back to his desk and slumped in his swivel chair. His eyes took on a far-off, somewhat gloomy look, "I wouldn't kick a guy in the teeth," he mumbled. "Not to his back . . . I heard the price went up. That's all."

"What's doing?"

Nathan Leitstein examined his nails. He wanted a manicure. Not a chance of the girl coming up in this weather. Should he send the car for her? Forget it. It would take hours. . . . Finally he cleared his throat and said, "The guy's a hoople, you know."

"Who? Katz?"

"The other hoople. Espensheid."

"What's Espensheid got to do with it?"

"I don't know exactly. He's talking big money, too."

"Espensheid?"

"Yeah. He wants to get down. The same deal Katz made with you," he said quietly, "but separate."

Mr. McManus imagined himself, Billy Light, "Katz," Major Espenwhatsit, Coombes, Herr Lemmer, and the big hoople in the ratty raincoat all in the same room. They were about to sit down at a table. What was the probability that Billy and Major Espenwhatsit would choose to sit by each other? Coombes and Katz? Himself and the big hoople? Lemmer and . . . I can handle it if all the favorable events are equally probable, but what the hell do you do about the unfavorable ones? Now I know why the Law of Insufficient Reason ought to be called the Law of Indifference. Material assumptions can be a pain in the ass.

"An extra two-fifty, right?" asked.

"Yeah."

"For what?"

"To make sure the fifty-five million don't go down the tube."

"How does Espensheid know it's going down the tube?"

"He don't. It adds up to the same thing, though. The money his people get, he wants to play it on a winner."

Mr. McManus whistled. "Why the hell didn't you tell me that to begin with? Jesus, you'd have thought there was some way you really could hang me up. Why was you being so slick about it?"

"Well," Nathan Leitstein said, puffing his cigar, "I still ain't figured out how everybody's going to get what they want. I mean, Katz wants to win with his sixty million and lose fifty-five—and the same fifty-five is what I'm supposed to win with for Espensheid. I'm fucked if I see how you can do it. Not on one game, not at this OTB—not unless they got the thing bagged."

"You think they're messing with the game?"

"Philadelphia-New Orleans?"

Mr. McManus nodded.

"I got a feeling they might've tried."

"To put in a fix?" Mr. McManus's mouth fell open. Slowly he reached in his pocket for a cigar.

"He asked a lot of questions, Espensheid. Mostly he wanted to know how good Snakehips would be Sunday, you know, as he was shot at and his buddy got nailed and everything."

Mr. McManus was about to bite the end of his cigar and stopped. "What are you getting at?"

"I don't know. Espensheid must be some kind of nut. I talked to him an hour, hour and a half. All the time he kept saying how colored ballplayers are second-rate, but at the same time he kept saying how if Davis was such a hot player, then Philadelphia would get left in the gate if he wasn't in there Sunday, Davis."

"What'd you tell him?"

"I told him you can't bet a game's been messed with."

"What'd he say?"

"He said he'd listen to me on getting down. When I told him how it works, he piped down about colored ballplayers and that. I think what he's really interested in, Espensheid, is fucking Katz."

"And Katz wants to fuck Espensheid—" Mr. McManus nipped his cigar and lit it. "What I can't figure is why they want to run this hoop-de-doop. Betting one game. I mean, it sounds like they're playing some kind of system."

Nathan Leitstein shrugged.

Both men were silent a moment and then Mr. McManus said, "You hear from your guy in Florida, yet?"

"Yeah. The indictment's still on the books. It's pretty much worthless, though. If they tried to prosecute, I'd get it knocked down like that. Hell, they'd never get an extradition through, much less bring you to trial. The worst could happen is you'd get your name in the paper."

"That's all? You sure of it?"

"A hundred percent."

Mr. McManus laughed. "I ain't had my name in the paper since 1933," he said and leaned back and blew a smoke ring. Then he eased himself from the armchair and walked to the telephone. He grinned at Nathan Leitstein as he punched his number. "You know, Billy," he said as he waited for an answer, "for a guy that gets up before nine in the morning, you can complicate the hell out of something simple."

An hour later they were in Nathan Leitstein's *pied-à-terre* in the East Thirties.

"That's him," said Mr. McManus as the buzzer rang.

Nathan Leitstein disappeared into the foyer and spoke to the doorman through the intercom. Presently he shouted, "The doorman says am I sure it's him. He says the guy don't look like somebody I usually see."

"Big guy? Looks like he missed a few paydays?"

Nathan Leitstein spoke into the intercom. Then he shouted again. "Yeah. Sounds like him. He's on his way up."

"Who is this Coombes, anyway?" he asked as he walked back into the room. He looked at the fruit in a bowl on one of the casual tables. It was turning brown. The housekeeper hadn't shown up since the snow started. The stuff needed throwing out.

"What else can I tell you? He ran my unit in Burma. Used to be a government type. One of them spy outfits, I guess. Retired. Comes on like a rubber-hose artist that don't get a kick out of his work."

The bell rang. Nathan Leitstein walked to the door. Moments later he returned, leading Coombes, who seemed to fill up the entire room.

There was an uneasy silence.

"Nat Leitstein," Mr. McManus said after a moment and nodded.

"We met," Coombes said gruffly. He took a seat at the end of the room. He did not remove his overcoat or hat. He needed a shave. His hooded eyes were lustrous. His nostrils flared as he breathed.

Mr. McManus and Nathan Leitstein exchanged cursory looks. They conveyed to each other that both of them wondered what to make of this wild, wasted, worn man. The only part of him they could make sense of was the bulge under his left arm.

"You want a drink?" said Nathan Leitstein. It was more of an invitation to conversation than a show of hospitality.

"Skip it," said Coombes. He bit a fingernail and looked neutrally at Mr. McManus. "You said we might have something to talk over. Something of mutual interest. What is it?"

Mr. McManus studied Coombes for a moment. The guy is sitting in a warm, soft apartment, he thought, and he looks like he's in a dead-or-alive hole in the middle of nowhere, trying to figure how long the ammo will last. At length he said, "Like I told you, I said I'd be in touch if I heard anything you maybe could use. Well—"

"What is it?" Coombes interrupted sharply. "What the hell have you heard?"

Mr. McManus raised his hand. "Slow down, for Christ's sake," he said. "Just take it easy a minute, will you? Me and Leitstein there, we ain't as tough and mean as we used to be. Couple of buckets like us got to slice up a pie so everybody thinks they're getting the biggest piece. Know what I mean?"

Coombes stared straight ahead. The uneasy silence returned. Mr. McManus thought of a poker game in a building on Ashland Avenue in Chicago. Years ago. Middle of the night and the sound of fire engines. Cries of panic and chairs scraping. One hoople, an insurance salesman who was having a rough night and who had two kings showing, whipped out a .45 and said for everybody to sit still, if the place is on fire they'll come and tell you about it. They played out the hand with the smoke boiling in under the door, and the hoople lost, and they had to scramble down a fire escape, and the hoople went crazy when they got to the street because he left twenty dollars on the table, and he pulled the .45 on the firemen and went back in the place, and the smoke got him before he could get out, and another guy passed the hat for the widow and children. . . . He wondered if Coombes were the type to run into a burning building for twenty dollars—or for a hundred and fifteen million. Probably not, he decided; Coombes wouldn't be in the shape he's in if he really cared about money; what it was that Coombes did really care about he dared not guess.

It was Nathan Leitstein who finally spoke.

"The idea is don't say 'Hurry up,'" he said. "It don't get you anywhere. For years my ma thought 'Hurry up' was the national motto. It was the first thing they said to her when she got off the boat."

Coombes glanced impatiently from Nathan Leitstein to Mr. McManus. He took a deep breath. "What was it you heard, Mac?" he asked sourly.

Mr. McManus folded his hands on his lap. "I heard you was on the right track," he began. "The thing you said about Israel and South

Africa. That's who it is, all right. But there's been a little switch. The hooples that was hanging around in the snow, they ain't hanging around anymore."

Coombes gnawed at a frayed cuticle. He nodded meditatively. "Why were they hanging around in the first place?" he said. He managed to sound as if he knew he would not get a straight answer.

"Who knows?" said Mr. McManus. "Maybe they was in Hawaii and got tired of it. Maybe they didn't know any better. Some hooples, who knows?"

Coombes bit harder at his cuticle and then spit out a speck of flesh. "The strange part," he said, "is that they came to you." He sounded as if he were thinking out loud rather than speaking to Mr. McManus and Nathan Leitstein. "I know you two move a lot of money around, but what can you do for them? Make book for them, I guess, or give them some good tips. For your usual big fee, naturally." He thought of his own financial condition and sneered with resentment. "None of which answers the main question—why did they come to you?"

"They wanted the best," said Nathan Leitstein. "Obviously."

Coombes stood up and took off his hat and overcoat. For a fraction of an instant the stock of his Colt Cobra was visible as the front of his wrinkled jacket was tugged open. His cuffs and collar were dingy.

"There are lots of gamblers," he continued, sitting down heavily. "There are files on them as thick as phone directories. The FBI, the IRS, the drug-enforcement people, everybody in Washington has files on the combination guys. If their money goes into a movie, for instance, or if they skim money out, the agencies know it. They usually don't do a hell of a lot, but they know about it."

"Don't give me that," snapped Mr. McManus. "We're clean as a new penny. No drugs, no movies. I been audited up one side and down the other. The IRS ain't found—"

Coombes sprang abruptly to his feet and flourished his horny fist a few inches from his jaw. "Shut up, God damn it!" he roared. "I don't give a fuck how much you paid in taxes! I don't care if every cent you've got to your name was made with loaded dice. I'm not getting paid to raid a God damned crap game. So just shut the hell up."

He bared his teeth and glared at the two men at the other end of the room.

After a few moments Mr. McManus gestured with his thumb toward Nathan Leitstein and said, "He's a lawyer, you know. He knows what we have to say and what we don't."

"He's no lawyer," Coombes growled. "I'm damned surprised none of his high-priced clients have checked him out. On the other hand, I'm not surprised. He's stayed down pretty low since he threw that fight to you in 1933." He unclenched his fist and chewed his fingernail and added in a milder tone, "You've stayed pretty low yourself, Mac. How did—"

"If you got no interest in the kind of stuff most of you people want to know," Nathan Leitstein broke in, "how come you claim to know so much? Not that I admit you do, but how come?"

Coombes plopped back into his chair. He blew a long, weary sigh. "Those files I mentioned. There aren't any on either of you except at IRS. If you went to every other agency in Washington and asked to see what they have, you know what you'd get? A hundred words here, fifty words there. In Washington that's nothing. You wouldn't even be considered listed." He rubbed his stubbly chin and added, "The point is, somebody—and I know it's Mossad—has built a file on you."

"Mossad?" said Nathan Leitstein. "Undercover types from Israel, right?"

Coombes nodded, "The file they put together came from bits and pieces," he said. He was calmer now. "I'd love to see it. Christ, the stuff they got is incredible. The funny thing, though, is that they were able to get it at all. They seemed to be tracking backwards. Every question they asked turned up a mother lode of information—and led them to even better stuff. That isn't possible unless you're working with letter-perfect early data."

"What's early data?" asked Mr. McManus.

"It means Mossad knew what they were looking for. They weren't simply fishing. You can't find out very much in Washington that way. You can't walk in—even Mossad can't do it, and they get damned near anything they want—you can't walk in and ask something like, how much does Hedy Lamarr spend for clothes? Even if he got the data, only a fool would trust it, because by now everybody knows the computer technician wouldn't take the trouble to update the addition record. What you ask is, how much did Hedy Lamarr spend at—well, wherever Hedy Lamarr shops—how much she spent at this place on 15 July in 1942. That's simple, and the technician can find it if he's got the subscript."

Mr. McManus's eyebrows shot up. "You mean this Mossad could

walk into one of these joints and find out what I paid for a suit twenty years ago?"

"With the right entree, anybody could—if he knew you bought a suit twenty years ago and there was data on it. Mossad has the right entree—and they knew where to look."

"It sounds to me," said Nathan Leitstein, "like anybody can find out anything down there if they spend enough time and knock on enough doors. What's it cost, anyway?"

"It doesn't cost anything," Coombes replied. "We're very cozy with Mossad—up to a point. You're right, though. They could find out a lot with enough time and enough people. We've done it for years. But we've always done it the other way around. We gather the data, analyze it, authenticate it if we can, and then try to figure out what we'd do if we were in the other guy's place. It's called hypothetical intelligence. I was never good at it. What Mossad has done is different. They seem to have done all the preliminary work and *then* gone to the agencies."

"Run that by me again," said Nathan Leitstein. "Are you saying these hooples were asking questions they already knew the answers to?"

"Damned near it," said Coombes. "I've seen an analysis of all the queries that Mossad asked at the agencies. They were substantive and to the point. None of the speculation or intuition that usually crops up. That means they must have done a lot of preliminary checking with nonclassified sources, too—libraries, public records, old newspapers, things like that. It's clear what they were doing. They were building profiles on both of you. Which wouldn't have attracted any attention, except that the questions were so detailed. It was almost as if they already had a damned thorough outline and were just looking to authenticate it with facts."

"Give me an example," said Nathan Leitstein.

"Well, I'd have to look at the archive to get all the particulars," Coombes said, "but this is something from thirty years ago, probably a year or two earlier. Right after the war. Mac won a fourteen-carat gold tie clip in a crap game in Pittsburgh. A guy named Scott. He marked the thing to you for twenty-five dollars. The guy was red-haired, spent four years in the Air Force, and he was born someplace in West Virginia. The game was at a fairly posh place called the—"

"Twenty," Mr. McManus put in quietly. He touched his arthritic thumbs together and tried without success to flex the knuckles. "It was twenty bucks."

"Anyway," Coombes went on, "the guy lost the thing. It turned out that the tie clip was some kind of family treasure and he wanted it back. He drove all the way to New York—with his wife—and offered to buy the thing back. Mac didn't have it any longer, and Scott reported it stolen. It was insured and the guy got his money."

"This kind of shit is in the records in Washington?" asked Mr. McManus.

"No," said Coombes. "What's there is the insurance stuff about the tie clip and a tax deduction. Somebody else knew about the crap game. That came up when Mossad was querying one of the agencies. Something to break the ice, probably. It's just a detail. It authenticates a profile."

"The U.S. attorney," said Nathan Leitstein, "he seen this thing?"

"Oh, for Christ's sake," said Coombes. His face constricted again.

Mr. McManus pushed himself from his seat and walked to the window. He stared at the blizzard for several moments. "Snowing like a bastard, ain't it," he said. He concentrated on lighting a cigar and then slowly turned around. "The reason you heard twenty-five bucks on the tie clip," he continued, gazing into space, "is that's what I said it was worth. Not to the hoople in Pittsburgh. To somebody else. I said to this other person, I know you got a wife, a couple of kids, take this and forget you seen me in this phone booth. I got it for twenty bucks but it's worth at least twenty-five. Thanks for the break and I'll see you around. The coffee's on me. Have a slice of pie. . . . Some people's memory ain't too hot. . . . You know who's got the thing, the tie clip?"

Coombes and Nathan Leitstein shook their heads.

"Would it do you any good to know?"

"It might," said Coombes. "Why?"

"Because," said Mr. McManus as he returned to his place on the sofa, "I still ain't got it straight why anybody would break their ass running down this rooty-toot crap. If the DA don't want it—and why should he when it ain't nothing but old boiler plate—then why the hell do these foreign hooples want it? I mean, you want to know the skinny on me and Leitstein, you sure as hell don't have to go through all that whatchamacallit to come up with stuff like I won a twenty-dollar tie pin throwing dice. How come they done that?"

"That's the only way they know to do it," said Coombes. He conveyed that he didn't think the practice was very efficient. "They also wanted to scout you out. You aren't listed in Dun and Bradstreet, you know."

"I ain't listed in the phone book, either."

"Will you can the double talk?" Coombes snorted. "We all know Mossad and BOSS are bringing at least a hundred million in cash to New York. It's here already, more than likely. If they're using you and Leitstein, they're gambling the money. I don't know when and I don't know how, but I sure as God mean to find out why."

"Why do you think?" said Mr. McManus.

"I don't have a clue. They want a bundle of money in a hurry, obviously. They can always use it. To buy arms, to buy something. What else is money good for? It's a waste of breath to talk about it. I've got to get on the other side of this thing. That's why I want to know how Mossad knew which questions to ask."

"You ain't out-and-out interested in what they do with the money, are you?" asked Nathan Leitstein. "I mean, if they want to bet a little of it, you don't care, right?"

"I care about why they're bringing that money here. If they're dealing with you, I assume they want to gamble. But why do they want to gamble when there are thousands of other ways to put money to work? If I knew how Mossad got prepared to ask all those questions, I could start finding out why."

"If you found out how they got the scoop," said Mr. McManus, "what would you do?"

"I'd tell the man who sent me up here. That's what I'm being paid for."

"And what would he do?"

"Tell the people who're paying him."

"If you found out this Mossad and . . . what's the other outfit?"

"BOSS."

"And this BOSS was playing a horse, would you stink out the joint?"

"That would depend."

"On what?"

"On why they were betting a hundred and fifteen million dollars on a horse . . . Do you know why?"

Mr. McManus blew a thin stream of smoke. "I can tell you why a man drinks," he said. "I can tell you why a man kills another man over a woman. I can even tell you how much Herbert Hoover paid for suspenders in 1930. But I can't tell you why a man plays a horse if he thinks he'll make money—unless he thinks he'll live forever."

Coombes bit hard at a fingernail. "How do you think they got that stuff on you?" he asked plaintively.

"From that tie pin," said Mr. McManus.

"What the hell does that mean?"

"Only one man in the world knows what happened to that tie pin."

"Who?" broke in Nathan Leitstein.

"Charlie Dolan."

"Who is Charlie Dolan?" asked Coombes. He sounded bewildered.

"The hoople with the tie pin."

"Who is he?"

Mr. McManus crossed his arms and exhaled an enormous cloud of cigar smoke. "You tell him, Billy," he said. There was a note of mischief in his voice. "You been bullshitting with Charlie for years. The gate-mouthed son of a bitch."

Captain Zanin dropped the box on the kitchen table. He bristled and brushed the snow from his black raincoat.

"What is it?" asked Jackie Dolan. He hovered a few feet away, in front of the stove. He had lit the oven for warmth, even though he knew the danger of fire should the pressure drop in the gas line.

"Explosive gelatin," said Captain Zanin as he ripped the pasteboard apart. "Gelatin dynamite. Like plastique. Is the detonator assembled?"

"Yes, sir."

"Where is it?"

"In the refrigerator."

Captain Zanin at last got the box open. He pointed to it with an open palm.

Jackie unobtrusively turned off the oven and said to himself, I can't even keep the stove lit with that shit in here.

"Have a look, Dolan."

Jackie stepped up to the table and peered into the open box. Immediately he moaned and jumped back a half step. "Christ all fucking mighty!" he shouted, frantically squeezing a new pimple on his chin. "How much you got in there?"

Captain Zanin looked at him with a superior smile. "Fifty kilograms," he said. "It's quite old, I believe."

"Fifty kilos! Christ Almighty! You can level this fucking block with fifty kilos of that shit!" Jackie's voice was a mixture of terror and excitement. "What'd you bring all that shit in here for? Christ Almighty!"

Captain Zanin's mouth turned down at the corners. He knew nothing of explosives. Perhaps he had committed some error in bringing this much. It galled him to think that Dolan might have seen him do something with less than complete competence. Dolan would be more difficult to manage if he detected some fallibility on his part. "Will you stop it, Dolan?" he said harshly. "What is the matter with you?"

"Christ Almighty, sir! Blasting gelatin is strong as hell. Even old blasting gelatin."

Captain Zanin folded his arms. "You're to use what's necessary," he said. "Not all of it, of course. Whatever is needed. How much would that be, for a rather small explosion?"

"How big is that, a small explosion?"

"Something that would, say, disable a small car."

"With somebody in it?"

"Not necessarily."

Jackie sighed and reached into the box. He dug out a huge, untidy handful. It was a waxy, brown dough as moldable as clay, a solution of lower cellulose nitrates in nitroglycerin. He fashioned the mess into a small bar and plumped it several times in his palm.

"That's about a pound and a half, maybe a little more," he said. "That's enough to take any car apart. You could take out a tank with that much."

"How much other damage?"

"It'd blow the center away. The whole thing. Anything else, it'd depend on how close it was to the center."

"If only the amount in your hand was detonated, what would be the range of damage?"

Jackie dropped the bar of explosive back into the box. He wiped his hands on his trousers. "If it popped from right here, right on this table, it'd blow that wall down"—he pointed to the wall opposite the stove—"and the floor would go and the ceiling and the other wall, the one on the alley. The wall on the house next door would get a hard pop, all the bricks would go, probably. That's not counting secondaries, gas mains, fuel oil, and that. All the windows from here to the corner would break. If it wasn't snowing, it would be a hell of a lot worse, the concussion."

"Would anyone survive? Anyone at the, ah, center?"

Jackie thought this over a moment and then said, "No, sir."

"We want no half measures, Dolan."

"What do you mean, sir?"

"I mean we have fifty kilograms. If it's necessary to use more than a handful, then we must use it."

"Sir, I can wire the whole thing if you want me to. But a pound or two will blow the hell out of everything. With it loose like that fifty kilos would . . . well, Jesus . . ."

"All right. Use what's needed but don't feel you have to stint. How does the detonator work?"

Jackie opened the refrigerator and removed a contraption that looked like a clock wrapped in masking tape. From the back protruded a small copper tube. "That's the primer," he said, pointing to the tube. "It's packed with fulminate of mercury. You stick the primer into the gelatin and set the timer. When the timer goes off, the blades inside here release a spring that kicks the plunger into the fulminate of mercury. That detonates the blasting gelatin. . . . It's no problem setting up the charge. The primer'll slip in like a knife cutting soft butter."

"How much time should be allowed?"

"No more than you have to. Two minutes at the most. Longer than that, a lot can go wrong. In weather like this, the timer might freeze up. If you put it in a place that's full of people, somebody might hear it ticking."

Captain Zanin nodded and then turned up the collar of his raincoat. "Have it ready by tomorrow night."

"It's ready now. All you have to do is—"

"Then be ready by ten o'clock Saturday morning. In the meantime do not leave this place on any account. No matter what you might hear from Van Hooff or anyone else, you are not to leave. Is that clear?"

Jackie put the detonator back in the refrigerator. He tried to think of someplace to store the explosives. Then he said, "Could I go around the corner for a sandwich or something, sir? I ain't ate nothing but those hamburgers since . . ."

Captain Zanin thrust his hand into his raincoat pocket and pulled out a hard-boiled egg. "Take this," he said. "It is very nourishing."

Jackie looked at the egg and then at Captain Zanin. "I got to have something else. I can't eat eggs. They make me fart."

"There is no need for crudeness," said Captain Zanin, peeling the egg. "Very well. You may go out. But it would be unwise to stay long. There was some difficulty with your unauthorized action. The police may no longer be completely in the dark."

Jackie's eyes grew wide and his lower lip began to twitch. "You mean they might have made me?" he said with a whimper.

"What does that mean?" Captain Zanin popped the egg in his mouth and flung the shell in the sink.

"They might have identified me?"

Captain Zanin took a moment to chew his egg and swallow it. Then he said, "There's no way of knowing. We don't know whether we're still in control of the police response. They may have learned something from Davis."

"He couldn't have made me," Jackie said in a voice of panic. He shook his head and rubbed his eyes. He shuddered involuntarily. Then he looked at Captain Zanin. His eyes pleaded. "You loan me a five, sir?" he asked forlornly.

"Why?"

"I'm tapped out. You know, broke."

Captain Zanin touched his jaw. He looked as if he were about to say it was out of the question when he shrugged and handed Jackie a five-dollar bill. "Have a bite," he said tersely, "but be quick about it. I can't have you wandering about. We're nearing the delivery hour of this operation. We don't want anyone out of place."

He left the apartment.

Jackie stuffed the five-dollar bill in his pocket and walked into the living room. He picked up the bottle of rye. Only a corner left. He tossed it onto the mattress. He picked up his parka and dug into a pocket. A couple of dollars and some change. He struggled into his parka. It was painful because of his shoulder. He walked to the front door. He cracked it and peeked out. The snow was solid. Captain Zanin could have been across the street and he would not have been visible. Fuck that Jew bastard, he said out loud. He slammed the door and locked it and headed for the nearest subway station. En route he ducked into a pizza parlor for a slice. "Sausage and extra cheese," he said, "and don't leave it in the oven too long."

Nearly two hours later he was in the Bronx. Wearily he made his way from the subway station up a hill and around a corner and into a block that looked ever so much better covered with snow. He trudged into the Cork House and stamped the snow from his feet.

He stepped up to the bar and placed his money in a neat stack in front of him. The place was virtually empty; because of the snow and the fact that it was early afternoon.

"A ball and a beer, Dermot," he called out.

The bartender looked up from the other end of the bar. "Oh, oh, Mr. Jackie Dolan. Back in the old neighborhood, are you, and so soon? Well, it's a pleasure to serve a businessman from the state of California. That's where you wish you were, I'll be bound, in the state of California taking God's sunshine."

He filled a glass of beer and poured a shot of Irish whisky and set them before Jackie. Jackie downed the shot, shoved the glass across the bar for a refill, and gulped some beer. He tossed off the second shot the instant it was set before him and immediately signaled for another. He finished his beer and ordered another glass.

The bartender was launching into a discourse on the Big Snow of 1947 and how this blizzard was nothing by comparison no matter what the eejit on the radio said, when the telephone rang. He smiled apologetically and walked away.

Jackie propped his foot on the brass rail and took an immoderate sip of beer. He was a soldier full of strange oaths. He stared at himself in the mirror behind the bottles. Am I doing my duty? I ask you. Am I? He studied the skin on his face. He saw only particles, chaff, the efflorescence of decay, a fishy anaglyph mocked by inflamed deviations in the sebaceous glands and hair follicles. He had imagined that women were ever kind to a soldier, but he couldn't help wondering whether a woman—other than his wife—would look at this face and be able to see a soldier. He quickly brought matters up to date. I'll let you in on a little secret. It ain't commonly known. I ain't a soldier. I'm a troopie. World of difference. I ain't exactly sure what, but there's a difference. I know from soldiers, I think. Soldiers speak English. Troopies speak gobbledygook. When a troopie speaks English, watch out, he's got something up his sleeve. It's a grave thing to deceive a man who's been chosen; the moment Jackie understood he was being assigned to a secret mission his body tingled with an earnest lyricism, and his notions of soldiering had assumed a new urgency; now he felt deception creeping up. I should've guessed. My kids could've told me. Don't trust a troopie when he ain't speaking gobbledygook. . . .

Remember Colin Kelly? Flew his plane down the smokestack of a Jap ship? Congressional Medal of Honor. He wouldn't've got it if he'd been a troopie. Troopies don't get the Medal of Honor. They get something else. Has a gobbledygook name. They don't give one to a guy named Kelly—or Dolan—that don't speak gobbledygook. No matter how good he done, no matter how many times he done it, if he don't speak gobbledygook, forget it. Lots of Mexicans, Puerto Ricans, they get the Medal of Honor and they can't speak English worth a fuck. They'd give one to a nigger if he deserved it. Niggers can't speak English worth a fuck, either. And you know what? Even the president has to salute a Medal of Honor winner. It's the law, no matter if the guy speaks English or what. Who knows what the law is over there. It's in gobbledygook.

"Set me up again, Dermot, when you got a chance."

It's a funny place to figure. Nothing at all like I thought it'd be. Great if you like scenery. A big switch, though. A very big switch if you grew up like me, right here in this neighborhood. It ain't the slightest bit like Cannon Heights. The locals are too much. Stand-offish cocksuckers, the Boers. The Brits, too, but at least you can halfway understand what the Brits are telling you. Boers and Brits. Hate each other's guts. Gobbledygook's a big part of it. The Brits think it's a shit language. They got a point. It gets to you after a while, the gobbledygook. Why can't the Boers speak English like normal people? English is what I'm used to. It's like white bread. You don't think much about the taste, but if you can't get it, you miss it. The kids speak it like a native, the gobbledygook. I don't know what they're saying. The wife don't know. Why should we? We're just a couple of dumb micks from Cannon Heights. Drive you nuts, kids speaking gobbledygook when you fucking tell them to speak English. Got no idea what it means to speak English, the kids. Got no idea what it means to be Irish, either, or Catholic. Got no idea what it's like to follow their old man into a bar. Scare up some change to come to the Cork House? My kids? No way. I'll tell you this. My kids'd make better troopies than me. Got a grip on the gobbledygook.

Snatches of conversation from one of the booths opposite the bar. Jackie picked up the drift. A book was asking for time to make good on a pay-up. He was short on account of the snow. Five hundred now and the rest Saturday, says the book. Five-fifty now and the rest Saturday, says the player, and the book says okay and thanks and please don't mention it to Mr. McSomething I was late on the pay-up on account of he knows I pay my bills. Jackie thought one of the voices sounded familiar. He glanced over his shoulder. The partition blocked his view. Micks, that's what they sound like. Everybody in Cannon Heights sounds like a mick.

Wonder how come the Irish came here instead of South Africa? Rather dig sewers than dig for gold, I guess. Heads screwed on crooked, the Irish. Always kissing ass. Scream a blue streak one minute and kiss ass the next. The Irish in South Africa are damned near every one of them priests. They kiss a lot of ass. To stay alive. Dead set on bringing the niggers into the schools. I never saw the point. When in Rome, right? You can't be a Catholic in South Africa and get anywhere. I seen that from the start. I'm still polite to them, the priests, out of habit, mostly, but I don't overdo it. What do they expect? I mean, everybody over there thinks Catholics are a piece of shit. How would you like it, have to take heat on account of what your religion was? The priests are out to lunch. This Father Kilgallen caught me one morning at the bus. You're Mr. Dolan from America, I believe. I'm a curate at Saint Somebody-or-other. Delighted to see you. Delighted. And from New York City, I'm told. You're no doubt a Catholic, in this loud mick voice. Every head on line snaps around and stares at me. Jesus, I could feel it. I says to him, me, a Catholic? You got to be kidding, father. I'm indefinite but I'm leaning strongly to Dutch Reformed. So's the wife and kids. He looked at me the way priests look at you when they know you're lying. Everybody seen that, too. I half expected him to say, right there at the bus, I'll be seeing you at Mass. He might just as well've said, you're no doubt a nigger lover. On the bus this guy I worked with, a Boer who ain't ever said two words to me, sits down in the same seat and says—in English—so you're RC, are you, Dolan? He says it like I might just as well confess and take what's coming to me. . . . Confess? Let's see. Bless me, Father, for I have sinned. It's eleven years since my last confession. I committed immodest looks, impure thoughts, all of that. Every day, all day long. No playing around though. Way I look, I'm lucky to have a God damned wife—who wouldn't lead no parades herself. Probably thinks she's lucky to have me. What I've done is kissed ass. That's led to all kinds of other shit—which I ain't about to mention even if you hit me with the "bad confession" crap—but basically I've kissed ass, which is how it started. . . .

"Hello, sucker," said a pleasant voice.

Jackie looked around wildly. He squinted a moment and then his face broke into a hungry smile. "Freddie! Was that you over—" He jerked a thumb in the direction of the booths.

"Big as life," said Freddie. He beamed broadly.

The two brothers embraced and then stepped apart. Jackie asked Freddie how he got the mouse under his eye, and Freddie said a chick hit him with a high-heeled shoe. They smiled and clucked several times and shook their heads.

"I'm on the way out," Freddie said, "and I look over and I says I know that dumb mick from somewhere. What the hell are you doing here? I thought you was in Africa someplace."

"What the hell are you doing here? You're the last guy in the world I thought I'd run into. I mean, in Cannon Heights. Jesus, you scared the shit out of me."

"Dumb mick luck, I guess. I come up here to talk some shit to a guy. He owed me and he wanted to cut down on the pay-up. I give him 'til Saturday. . . . A thousand people I could've seen, but you . . ."

"I mean, what're you doing in New York? I thought you was in California."

"It's dead now, California. Christmas and that. Christmas, everybody leaves California."

"You seen the old man?"

"Nah. You?"

"Nah."

A silence fell between them. They stared at themselves in the mirror. Jackie finished his beer. Freddie rested his elbows on the bar, adjusting them several times. Then he looked back at his brother. "What the hell are you doing here?" he said.

"Last-minute thing," Jackie said with a foolish grin. "You know how it is. You get a break, you take it."

"Dumb mick luck . . . What're you drinking?" Freddie took a hundred-dollar bill from his pocket, snapped it like a shoeshine rag, and placed it Franklin-up on the bar. Jackie stared at it and then raised his hand over his head.

"Hey, Dermot," he shouted. "Give us a drink. This fancy-looking mick asked me to be his guest and I said it's my pleasure."

The bartender advanced from the other end of the bar. As he did Jackie was suddenly overtaken by what he had drunk already. He slouched against the bar, his hair fell across his face, and his eyes slipped out of focus.

"What'll you have, sir?"

"Red Label on the rocks."

"Nah," Jackie said thickly. "Give him a ball and a beer. Like me. Ball and a beer. Don't think nothing of all that money. Just another mick from the neighborhood, this guy. Hey, Dermot, know who this is? This fancy-looking mick with the hundred-dollar bill?"

The bartender's brow lowered. His eyes darted from one man to the other. He forced a tentative smile.

"This my kid brother. He's big shot—"

"You're the gentleman's brother?"

"Freddie Dolan. Been a long time, Dermot."

"Freddie Dolan! Oh, oh, oh! Freddie Dolan! And aren't you the spit and image of your father! A grand man, your father. Yes, yes, yes. Charlie Dolan, the policeman."

"Freddie's hot shit. Makes a pile in California. Big bucks. Hundred bucks nothing to you right, Freddie?"

"It's a grand thing, young people move away and still they drop by for a glass. A grand thing. And it Christmas time. Here's you man, sir. Red Label and ice."

"Have one yourself, Dermot."

"Mustn't. Me stomach. And here's yours, sir. A ball o' malt and a jar. God bless. Look at the two of you. A balm for me old eyes. Two famous businessmen from the state of California, taking their custom in the Cork House."

"Well, Jackie's—"

"Freddie's teaching me the ropes. He's a big deal, Freddie. I'm just learning the ropes. See, Freddie's got a hundred-dollar bill. I got this. I ain't got a hundred-dollar bill."

"Might I ask the nature of your business, sir?"

Freddie lowered his head to his drink. "Investment," he said. "I'm an investment counselor."

"A grand thing, investment. A grand thing. Not atall like the saloon business, I don't suppose. And you must be looking forward to a grand Christmas with your father the policeman. A grand man, your—"

"Invest the hell out of it, don't we Freddie? Out in California there, don't we?"

"Yeah . . . Thanks, Dermot. Here's to a Merry Christmas."

"I appreciate it, sir. And may God grant us a joyous New Year."

"God damned right. Happy fucking New Year."

"You may not have heard," said the bartender, leaning over the bar and addressing Freddie out of the side of his mouth, "but there's a savage at large. A murdering darky. The eejit's blazing away like a Wild West rodeo. The peelers, protectors of the public peace though they are, aren't of the caliber of your father—they don't know how many blue beans make five. Not hampered by the weather, either, he isn't. Terrible effect on the boys. They're scared stiff."

"It's a bitch," said Freddie.

Jackie's face paled. He gulped some beer and at once was seized by a fit of explosive coughing.

The bartender moved away. Presently Jackie caught his breath. Freddie looked at him sideways. "You all right?" he said.

"Yeah. Must've swallowed some beer the wrong way." He sounded not quite so drunk.

Freddie stuck his finger in his drink and splashed it with the ice cubes. "How're Kath and the kids?"

"Fine."

"Where you staying? With her folks?"

"They couldn't make it. It's just me."

"What about Christmas? How long you here for?"

"Few days."

"Where you staying?"

"Here and there. You?"

"You need a place?"

"I look like I need a place?"

Freddie glanced at his brother in the mirror. That face, Christ. Then he said, "What's this shit with Dermot?"

"What shit?"

"California businessmen."

"Oh, that. Dermot must've got it mixed up. I told him you was in business in California."

"What'd you tell him that for?" Freddie asked hotly.

"You are, right?"

Freddie looked into his drink and sighed. "Like I told you. Things're dead right now. How come you think I'm back here? I got a couple of thing's cooking. Friend of mine's working on the financing. Takes time, you know, to get a movie deal lined up."

"How come you told Dermot you was an investment counselor?"

"My business ain't Dermot's business."

"What're you, making porno flicks?"

"You're putting a deal together, you don't blab it all over New York, that's all."

"A movie, Jesus."

Jackie shrugged apologetically. He looked around to see who might have heard them. There were only two other customers. Who would they tell about Freddie's movie, he wondered, Cecil B. DeMille?

Freddie tasted his drink again and then set the glass on the bar with a bang. He inclined his head and gazed at his brother with an indulgent smile. "I got an idea," he said. "Let's get out of here. We'll go to Manhattan, bounce around, hit a few joints. Christ, we ain't seen each other, what is it now, four, five years?"

Jackie looked at his remaining funds. Two bucks and some change. He'd have to stiff Dermot on the tip. No class, not leaving a tip, and it Christmas, too. He thought of Captain Zanin—and Major Espensheid and Lieutenant Van Hooff. If Captain Zanin dropped by the apartment and he wasn't there . . .

"Better not," he said dejectedly. "I got to get going."

"Ah, come on, for Christ's sake," said Freddie. He looked closely at his brother and then added, "Don't worry about the fucking money. Hell, I'm loaded. You know what I'm holding? More than five hundred bucks. Come on. Let's blow it out. You're only here a couple of days, right?" He gave Jackie a playful punch on the right shoulder.

Jackie shuddered. A constricted moan forced itself from his throat. He looked as if he were about to collapse when he managed to catch himself on the bar with his left elbow. Slowly he righted himself with Freddie's help.

"Jesus, what the fuck's wrong with you?" Freddie asked anxiously. He told the bartender to bring Jackie another round.

Jackie gasped for breath. "Shoulder," he muttered. "A little sore is all."

"Thanks, Dermot. Here. Drink it. Best medicine there is."

Jackie bolted the shot and immediately chased it with the entire contents of the beer glass.

"What happened to it, your shoulder? You sure you ain't got heart trouble or something."

Jackie looked a long moment at his brother. Then his eyes widened and his forehead wrinkled and his mouth began to quiver. He looked at his feet and his body began to shake. Then he put his left arm on the bar and buried his face in it.

"You crying, for Christ's sake?"

Jackie snuffled and bobbed his head without lifting it.

"Jesus. Let's sit down. Dermot! We're taking a seat. Bring my drink over, will you. Thanks."

They slid into a booth and seated themselves across from each other at a small table. The bartender brought Freddie's scotch and another ball and beer for Jackie, which he said was on the house. "Good luck, sir," he said. He placed Freddie's thick stack of change and Jackie's thin one on the table and walked away.

Jackie shook his head and wept some more. Gradually, he caught his breath and sipped the whiskey. Some of it slopped onto his parka. "You seen the papers?" he mumbled.

Freddie nodded and grunted affirmatively.

"The thing about the 'Finger of God?' You seen that?"

"I ain't seen it in the papers. It's been on tv. Remember that guy Burns, used to be the old man's partner? He's been on tv. He's ramrodding it. Cops don't know shit."

Jackie stared at his whisky glass. He tilted it this way and that without lifting it from the table, as if he were trying to see how far he could go without spilling any. Then he drank it off and looked at Freddie. His eyes pleaded. "I know who it is," he said pitifully.

"Know who what is?"

"The guy."

"What guy?"

"The 'Finger of God.' "

Freddie frowned intensely. "It's a scum-bag nigger. Everybody knows that. What the fuck do you mean, you know who it is?"

"I know who it is!" Jackie blurted out and fought back tears. He leaned forward and went on in a quieter voice. "I'm telling you, Freddie. I know who the fuck it is. It could cost me . . . knowing who is it, I mean."

Freddie continued to frown. At length he said, "Are you shitting me?"

Jackie shook his head and looked at the table.

"What the fuck?" Freddie snapped. "I mean, what the fuck? You're full of shit, you know that? How would you know who the fuck it is? Tell me that. How the fuck would you know?"

Jackie slowly lifted his eyes. "I know," he said simply.

"Put your dough in your pocket," Freddie said. "We're getting out of here. Cannon Heights is a shit place. You look like you ain't had a meal in days. We're going somewhere. Get something to eat. Have some drinks. Have some laughs. You're full of shit. That's all there is to it."

Jackie stayed put. "I got to talk to the old man," he said.

Freddie slumped back in his chair. "What do you want to talk to him for?" he said with a note of disgust.

"I got to talk to him."

"What the hell good is *he*? He's useless, fucking useless. He done what ma said, you know . . . and walked away from me and you like we'd never been born."

"I got to talk to him," Jackie said fiercely.

Freddie drank some scotch. "So talk to him," he said with a sneer. "You want to talk to the turkey, go ahead. What do you think it'll get you?"

"I don't know. He'll give me a tip on what to do."

"Call Burns, why don't you? Tell him your old man's Charlie Dolan. That'll impress the hell out of him. Tell him you know who the guy is and where to get him."

"You got a number for him?"

"Who? Burns? Why the hell should I—"

"For the old man."

Freddie stared into space. "Yeah," he said after a moment, "I got a number. He ain't there, though. I know for a fact he ain't there. Guy who's been doing some work for me"—he thought a moment of Mr. McManus's wrath if he was unable to repay the loan—"he's been trying to reach him. He ain't around." Suddenly he thought of the men who barged into Mr. McManus's apartment and beat him up; he thought of Mr. McManus's discussion with "Katz" and the enormous scheme that was unfolding; he restrained himself from telling Jackie; he felt the hair bristle on the back of his neck. "Say, Jackie," he said, "where is it you live in Africa?"

"South Africa," Jackie replied complacently. "Place called Alberton."

Freddie touched his bruised eye. "You ever hear of a guy named Espensheid?"

Jackie bolted upright as if he had received an electric shock. He upset his glass of beer. His eyes glistened with panic. "He's my—" He clapped his hand over his mouth.

"He's your what?"

"I heard of him. That's all. I heard of him."

"He the guy?"

Jackie felt the muscles knot in his throat. "Look, Freddie," he said, breathing heavily, "there's a lot to this. It's fucked up six ways from Sunday. If I tell you, what good's it going to do? I need to talk to the old man. He knows how to fix this shit."

Freddie looked a moment at his brother and then made up his mind. Mr. McManus would be impressed, he thought, if he knew how I'm going to handle this. "I think I can track him down, the old man," he said. His voice had a ring of optimism and competence.

"How?" Jackie said helplessly.

Freddie smiled smugly and touched his temple lightly with his forefinger. He did this several times. "If he ain't left town," he said, "he's probably trying like hell. Waiting for the snow to stop. We'll call the airlines. When we find the right one, we'll tell them to change his reservation to next week or next year or something. Then we'll ask what call-back number he give them. Then we'll have him."

"What if they ain't got him down for a ticket?"

"We'll try something else. But I'll bet you twenty bucks he's booked on a flight."

"How come?"

"That's how they found me."

"Who?"

"The shylocks in LA. I owed them and I didn't have it. I told them I didn't know where I was going to get it because I was getting down to the bottom of the barrel and I couldn't go to too many more places to get the money."

"You down by much?"

"Eight yards. It was a Friday and I told them I'd settle up Monday. Most of them said okay but this one guy says it's now or else. I told him I'd meet him at this massage parlor in Hollywood and then I called the airline and made a reservation for Saturday. That's where I fucked up. I get to the airport and they tell me somebody's canceled my reservation. I start to argue and this cocksucker walks up behind me. He says let's talk. He says he knows I'm running on hot plastic and he says he'll tell the ticket guy if I don't settle up on the spot. I give him four bills. Last cent I had on earth. Smart cocksuckers, shylocks."

"How come you think he's on a flight, the old man?"

"Don't rush me," said Freddie, very full of himself. "I'll tell you in a minute. . . . Dermot, give me three bucks worth of change."

Steam hissed in the radiator. It gave the air in the small hotel room a dry, insipid quality. The windows were sealed and could not be raised except with a special device that was used only in emergencies. The hotel was in the West Fifties on Seventh Avenue. It catered to low-budget conventions and touring high school students. In previous years the police had been summoned nightly in response to complaints of beer bottles, water-filled balloons, and other objects being dropped on pedestrians from the upper stories. Once a chemistry teacher from Ohio was dangled stark naked by his heels from the fourteenth floor. Hence the sealed windows. The carpet was dank and springless.

Coombes lay on one of the single beds. His eyes were closed, but he was not asleep. His huge body heaved as he breathed. He tried to relax. Every second or two he forced himself to slacken his jaw and unclench his fists. He had no affinity for contract work, he reflected, no talent for new techniques. Putting an old dog up to new tricks is a desperate thing, like marriage or composing music—neither of which Coombes had a flair for. In any case it was a poor way to pay your debts. He thought of the lawyer. Adley, the glorified bill collector. That was an old technique put to use in a new way. Get a man beyond or almost beyond hope and then wave a lump sum of capital in front of him. Why, he wondered bitterly, had Headlight thought it necessary to have him pushed into a corner before offering help? It was Headlight's notion of control, his way of manipulating an agent. That was Headlight's technique. He had done it in Burma. . . .

He thought of his meeting with Mr. McManus and Nathan Leitstein. He deeply regretted he had not been rough with them. *That* was a technique he had confidence in. Instead he had let them slip away, retreat behind their outlandish jargon—and force him to back into this operation. Backing into things was not Coombes's style.

The telephone rang.

Coombes swung his feet off the bed. Automatically, he reached into his valise. It was unzipped on the other bed. He felt for his Colt Cobra. It was an old habit. Once in Guatemala he had answered the phone in a hotel room and at the very same instant a man with a stocking on his face had kicked in the door and fired a submachine gun at him. The man had missed and fled. Coombes had always been certain that he could have killed the man had he thought first of his own weapon and not the telephone.

He seized the receiver.

"This is Major Hunt," said the voice.

"Who?"

"Major Hunt. I believe you have some lacquerware I might be interested in. Is this Mr. Walker?"

"This is Mr. Walker. Can we discuss the Hintha bird?"

"Yes," said Headlight. They were using an old identification code. Headlight had an extensive collection of lacquered betel-nut canisters. They came from Burma. He particularly prized those with Hintha-bird decorations. "The phone is secure," he added a trifle irritably. "Why didn't you call on this line to start with?"

"The number," said Coombes; his voice was raspy, "I can't find it. Does it matter?"

There was a silence and then Headlight said, "Do you have a hash total?"

Coombes sighed. He hated it when Headlight used computer jargon. He was never quite sure what it meant. "I've had two contacts with McManus," he said. "The second one was with Leitstein, too."

"Well?"

"It pretty much tracks with your summary. McManus and Leitstein are going to bet the money somehow. I don't have it confirmed, but it's obvious."

"How so?"

"Oh, for Christ's sake . . ."

"I mean, what are the indicators? What makes you so sure that's what's going to happen to it? There are any number of things—"

"That's all they talked about, for God's sake. That and making sure they won't be prosecuted. They haven't seen the money, though. That's a problem. I think you'd better get Treasury onto this. Have them watch for unusual currency transfers. In this weather—"

"State's monitoring that. They have been from the first. I think they're wasting their time."

"Why?"

"I think the money's here already."

"But—"

"I saw an FAA thing. State got it. Request to proceed with administrative action against a pilot for a foreign carrier. An El Al charter. Landed night before last at Kennedy. The pilot is military, no civilian flying status. Shlomo Harian. Do you know the name?"

"The high-low-high man?"

"Yes. It's typical of Mossad. A conceit, really, not bothering with cover . . . They imagine they're being tricky, choosing a noncommercial pilot, and then they use the most visible combat pilot they've got. Of course, it's such a small country."

"Where do you think the money is?"

"How should I know? *You're* in New York."

"I'm in the middle of a God damned blizzard. How the—"

"All right. All right. Have you seen anything of BOSS?"

Coombes squeezed the receiver until his knuckles turned white. He bit at a fingernail on his other hand. "No," he snapped. "If they're here, they're folded in with Mossad. Mossad's doing all the work, as far as I can tell. Until today they were watching McManus's apartment house in relays. They had what amounted to a command post in a restaurant around the corner. Twenty-four of them in all. They ate the entire time."

"Any old faces?"

It was the question Coombes had been dreading. Mossad always sent a high-ranking officer to oversee priority-interest operations. They usually did their work in the open, leaving the details to others. Coombes had spotted no one familiar. "No," he said. There was a note of dejection in his voice. "The surveillance phase seemed contained. Fixed schedules, fixed reporting. They didn't use the telephone. A courier came to the restaurant every three hours. A woman."

"What did she look like?"

"A blonde. Young. Thirtyish. Maybe a lot younger. I can't tell anymore."

"Pretty?"

"I suppose so. The thing is, the surveillance merry-go-round has rolled up. The operation is shifting gears, I guess. Mossad will bring up another team. That's their technique. Compartmentalization. No crossover."

"Any ideas?"

"Well, McManus doesn't know *why* they want to bet. Neither does Leitstein. That leaves the only other source I know of. A man named Charlie Dolan. Retired cop. He works for them, odds and ends, police gossip, things like that. But he's dropped out of sight."

"What's so interesting about him?"

"He's the one who prepped Mossad."

"*He's what?*"

"The questions Mossad was asking the agencies. The prep came from this Charlie Dolan."

"How do you know that?"

"McManus saw a profile. It tracked out of the questions Mossad asked the agencies."

"How did he see it?"

"I don't know really. McManus was evasive. All he would say about it was that the man who showed it to him was thorough and well briefed. He didn't know much about gambling, not in a working sense."

"Name?"

"Katz. It can't be genuine, though. The only remarkable thing about him is he points with two fingers."

"*Two fingers?*" Coombes could hear Headlight put his hand over the receiver and say something. This was followed by the sound of muffled laughter. "Now we're getting somewhere," Headlight said when he came back on the line. "The trouble is finding anyone in this weather. There are several directions we can take. As I see it, what we have to do immediately is find this man Dolan."

"In this weather? You must be—"

"It might not be as difficult as you think. If you were in Dolan's place, what would you be doing?"

"Leaving the country. But—"

"Exactly. But he can't do it right away because of the weather. So what we'll do is work the phones. All the airlines and hotels. We'll do it from here. I've got a few extra hands."

Coombes was silent a moment. Then he said, "Why do that?"

"Oh, for God's sake, Coombes. We've been doing it for years. Before Counter Intelligence went down the tubes, they did it all the time. It's basic. Even loan sharks and bill collectors do it. Adley told me."

Sergeant Mazibuko trudged down Broadway. He had been crouching in the elements for two days and two nights. He was on the West Side of Manhattan. In fact he was within walking distance of Mr. McManus's apartment, but he was unaware of it. His sense of where he was had been shattered by the weather. The snow and wind lashed him. He wondered how long he could stay conscious, lacking sleep and being so cold. Every step was painful, an act of will.

Finally he reached his hotel. It was old and cheap—and unquestionably a place where the police regularly asked questions. Most of the guests were black. He had concocted a plan for getting to his room without being noticed. His experience told him he had an even chance of bringing it off.

He was about to push his way through the heavy glass door, when abruptly he stopped. Directly ahead of him, seated in a chair against a column in the middle of the small lobby, looking conspicuously ill at ease under the gaze of two black prostitutes, was Lieutenant Van Hooff.

Sergeant Mazibuko recoiled. He backed away and headed again into the blizzard. He weighed two courses of action. He would wait until he had warmed himself before he decided. Several things were clear. Lieutenant Van Hooff had not seen him. Nor was Lieutenant Van Hooff leaving the fate of Special Branch Detective Sergeant Mazibuko to the local police. No. Lieutenant Van Hooff meant to tend to this problem himself. That had a number of advantages, especially in view of the fact that Sergeant Mazibuko was registered under a false name. A false name known only to him and Lieutenant Van Hooff.

Mr. McManus eased himself out of Nathan Leitstein's limousine. He held on to his hat and walked into the candy store. There was a trace of bounce in his step. He leaned over the counter at the cash register and said, "I want the phone for a while, Leo. Can you put up the sign?"

The candy-store owner dried his hands and walked to the booth. He hung the frayed "Out of Order" sign over the coin slot.

Mr. McManus sat down on a stool at the far end of the counter.

"You dealing the line?" asked the owner.

"Yeah," said Mr. McManus. His voice was clear and firm, without a hint of a crack in it.

A brief, expectant smile lit the owner's face. "Laundry list?" he asked with furtive eagerness.

"Something special," said Mr. McManus. "Different kind of player. Heavy hitter with bells on. He's got enough on him to shake the thing for a while. I'll give you the word when it's time."

"You need change?" The owner had been making change for Mr.

McManus for a long time. He knew to the nickel the cost for the first three minutes of virtually every long-distance in the country.

"No. This is local."

The owner frowned. He was astonished. He was also disturbed. He took great satisfaction in his ability to anticipate Mr. McManus's professional needs—newspapers, cigars, telephone change. It was one thing for Mr. McManus to have a heart attack. It was another thing altogether for him to decline change. Was it a rebuff? Was Mr. McManus telling him he was no longer useful? Was Mr. McManus making a move toward independence without so much as a fare-thee-well?

Mr. McManus smiled. "I know, Leo," he said. "Sounds oddball. It's a new one on me, too. . . . What's doing? Seen anything?"

The owner shrugged. "Remember the egg-cream *nudnik*?"

"The hoople in the black raincoat?"

"Of course, the hoople in the black raincoat. He sticks his head in this morning. Does he spend a thin dime? Hah! He holds the door open until the wind makes a *kasheh* of the newspapers."

"Anything else?"

"Anything else? After that do I need anything else?" The owner walked away. "Is this what I had to live for?" he muttered. "I should have died with the rest of them."

The telephone rang.

Mr. McManus slid off his stool and sat down in the phone booth.

"Mac?" said a female voice.

"Yeah, Lula."

"How you feeling?"

"Great."

"I mean really how you feeling? You always say you're feeling great. Been saying that for fifty years."

"That's how I feel. Great."

"Got your strength back?"

"I ain't doing bad. I been on the go since Monday. Down to one pill a day. I ain't sure I need it, but the doc says take it, so I take it."

"Laying off the cigars?"

"I cut down."

There was a pause. Then Lula said, "You surprised me the other day, Mac. Old woman like me don't need surprises."

"Time I was on my feet."

"I been missing you, Mac. I'm glad you ain't dead."

"I been missing you, too. I'm coming up Saturday."

"Saturday? That's day after tomorrow. You sure you up to it?"

"I hope the hell I am."

"Me, too. I was afraid you'd gone and died without getting my pants down one more time. You ain't going to die before Saturday, are you?"

"Jesus, what kind of a way to talk is that? You ain't no spring chicken. What're you, close to seventy yourself? Did I ask you if you was going to die?"

"I ain't the one had a heart attack."

"Well, God damn it, we'll see who—"

"I'm just teasing. I can't wait to get your thing up between my—"

"Jesus Christ."

"Now, Mac. Don't get yourself all excited. All you'll do is mess up your clothes."

"Will you shut up with that? What the hell's wrong with you, talking like that?"

"Why?"

"Well, Jesus, don't you know by now what—"

"Getting a hard-on, Mac?"

"What do you think?"

"Feel good?"

"Feels damned good. What am I supposed to do with it? I'm too old to be whacking off."

"Where are you?"

"In a phone booth."

"Room in there for both of us?"

"Knock it off, Lula, for Christ's sake. Let's figure the other thing. Give me the dope on Hips."

"Well," she said; the playfulness left her voice, "he's still upset. Real upset. About Ernie. But he ain't dreaming about rats anymore. Said he dreamed last night he had on a new suit with a flower in the buttonhole. You heard how he got back to Philadelphia, didn't you?"

"Yeah. The Navy or somebody took him back in a boat. What about the new suit and the flower?"

"Prosperity. For him, anyway. I don't know about the team."

"Can he go the full game?"

"They're still working on his toe. He'll play, but it ain't no way of telling how long. Except long enough to get what he needs."

"Seventy-four yards?"

"Uh huh."

"You figured a setup?"

"How high can I go?"

"Name it."

"Hundred thousand?"

"Make it two-fifty."

"Two hundred and fifty thousand dollars?"

"And here's for your lungs. Watch the OTB line. Just Philadelphia-New Orleans. Forget the card. When I see you Saturday, I'll tell you which way to hit it."

"Why OTB?"

"Never mind. Just watch it. Send your girl down to watch it for you. Good practice for her."

"What time you coming up?"

"Let's go to the hotel."

"The hotel? Mac, the last time we was in the hotel we didn't leave for three days. Maybe we ought to wait on the hotel."

"I'll see you Saturday. At the hotel. Noon."

"I'm bringing a suitcase this time."

"Good."

He hung up and immediately dialed one of the numbers Katz had given him.

"Providence Precision Grinding," said a male voice. "May I help you?"

"My name's McManus. Katz said you'd be expecting my call."

"Yes, Mr. McManus?" said the voice. It had an Eastern European accent. It reminded Mr. McManus of his mother.

"Yeah, good. First of all, about my money—"

"Yes?"

"Will you stop interrupting? You hooples owe me a total of five hundred thousand dollars. I—"

"One moment, please . . . Yes . . . Yes, that's correct."

Mr. McManus rolled his eyes toward the top of the phone booth. "I want all of it—that's a half million iron men—I want it delivered at noon Saturday to the lobby on the Fifth Avenue side of the Plaza Hotel. I want it in hundreds and fifties, mostly fifties, nothing smaller, nothing larger. Cash. Got that?"

"Yes. You want five hundred thousand dollars in cash—fifty- and one-hundred-dollar notes—delivered at noon Saturday at the Plaza Hotel in the lobby on the Fifth Avenue side."

"Good. Now, about getting down. Here's—"

"Pardon me?"

"Betting."

"Yes."

"Here's how we're playing it. It's Philadelphia-New Orleans. That's the game. Play it ten units a throw. That's two hundred bucks each time a player steps up to a window. Use both the ten- and twenty-dollar windows. They'll think you're judges from out of town. You lay a total of two and a half million. You got something under two hours before the OTB windows close. Here's how you lay it. You take the two and a half million and you put it on the short."

"The short?"

"The short. The underdog. New Orleans, for Christ's sake. You got that?"

No reply. "I said you got that?" Mr. McManus repeated impatiently.

"Excuse me, sir. I think you've made a mistake. I'm looking at a form issued by the Off-Track Betting Corporation. It lists the professional football matches for Sunday. It says the favored team is Philadelphia. In fact it says Philadelphia is favored by ten points. Don't you think it's extremely foolish to—"

"Listen. I don't know who you are or why Katz has you sitting. But you better write down what I just told you. No verbal shit. Write it down. And get the money on the line. Quick!"

There was some confusion at the other end. A hand was held over the receiver. At length another voice came on the line. It was Colonel Garovsky.

"Good afternoon, Mr. McManus. Forgive the—"

"Good afternoon." Mr. McManus shoved his hat back. "Katz, either you're overworked or you're the dumbest son of a bitch I run up on in I can't think when. What're you, insane, letting a hoople like that handle the phone?"

"The person assigned has been delayed. The snow. But you must admit it all sounds rather illogical. I mean—"

"I'll tell you what I admit. I admit you hooples better stop yakking so God damned much and get to work. And you better stop answering back when I'm telling you where to put your dough."

"Please bear with us, Mr. McManus. There's no need to be alarmed. My people are on their way. It shouldn't take them more than an hour and a half. They have the essence of their instructions.

Two and a half million dollars. On New Orleans. Since we are having some difficulty understanding each other, I think you should give me the instructions on the ah, other bet."

"The loser?"

"Yes."

"OK. I'll deal with you on both of them from now on, right? The other hoople, he got it right about my money, didn't he?"

"Yes. The lobby of the Plaza Hotel. Saturday—"

"That's it. Now, on the other bet. It's no sweat. Losing money is simple. You bet another two and a half, same units, same everything, except you put it on Philadelphia."

"To lose we bet on Philadelphia? But Philadelphia is favored by ten points . . . to win."

"Jesus Christ!" Mr. McManus looked out the door of the telephone booth. The candy-store owner was staring at him. He lowered his voice. "You said you wanted to lose, didn't you? So put the two and a half on Philadelphia."

"But—"

"It works like this. Philadelphia couldn't whip the Little Sisters of the Poor by ten points. Not this Sunday."

"Ah. Now I see. Philadelphia will not be able to cover the spread."

"Very good, Katz. Very good. You ever get tired of the spy business, you let me know. I can set you up in costume jewelry. You'd love it."

Nathan Leitstein leaned back in his elevated swivel chair and puffed a cigar. All in all, it had been a gratifying afternoon. He had approved a client's plan to blackmail a United States senator; arranged a series of bribes to local judges; advised against a campaign contribution to a state legislator ("The bum's finished," he had said. "He'll be indicted before the session starts and this time he won't beat it."); informed the president of a motion picture studio that the details had been settled with an off-shore bank for financing a movie; and cautioned the owner of a supermarket chain who was negotiating with a union he represented "not to walk alone at night." All by telephone. A terrific gadget, the telephone.

The telephone rang. He glanced at his watch. The hoople said let it ring four times. So let it ring four times. For what he's paying he's entitled.

. . . Two rings. Three rings. Four.

He lifted the receiver.

"Mr. Leitstein? Major Espensheid here."

"Yeah, Major. I got a fat one for you. Big ass, big tits, strong and healthy. Good as money in the bank. How much you dropping?"

"We've had an extraordinary spot of luck. My chaps were told to bet on the Philadelphia-New Orleans match. They were told to place their money on Philadelphia. Extraordinary, isn't it? Philadelphia is predicted to win by ten points. And my chaps were told to place their money on the Philadelphia side. Extraordinary spot of luck, wouldn't you say?"

Nathan Leitstein tapped the ash of his cigar in an ashtray. "It's extra something," he said. "Extra wide open is what it is. You put that dough on Philadelphia and you know what you'll get? A handful of dead tickets."

Major Espensheid muttered something in a language Nathan Leitstein did not recognize. Then he said in a very cool voice, "What should we do?"

"Well, I'll tell you, Major. That's a good game there, Philadelphia-New Orleans. You got a short at home, and, well, there's a couple of other things. I don't want to worry you with them, but it's a good game, Philadelphia-New Orleans. How much you going for?"

"My chaps have a total of two and a half million dollars."

Nathan Leitstein ran his cigar under his nose and sniffed it. He wondered if this hoople had any idea . . .

"They know the setup? What units they're using and that?"

"I believe they understand the drill. They're to approach the betting windows with wagers of two hundred dollars each and—"

"Okay. I got the picture. What we got to do is shake the line. Remember how I explained you it? So you tell your guys here's the way to go. New Orleans. No fooling around with the chalk. That's Philadelphia. They're the buckshot, and you want to go big, right? So you take the points."

"So we are to bet New Orleans?"

"You got it."

"But New Orleans is the poorer side."

"Believe me, Major, it's worth it."

They dined at a restaurant in an East Side hotel. The placed used to be a simple, matter-of-fact bar and grill, a haunt of the sporting crowd and a refuge from process servers, brightly lit, noisy, and smothered in a thick, stagnant haze of cigar smoke and whiskey; the food had been hotel food. Now it was under new management and had a French name. The bar was dim and quiet. The tables had marble tops and the windows had white curtains that were gathered and sewn at the top.

"What's this say, Burt?" said Mr. McManus. He was studying the "nouvelle cuisine" menu. It was in French.

"It's a lamb chop," said the waiter. He was a holdover from the old days. The new owners had been on the verge of firing him when they noticed that many customers, particularly the older ones, asked for him by name. "They're not bad. Not like they used to be. Not the quality. But not bad."

"That's what I'll have. Medium well. And whatever comes with it."

"Same for me, Burt," said Nathan Leitstein. "And a bottle of beer."

When they were alone, Mr. McManus said, "What'd you say the price was now?"

"Philadelphia by seven and a half. They were slow closing it up, though. Took them 'til just before they shut the doors. Takes them forever to move the line, this OTB."

"They never seen five million balloons in two hours before."

"That's what I mean. What would you do, you seen that much on a ten-point short?"

"They'll get the hang of it, the work they got coming."

Nathan Leitstein swirled the ice in his scotch. "What do you think these hooples are going to do? They're bound to find out this screwing they're trying to give each other is working ass-backwards."

"Who knows? It was me, I'd be damned glad it happened." Mr. McManus sipped his seltzer water. "You thinking what I'm thinking?"

Nathan Leitstein finished his drink and motioned to Burt for another. "A middle?" he said.

Mr. McManus nodded. He looked into his glass and watched the bubbles. He computed the number of ways in which a hundred and fifteen million could be expressed by the sum of two or more consecutive numbers. "Maybe a three-way middle," he said.

"Something tells me it ain't going to get to that. They're too up and down, these hooples."

Over dinner they discussed their holiday plans. Nathan Leitstein said he was flying to California to dispose of his house in Palm Springs, which he had rarely used in the years since his wife died. Mr. McManus said his plans for joining his family in Florida were still tentative.

"You know how it is," Mr. McManus said. "You been laid up for a while, you want to stretch, do some catching up. I'll get down there, sooner or later. Florida's Florida. I want to spend a few days with Lula first."

Nathan Leitstein frowned. "You sure you can handle it?"

"Handle what?"

"Well, I mean, these colored women—"

"Jesus Christ. You and Lula should have a talk, you know that? The both of you think I ain't got enough sense not to hump myself to death."

"It's like roadwork," Nathan Leitstein said shortly. "You think you could do roadwork?"

"Where'd you get the idea humping was like roadwork? Humping is humping. It ain't like playing pinochle, but it ain't roadwork."

"But these colored women—"

"What is this shit about colored women?" Mr. McManus snorted. "You talk like you never spent the night in a Havana whorehouse."

"I never humped a colored." Nathan Leitstein cast his eyes at the table.

"Like hell. Every whore in Havana was colored one way or another."

"Well," Nathan Leitstein said vaguely, "I was a lot younger. So was you. I couldn't do it today."

"Why not?"

"Because I'm damned near seventy-five years old. The same as you."

"Maybe you ought to try."

"Try what? A colored woman?"

"A woman, period."

Nathan Leitstein suddenly looked very tired. And elderly. As if time were drawing his spirit from him, like the tide, and taking with it his boulders and pebbles and cliffs. He tossed back a slug of scotch. "You know, Kid," he said, shaking his head, "I was in Vegas last month. Couldn't stand the idea of Thanksgiving at my daughter's. She's all right, but my son-in-law, he's a pain in the ass. Very big in poultry, my son-in-law. Him and the kids watch television. Dumb shows with the laughs on tape so they won't miss it's funny. So I call Izzy, tell him I'm coming, and I don't want turkey except if it's in a sandwich. He fixes me up, Izzy, with this number. Well, she comes on like a house afire. I say let's catch a couple of shows, play some blackjack. She says later, and right there in the hall she grabs my schlong. Right there in the hall! I no more than get her in the room than she's on her knees, giving me a blow job. Have some champagne, I says. She just looks up and smiles. After that I says I'm taking a bath. I come out of the bathroom and she's standing there with a jar of salad oil. Naked as the palm of your hand and standing there with a jar of salad oil. Must've called down for it. Rubbed it all over the both of us. I never seen anything like it. She done the thing with the string, too. She don't leave me alone. . . . You know what? In the morning I called Izzy. I told him, Izzy. I said the number is going to kill me. Two thousand bucks and I had to call Izzy after one night. . . . She never touched the champagne."

"She colored?"

"Irish. O'Neill her name was. What she really was, though, was twenty-six years old."

Mr. McManus stared across the room and narrowed his eyes. "We'll hold hands, me and Lula, if I ain't up to it," he said. "You been around the block as many times as we have, you like it if it's just holding hands."

Nathan Leitstein looked astonished. "You mean you'd sit around with Lula the same as you sit around with your wife? Watch television and that, you and Lula?"

"I ain't held my wife's hand in thirty years," Mr. McManus said. Then his face brightened. "Maybe I won't go to Florida. Maybe me and Lula'll pack up and go to Puerto Rico. Acapulco, maybe. Throw some of this money away. That's what you ought to do with that extra two-fifty you're getting from Espensheid. Just throw some of it away."

Nathan Leitstein's expression grew pensive. "Do colored women hump the same when they get . . . to be our age?"

Mr. McManus laughed. "No," he said. "Lula, don't anyway. She's slowed down and so have I. But we slowed down at the same speed. When you been together as long as we have, you get used to yourself."

When the dishes were cleared away, Nathan Leitstein ordered an Armagnac.

"Me, too, Burt," said Mr. McManus.

Nathan Leitstein raised an eyebrow but said nothing. If Kid Sweeney thinks he can hump Lula in the shape he's in, who am I to say he shouldn't drink Armagnac. He's free, white, and going on seventy-five.

They sipped their brandy and smoked cigars.

"How do you think OTB is going to handle the pay-up?" said Mr. McManus.

"Pray for a miracle, I guess. Or an accident."

"Time was, you found yourself holding everything on straightening-out day, you did one of two things. You claimed you was robbed or you left town. What the hell's OTB going to do?"

"Try and work a deal. What else?"

The snow had stopped. Friday broke with a burst of
sunlight and a near vernal stillness. Almost at once the thaw began.
Mountains of snow, dense and crunchy the night before, were tugged
down by preternaturally high temperatures; they slid, tentatively at
first, then with spiteful ease, forming vast puddles of gray ooze at
street crossings. Melting ice dripped from everything. Pavements
glistened, inverting the reflections of buildings and causing them to
appear as if they were suspended in the sky.

Mr. McManus handed the doorman a ten-dollar bill. He stood
under the canopy and rocked gently on his toes. He squinted at the
excess of light as it bounced off the dissolving snow in Central Park.

The doorman, wearing knee-high rubber boots, waded into the
street and blew his whistle for a cab.

Mr. McManus was irritated with Freddie. The young punk hadn't
come home last night. Not a word from him, no phone call, nothing.
Probably trying to pick up another bimbo. Let that be a lesson to me,
he said to himself, never lend Freddie another cent. . . . Otherwise,
he was inclined to put the best possible construction on the outcome
of the day. He was full of vigor. His spirits were further enlivened by
the break in the weather. The middle of December, and this could be
the first day of May.

A cab skidded to a halt in front of the building. The doorman had to tell the driver, a smiling, young, out-of-work actor, to back up and pull closer to the curb so Mr. McManus could get in without stepping in the ankle-deep slush.

The ride was wild and jarring. The driver seemed to be making up for the period of restraint that the blizzard had forced on him. He turned corners with wanton sharpness, splattering slush on pedestrians as they waited for the light to change. "Jesus fucking Christ!" Mr. McManus shouted as he was slung from one side of the back seat to the other. Twice they were stalled briefly in traffic; the driver leaned on the horn with a fury, startling a knot of schoolchildren in navy blue blazers and moments later a sleek young man with a tiny dog.

The driver reached his destination and stopped with a jolt a yard or two from the curb. Mr. McManus told him to back up and pull closer. This he did with insouciant recklessness, smiling gleefully. He accepted his tip, which Mr. McManus kept to a minimum, with effusive thanks.

Mr. McManus disappeared into the candy store. The Christmas trees on sale outside the adjoining florist shop were brilliant with melting snow.

He grabbed a number of newspapers, both local and out-of-town, and began tearing through them as he plopped them on the counter. "Cup of tea, Leo!" he shouted, "and some cigars!" He rapidly flipped through one sports section after another, diagnosing the mosaic of statistics, chance comments, and frivolous asides, and absorbing them, universally, individually, and categorically.

"You want the sign?" asked the owner. He delivered the tea and extended the box of cigars.

"No," said Mr. McManus. He stuffed several cigars inside his jacket. He took another one and lit it and added, "You want a trip to Florida, Leo? A trip around the world, maybe?"

The candy-store owner furrowed his brow. Mr. McManus nodded for him to lean closer. The owner propped his elbows on the counter. "Skip the list," Mr. McManus said quietly, "It's Philadelphia-New Orleans. Take the short."

The owner looked puzzled. "New Orleans is a ten-point short," he said.

"Not in the new line, they ain't," said Mr. McManus. "I was on the phone early. It's nine and a half now most places. You know why? They seen last night's OTB price. It's down to seven and a half."

"OTB?" The owner continued to look puzzled. "What do they know, OTB?"

Mr. McManus half smiled. "They know something. Keep an eye on it. Don't touch it, but keep an eye on it."

The owner raised an eyebrow. "Big?"

"Very big."

Mr. McManus drained his cup of tea and stepped into the phone booth.

"Providence Precision Grinding. May I help you?"

Mr. McManus recognized the voice. It was the woman who had duped Freddie Dee. "Hello, doll-face," he said. "How's business? Still in line for the no-clap medal?"

"Who's calling, please?" the woman said coolly.

"Old friend of Freddie's," he said. "You ain't forgot him already? Freddie says you're some piece of work. I didn't get a chance to tell you how glad I was you could stay over. Freddie speaks very highly of you. He's got a thing for foreign ass, Freddie. Says you know more tricks than a sideshow magician. What can I tell you? He's a real swordsman, Freddie. That's what the women say."

There was a pause. Mr. McManus could hear the woman lighting a cigarette. At length she said again, "Who's calling, please?"

"Name's McManus. You remember me. I'm the guy who's learned not to touch wet-paint signs."

"Do you—" Suddenly there was shouting on the other end. It was in a foreign language, which Mr. McManus guessed was Hebrew. The only thing he recognized was the word "Espensheid." It was spoken a number of times with varying degrees of vehemence. At one point one of the voices said in English with a heavy accent, "Espensheid is a hoople and a *shlemiel!*" Then a hand was clapped over the receiver.

Finally another voice came on the line. It was Colonel Garovsky. "There has been a delay," he said. His voice was harsh and tense. "Please call back in an hour."

"Wait a minute, Katz," Mr. McManus replied hurriedly. "You're acting stupid again. You ain't got an hour. You got to get your people out now. OTB opens in forty-five minutes. I want them to put—"

"I repeat," Colonel Garovsky snapped, "there has been a delay. . . . We have encountered difficulties."

"Not with the money?"

"Not exactly. We have just audited yesterday's operation. The money that was to be bet on Philadelphia was mishandled."

"What do you mean?"

"I mean the money that was supposed to be bet on Philadelphia was bet on New Orleans."

"The two and a half you wanted to lose?"

"Of course."

"No shit."

"There are some matters to resolve. You must call back in an hour."

"If you wait an hour to hit the line again, you can fold it up and walk. You got to be ready to pop the minute OTB opens for business. We're talking about closing up a short, Katz, not—"

"It is impossible. Decisions must be made. You must—"

"It's now or forget it. You seen what happened, didn't you? You don't shake the line right now—and hard—the price'll stretch again. We got the line moving. Don't be a hoople and let it go back up."

Colonel Garovsky sighed. He said something in Hebrew. This was greeted by much shouting in the background. Then he came back on the line. "Very well," he said in a tone of acquiescence, "what are our instructions?"

"Now you're making sense," said Mr. McManus. He drew on his cigar and opened the door of the phone booth for ventilation. "Use the same units as yesterday. Ten- and twenty-dollar bets. Two hundred bucks a pop. This time you go a total of five million on New Orleans. Since you ain't having much luck on the other thing, go cheaper on Philadelphia, say, three and a half million."

There was a pause. Then Colonel Garovsky said, "I think we should omit the Philadelphia bet."

"How come?"

"I have reason to believe it won't be placed on Philadelphia."

Mr. McManus smiled and thought of the "separate arrangement" that Nathan Leitstein had worked out with Major Espensheid. Then he said, "How come you think that?"

"I have my reasons."

"Then here's what you do. The money you want to flush, you tell them to put it on New Orleans. If they're switching up on you, they'll drop it on Philadelphia if you give them New Orleans, right?"

Colonel Garovsky thought this over. Presently he said, "It might work. It might just work." The gloom had vanished from his voice. He sounded as if he had thought of the new tactic himself. "Tell me,

Mr. McManus," he went on heartily. "Are you a disciple of 'Raffles' or
of 'Arsene Lupin?' "

"Never heard of them."

Colonel Garovsky laughed. "I mean to say, would you settle down
as a solid citizen—for good—if you could get away with a big enough
haul?"

"For Christ's sake, Katz. Get them hooples of yours on the street.
Next thing I know, you'll be asking me if I'd hit a guy when he's
down."

"I admit it has crossed my mind. I mean, gambling *is* a thing of
forlorn hopes, isn't it? Sudden changes of fortune and so on. The
rules, as I understand them, seem so ill defined that sorting them out
must be at least partly an ethical business. Am I right?"

"If your idea of ethical is a pigeon that don't crap on a statue every
day of the year, then it's ethical. . . . Get them hooples of yours on
the street."

"When might I expect your next call?"

"Two o'clock this afternoon. On the nose. And Katz. Cease fire with
the bullshit, will you? I heard it all before."

He hung up and drank another cup of tea. He walked to the end of
the block to a barbershop. He got a shoeshine and a manicure and
used the toilet. A half hour later he returned to the candy store and
called Nathan Leitstein.

"This Espensheid," said Nathan Leitstein, "I thought he'd have a
hernia. I tell him New Orleans and he says that's what Katz told him
and it must be Philadelphia. Jesus, I thought he'd never get off the
phone."

"But he did it, right?" said Mr. McManus. "He popped the price,
didn't he?"

"I don't know. He can't figure which way is up, Espensheid. I give
it to him straight. He won't shut up. Argues back like a maniac. He
says he knows for a fact Katz is zinging him and if Katz tells his
hooples New Orleans, he just knows his money ought to go on
Philadelphia."

"It's three and a half million out the window if he does. Three and a
half million, that could shove the price up again. Katz dropped five on
New Orleans, that's in the box, but it won't shake the line if there's
three and a half coming back the other way on Philadelphia."

"Up a half, maybe. What the hell? Espensheid's paying for advice.
If he don't take it, fuck him, right?"

"Yeah. It's just I hate like hell to get beat on a fruitcake overlay. Jesus, the price on Philadelphia is so full of air it'd blow away in a strong wind."

"What do you care? You get paid as long as both teams show up, right? They could start my son-in-law the poultry king and you'd still be up half a million balloons."

"I don't feel right about it. If I can't shake a line the right way, I say forget it."

"Forget it? Look; we shook the line and we done it right. It's these other hooples're screwing up. So what? We done it right because that's the way we do business. How they do business is up to them. . . . Listen to me, would you? I sound like a God damned Catholic. What time you getting down again?"

"Two o'clock. If Espensheid fucks up, I'm going to hit Katz with a double come-on."

"Ten million?" Nathan Leitstein sounded doubtful. "What about the tub money, the losing bet? You going ten on that, too?"

"I don't know. I'll wait and see what OTB does with the shot they're getting this morning."

"Okay, Kid. Who said Lana Turner couldn't wear a sweater just to keep warm?"

For a big man, and an ex-cop at that, Charlie Dolan looked strikingly soft. He had thick, gray hair, pomaded back, and coarse, bright skin. Unnaturally deep wrinkles ran from the top of his cheeks to the corners of his mouth. At a distance he gave the impression of a man on his way from a congenial meeting with a poor relation for whom he had been able to do a kindness. Up close he looked like the poor relation. It was his eyes that made the difference. They were prominent and gray and had a glazed quality that hinted of incipient cataracts; they got that way from a lifetime of sycophantic imitation and neglecting to follow up.

At the moment he was enjoying a cup of coffee in a motel room near Kennedy Airport and talking on the telephone. He was dressed in a pair of well-cut polyester slacks and a fresh white shirt, unbuttoned at the neck. He was lying on the bed, two pillows propped behind him, his legs outstretched and crossed. The morning papers lay beside him in an untidy pile.

"I know it sounds a little dopey," he said, shifting the receiver a fraction, "but if Nat Leitstein says play it that way, that's the way to play it. I been with him for years, Nat, and I never seen him screw up. If a line is soft, Nat Leitstein knows just where to hit it."

"I've no doubt of that," said Major Espensheid, "but in this case I'm not certain that Leitstein is aware of all the facts. You see, Garovsky told my men to bet New Orleans. Yesterday they were told to bet on Philadelphia. Garovsky is playing a deep game, I'm afraid."

"I wouldn't worry too much," Charlie said in a tone of unctuous reassurance. "Know what I'm thinking of doing? I'm thinking of putting most of my fifty grand on New Orleans. All of it, maybe."

"Your entire commission? I think that would be most unwise, Mr. Dolan. Especially in view of the fact that—"

"Oh, I wouldn't think of playing it at OTB. Not after you told me what kind of shape OTB'll be in Monday morning. No, I'm going to a regular book. You want me to get a bet down for you, Major? Be more than glad to."

"No, thank you," Major Espensheid said curtly. "Gambling is a pastime for Kaffirs."

"I don't get you."

"No, I expect not. Americans never do."

"Well, thanks anyway, Major. I appreciate the call. I really mean that. Stick with Nat Leitstein's picks. They're solid. People pay through the ass for them. The heavy hitters, they don't drop a nickel without they buy the pick from him and McManus. And they drop a lot of nickels. What time you hearing from him again?"

"The early afternoon."

"You'll be in touch again after you hear from him, right?"

"If you wish."

"I'd appreciate it, Major. I'd certainly appreciate it. It's a pleasure doing business with you. A pleasure."

Major Espensheid grunted and hung up.

Charlie quickly dialed again. After ten minutes of busy signals he got through.

"Yeah, this is Charlie Dolan. Friend of Sheldon's from Massapequa."

"Hold on . . . Yeah?"

"Lennie?"

"Yeah, Charlie?"

"Give me the line for Philadelphia-New Orleans."

"Philadelphia by seven and a half."

"Seven and a half? It was ten last night. What are you, jumping off your own price? I mean, that's two and a half—"

"Seven and a half, Charlie. I'm getting a ton of short action on Philadelphia-New Orleans. So's every book in the country. Seven and a half or sue me."

"Well, Jesus—"

"You playing or what? You're tying up the line. What can I tell you? New Orleans's coming on. Everybody's seen OTB. The fuckers dropped the price to seven and a half last night."

"You getting your line from OTB, for Christ's sake? I never heard of a book—"

"Hell, no. You know what OTB is now?"

"What?"

"Philadelphia by six and a half. Somebody's loading them up on New Orleans . . . Come on, Charlie. I ain't got all day."

"Okay. Give me New Orleans fifty times."

"Fifty times? That's five thousand bucks. You went fifty times yesterday. Where you getting that kind of money?"

"Have I ever stiffed you, Lennie?"

"Okay. New Orleans fifty times."

"I'm on the sheet?"

"You think I keep this shit in my head?"

Click.

Charlie hung up and made a notation of his bets on a small note pad next to the phone. He stuffed it in an airline flight bag that contained his fifty thousand dollars, his commission for briefing the Mossad and BOSS on Mr. McManus and Nathan Leitstein. He walked to the mirror and smoothed his hair. He observed his teeth from several angles. Need cleaning, he thought. Wonder what the dentists are like in . . .

A knock at the door.

He frowned. He thought of his service revolver. He hadn't brought it along. He wanted to attract no attention when he boarded the plane or when he cleared customs at the other end.

"Yeah?" He placed his hands on his hips and continued to frown.

"Laundry," said the voice beyond the door.

Laundry? Charlie stroked his cheek. Did I send anything to be cleaned? I guess I did. Must've forgot. Yesterday was a rowdy-dow from beginning to end. He walked to the door, slid back the chain, and opened it.

There stood his two sons. Jackie, weary with fright, grinned weakly. Freddie scowled, feet planted and arms folded.

Charlie looked startled, glancing first at Jackie and then at Freddie. Then he broke into a qualified, bluff smile that required only one side of his mouth. "Well, I'll be damned," he said. He kept one hand on the doorknob and made no move to admit them. "As I live and breathe. If it ain't the pride of Cannon Heights. What brings the two of you—"

"How you doing, Pa?" Jackie said sheepishly.

"Fine, Jackie," said Charlie, maintaining his bluff smile, "I'm doing fine. Never been better in my life. You're looking great yourself. Best I seen you look in your life. You, too, Freddie. Life's agreeing with you, shows all over your face. . . . Tell you what. I got a couple of things to do. You know, the bank, guy I'm doing some work for and that. Take a few hours. Then we'll—"

"That's too God damned bad," Freddie snarled. He lunged and struck his father in the chest with his forearm. Charlie staggered backward into the room. Freddie charged after him.

Charlie caught his balance and put up his fists. His mouth twisted viciously. "You scummy little fuck," he growled. "I don't know what you come after, but I'll tell you what you're going to get. The stomping you been asking for for years."

Freddie threw up his own fists. His eyes blazed with anger and hatred. Over his shoulder he shouted, "Jackie, get your ass in here and shut the door and lock it!" At once he turned back to Charlie. "You want to try and stomp somebody, you flabby bastard, come ahead!"

Charlie touched his nose with his fist. "Never got it through your head you can't take me, did you?" he said. He smiled maliciously. "Always telling your ma how you're going to bust me open one day after I give her what she deserved. You ain't got what it takes, kid. Never did . . ." Abruptly he shifted his weight and feinted with his head.

Freddie countered and stepped back. Charlie swung, haplessly, and Freddie caught him by the throat of his shirt with his right hand—and with his left he punched him flush in the face.

Charlie sank to the floor. Blood poured from his nose.

There was a towel draped across the back of a chair. Freddie seized it and flung it at his father.

"You're fucking lucky I didn't kill you," Freddie said.

"What'd you hit me for?" Charlie mumbled through the towel.

"Jackie needs a favor. Jackie, your son, remember? He's in town a few days and he needs a favor. Tell what it is, Jackie."

Jackie had seated himself in a chair next to the television set. "You tell him," he said. He held his head in his hands.

Freddie looked at his brother and then at his father. "Jackie's in the shit so deep he had to come to *you* for a favor," he said, his voice rising in rage. "He'd rather eat broken glass than ask you for dick, but he ain't got no choice. He needs help"—he knelt down and put his face less than an inch from Charlie's ear and screamed at the top of his lungs—"and you're going to give it to him! You hear me, you low-life cocksucker? You're going to give it to him or I'm going to stomp your fucking brains out!"

Charlie buried his face in the towel. He held up one hand weakly and waved it. "You're going too fast for me," he said with a muffled whine. "What the fuck's he want, Jackie?"

"Tell him what you want, Jackie."

"You tell him."

"Will you tell him, for Christ's sake? You're the one need's the fucking favor."

Charlie struggled to his feet. He trudged to the bed and sat on the edge. He looked a moment at the bloody towel and then put it back to his nose. "Make up your mind, will you?" he said dismally. "I got to go a couple of places."

"You ain't going nowhere," Freddie snapped. "Not Brazil. Not nowhere."

"What do you mean, I ain't going nowhere?" Charlie shouted. He flung the towel to the floor. "I'm taking a God damned vacation and—"

"I said you ain't going nowhere. That plane ticket of yours, me and Jackie, we canceled it."

"We told them to cancel it," Jackie mumbled from his chair.

"What do you mean, you canceled it?" Charlie shouted indignantly. "Who told you you could cancel my fucking plane ticket?"

"It's canceled," Freddie said. "I called them and said cancel it. They said you want to rebook and I said forget it. I told them a shit-head mick's got no business in fucking Brazil."

"You little prick," Charlie said sullenly. He picked up the towel and held it to his nose.

Freddie stalked over to the bed and snatched the towel from Charlie's face. "What Jackie needs," he said; his teeth were clenched, "is for you to fix something."

Charlie looked up. His prominent eyes shone with astonishment. "He wants *me* to fix something?" he said, pointing to himself. "Why the hell ask *me* to fix something?"

"On account of you're his old man, that's why?"

Charlie shook his head violently. "My God, boy," he said; his voice was shrill, "you're staying with one of the slickest guys in town. Old Man McManus can fix anything. If I was jammed up—and I been jammed up plenty—who do you think I'd go to? McManus, that's who. I'd look him up like that."

"This ain't no Mickey Mouse gambling thing."

Charlie glared a moment at his youngest son and then glanced about the room. At length he said wearily, "Fill me in."

"You know where Jackie's living now, don't you?"

"Middle Village, Corona, in Queens some place."

"No, God damn it!" Freddie screamed. "He ain't lived in Queens in five years! He don't even live in the country! You know he's got another kid? You know you got another grandson, you useless fuck?"

Charlie looked at the floor. He rubbed the back of his neck. "What's the rest of it?" he said without evident interest. "Where's he live now?"

There was a pounding at the door.

Charlie and Freddie looked at it wide-eyed. Jackie managed to lift his head.

The pounding continued.

Charlie and Freddie exchanged nervous glances. Freddie motioned for Charlie to stay where he was. He walked to the door.

"Yeah?" he said, inclining his head.

"I want to see Charlie Dolan," said a gruff voice from the corridor.

Freddie looked frantically from side to side and then said, "There's no Charlie Dolan here. Beat it."

"Is that you, Dolan?" demanded the voice.

"I said we don't know any Charlie Dolan!" Freddie shouted, squaring his shoulders. "Now beat it before I come out and kick your ass!"

"Dolan, I know you're in there! Listen, and listen good! This is the

FBI! We're armed and we have a warrant for your arrest! It's signed by Judge West of the Eastern District! We have shotguns and tear gas! Put your weapons in the middle of the floor! Open the door and file out one at a time! Lock your hands behind your head! If we have to break down this door, anybody who gets hurt is your responsibility! It's up to you!"

Freddie looked at his father. His face constricted in terror. Charlie seized his flight bag full of money, clutched it a second to his chest, and then swung it under the bed. Jackie hauled himself to his feet and rolled open a window and put one leg through it. Charlie grabbed him by the collar and pulled him back. "This is the eighth floor, you fucking idiot," he said in a hoarse whisper.

Freddie gestured wildly at the door. He mimed turning the knob and made a pleading face at his father. Charlie ran his hand through his hair and flicked his tongue at the corner of his mouth. Then he nodded jerkily. Freddie opened the door.

There stood Coombes.

He was in a partial crouch. He held his Colt Cobra, cocked, in his right hand. He drove a knee toward Freddie's groin. Freddie arched his body at the waist and turned a degree to avoid the blow. In a fraction of a second Coombes brought up the foot of his other leg. It caught Freddie squarely in the crotch. He dropped to the floor. He doubled up, groaning, and held himself between the legs with both hands.

Coombes slammed the door behind him. "On the floor!" he shouted at Charlie and Jackie. "Both of you! On your stomachs! Hands stretched above your heads! Move!"

Jackie dived to the floor and spread-eagled himself face down. Charlie hesitated. Coombes leveled the revolver at him. Charlie got to the floor, one knee at a time. He smoothed the front of his shirt before flattening himself. Freddie remained curled up holding his groin. Coombes put a heavy shoe against the small of his back and pressed sharply until he was stretched out like his father and brother.

Swiftly, Coombes patted them down for weapons. He removed their wallets and shook the contents on the floor. He scanned credit cards and drivers' licenses and established which one was Charlie Dolan. Who is Freddie Dolan? he wondered. Jackie had no wallet and not a single item of identification. Coombes seized his hair and twisted his head and pressed the muzzle of the Colt against the base of his skull behind his right ear.

"What's your name?" he snarled.

Jackie looked into Coombes's hooded eyes. He tried to swallow but couldn't. "Jackie Dolan," he gasped. Coombes released his grip and Jackie's head fell to the floor.

Coombes then upended Charlie's suitcase. He found Charlie's passport. He saw that it was stamped with a Brazilian visa. He opened all the drawers. He went through the suits and jackets in the closet and emptied the pockets. He found nothing of interest. He peeked under the bed and dragged out the flight bag. He opened it and dumped the money on the floor. He flung the bag across the room and sat down in the chair where Jackie had slumped before.

"Who are these other Dolans, Charlie?" said Coombes. He took the silencer from his pocket and attached it to the muzzle of the revolver.

"My sons."

"Whose money is that and where did it come from?" He cocked the revolver. The three men on the floor gave a start at the sound. "Charlie, is that your money?"

Charlie lifted his chin. He grasped the carpet for support. "You ain't FBI, are you?"

"No," Coombes said, training the Colt at Charlie's face. "But I'm close enough. Where did you get that money?"

"What's it to you?"

Abruptly Coombes leaned forward. He held the Colt straight ahead and aimed at a point in the middle of Charlie's forehead. Charlie ducked his face to the floor.

"You're in over your head," Coombes said fiercely. "I know where you got the money. I know you got it from Mossad or you got it from BOSS. Or both. What I want from you are some simple, direct answers."

"Like what?" Charlie said, pressing his head against the floor.

"Like what Mossad's interest is in a history of McManus and Leitstein."

"I don't know."

Coombes sighed angrily. "I'm in a hurry, Charlie," he said. "I'll put a bullet in your head if you don't give me some straight answers. . . . Now!"

Charlie reared his head. "Can I sit up?"

"No! Start talking!"

"All right. All right. Be careful with that thing, will you?

Jesus . . . To start with, it's the truth I don't know why they wanted all that stuff. What they asked me was—"

"Why do you think they wanted it?"

"It's something to do with gambling."

"What?"

"They want to bet money at OTB," Charlie replied hastily. "McManus and Leitstein are the best in the business. They figured McManus and Leitstein could show them how to get a lock on a price."

"OTB? That's the public betting outfit, isn't it? How much are they betting?"

"I don't know."

"How much, God damn it?" Coombes screamed.

"A hundred and fifteen million bucks." It was Freddie. He moaned and curled up again and held his groin.

"How do you know that?" Coombes snapped.

"I heard Mr. McManus and a guy," said Freddie, uttering little cries of pain. "They was talking about it."

"Who was he?"

"A jerk named Katz."

Coombes's hooded eyes widened with perplexity. "Does he have a habit of pointing with two fingers?"

"Yeah," said Freddie, groaning softly. "The jerk."

Suddenly Charlie rolled over onto his back. His arms flopped. "Let it go, Freddie," he said in a tone of resignation. Then he continued. "This Katz. That ain't his name. His name's Garovsky. He's running the thing. Him and a South African."

A sound of pain and boiling rage filled the room. It was a noise of the sort heard on hospital wards when an accident victim learns he had lost a limb or when a cancer patient hears that his therapy has proved futile. It was the sound of a man pleading for time to back up and for God to redesign the map of chance.

It was Jackie.

He uncoiled from the floor. His thin shoulders were curved forward. His arms swung at his side. He sprang and crashed onto the prostrate body of his father, flailing him with both fists.

"I'm the 'Finger of God,' Pa!" he cried as tears of fear and anger flooded down his mottled face. He pounded and pounded, and Charlie drew his arms across his face and tried to struggle free. "I'm the 'Finger of God,' Pa, and you got to help me! You got to help me!"

Coombes leaped from his chair. He seized Jackie by the hair and sent him sprawling. Jackie pulled himself into a sitting position. He doubled his knees under his chin and continued to weep.

Coombes quickly surveyed the situation. He saw that neither of the others was disposed or in condition to cause him trouble. He walked to the bathroom and returned with a glass of water for Jackie. Charlie was duck-walking about the room gathering his money. Freddie had managed to get to his feet. He was leaning against a wall.

"We'll start with you," Coombes said to Jackie. He returned to his chair. He gripped the Colt tightly. "I want names, dates, and details. Don't fuck around. You hold back anything and I'll pick up that telephone and call the police."

Jackie gradually stopped crying. He regained his breath and sipped some water. He looked at Charlie, and then at Freddie, and then at Coombes. He squeezed a pimple and began. He laboriously recounted, step by step, the past three months—from the moment Major Espensheid had delivered him to Captain Zanin at the Grootfontein airstrip to his chance meeting with Freddie the day before in the Cork House. It took a good deal of time. Coombes interrupted frequently, questioning him on such points as how he had entered the country, how much advance notice he was given before an "elephant gun" action, the reaction of Captain Zanin to the unscheduled attempt on Snakehips Davis.

"What's the target of the bomb you built?" Coombes asked. He sounded a bit distracted. He was afraid he wouldn't be able to remember all he had heard.

"I ain't got any idea," Jackie said. "I ain't sticking around to find out either. I'm through with the whole fucking thing. South Africa, everything. That's how come I want Pa to fix it for me."

Charlie massaged his temples. He was again seated on the edge of the bed. "You want me to fix *this*?"

"What can I do, Pa?" he begged.

"Do?" Charlie pulled a face. "You better find Espensheid. Tell him you want to get back to your wife and kids. You better—"

"Thanks a lot, you toilet," Freddie broke in sourly. "I told Jackie you was useless. I told him." He turned to Coombes. "Can we go now, me and Jackie?"

Coombes nodded. Freddie walked stiffly across the room.

"What's your next move, son?" said Charlie.

"What the fuck do you care?" said Jackie, joining his brother at the door. "You're a scumbag, you know that? You're the same kind of old man that you was a cop. A scumbag."

He and Freddie left the room.

Charlie looked at the floor. His nose was bleeding slightly again. He found the towel and held it to his face. "You want to tip the cops?" he said. "I know the guy who's honchoing the case. Used to be my partner."

Coombes hated Charlie Dolan. He knew he could kill him and the police would never be able to put the case together. For one thing his Colt Cobra wasn't registered in the Federal Supply Control System. For another . . .

"Why do Mossad and BOSS want to bet the money at OTB?" he asked. He felt his body shake with anger.

"You got me, mister."

Coombes stood up. He leveled the revolver and fired a muted shot that struck the mattress a few inches from where Charlie was sitting. The smell of gunpowder filled the room.

"Are you crazy?" Charlie cried. "I mean, are you some kind of fucking yo-yo? Jesus Christ! What the fuck—"

"Shut up, Dolan! Why are they betting that money at OTB?"

"Oh, Jesus." Charlie was breathing heavily and his mouth was quivering. "They want to break it," he blurted. "They want to break OTB. They want to run it into the fucking sidewalk!"

"Why?"

"How the hell do I know? They didn't tell me. I didn't ask. Garovsky, he looks me up five, six months ago. Why he comes to me, I don't know. He says he knows I work for Nat Leitstein. He also says he knows I took a fall for him and McManus and I know from wiretaps and that. He knows I done a lot of illegal shit. He asks me if McManus and Leitstein can tell him how to break OTB. I says, if anybody can it's McManus and Leitstein. That's all he said about it and that's all I told him. I swear to God, that's all."

"What happens if they break OTB?"

"What're you asking me for? Ask OTB. If it was a book that stiffed you, you'd lean on him 'til he paid off. OTB ain't a book. I don't know what happens, they don't pay off. It's never happened before."

Coombes removed the silencer from the Colt and slid the revolver into its holster under his left arm. "What about Espensheid?"

"He set Jackie up, I guess. Hey, that what Jackie said, that 'elephant gun' business, I didn't have no idea. I swear to God I—"

"What else?"

"What else what?"

Coombes glared at him.

Charlie nodded vigorously. "Yeah, right. Well, this Espensheid, I don't know exactly what he's doing. I only seen him a couple of times. He's—"

"When was the last time you saw him?"

"Two days ago. I didn't see him. We talked on the phone."

"And?"

"He says could Nat Leitstein figure a way for him to bet the money without the Jews—that's Israel—without them finding out about it."

"What did you tell him?"

"I said Leitstein's almost as good as McManus. You can't tell the difference, really. That's what I told him. He give me a break, Espensheid. He's telling me how Leitstein's playing the line. They're betting Philadelphia-New Orleans. Did you know that?"

Coombes bit a fingernail. "Do you know what they're going to do to Jackie?"

Charlie shook his head. He stood up and walked to the window. "He turned out rotten, Jackie. Him and his brother both. They're bums, the two of them. Broke their mother's heart. I give them everything I could and look at them. Rotten. You never saw a pair of kids had more than they did . . . and look at them."

Coombes did not hear him. He had stormed from the room and left the motel. He squinted in the cool, brilliant sunlight and hailed a cab.

Detective Second Grade Tedesco eased the car into a small street in Flushing. The sun cast dazzling light on the melting snow—which had turned the street into a treacherous sea. The slush rose to the hubcaps. Tedesco knew this part of Queens well. He had been born here. Lived in that house on the left until the folks moved to Corona. Played stickball on this very street. Got his first hand job in that alley over there. Sandra Ricciardi. Silky Sandra. Married a guy owns a shoe store in Merrick. Got five kids and looks like she swallowed a set of dishes.

He pulled up as close as possible to the curb in front of a small house whose stoop was reticulated with white grillwork. It looked like every other house on the block. A man about his own age stood stiffly on the sidewalk. He wore a suburban jacket. His eyes were set in dark, bulgy pouches. He slid in next to Tedesco and lit a cigarette and sucked it twitchily.

"How you feeling, Artie?" said Tedesco as he drove away. "Great looking day, huh?" He switched on the radio. A hit song, jumpy and loud, blared through the car.

Artie cupped his hands around his cigarette and lowered his mouth to it. He seemed the kind of man for whom one phase of the climate was much like the next. "To tell you the truth," he said, "my nerves are a little out of commission. Could you turn that down a little? Off would be better."

"Sure," said Tedesco. He switched off the radio.

"Thanks. Gets to you sometimes, the radio."

Minutes later they wheeled onto the Grand Central Parkway. At once they were stuck solidly in traffic.

"It's like this all over," Tedesco said. "The fucking snow, you know . . . You called the place, didn't you, let them know you'd be late? I mean on account of the snow and all. Did you—"

"Jesus Christ!" Artie shouted. His face grew taut. He slammed his fist against the dashboard. "Are you going to start in on me, too? Linda, she starts in first thing. Then her ma. The both of them. Why don't you call, Linda says, let them know you might be a little late. I'm drinking coffee, reading the God damned paper, and she starts with this shit. And her ma. That cunt. She comes down. 'Arthur, don't you think you ought to call the clinic?' I mean, *shit*! How much of this am I supposed to fucking take?"

Tedesco said nothing. He knew Artie was having a rough time. Which was in no way the fault of his wife or mother-in-law. Artie was an alcoholic. He was also a cop. He and Tedesco had been childhood friends and had graduated in the same class from the police academy. At the moment Artie was on the "bow and arrow squad." This meant he was assigned to clerical duty and not permitted to carry his service revolver. Artie was a mounted patrolman. Two months ago he had ridden his horse, a gelding named Hugo, to the Penn Central freight yards at the foot of West Sixtieth Street. He had coaxed Hugo into an empty boxcar, climbed in himself, and then proceeded to polish off a fifth of vodka. He came to when he heard Hugo neighing and he felt something under him move. He scrambled to his feet and looked out. He was in Poughkeepsie, eighty-five miles away. A van was dispatched to return Artie and Hugo to New York. Only the vigorous intercession of the local city councilman, a family friend, averted Artie's dismissal from the department. A condition of his continued service was that he attend weekly therapy sessions at an alcoholic rehabilitation clinic. At the request of Artie's wife Tedesco agreed to drive Artie to the clinic every Friday and then to drive him back home.

"The thing with this clinic," said Artie, a fraction more composed, "is it's no booze. I mean, *no booze*. When I first went in, you know what I was hoping? I was hoping they'd show me how to cut down. That's what I was really hoping. I figured they'd show me how to get it under control—the booze, you know, how to lay off the stuff on the job and like that, how to have a few and then stop before you get shit faced. Just keep it under control so you don't fuck up. This clinic, they don't tell you how to cut down."

"Maybe it's a good idea to quit," Tedesco said. "Everything else, it just piles up on you when you're hitting the sauce, right?"

"For some reason or other," Artie said, tossing his cigarette out the window, "I always want to drink everything in the gin mill. I quit two other times, you know, but the time before was the longest. Year, year and a half. And I just got disgusted, you know. I was boning up for the sergeants' exam and I just got disgusted. I walked out of the house and I poured as much down my throat as I could get my hands on. Linda was pretty sore."

Tedesco wanted to change the subject. "We thought we had a break in the case," he said. "It ain't turned out to be much."

"Oh, yeah?" Artie said, trying to sound interested. "What was it?"

"We found the rifle."

"Hey, that's something, right?"

"It looked like it at first. I mean, you find the weapon, you're in business, right? This thing is off the wall, though. It's a cannon and it's fifty years old. The nut was using homemade cartridges, so we're out in the rain on finding him that way."

"So what're you doing?"

"Burns is going to release it this afternoon. Press conference. Watch the news tonight, Artie. I'm going to be on television. Burns wants me to describe the nomenclature."

"How come he's releasing it, Burns?"

"He's getting heat. He ain't clearing the case and he's getting heat.

He shows this cannon on television, it looks good, you know, like we're closing in or some fucking thing. It don't mean shit, but it looks good. Takes the heat off for a few days."

Presently they turned off and made their way along a slush-filled side street. They turned onto Roosevelt Avenue in Jackson Heights and drove under the elevated train tracks. A few minutes later, Tedesco backed into a recently cleared parking space.

Artie was tense again. "Here it goes," he said. "For one solid hour I got to admit I'm powerless over drinking and my life is unmanageable. A solid fucking hour. I also got to admit I'm entirely ready to have the defects in my character removed."

"See you in an hour," Tedesco said. "I got to get a couple of bets down. Burns is going twenty bucks. Philadelphia. He was going to take New Orleans 'til they moved the line. I'm taking Philadelphia, too."

"Betting football is one of the few problems I don't have," said Artie.

They parted in the narrow, dingy concourse of an irregularly shaped building. The door to the alcoholic rehabilitation clinic was on one side. An Off-Track Betting Corporation parlor was on the other. Downstairs was a subway station.

The OTB parlor was a complexity of converging, impervious bodies; men and women; reticent and anxious; pensioners, housewives, shop clerks, general idlers; chalk monsters sticking with favorites, spot players getting down mostly out of curiosity, compulsive gamblers constantly in need of money; some extravagant, some feebly pretentious, some corrupt in taste, some not memorable in the least; all in one state or other of expectation, dreaming of power. The light was faded yellow. The floor was pulpy—betting slips, old newspapers, and losing horse-race tickets emulsified in tracked-in slush. Layers of tobacco smoke like a mackerel sky hung in the air.

Activity was focused on the football windows. Lines were shifting and deep. Most of the bettors clutched tip sheets, "newsletters," and other printed matter containing information on the weekend's professional football games. The ten-dollar and twenty-dollar windows had unusually long lines.

Tedesco took in the scene. He was bombarded by sounds of hope and fear, envy and jealousy.

"I seen a car from Louisiana. I'm taking New Orleans."

"I'm going to have to face up to my wife. She got a phone call. I'm late with the finance company."

"What do you mean, what am I playing with? I claimed a back injury. I got four hundred bucks."

"How come you didn't tell me that last week? I got checks bouncing all over the place."

He saw the security door open. A cashier emerged. The man had a driven, persecuted look. He elbowed his way through the eddying mass as if he were escaping from a fire.

"Hey, Ralph," Tedesco called out. He had known Ralph for years. Ralph was from the neighborhood.

Ralph stopped. His expression changed briefly to a faint smile. "Hello, buddy," he said. "You think you're in a tough line of work? Look at this zoo."

"How's it going, Ralph? Heavy action, huh?"

"Heavy? You don't know from heavy. All you got to do is fight crime. I got to work the twenty-dollar windows."

"The twenty-dollar windows? That's work? I thought the twenty-dollar windows was the milk run for you guys."

"Oh, yeah? Well, you thought wrong. We're getting more twenty-dollar action than I ever seen. See that bunch?" Ralph pointed to a line thirty deep at the window he normally worked; his lunch-hour replacement was accepting bets. "Every one of them's going two hundred bucks apiece. Same down at the ten-dollar windows. Crazy, every one of them, crazy as bedbugs. Know who they're taking? New Orleans. They don't speak much English and you have to explain the fucker to them every time they place a bet. And they keep throwing it in there like there's no tomorrow. They was in here late yesterday, too, some of them, it snowing like hell, and they're screaming for New Orleans . . . I don't know what it is with this New Orleans."

"What do you mean?"

"We're getting more action on New Orleans than you can imagine. More than anybody can imagine. I mean, in two hours yesterday we got five million on New Orleans. *Five million dollars.* It's coming in again today . . . New Orleans. New Orleans. Jesus."

"I'm putting twenty on Philadelphia. For my boss. The guy that's been on television. How does that sound? Good bet?"

Ralph glanced from side to side and then lowered his voice, "Give it another fifteen minutes. We're adjusting the line again. The supervisor got the call just as I was walking out."

They both looked at the computerized flashboard above the betting windows. It displayed a schedule of all of Sunday's National Football League games. Alongside each game was the name of the favored team. Next to the entry, "Philadelphia-New Orleans," was the listing, "Philadelphia 6½-point favorite."

"The new line," Tedesco said out of the side of his mouth. "What's it look like?"

"Philadelphia by five."

"Down a point and a half? Christ, Ralph—"

"They should've dropped it to four, you ask me. We're getting hit hard again. Real hard. The supervisor checked the computer a little while ago. We seen close to four million on New Orleans this morning already."

"What do you think, Ralph? Should I lay the points or what?"

"It's your boss's money, ain't it? He wants to lay the points, he should get what he wants, right?"

"I guess so, but I want to get down, too. Twenty bucks, maybe. It look good, this New Orleans thing?"

"How the hell do I know? I'll never understand gambling, not if I work here fifty years. All I know is somebody's going ape-shit over New Orleans. . . . I'll see you later. It's my lunch hour. I want to read the paper. Maybe they'll have something about another plane landing in the blizzard, the Brooklyn Bridge breaking in two, you know, something simple."

Tedesco took his place at the rear of the line at a twenty-dollar window. The players ahead of him were speaking a language he did not recognize. They all seemed to know each other. Each carried an airline flight bag on his shoulder. They were soon joined by others, who fell in behind Tedesco. Each time one of them stepped up to the window, the cashier had to explain in detail how the betting was accomplished. Every one of them put two hundred dollars on New Orleans to win. Tedesco gazed at the flashboard. He guessed that the point spread would drop by the time he reached the window. He was right. As the man ahead of him announced in awkward English that he wished to bet two hundred dollars on New Orleans, the flashboard blinked. A second later, the listing next to Philadelphia-New Orleans read, "Philadelphia 5-point favorite."

Suddenly there was an outburst of savage screaming at the entrance. Tedesco glanced over his shoulder. So did the men behind him. He could see nothing. The raft of humanity blocked his view.

Presently the screaming drew closer—and it was apparent who the screamer was.

It was Artie. His hollow-eyes, contorted face was less than a foot from the ear of a woman. She was wearing a trench coat and a scarf and carrying a flight bag. Her face was cast resolutely at the floor as she dodged her way through the parlor. She was approaching the twenty-dollar window.

"Who the fuck do you think you are, you cunt?" Artie bellowed. He was dogging the woman in the fashion of a baseball player arguing with an umpire. Each time the woman averted her head to give the impression that his fury would get him nowhere, Artie did a frenzied two-step across her path and launched afresh into her other ear. "Answer me, God damn it! Who the fuck do you think you are? I'll break your fucking jaw, you don't answer me!"

Tedesco looked quickly at the digital wall-clock. If I lose my place on line, he thought, I'll be here another hour and late for work. On the other hand . . .

"Do you think I'm just a piece of shit, you fucking cunt?" Artie roared. "Do you? Who the fuck do you think you are? You think you can shove people this way and that? You think you can shove *me*, you cunt?"

Tedesco detached himself from the line. He noticed that several of the men behind him broke away at the same instant. He breasted the crowd, struggling to get to Artie before real trouble started.

"Artie! Artie! Artie!" he shouted. "How come you ain't upstairs, for Christ's sake? What're you, stupid? Get upstairs!"

Artie was arched forward from the waist, screaming in the woman's face. His body was between Tedesco and the woman, blocking her progress. He shot a glance over his shoulder at Tedesco—his eyes were afire—and then turned back to the woman. "I'm trying to buy a fucking paper and this cunt pops me in the fucking ribs and says she's in a hurry! She wants cigarettes and she pops me in the fucking ribs like I'm a piece of shit!"

Tedesco placed a firm hand on Artie's shoulder. Artie jerked free. "Don't fuck with me, Teddy!" he screamed. "I want this cunt to answer me!"

As Artie pulled away Tedesco could see the woman's face. It was delicate, with wide, round eyes and high cheekbones. He was about to apologize for Artie when he realized who she was. His mouth dropped open.

Tedesco shoved Artie ferociously aside. "It's you!" he shouted. "You're Meyers! You called Schmidt. You made the nut at Lexington and—"

"I was upstairs, Teddy," Artie broke in, his voice suddenly plaintive, "but I was late for the session. I'm in trouble on account of I didn't call. I should've called, but Linda jumped my ass and then her ma. So I come down, you know, and this cunt . . ."

Tedesco was aware of being jostled. He saw the men who had been in the betting line behind him form a rank in front of the woman—who spun around and began to walk hastily toward the exit.

"Stop her!" Tedesco shouted. "That woman with the bag! Stop her!" He started to run when his feet went out from under him. He had been tripped. He broke his fall and rolled over. He saw the other men with the flight bags running after the woman. "Artie! Grab that woman!"

Artie snapped back to life. He dashed off in pursuit. He sent a number of people sprawling.

Two uniformed policemen, both beefy men, burst in the door. They had been summoned by the management to deal with Artie. They glanced about warily. Cries of "That's him! That's him!" went up.

Patrons who had been knocked to the floor shook their fingers at Artie.

The two policemen spotted what was bearing down on them: the woman in the trench coat, the other men from the twenty-dollar line, and Artie. They exchanged perplexed looks and simultaneously drew their service revolvers.

Bettors retreated to the walls. Those at the two-dollar horse windows dropped to the floor.

Across the room Tedesco scrambled to his feet, waving his gold detective's shield over his head.

"Hold it!" ordered one of the policemen. He raised his left palm and leveled his pistol. "That's far enough! What's going on?"

The woman, the other men, and Artie, pulled op to a dead halt.

A clamor arose, the crowd was animated and snarling.

The woman complained she had been assaulted by Artie. The other men accused Artie of trying to rob them. Artie shouted that he was a policeman and was trying to apprehend the woman.

Other bettors joined in. Shoving matches broke out. More

policemen arrived. The shoving grew more violent. Blows were swapped.

Tedesco shouldered his way to the center of the confusion. The woman was trying to squeeze past one of the policemen blocking the door. He seized the woman by the arm and flashed his detective's shield as another policeman was about to lower a nightstick onto his head.

"I want her!" Tedesco shouted. The woman squirmed and brought up an elbow behind her. Tedesco felt it graze his ribs. He recognized it as a practiced, professional attempt; judo, karate, one of those. He slammed the woman in the kidney with the heel of his palm. She sagged but kept her feet.

"That guy over there!" Tedesco shouted to the policeman. He retained his grip on the woman's arm. He pointed with his other hand at Artie. Artie was arguing vehemently with another policeman. "That guy!" Tedesco repeated. "The one in the jacket! He's a—" He didn't trouble to finish his sentence. He saw Artie go down. A nightstick struck him from the rear. It landed on the tender spot between his neck and shoulder.

Unnoticed in the tumult, the men who had stood behind Tedesco in the twenty-dollar line slipped out the door and vanished.

Tedesco dragged the woman into the dingy concourse. It was teeming with curiosity seekers. They watched silently as he slipped her flight bag onto his shoulder and handcuffed her hands behind her.

More policemen arrived. They ran toward the entrance of the OTB parlor. They held their jouncing revolvers to their hips. Tedesco stopped one of them. He told him to return to his radio car and signal the Special Homicide Task Force that he was bringing in "Meyers."

He marched the woman to his car. He hustled her through a rippling pool of slush into the passenger seat. He tossed the flight bag into the back seat. He yanked off her fur-lined boots. He pulled another pair of handcuffs from the glove compartment. He snapped them on her ankles.

They drove toward the Queensboro Bridge. Overhead were elevated subway tracks. Periodically chunks of snow dislodged above and splattered on the hood. Tedesco glanced at himself. His suit was blotched and wet from his tumble on the OTB parlor floor. Ruined probably, he thought with disgust.

He inclined his head toward the woman, keeping his eyes on the roadway. Traffic was dense and crawling. "You want to tell me what you're up to?" he asked. He forced himself to sound casual. He restrained himself from reaching over and backhanding her across the mouth.

"I want to know why I am being treated this way," she snapped. She looked grim. "I am an Australian citizen. I demand to know why I am being mistreated."

Tedesco sighed. A few moments later he said, "Your feet cold?"

The woman said nothing. Tedesco shrugged. He switched on the heater. "There," he said. "Your feet'll be warm as toast in no time."

They crept onto the approach to the bridge to Manhattan. Tedesco tried again. "I don't know Australia," he said. "Where do you live? In Australia, I mean?"

The woman snorted. "I am a child psychologist in Sydney. I am on holiday."

"Enjoying New York? Taking in some shows and that?"

"Until today I was enjoying it thoroughly. The tales of the rudeness of New York, I did not believe them. The tales of the brutal methods of the police, I did not believe those, either. Until today. Now I believe all the tales." She snapped her head toward Tedesco. She glared at him. "You are a beast. I will make difficulty for you. Much difficulty."

They were in the center of the bridge. Traffic came to a halt. "You know, you don't sound like an Australian," Tedesco said. "I thought all Australians talked like, what's her name, the tennis player. You don't sound nothing like her. What kind of accent's that?"

The woman shifted in her seat. "These manacles are becoming painful," she said. She peered primly down her nose. "Would you be kind enough to loosen them?"

"Can't," he said, "Not and drive at the same time. Just relax. We'll be there in a few minutes . . . ah, I didn't get your name."

"I'm called Leslie Hammond," she replied. There was a note of anxiety in her voice. "I'm in New York on holiday, you see. When that man accosted me in the football office, I became frightened. Don't you see? I became frightened. Well, I ask you, who wouldn't have? A visitor in a foreign country is approached in the most awful way. Naturally she becomes frightened. Don't you see?"

"Where you staying, Leslie?"

"With friends."

"Where do they live, your friends?"

"Oh, must they be dragged into this? It's most embarrassing."

"Be a good idea to tell me. We'll send somebody around, tell them not to worry."

She dropped her chin to her chest. "This is a dreadful mistake. Dreadful. Will I be detained?"

"Just relax, Leslie. Not a thing to worry about. Not a thing. We got a few questions for you. That's all. Nothing much. Just a few routine questions."

"Can't I answer them now?" she asked fretfully. "You can't imagine how awkward this is."

"Where'd you get that accent?" Tedesco asked sharply.

The woman looked at him. "It's all mash, mate," she said out of the side of her mouth. "I've 'ad nothing but duck's dinner for days and I want to make me marbles good. . . . Don't you want to get among it, copper?" She smiled brightly. "There. That sounds like a good Australian, doesn't it?"

Tedesco shook his head and frowned. "What the hell does it mean?" he said.

"It simply means this is a lot of nonsense. I've missed a few meals and I'd like to improve my condition." She slowly turned her head toward him. She ran her tongue along her upper lip. "I also asked if you'd like to go to bed with me."

Tedesco looked startled. He wondered whether the woman could give a blow job with her hands locked behind her back. Probably not. Should I uncuff her? The key's in my left pocket. No, the right . . . He was jolted back to reality by the blaring of horns behind him. The car ahead of him was nearly fifty yards along the bridge. He stepped on the accelerator. The car lurched forward.

They drove off the bridge and turned onto a crosstown street. "I meant what I said about going to bed with you," the woman said demurely. "Can't we go somewhere? The questions can wait, can't they?"

"Later," Tedesco said gruffly. "Later . . . maybe."

They pulled up in front of the precinct where the Special Homicide Task Force had its headquarters. Detective Lieutenant Burns and the other detectives were standing on the sidewalk. Burns seized open the door. He stuck his head inside. He looked inquiringly at Tedesco. Tedesco nodded.

Burns leaned close to the woman. He rapidly recited the brief statement of a suspect's constitutional right to remain silent and to summon a lawyer.

"It's a pleasure to meet you, Mrs. Meyers," he added. "Lieutenant Schmidt speaks very highly of you. He says you got X-ray vision. See around corners, too, in a blizzard. Too bad us cops ain't gifted like that. . . . Tedesco! Unlock her and get her upstairs! Put her shoes on her and don't look up her dress!"

Forty-five minutes later, the woman was seated in front of Burns's desk. Her face was grave and drawn, but still beautiful. Burns stood across from her patting his stomach. The other detectives surrounded them. They stood with arms folded. Concealed beneath the desk was a microphone. It was linked by a long cord to a tape recorder in an adjoining room.

Laid out on the desk were the contents of the woman's flight bag: Twenty-dollar bills, all used, in packets of two hundred dollars each; stacks of betting tickets.

Burns was examining the woman's passport. "Leslie," he said, suppressing a burp, "I can't think of but one thing. I ought to take up child psychology in Australia. I ain't a whiz at arithmetic, but a rough count makes that pile there in the neighborhood of a hundred and thirty thousand dollars. Plus twenty thousand in OTB football tickets. This your life savings or what?"

"I want to see a lawyer," the woman said flatly.

"Of course, of course. I already talked to the DA," Burns lied. "He's making some calls. He told me he'd have a lawyer up here quick as he can arrange it."

"I refuse to say anything further until I have consulted with a lawyer," she said angrily. She clasped her hands in her lap. "I have been mistreated. A lawyer will advise me on what steps to take. You will regret this," she added, looking fiercely at Burns. "I assure you of that."

"I regret it already," Burns said nonchalantly. He walked to the edge of the room and leaned against a filing cabinet. He tapped the passport against his palm. "I took the liberty of doing us both a favor. I called the Australian consulate," he continued to lie. "I gave them the details of the charges—you know, assault on a police officer and so on—and they said they'd send somebody over as quick as they can. I thought you'd be happy about that. Somebody from your own country taking a personal interest in you. We always do that when we're holding a foreign national. Department policy."

The woman's eyes widened. "Who authorized you to do that?" she said. Her voice cracked a fraction. "What good can come of it? This isn't a diplomatic incident. There was a *mishegoss*. I was inadvertently involved. Your assistant mistook me for someone else. Why did you call the consulate?"

"It's a service we provide," Burns said. "I had to do it. When you call the Immigration and Naturalization Service, you got to call the subject's consulate. Regulations. This way, we'll check out your ID and confirm you entered the country with at least a hundred and fifty thousand dollars or equivalent currency. It'll clear some things up and we can get this over with and you can go back out and have a good time. That's what you're doing in New York, right? Having a good time?"

"May I have a cigarette?" the woman asked.

Burns took a pack from a detective and gave her one and lit it for her. She drew on it deeply and then said, "Would you please call the Israeli consul?"

Burns narrowed his eyes. So did the other detectives.

"The Israelis don't handle Australian nationals," he said. He turned and whispered to one of the detectives to go to another office and call the DA's office and tell them to get somebody up here fast.

"That is the consulate I wish you to call," the woman said. Her voice was without emotion.

Burns motioned to another detective. He handed him the passport and whispered to him to get to a phone and call the Australian consulate and get everything he could on one Leslie Hammond, born Feb. 23, 1953, in Perth, current address Sydney, and tell them it was urgent.

"You're carrying an Australian passport," Burns continued. "You got to give me a damned good reason for calling the Israelis when I got an Australian national on my hands."

"They will know what to do," the woman said.

Abruptly Burns strode to where the woman was sitting. He bent over and put his hands on his knees. "Look, lady," he snarled. "It's time to stop futzing around. My man"—he pointed across the room at Tedesco, who was talking on the phone at his desk—"he made you. That was me called you back the other night after you talked to Schmidt. Tedesco listened in. He made you. He saw you two other times. You been a witness three different times. Phony names, phony addresses, phony everything. You're going to tell me what's going on and you're going to tell it to me straight. So let's hear it from the top."

The woman inhaled. She lifted her chin as she blew out the smoke. "I want to speak to a representative of my country," she said. "That is my wish."

"Your country?" Burns stood up and placed his hands on his hips. "First it's Australia, now it's Israel. Who you want me to call next? San Salvador?"

The woman said nothing and puffed her cigarette.

"You see that rifle over there next to the wall?" Burns shouted. "At three o'clock I'm supposed to go on television and tell the media boys I got a king-size break in the 'Finger of God' case. That thing is the murder weapon."

He seized the woman's chin and twisted her head in the direction of the H&H. "*That's* the murder weapon." He released her chin with a snap.

"You been a witness to three homicides perpetrated by that God damned thing. Or so you said. I know for a God damned, fourteen-carat fact you was lying about the last one. I want to know why! Because when I go on television I'm going to tell them I got another king-size break in the case. I'm going to tell them I got a woman from Sydney, Australia, who wants me to call the Israeli consulate to get her out of the shit. I'm going to tell them I got this woman from Sydney, Australia, named Leslie Hammond and she's been charged with interfering with the administration of justice, assaulting a police officer . . . What else, Tedesco?"

"Incitement," Tedesco called out from his desk. He hung up the phone. He had just finished persuading a sergeant at a Queens precinct that Artie had assisted in making an important arrest and should not be booked for disorderly conduct. "Conspiracy to interfere, violation of the Traffic Safety Act . . . and ruining my fucking suit."

"The traffic safety thing is federal," Burns said. The emotion went out of his voice. He sounded like a director at a rehearsal giving an actor another chance to get his lines right. "Try again. I want something else local. Something that'll stick."

Tedesco leaned back in his chair. He gazed a moment at a grimy spot on his sleeve. "Attempted bribery," he said, "resisting arrest. I'll think of a couple of other things before we get downtown."

"What else?"

"Criminal solicitation. I can always fix up a narcotics thing if I have to. If she don't start cooperating."

"I took care of that already," put in one of the other detectives. "More than an ounce of coke in the bottom of her bag."

"You hear that?" Burns turned back to the woman. "We'll shove it so far up your ass you'll get terminal earache. I'm going to try one more time. How come . . . No. How come you knew to call Schmidt when Ernie Parks got shot?"

"I must see a representative of my country," said the woman. She swallowed with difficulty to hold back tears.

"As far as I can tell you ain't got a country. What you got is a shit-load of trouble." Burns reached into his desk drawer and retrieved a bottle of antacid tablets. He popped two of them in his mouth and resumed. "Let's try it this way. If I was to call the Israeli consulate, who would I say is asking for representation?"

The woman looked up. Her expression was painful and dubious. "Must I tell you that?"

Burns emitted a resonant burp. "What can I tell you?" he said. "Think how it'd sound. I call the Israeli consulate and say I got an Australian here. She's in the shit up to her eyebrows. She wants consular help. She said call you. Name's Leslie Hammond." Burns sat down and put his fingers together in a peak. "Know what the Israelis would say? They'd say why the hell are you bothering us? We don't handle Australians. . . . If you want me to call the Israelis, you got to give me a reason."

The woman carefully butted her cigarette. "My name is Ayala Evron," she said quietly.

"So what does that mean?"

"It means my name is Ayala Evron," she snapped, suddenly combative again.

"Then how come your passport says Leslie Hammond? How come you're traveling on an Australian passport? How come the other night you said your name was Meyers? How come you gave different names the other two times you volunteered as a witness on these 'Finger of God' things? How come, lady, *how come*?"

A detective stuck his head in the door. "Can you come out here a minute, Lieutenant?" he said. "Somebody to see you."

"Tedesco!" Burns shouted. He jumped to his feet and slipped on his jacket. "Take over for me, will you?"

He walked out and closed the door behind him. A young man, sprucely turned out in a three-piece suit, was standing in the narrow corridor. He introduced himself as Gerald Pollack from the district attorney's office.

Burns took an immediate dislike to Pollack. He knew this type of assistant district attorney. Pollack fell into the category that Burns referred to as "the wash-and-wear boys."

"No, it ain't a suspect," Burns explained impatiently. "It's a woman we collared at an OTB parlor in Queens. One of my guys grabbed her. He made her as one of these bullshit witnesses who's been—"

"A woman with an Australian passport?" Pollack put in. He smiled archly. "Leslie Hammond? Carrying an enormous amount of currency?"

A scowl and a look of astonishment spread over Burns's face. "How'd you know that?" He looked angrily at the detective who had summoned him from his interrogation. "Did you tell him, God damn it?"

"Not me, Lieutenant," the detective replied defensively.

Pollack raised his hands, still smiling archly. "Let me tell you what you've got in there, Lieutenant. You've got a mentally unstable linguist from the Israeli consulate. Believe me, I know. We had a call from them at least two hours ago. They've been—"

"At least two hours ago was when Tedesco grabbed her," Burns retorted.

"I didn't come up here to argue. Here's the deal. You've got to release her."

Burns looked stunned, as if he had received a stiff, breath-taking blow. "*Release her*? Are you out of your fucking mind? This is the first break I've had in this thing. We let her go, we just as well roll it up and go play with our goldfish."

"It's a diplomatic thing," Pollack said evenly. "You have to release her. If you don't, we'll all have our cocks in the wringer."

Burns set his jaw. "Wait a minute," he said. He lowered his brow and gestured firmly. "I got this interrogation on tape. What we've done so far. I want you to listen to it and *then* I want you to tell me I got to release her."

Pollack shook his head. "I don't care if she's confessed to every homicide in the past ten years. You've got to release her."

"Will you listen to the fucking thing, for Christ's sake?"

"No."

At that moment Tedesco stepped into the corridor. He eased the door shut and waved his arms frantically. "She said it," he whispered loudly, making an effort not to shout. "She said she was Meyers. She said she called because she was supposed to."

Burns turned away from Pollack. "She admitted she made that call to Schmidt?" he demanded. "How about the other two times? She say anything about those?"

"Not yet," Tedesco went on excitedly, "but she will. They're still working on her."

Burns turned back to Pollack. "Satisfied?" he said acidly. "Let's go listen to that tape."

"We aren't listening to any tape," Pollack shot back. "Somebody from the Israeli consulate will be here any minute. When they get here, you're going to release that woman. Period. No more questions. No more crap about this being a major break in the case. Listen to me, Burns. That woman is unstable. The Israelis are looking for her. You've got the murder weapon. You said so yourself. What you need to clear this case is the maniac who's been using it, not some birdbrained woman who's been running around town with stolen consulate funds betting on football games."

"That woman is a witness," Burns said desperately. "She's more than that. I don't know how much more. Not yet. But she's more than just a witness."

"I'll tell you what she is," Pollack snapped. "She's a flake."

"Have you seen how we're developing this case?" Burns said. "We've just figured out that all these God damned witnesses are some kind of front. They're all phony. We don't have an accurate name or address for a single fucking one of them. This woman, this Hammond or Evron or whatever her name is, she's the break we need, for Christ's sake."

"Sounds like second-rate police work, if you ask me," Pollack said with a sneer.

"You asshole!" Burns screamed. Tedesco and the other detective seized him by the arms when they saw he was about to take a swing at Pollack.

"I'm glad you didn't do that, Lieutenant," Pollack said. "I would've personally seen to it that—"

A uniformed policeman appeared at the head of the stairs. "Two guys from the Israeli consulate," he said. "They're downstairs. They say they're here to pick up some woman. That woman you got in there, Lieutenant?"

"Send them up," said Pollack.

Presently two men walked up the stairs. One of them was Colonel Garovsky.

"My name is Katz," said Colonel Garovsky. He gestured with two fingers at the other man. "This is Dr. Hirsch, a physician on our staff. Miss Evron is under his care."

"What the hell's wrong with her?" said Burns. "Except she's lying through her teeth."

"Shut up, Burns!" shouted Pollack.

"Stay out of my way, you little bastard," Burns said savagely. He turned to Colonel Garovsky. "That woman in there, she's a witness in a case. She might even be connected with it. I need some more time with her. Another hour. That's all. Another hour. What do you say? Another hour, OK?"

"Burns, for God's sake," Pollack broke in. "These men are diplomats. They have every right—"

"What do you say, Katz?" Burns pleaded. "Another hour?"

"I'm sorry," Colonel Garovsky replied kindly. "The woman has severe mental problems. Dr. Hirsch says she will probably have to be institutionalized. We thought she had recovered sufficiently to perform her duties without reverting to her old patterns of behavior. Apparently—and sadly, I'm afraid—that is not the case. May we see her now?"

Burns thrust his hands on his hips. He closed his eyes. He sighed deeply.

Pollack opened the door. At the other end of the room Ayala was surrounded by detectives.

". . . Yes, yes, yes," she was saying. Her voice was shrill. "It was the plan from the start, you see. We were told when the shootings would occur. An hour beforehand we would assemble for our instructions. We would be told the location and the description we were to give to—"

"Ayala," said Colonel Garovsky. "We've come for you."

She stopped talking and looked over her shoulder. "Yakov!" she cried. She leapt from the chair and ran into his arms. "Oh, Yakov! They have been awful to me! They made me—"

Colonel Garovsky pulled her close. With one hand he pressed her face against his chest, effectively muffling her. "There is nothing further to worry about," he said in a not quite soothing tone. "Dr. Hirsch is here. He will see to you. It's time to go now."

Ayala pulled away a fraction. "Dr. Hirsch?" she said. Her voice was still filled with fright. "Who is Dr. Hirsch?"

Colonel Garovsky smiled. He nodded toward the man at his side. "See. I've brought Dr. Hirsch. You must get a grip on yourself."

Dr. Hirsch stepped forward. He took her by the arm. "Some rest, Ayala," he said. He smiled professionally. "You must have some more rest. I think we shall send you home. That will be good for you, won't it? After a rest you can return to your duties." He handed her a handkerchief. She dried her eyes.

She returned the handkerchief. She straightened her clothes. She ran her hand through her hair. Almost at once she appeared cool and composed. She and Dr. Hirsch left the office.

Colonel Garovsky asked whether the money on Burns's desk belonged to Ayala. One of the detectives said it did. Colonel Garovsky began stuffing it into the flight bag.

"Ain't you going to count it?" Burns asked from the door. "Don't forget the tickets. Lots of tickets there."

Colonel Garovsky said nothing. He went on putting the money and the tickets into the bag. At length he finished. He slung the bag over his shoulder.

"We'll sign the necessary forms when you've prepared them," he said to Pollack. "This will mean some sort of protest, I'm afraid. A minor thing, but it must be done. Diplomatic procedure, you understand."

"Of course," said Pollack. "I'm really sorry about this, Mr. Katz. Policemen sometimes go overboard when they get frustrated on a case." He ushered Colonel Garovsky to the door. "Our office will be in touch with you later today," he said as Colonel Garovsky descended the stairs. Colonel Garovsky looked over his shoulder. He said thank you and walked out of the precinct.

"I want the tape," Pollack said.

Burns sent a detective to fetch it. When he returned, Burns shoved the cassette into Pollack's hand. "If it ever occurs to you clowns to find out what this 'Finger of God' shit is about, listen to the thing. It'll make you look in both directions next time you run a red light."

"Oh, for Christ's sake, Burns," Pollack said. He dropped the cassette into his jacket pocket. "Anybody can make a mistake. You jumped too quick and you made a mistake. It could happen to anybody."

Burns said nothing.

"Look," Pollack said. "You've got the murder weapon. That's your best chance of clearing this case, right?"

"We had our best chance," Burns replied evenly. "We don't have it anymore. It just walked out the door."

Pollack turned to leave. "Well, good luck," he said. "I understand you're having a press conference this afternoon. Explaining about the rifle and all. I'm taking off early so I can watch the news. You've been doing a hell of a job handling the media, by the way."

"Don't bother."

"What do you mean?" Pollack stopped halfway down the staircase.

"There ain't going to be any press conference. I'm putting in for retirement the minute you get your ass out of here. I got sick days coming, accrued overtime, all them times I gave blood, vacation, terminal leave. That's a year right there before I start drawing my pension. A retired cop don't hold press conferences."

Pollack's expression contorted with consternation. "You can't do that," he said with a whine.

"Watch me," Burns said. He walked into his office. He slammed the door with a reckless heave.

They sped through the Queens-Midtown Tunnel. Colonel Garovsky was at the wheel. Ayala was beside him. She wore sunglasses. She drew on a cigarette.

"I should have known better," Colonel Garovsky muttered. "I, of all people, should have known better."

Ayala stared out the window. The sunlight was lustrous on the melting snowdrifts. "Oh, Yakov, don't be hard on yourself. How could you have known?"

"I have been in this business since before you were born," he snapped. "That's how I could have known. I violated a cardinal rule. A rule *I* invented."

"But—"

"There's no point in discussing it. We were lucky. In any number of ways we were very lucky. . . . There are still Espensheid and the Boers to contend with. They're onto it, you know."

They drove on in silence. Presently Ayala said, "I only wanted the experience. That's why I wanted to bet some of the money."

"Experience!" Colonel Garovsky exploded. "I allowed myself to violate one of my cardinal rules so you could have an *experience!*"

"Oh, for heaven's sake. No real harm has been done."

"No?" he said caustically. "Let me explain something to you. I run only successful operations. The reason they're successful is extremely simple. I compartmentalize everything. I established three teams for this operation. Surveillance, disruptive action, and financial. When I agreed to let a disruptive-action member take part in the financial action, I violated my own operational rules."

"You let me take part in surveillance, didn't you?"

"That was a mistake, too."

"I still fail to see where any actual damage has occurred. The consulate cooperated—"

"The consulate was obstructive. Why shouldn't they have been? They aren't a part of this operation. They almost fainted when I turned up and told them it was urgent that I pose as a diplomat to deal with a police matter. I had to call Jerusalem. Everyone at the consulate is most upset. They were very reluctant to go along with the mental-illness story. They said the police could easily find out whether you were an employee. They refused to allow their doctor to accompany me to the police station. That's why I had to bring Zvi along to impersonate Dr. Hirsch."

"There really is a Dr. Hirsch?"

"Of course. He's at least seventy years old. He doesn't look a thing like Zvi."

They drove through the maze of roads at Kennedy Airport. They pulled up at the El Al terminal.

"They're holding a flight for you," Colonel Garovsky said. "It stops in Rome. Why don't you go to the flat and relax? I'll be able to join you in a few days."

"The operation will be a success regardless," Ayala said cheerfully. She leaned over and kissed him. "I shall miss you, Yakov."

Colonel Garovsky smiled at her. "I shall miss you, too. Now hurry. They don't like to hold a flight any longer than necessary. Even for Mossad."

Ayala walked into the terminal. She was greeted by a woman with a hospitable smile, who escorted her to the boarding area.

Colonel Garovsky watched until she had vanished up a flight of stairs. Then he drove away.

* * *

Sergeant Mazibuko sat on a bench on the promenade overlooking the Seventy-ninth Street boat basin. He basked in the sunlight. The warmth penetrated his body. He felt his muscles loosen.

He watched the strollers. They sauntered, singly and in pairs, luxuriating in the springlike air. He was particularly interested in a pair of young boys; they were racing their ten-speed bikes back and forth in front of him.

"Let's go no-hands!" shouted one boy. "Bet I can beat you to the water fountain!"

"Bet you can't!" shouted the other.

They were off. They held their hands to their sides. Sergeant Mazibuko leaned forward.

They drew even with where Sergeant Mazibuko was sitting. The bike in second place began to wobble. The rider moved to grasp the handlebars.

"Not yet! Not yet!" Sergeant Mazibuko shouted. "Look at me!"

The boy jerked back his hands. He shot a glance at Sergeant Mazibuko. His front wheel jackknifed. The bike clattered to the pavement. The boy went sprawling. He jumped to his feet. He was furious but unhurt.

Sergeant Mazibuko rose. He walked over to the fallen bike. He saw the boy was growing anxious. He smiled broadly.

"Do you know why you took that fall?" he asked. He knelt down and appeared to examine the front wheel.

The boy shook his head. The winner of the race pedaled up and dismounted.

"You fell because you have all the spokes in the wheel," Sergeant Mazibuko said. "It is well known among trick cyclists that you must remove a spoke if you wish to retain balance. Did you know that?"

The boy shook his head again.

"Do you often attempt tricks like that?" He looked from one boy to the other.

"Sometimes."

"And you?"

"Sometimes."

"Then let me show you how you can perform this trick and greatly minimize your chances of a fall." He reached his huge hand into the front wheel. He wrenched loose a spoke.

"Hey, my dad paid a hundred and twenty dollars—"

"It is only one spoke," said Sergeant Mazibuko. He lifted the bike upright. He handed it to the boy. "Now you will be able to perform tricks with much less risk of falling. Of course, like everything in life, it requires a great deal of practice."

The boy held his bike. He looked dubiously at Sergeant Mazibuko.

"Try your stunt again," Sergeant Mazibuko said. "You will find your bike far more manageable. Go ahead. Try it."

The boys looked at each other. They mounted their bikes. They pedaled some distance and turned around.

They pedaled forward. For reasons that had nothing to do with the missing spoke, the boy who had taken the fall sailed past in the lead, hands held high.

Sergeant Mazibuko resumed his seat. He held the spoke beside him. Unobtrusively he honed one end on the stone leg of the bench. He felt the tip. It was needle sharp. He slipped the spoke, sharp end down, up the sleeve of his overcoat.

The sun was dying. A chill gripped the air. Sergeant Mazibuko walked back to his hotel. Loiterers leaned against the facade. A pair of transvestites admired the wigs in an adjoining shop. A knot of men leaned against a car. They shared a bottle of wine concealed in a paper bag. Another man, much older than the others and dressed in rags, ranted about an injustice done him by the telephone company in 1948. Prostitutes gave the eye to male passersby.

He pushed his way into the tiny lobby. There sat Lieutenant Van Hooff. He was in the same chair he had occupied the day before. Also as on the day before, two black prostitutes stood over him. They regarded him with lustful, evaluating gazes.

"If you want chops, honey," said one of them, "you best get over to Amsterdam Avenue."

"Unless you want some hot, tan pussy," said the other, "which I'm beginning to believe you can't handle. You been sitting here going on two days and you ain't said *what* you want."

Sergeant Mazibuko paused and then walked forward.

"Good evening, my boss," he said. "Are these women annoying you?"

Lieutenant Van Hooff looked up. He jumped to his feet. He looked relieved to see Sergeant Mazibuko. Abruptly his expression turned grim. "Come with me," he said sharply. He nodded toward the entrance. He thrust his right hand in his overcoat pocket.

Sergeant Mazibuko smiled pleasantly. "I must go to my room first, my boss," he said. "It is wise to see to one's things now and then in an establishment such as this."

Lieutenant Van Hooff's mouth tightened. He saw he had no choice but to accompany Sergeant Mazibuko. What he had to do would be impossible here. These cheeky Kaffir women knew his face. They might even summon the authorities.

"I knowed it was chops," said one of the prostitutes. "Red-headed motherfucker always wants chops."

"His asshole going to look like a train run through it when that dude done with him."

"Mixing peanut butter in a whorehouse. What's the world coming to?"

Sergeant Mazibuko allowed Lieutenant Van Hooff to enter the elevator first. The elevator was self-service. Sergeant Mazibuko pressed the button for the twentieth floor. The ascent was slow. He kept an eye on Lieutenant Van Hooff's right hand. He guessed Lieutenant Van Hooff wouldn't make his play in the elevator, but he was uncertain.

The elevator stopped. The door slid open. Still observing custom, Sergeant Mazibuko bade Lieutenant Van Hooff step off first.

Lieutenant Van Hooff flinched. Sergeant Mazibuko gently touched his elbow, urging him forward.

The corridor was dimly lit, windowless, and gorged with people. The smell of sweat and cosmetics, mingled with wine and the smoke of tobacco and marijuana, saturated the air. The noise was blatant and engulfing—ear-splitting music from a dozen inexpensive electronic sources, occasional whoops and deep, raucous intonations, screeches of pain, grunts that hardened into groans and reverberated as howls or fits of wheezing. Men and women, of all ages, clothed, half-clothed, unclothed, stood, leaned, or reclined on the threadbare carpet, conversing on the prospects of employment, the success or failure of relatives and acquaintances, the sale of flesh. Children darted about. Everyone was black.

At the sight of Lieutenant Van Hooff all sound except the music vanished. A few people disappeared into their rooms. Sergeant Mazibuko stepped into view. There was murmuring here and there.

"It's me," Sergeant Mazibuko announced in a huge voice. "Maz, the Big Blood from Georgetown. Don't fret about this white man here. He's my very good friend. A happy Dutchman, he is, a gentleman who likes his pleasure."

He threw an arm tightly around Lieutenant Van Hooff's waist. Lieutenant Van Hooff stiffened. He tried to pull away. Sergeant Mazibuko held him close. He ducked his head and kissed Lieutenant Van Hooff wetly on the cheek. Lieutenant Van Hooff shuddered.

"Everyone step up! You, there, Gwendolyn, step over here! Sylvester, R.J., everyone, step up and greet my friend, the happy Dutchman! You may call him Van!"

Everyone stepped up. "See how happy he is?" Sergeant Mazibuko smiled widely. "Now who could say this is not a very happy man?"

A woman clad only in bikini panties and knee-high black boots pushed close. She pressed her fingers against Lieutenant Van Hooff's groin. "Ain't much there," she said, "but it'll be all right once you get strapped on."

Lieutenant Van Hooff tried to struggle free. He was locked in Sergeant Mazibuko's arm. In desperation he took his hands from his overcoat pockets and shoved the woman away. As he did, Sergeant Mazibuko unceremoniously slipped his hand free and removed Lieutenant Van Hooff's automatic and slid it into his waistband.

Lieutenant Van Hooff felt it happen. He looked up at Sergeant Mazibuko. He was so bewildered that he did not notice a child reach inside his coat and remove his wallet.

"What's wrong with this jive cracker?" demanded the whore who had been rebuffed. "I thought you said he was up here to get into somebody. What the hell's wrong with him, Maz?"

Sergeant Mazibuko, still smiling, looked at Lieutenant Van Hooff. "Oh, Van's for the pleasure," he said. "Oh, yes. I think Van's bloody well for the pleasure. All of it. He likes to start with the he-she."

At that, the man named Sylvester elbowed his way forward. "I want him!" Sylvester shouted. He was gasping and drooling. "I'm a bull, Maz! I love white chops! Love them! Let me have him! I'm a bull! I got to have me some round-eye! I'm a bull! Let me have him! I'm a bull! I ain't had me a pale ethel since I got out of the joint! I'm a bull! Let me have him, Maz!"

Sergeant Mazibuko shook his head. "No," he said; he drew the word out. "He wants me first. Isn't that so, Van?" He seized Lieutenant Van Hooff by the arm and spun him halfway around. "Isn't that so?" he repeated. His gaze was steady and hard.

Lieutenant Van Hooff glanced horrified at the faces surrounding him. His throat was dry. It had all happened too fast. He imagined for a fraction of a second that if he closed his eyes it would all go away. He knew danger. You went into the field. You killed and did the best you could not to be killed yourself. He knew torture. You tortured Kaffirs because they defied the government. Torture was deliverance for a Kaffir. It delivered him from the sin of identity, the sin of holding a difference of opinion with authority. What he did not know was sympathy. His world protected him. If there was misery in somebody else's world, it was the fault of those who suffered it. Humiliation and vulnerability were foreign to him. . . .It suddenly dawned on him that he was in somebody else's world. He screamed something in Afrikaans.

"What's that shit he's speaking? Sounds like one of them old Jews down to the food stamp."

"A special language," said Sergeant Mazibuko. "He speaks it when he's ready for his he-she."

He propelled Lieutenant Van Hooff down the corridor. Several of the men, led by Sylvester, trailed them. "Let us watch, Maz," said Sylvester. "Watching's just as good . . . sometimes anyway."

"Well, God damn!" shouted a woman from the other end of the corridor. "You sure fooled me, Maz! *You* going for grayboy chops! Ain't this some everlasting shit!"

"I crave diversity, my love."

"It's going to be diversity, all right," Sylvester said enthusiastically. "Maz going to chop this fay so low he going to have to look up to tie his shoes."

Sergeant Mazibuko unlocked the door to his room. He heaved Lieutenant Van Hooff inside.

"Perhaps I won't be enough for him," he said with a wicked grin. "If not, I'll call for you, Sylvester." Sylvester grinned wickedly, too.

Sergeant Mazibuko slammed the door in his face and locked it.

Lieutenant Van Hooff was across the room. He had recovered somewhat. He seized a lamp from the small dressing table.

"You've taken leave of your senses, you Kaffir bastard!" he snarled. He brandished the lamp. "Let's have the gun. Use your head, Kaffir. You'll get off with a jail stretch if you drop this nonsense. Otherwise, you'll hang. I promise you that. . . .The gun, give it to me."

Sergeant Mazibuko slowly took the automatic from his waistband. He aimed at Lieutenant Van Hooff's chest. "Take off your clothes," he said without emotion, "and lie face-down on the bed . . . my boss.

"Do you mean you're actually—"

"Now, my boss."

Lieutenant Van Hooff shivered a moment like a thin dog in the cold. He tried to speak. The words caught in his throat. He dropped the lamp. He gasped, and then he doubled over and vomited. He straightened up. Again he tried to say something. His eyes bulged. Then he vomited some more.

Sergeant Mazibuko walked over to him. He shoved the automatic back in his waistband. He looked closely at Lieutenant Van Hooff—who appeared as if he were about to collapse from retching. Sergeant Mazibuko lifted him by the lapel of his overcoat and punched him with all his strength in the solar plexus. Lieutenant Van Hooff sank to the floor. His legs were sprawled in the pool of vomit.

It was the first time he had ever struck a white man. Nothing to it, really, he thought.

Sergeant Mazibuko lifted him to the bed. Lieutenant Van Hooff was conscious but helpless. Sergeant Mazibuko stripped him to his waist and stretched him out on his back. He reached into his overcoat sleeve. He pulled out the bike spoke.

He lifted Lieutenant Van Hooff's left arm above his head and let it fall. He probed the armpit until he found the place. Lieutenant Van Hooff stirred but offered no resistance. He felt the place again. The space between the third and fourth ribs.

He held the point of the spoke against the soft flesh. He covered Lieutenant Van Hooff's mouth with his other hand. He tightened his grip on the spoke. He lunged. He drove the spoke into Lieutenant Van Hooff's body at an upward angle. Lieutenant Van Hooff writhed. Sergeant Mazibuko fell across him, pinning him down. He felt his arm quiver as he forced the spoke deeper and deeper.

The writhing stopped. The aorta had been penetrated. The tip of the spoke protruded from the lifeless body. Sergeant Mazibuko walked to the bathroom and returned with a handful of toilet tissue. He extracted the spoke, pressing the tissue against the spot of the puncture. Only a speck of blood showed on the skin. The mass of muscle and tissue contracted instantaneously, sealing the tiny wound. Sergeant Mazibuko daubed the speck with the toilet tissue. Within moments it looked like nothing more than an insect sting.

For all anyone—the police, the medical examiner, or anyone else—would ever know, Lieutenant Van Hooff had died of a cardiac arrest. The evidence was identical.

Sergeant Mazibuko wiped the spoke clean. He dropped it out the window. It landed in an accumulation of soggy garbage at the rear of the hotel. He flushed the tissue down the toilet. He stripped off Lieutenant Van Hooff's shoes, trousers, and briefs and placed his body stomach-down on the bed. He searched the clothes and found nothing. He wondered what had happened to the wallet.

There was a final detail. Sergeant Mazibuko rejected authenticity and searched the room for a credible substitute. He decided on a section of the shower-curtain rod. He returned to the bedroom and completed what he had to do. It was all the more unpleasant because Lieutenant Van Hooff's bowels had given way. When he was finished, he cleaned the rod and reattached it. He threw the covers over the body. He replaced the lamp on the dressing table and sat down in the room's only chair. He would leave after a plausible interlude. He guessed that even he-she liaisons were expected to take a bit of time. He touched his watch.

Nathan Leitstein's limousine nosed through the traffic at Columbus Circle and turned onto Central Park West. The streets were awash with melting snow. The gutters could not contain the swollen streams of water. They overflowed and splashed onto the sidewalks.

Twilight was deepening. The sky was a sharp, dark blue. The remnants of the radiant sun glowed dimly beyond the New Jersey horizon. Pink clouds tinged with gray billowed aimlessly along a line of least resistance.

Mr. McManus and Nathan Leitstein sat in the back of the car in a state of pleasant excitement. They had dined early for the second straight night at the hotel restaurant with the recently acquired French name. They had again eaten lamb chops. They had given Burt, the waiter, a betting tip. They had discussed the disappearance of Freddie and Charlie Dolan, speaking of them in terms they usually reserved for racetrack touts, degenerates who tried to straighten out with personal checks, and people who appeared before grand juries. For the first time in years Mr. McManus wore galoshes. Nathan Leitstein had insisted on it. "You can't be running around in this slop in just your shoes," he had said. "You'll catch no telling what." Mr. McManus had kept his feet well under the table.

Nathan Leitstein puffed a cigar and shook his head. "I never seen anybody so slow to move a line," he said. "I mean, this OTB *deserves* to take a bath, the way they move the line. You'd think they'd learn sometime."

"It ain't that bad," said Mr. McManus. He gazed out the window.

"We hit them with eight and a half first thing this morning. That got it down to what, Philadelphia by five, right? Middle of the afternoon it was down to Philadelphia by four. That ain't bad."

"Too slow. Way too slow. Amateurish."

"Let's see," said Mr. McManus. "So far there's thirty-three and a half million bucks on New Orleans. It must have taken them hooples all afternoon. They was laying a total of twenty million. That's after two o'clock. It takes a lot of footwork, laying twenty million bucks at two hundred bucks a pop. In one afternoon."

"Don't bet that all of it went on New Orleans," said Nathan Leitstein. "Espensheid, he was acting funny again. He still wants to argue back, Espensheid, when I tell him New Orleans."

"Let's check the line."

Nathan Leitstein spoke into the intercom. He told the driver to tune in an all-news station that gave a sports report every quarter hour. First came the latest developments on a high school basketball scandal in Georgia. Then the announcer read the latest OTB point spreads. The Philadelphia-New Orleans game now had Philadelphia favored by two points.

"Shut it off!" Nathan Leitstein shouted into the intercom. The driver switched off the radio. "Jesus," he exclaimed. "Two fucking points. They moved it again. Espensheid must've listened to reason."

Mr. McManus shifted and looked at Nathan Leitstein. "That's down from ten since Thursday," he said. "We're putting it together, Billy." His voice was charged with enthusiasm. "When was the first time you saw a really heavy middle?"

"UCLA-Southern Cal," Nathan Leitstein replied immediately. "It was in—"

"That's it!" Mr. McManus went on. He gestured fervently. "That's the one! We knew UCLA would take it, remember, but not by no seven points?"

"Oh, yeah," said Nathan Leitstein. "Oh, yeah. We loaded up Southern Cal like somebody'd knocked on the door with the key to J.P. Morgan's safe."

"The book? Remember him? Morty Somebody. A hoople. Had one wife too many. He seen all that Southern Cal money and moved the line *down*. He was big back then, Morty. The other books, they all watched Morty. Morty pulls the line, and the other books pull it right behind him."

"Yeah. It was like an elevator. UCLA by seven, then six, five, four, three, two, one, pick-'em. Morty and the other books, they like to have shit when they had to sell Southern Cal as a one-point favorite and it three hours before kickoff."

"You know," said Mr. McManus, "I never thought Morty and them'd go for it when I went back and said I wanted to put three hundred grand on UCLA. Not after they'd moved the price to Southern Cal by one."

"Hell," said Nathan Leitstein, "I thought the hooples'd have sense enough to scratch it. They wrote me down for three hundred, too, and it was clear as a bell there was no way I could lose. If Southern Cal wins, I'm covered on the first bet, right? If UCLA wins, I'm covered on the second. A tie and I win them both. Same if UCLA wins by seven or less."

"A sweet day, Billy," said Mr. McManus. There was a trace of a purr in his voice. "A sweet day . . . Remember the score?"

"Twenty-one–twenty UCLA," Nathan Leitstein said. He smiled. The tip of his cigar glowed richly in the darkened car. "That kid, what's his name, run the extra point on account of the other kid, the kicker, broke his leg. . . .You know what it's like hitting a middle? It's like somebody tells you something nice about yourself and you know it's the truth."

Mr. McManus was quiet a moment. Then he said, "Sounds like Morty is telling OTB how to move the line."

Nathan Leitstein shook his head. "Not Morty," he said. "Don't you remember about him?"

"Morty?"

"Yeah. The hoople. Opened a fruit stand in Bensonhurst. Writes a two-hundred dollar sheet. High school basketball and the Milrose Games. Goes to the track once a year. Christmas."

They approached Mr. McManus's apartment building. The driver made a near-miss U-turn. The lights from inside reflected on the darkened wet sidewalk. There was a minor commotion at the foot of the steps under the canopy. The doorman was shouting and gesturing. A seedy, very old woman, a wrinkled, filthy shopping bag in each hand, was shouting back.

"I'm telling you for the last time," said the doorman. "If you ain't out of here when I come back out, I'm calling the cops. You know what they'll do, the cops? They'll take them shopping bags away from you. All your string and paper. All your junk, they'll take it away from you. You don't want that, do you?"

"Am spitting on you," said the old woman. She gave no indication she intended to heed the doorman's warning. "Am not listening to you. You are Irish ninny. Am waiting for important person. Man of affairs. Is not *servant* wearing silly costume. Is man of affairs . . . Go peddle papers, fool. Am having important business. Am not budging."

She set down one of her shopping bags. She pressed a bony finger to one side of her nose. She blew the other nostril and wiped it with her tattered sleeve. She picked up her shopping bag and jutted her chin.

"Oh, Jesus," said Mr. McManus. He told Nathan Leitstein he would be in touch first thing in the morning unless there was a reason to call in the meantime. The doorman held the door. Mr. McManus got out. The limousine pulled away into the river of slush.

"Just some crazy old broad," said the doorman. He smelled of whiskey. He motioned to the old woman. She had set her shopping bags on the sidewalk. She was scratching herself energetically. "I'll have her out of here in no time. Nothing to worry about."

"Let it go, Mike," said Mr. McManus. He pressed a bill into the doorman's hand. "I know her. I'll take care of it."

He turned to the old woman. "Hello, Ma," he said warmly. "How come you're so far from the neighborhood? It's thirty years since you was above Houston Street."

His mother looked at him with an ancient, giddy grin. "Change of scene," she said. She retrieved her shopping bags. "Am believing travel is educational. Am also believing uptown is generous at Christmas. Hah! Is easier to panhandle in Delancey Street. Is not puffed-up fool like *him*"—she thrust her chin toward the doorman and spit—"in Delancey Street."

"Come on upstairs, Ma," said Mr. McManus. "I'll give you a cup of tea or something."

"No!" she said fiercely. "Am not putting my eyes on *her*!"

Mr. McManus smiled. "She ain't here. Out of town. Her and the kids, they're in Florida. For Christmas, you know. Come on up. It'll just be you and me. You might even want to take a bath." He took her arm and guided her toward the steps.

"Okay," she said. "But no bath. Am not taking baths. Is bad for the blood. My uncle the king did not bathe once in entire life. Of course, was unworthy man. But still king."

The doorman stepped in front of them. "You ain't bringing her in, are you, Mr. McManus? She's got fleas, lice and that. Maybe even rats, for all you know. Don't bring her in here."

Mr. McManus stopped. He moved a step or two away from his mother. He looked coldly at the doorman. "You like your job, don't you, Mike?"

"I don't get you."

"I said you like your job, don't you?"

"Yeah, but . . ." He folded his arms and frowned.

"Get this through your thick head," Mr. McManus snapped. "You ever give this lady a hard time again, I'll have your ass bounced. Keep that in mind. You're too old—and too God damned dumb—to try and get another job. Open the door."

The doorman obeyed.

The old woman looked at him over her shoulder. She made a grotesque face. The doorman made an obscene gesture.

In the elevator the operator did his best to hold his breath. The old woman smelled of decomposing organic matter and oppressive, treacly perfume.

In the apartment Mr. McManus said, "Go have a bath, Ma, why don't you? Give yourself a treat."

"No bath," she said. She took a seat on the sofa. "Am not making trip to West Side for bath. Is inconvenient a bath. With no bath I am easy getting seat on subway. Car of my own. Everyone runs to next car when I get on. Am having private car. Is luxury. What is bath? Bit of soap, water. And no seat on subway."

"You want something to eat? There's some—"

"Am no eating Irish food. Thins the blood. You are having maybe *cevapcici*?"

"No."

"Am not eating, in that case. Must have *cevapcici*. Montenegrin sausage keeps the blood warm and rich. If your Irish wife feeds you *cevapcici*, you are not having the assault of the heart."

Mr. McManus lit a cigar. "What brings you uptown, Ma?"

"Some Christmas joy, yes? A visit with my clever son. What else?"

"Well, I don't know. You ain't here on account of you been missing my wife and family. You seen me a couple of days ago."

"You are ill. Assault of the heart. Weak Irish blood."

"I'm doing okay. Taking it easy and that . . . What's up, Ma?"

"Yes," she said. "You are clever boy. Strange powers of the mind. I look at world, I see strange things, hear old voices. Voices telling old tales. I think some of the tales are lies, but they sound like truth. Is confusing. I am looking at young man in subway. I am thinking what? I am thinking what? I am thinking, 'Unworthy Liverpool Irishman. Beautiful man with the red hair. Playing the *gusle*. Your father' . . . You look at world and see digits, yes?"

"I add and subtract. You know how it is."

Suddenly she reached down and dug into one of her shopping bags. She retrieved a greasy scrap of paper. Her withered face looked perplexed. "Have confession," she said. "Most embarrassing. Mistake."

Mr. McManus was about to put his cigar to his mouth. He arrested it in midair. He looked closely at his mother. "What kind of mistake?" he asked sharply.

"The life pulses," she said. She waved the scrap of paper. "Snakes Hip. A mistake. Miscalculation."

"What kind of miscalculation?"

"The body pulse. On Sunday Snakes Hip is having severe body pulse. Is weak. Is having trouble getting out of bed. Must be calm. Must sit in park and feed pigeons."

"But he's playing a football game."

"Maybe. But should be day of rest for Snakes Hip. So. Sunday is day of severe body pulse for Snakes Hip. Also severe mind pulse, severe soul pulse. Terrible. Bottom of barrel. Living end. Oh, brother."

"You mean he's going to have a bum day?"

"Worse. Snakes Hip cannot break matchstick on Sunday. Small girl can punch him out."

Mr. McManus inhaled deeply on his cigar. "I'll be damned," he said.

10

Nathan Leitstein's limousine dropped Mr. McManus at the hotel shortly before eight in the morning. The sunlight was piercing. The air was freshly invigorating. He carried only a small suitcase. The manager greeted him in person.

"A delight, as always," said the manager. He was elegant in a dark suit and striped tie. He took the suitcase and escorted Mr. McManus to the desk.

"The special form, Raymond," he said to the clerk. "The one I prepared last night. No, no, the other one. The one in the envelope."

The lobby was deserted except for a red-eyed disheveled young couple making their way to breakfast from a night on the town. They were bickering desultorily.

Mr. McManus covertly slipped the manager a packet of crisp, new bills, two thousand dollars in all. The manager pocketed it without any change of expression.

"Your usual suite," the manager said. He had the smile and manners of a diplomat. Or a gigolo. He filled in the registration form. He asked for no credit cards or other identification. He did not ask Mr. McManus to sign. He snapped his fingers in the direction of a bellhop and pointed to Mr. McManus's suitcase.

"Skip it," said Mr. McManus. "Nothing much in it, anyway. Give the boy something, will you?"

"Certainly."

He took the key and led Mr. McManus to the elevator. "Everything's in order," he said. "Just as you requested."

"Champagne?"

"Two bottles. *Moët et Chandon*. Chilled. And flowers."

"How about the newspapers?"

"All of them. I included the Chicago *Defender*."

"Any trouble with the phone?"

"None to speak of, I'm happy to say. It was short notice, but the telephone company usually cooperates with us. They know our guests often ask for special lines. What time shall I expect Miss, ah . . ."

"Ten-thirty, eleven."

"Any special message?"

"Tell her to come straight up. She'll probably have a lot of packages and that. See to it a boy gives her a hand."

"Of course."

The manager hesitated. He seemed reluctant to let Mr. McManus board the elevator. His face was eloquent with expectation.

Mr. McManus smiled. "New Orleans," he said in a low voice. "Heavy—if you're in the mood."

The manager looked dubious. He gently tugged Mr. McManus aside. "Are you quite sure that's wise?" he asked. He glanced from side to side, and abruptly his voice changed, "The morning line's Philadelphia by two. Been dropping like it had a brick in it. The frigging thing'll be pick-'em before—"

"New Orleans," Mr. McManus repeated firmly. "Stick with it."

The manager resumed his professional air. "Thank you, very much," he said. "I do hope you enjoy your stay with us. If you require anything, please call me personally."

The elevator delivered Mr. McManus to the fourth floor. His suite was down the corridor and around two corners. It was a large living room and a bedroom. It was on the north side of the hotel. The view was spectacular. The trees in Central Park were at eye level, dripping and sparkling. Fifth Avenue was a misfit river, overflowing magnificently with melting snow.

The flowers were arranged in a crystal bowl by the window. An ice bucket on a pronged frame held the champagne and two tulip glasses. A stack of fifty newspapers sat on the coffee table.

Mr. McManus dropped his suitcase and turned on the gigantic

television set to a special channel that broadcast sports news ticker-tape style. He was a stockholder in the company that operated the channel. He watched the latest OTB point spread and tore through the sports sections of the newspapers. He littered the floor around him. Presently he summoned a cleaning woman to remove the newspapers. He stood at the window and took in the view until she had finished. He tipped her and then picked up the specially installed telephone. He stretched out in an ornate chair next to the writing table as he waited for his number to answer.

"Providence Precision Grinding. May I—"

"Give me Katz."

Colonel Garovsky came on the line. "Yes. What do you want?" he said. His voice was strained, as if he were suppressing an urge to scream.

"What do you mean, what do I want? This is McManus. You seen the line?"

"No. Why should I have?"

"Oh, I don't know. If it was me dropping all that dough, I think I'd take a look at it. Just for the hell of it, if nothing else."

Colonel Garovsky sighed testily. "Get to the point, please."

"Okay. It's time for you hooples to get off your ass. The way I count it, so far you got seventeen and a half down on New Orleans. That's seventeen and a half million down to win. And you got sixteen million on Philadelphia—to lose, right? So what you got to do this morning is give OTB a stiff kick. I mean, a real stiff kick."

"Why?"

"Jesus Christ, Katz. This is Saturday. The last day. No more bets at OTB for Sunday's games after seven o'clock tonight. That means you got thirty-seven and a half million dollars' worth of winning tickets left to buy. You also got forty-four million left to bet on Philadelphia—you know, to throw in the tub. Like I already told you a thousand times, you got to hit the line early if you want it to move. You know what early means, don't you? It means when the God damned doors open."

After a long pause Colonel Garovsky said, "There have been developments. Developments that do not concern you."

"What do you mean, developments? You ain't scratching, are you?"

"No. Nothing like that. We intend to go ahead with the—"

"Will you stop pulling your putz, for Christ's sake, and tell me what you're talking about?"

Another pause. Then Colonel Garovsky said, "Frankly, we are in something of a quandary. There have been a number of, ah, misunderstandings. We—"

"What is it you ain't understood? I give it to you straight. I told you *exactly* how to play every fucking nickel and how to—"

"The quandary is *here*." Colonel Garovsky interrupted, suddenly angry. "The wagers have been placed improperly."

"Now wait a God damned minute. I give it to you right. Every time. If something's screwed up, you must've done it. What've you been doing, working with a beard or something?"

"What I mean to say," Colonel Garovsky snapped, "is that not a single bet has been placed on Philadelphia!"

Mr. McManus smiled. He gazed at the window. Sunlight slanted into the room. "How do you suppose that happened?" he said. "Them hooples of yours, they know how to read, don't they?"

"The situation, as I understand it, is this," Colonel Garovsky went on, a bit calmer. "We now have a total of thirty-three and a half million dollars bet on New Orleans." Then his voice rose again. "There is not a cent of our money on the Philadelphia side. Not a cent, not a farthing, nothing. I mean to say, what is our position? Are we—"

"—up shit creek with your pants down? Depends on how you look at it. . . . Hold on." He put down the receiver and lit a cigar. Then he continued, "If you ain't scratching, the thing now is what you want to do with the rest of your dough."

"We wish to play it all to win," Colonel Garovsky answered immediately.

Mr. McManus blew a smoke ring. "Katz," he said, "that's the first smart thing I ever heard you say. You ready for the down payment on the next favor?"

"Pardon me?"

"You ready for your hooples to hit the street?"

"Yes."

"All right. The OTB line opened this morning with Philadelphia by two. That's what the books're offering, too, but you don't care about that, right? Now. What've you got left. Eighty-one and a half million, right? Here's what you do. You take twenty of it right now. You take it and you hit New Orleans again. Same units. Two hundred a throw. It ought to take you all morning, right?"

"New Orleans?" Colonel Garovsky's voice was filled with extreme annoyance. "Shouldn't we place at least a portion of it on Philadelphia? In view of the fact that—"

"Stop answering back. Put the fucking money on New Orleans, understand? That'll leave you sixty-one and a half."

"How are we to play that? The remaining sixty-one and a half million dollars?"

"Don't get in a hurry, Katz. I'll tell you in plenty of time. You're forgetting something, ain't you?"

"Am I?"

"Yeah. A little matter of a half a million bills, remember?"

"Of course. The money will be delivered to the hotel lobby at noon."

"On the dot, right?"

"Of course."

"Good. It ought to take me a couple of hours to count it. Old man like me, it takes a while to count that much dough. When I've checked it out, I'll tell you how to play the rest of it, the other sixty-one and a half and whatever change you got left."

"As you wish."

"Time to get them moving, Katz."

"Who?"

"Your hooples."

Mr. McManus replaced the receiver. He puffed his cigar. A small grin spread across his face. Who do these hooples think they're kidding? he thought. He tapped his palm lightly against his forehead. It was clear as the way to church. From day one these hooples was going wide. I seen it before. A thousand times I seen it. It was the la-la-la that threw me off. I mean, the proposition wasn't self-evident. Most hustles, you play relaxed and talk a lot. These hooples, they just talk a lot. That's how come they got this far. I spent so much time telling them to shut up, I took my eye off what they was doing. Then there was all the other stuff. Freddie and Charlie. And Coombes. No wonder I couldn't keep my mind on what was going on. It's been like skinning suckers at a pool hall. Only this time, the suckers had the hustlers parked outside. Hell, anybody can see through this simple shit. These hooples, they ain't ever caught on that money don't buy a God damned thing. Never has. Never will. They want goods and services, and there ain't but one thing ever buys goods and services. That's goods and services. They think I ain't onto them. My bleeding ass. Who do they think they're diddling with, a couple of sideshow guess-your-weight artists who're too old to be Boy Scouts? Me and Billy Light, we been skinning hooples like this since before they invented stupidity. If we was booking vaudeville, we'd feature these hooples. Top of the Bill. Katz and Espenwhatsit Moving It Around— If, Reverse, and Chop the Pot. He chuckled. Will these hooples ever be surprised, he thought, when I . . .

Oh, Jesus . . . Oh, Jesus Christ on a crutch . . .

It was the pain. It was sharp, sudden, and deep. It was as if a giant hand gripped his left breast, nipple and all, and was squeezing the living hell out of it. It shot down his left arm like a pellet of white hot lead. His cigar fell to the plush carpet. He groaned and gasped for breath. . . .

Son of a bitch . . .

He reached into his jacket pocket. He felt for the aspirin tin. . . .

Son of a bitch . . .

He fumbled with the tin. He struggled to open it. . . .

God damn my fucking thumbs! Stiff as . . .

The tin popped open. He pinched out a digitalis tablet. . . .

Jesus, just don't let me pass out before I get this little fucker in my mouth. . . .

The pain roared again. It thundered from his chest down his left arm. It slammed into his pinky. . . .

Son of a bitch . . .

He slipped the tablet into his mouth. He gulped . . .

Son of a bitch . . .

He gulped again and gasped . . .

Son of a bitch . . .

The digitalis took effect. His blood pressure dropped. His breathing was easier. . . .

Son of a bitch . . .

He smelled something burning. It was his cigar on the carpet. With a difficulty he had not imagined possible for a human being to experience he leaned over and picked it up. He was scarcely able to hold it. But he did. He closed his eyes. . . .

Son of a bitch . . .

Colonel Garovsky massaged his temple with two fingers. His expression was stern. "Are you satisfied?" he demanded.

"Not entirely," replied Major Espensheid. His roast-beef face was drawn in a scowl. "I must confirm this with Leitstein."

They were in a large room off the main downstairs hall of the historic mansion in Queens. The windows were shuttered. The light came from a single, bare bulb overhead. A huge, detailed map of the city was fastened with masking tape to one wall. It was covered with red dots marking the locations of the OTB parlors. Next to it were lists of the Mossad and BOSS agents who were placing the bets.

Against the other walls were trestle tables. Each was laden with stacks of currency. On one of them they reached nearly to the ceiling.

Minutes earlier a team of agents had finished ripping apart the cushions and seatbacks of another El Al jetliner and stacking the remaining fifty-five million dollars on the tables. A half dozen men from BOSS were counting the new money, while a Mossad crew cleaned up the tattered airplane upholstery. In a smaller adjoining room were trestle tables covered with stacks of betting tickets.

Major Espensheid completed his call to Nathan Leitstein. "His advice is the New Orleans side again," Major Espensheid said as he hung up. "So there you have it."

Colonel Garovsky signaled a Mossad agent. Quickly, operatives who had been elsewhere in the mansion awaiting instructions filed into the room. Each carried an airline flight bag into which another agent stuffed currency as they passed in front of the trestle tables. Someone called attention to a handwritten sign taped above the door. The agents made their way from the mansion.

More agents with flight bags arrived. "Shall we go upstairs?" said Colonel Garovsky. There was distaste in his voice.

"The sooner the better," said Major Espensheid. He motioned to one of the BOSS men who had accompanied him to the mansion to stay in the room and keep an eye on things. "There are certain people who take liberties with composite operations," he added sullenly.

Colonel Garovsky closed the door behind them in his room on the second floor. He omitted the meager amenities such as offering Major Espensheid a cup of instant coffee.

"These threats of yours," Colonel Garovsky said harshly, "they're rank, utter nonsense."

"Are they?" said Major Espensheid; his voice, too, was harsh. "*Are they*? I suppose the authorities will think them nonsense, too. These witnesses, I suppose they're nonsense, and this string of murders that your chap arranged, I suppose *that's* nonsense!" He jutted his thick chin.

"My dear Major, don't you ever listen to the wireless? Just yesterday afternoon the police announced they have found the weapon. It was part of the item about the retirement of the policeman who's been leading the investigation. That weapon is your personal property, I believe."

Major Espensheid's scowl deepened.

"And the fellow who's been using it," Colonel Garovsky went on, "Dolan. He's one of yours. So please—" he clenched his teeth and pointed two fingers at Major Espensheid—"belt up about making trouble for us with the authorities."

Major Espensheid folded his arms. "This betting scheme was Mossad's idea from the start. I warned my people. I warned them. I said we'd be pulling with a strung trotter if we fell in with a lot of Jews in New York."

"In that case, Major, why don't you go downstairs and tell your people to bundle up their dollars and take them back to South Africa?"

"Because," Major Espensheid shot back, "if you haven't realized it, we have your backs to the wall. Think of it, Colonel, the reaction of the authorities here when they learn that Israel, their little pet collection of Jews that holds off the world against every difficulty, when they learn that Israel has tried to take control of their city. Think of the reaction."

Colonel Garovsky snorted. "I think you'd better consider a defense for cold-blooded murder. Unless you abandon this nonsense this instant, I'll telephone the police. I shall inform them that the Holland and Holland .375 magnum in their possession belongs to a member of the South African Bureau of State Security who is in this city at this moment. I shall also inform them that a member of the South African Defense Force is the man responsible for these senseless killings—a man who is a member of a unit that *you* command."

Major Espensheid's nostrils flared. He realized that, in fact, it was *his* back that was to the wall. The Jews had manipulated him. He silently cursed that ass Dolan. What on earth had driven him to try and get rid of the H&H. Of all the idiotic . . .

"What do you propose, Colonel?" he said at length.

Colonel Garovsky sat down in the chair behind his desk. He carelessly shoved aside some of the forged documents on architectural history. "I propose that we proceed with the original scheme."

"Does that include the disruptive action?"

"Yes."

"Even without Dolan? We've had no luck tracking—"

"Neither have we," Colonel Garovsky said; he sounded vague. "Zanin will take charge of it."

"Does he understand explosives?"

"Well enough . . . That leaves us with one loose end, Major. Your man Mazibuko. Has Van Hooff—"

Major Espensheid walked to the window. He was about to say he had no idea what had become of Lieutenant Van Hooff or his efforts to dispose of Sergeant Mazibuko—when his eyes widened.

"Come here, Colonel!" he said excitedly. "There's a man walking across the park! I think it looks like . . . "

Colonel Garovsky leaped from his chair. He stepped quickly to the window. He squinted. "Damn! It is! It's him!"

A Mossad agent stuck his head in the door. He held a .22 caliber Beretta. It was the same kind of pistol that Captain Zanin had held on Nathan Leitstein. "There's someone approaching!" he shouted. "Identity unknown! I'll assemble a disposal unit! We can bury the body behind the house! Shall I—"

"No!" Colonel Garovsky interrupted heatedly. "Absolutely not! Put away your weapon!"

The agent disappeared. He shouted in Hebrew as he bounded down the stairs.

Indistinct, angry shouting arose from the ground floor. It was a dissonance of Hebrew, Afrikaans, and English.

Colonel Garovsky and Major Espensheid exchanged glances of astonishment. Hurriedly they peered out the window again.

They saw a tall man with iron-gray hair. He was wearing a well-cut raincoat. He was making his way toward the covered front porch. He pushed past a dozen Mossad agents, three or four of whom had drawn guns.

They rushed down the stairs and into the room where the money was stored.

There stood the man. It was Headlight.

He looked around. He smiled wryly at Colonel Garovsky and Major Espensheid.

"Well, I'll swear," he said in a rich, exaggerated southern drawl, "if it isn't the world's highest-ranking uncircumcised Jew and the only

Boer to have his brains scrambled three times by Max Schmeling. Why aren't you boys staying on Park Avenue?" He gestured at the trestle tables covered with money. "It sure as hell isn't because you couldn't afford the rent."

Colonel Garovsky and Major Espensheid glared at him in silence. They had both known Headlight for years. Rhodesia, Angola, Mozambique, Lebanon.

Finally Major Espensheid asked harshly, "What are you doing here? You have no official status. We know you've retired. You were given the sack, to be precise."

Headlight continued to smile. He took an English cigarette from his gold case and lit it in a deliberate, leisurely way. "I heard the Shriners were having a parade," he said. "Wouldn't miss it for the world."

"Would you be kind enough to leave?" Colonel Garovsky said coldly. "This doesn't concern you."

"I'm afraid it does," Headlight said affably. "My wife's an astrology nut. She read my chart last night. Know what she told me? She said today was going to be one of the luckiest days of my life. She said the only thing for me to do was to fly up to New York and bet on a football game. I thought maybe you boys could put me on to something."

"You've blundered into an active operation," Major Espensheid snapped.

"Looks like it," said Headlight. He inhaled deeply on his English cigarette and blew the smoke out through his nose. "These aren't half bad," he said. "You boys don't smoke cigarettes, do you? I know you wouldn't touch one of these, Espensheid. They're made in Britain."

A Mossad agent rushed into the room. "He has no backup," he said, motioning toward Headlight, "no support of any sort."

Headlight raised his hand. He looked directly at Colonel Garovsky and Major Espensheid, "Your man's right," he said. His drawl diminished. "I haven't thrown up a perimeter around this place. But I've got support. So let's start talking."

Colonel Garovsky and Major Espensheid frowned. Colonel Garovsky gestured toward the stairs. He, Major Espensheid, and Headlight returned to the room on the second floor.

"Do you have official status?" Colonel Garovsky asked over his shoulder as he closed the door.

"I've got a contract," Headlight replied. "I've also got quite a bit of data."

"What sort of data?"

"For openers I know exactly what you're doing with all that money." He pulled a face and added, "Are you serious?"

"Do you have a reporting schedule?"

Headlight nodded. He looked for some place to butt his cigarette. Then he dropped it on the floor and ground it out with his heel.

"We are serious," Colonel Garovsky replied evenly.

Headlight looked first at Colonel Garovsky and then at Major Espensheid. Then he said, "If you're serious, why in the hell are you risking all that money on something as wobbly as betting on a football game? My God, why not real estate, or candy bars, even a herd of cows? Hell, why not a bank? That's what every other foreign investor is doing in this country. But betting at OTB? What's happened to Mossad and BOSS? Are you out of your minds?"

"We're not investing!" Major Espensheid blurted. "We're taking control! We're—"

"Shut up, Major!" Colonel Garovsky interjected vehemently.

"We're not betting money for the purpose of simply fattening our purses!" Major Espensheid went on wildly. "We're doing the same thing that you chaps have been doing for years! We're just a bit cleverer. When the dawn comes Monday morning, we'll own this state. Do you realize what that means? We'll be in charge of the state of New York of the United States of America! As its proprietors we will have effective control of one of the most influential political and economic entities in the *world*."

Colonel Garovsky threw up his hands and turned his back.

"From Monday morning on," Major Espensheid continued imperviously; his face grew redder and redder, "there will be no more concern in the United States about pushing South Africa to change its ways. We're on the bloody edge of a Kaffir takeover at this very moment. Please keep an eye on the telly Monday night. Your reader, Brinker or whatever he's called, he won't be using terms such as 'white-supremacist rule in settler Africa.' These corporations of yours, they won't be announcing a lot of rot about better wages for the Kaffirs. Come Monday, all that will stop. And much more. Your man at the United Nations, he will shut his mouth about human rights and all the other claptrap. Your banks will lend us more money, your Congress will vote away these monstrous embargoes, and your diplomats will stop making a lot of noise about how we should conduct the affairs of our *own* country. . . . The Jews have their own ideas about what they want. We both want much the same thing. For different reasons, naturally. We both need oil, of course. We'll expect you to twist the wogs' arms, tell them they must sell us petroleum or you'll cut them off from American technology. You must tell the . . ."

Major Espensheid was breathing heavily. He clasped his hands behind his back.

Headlight nodded. He raised his eyebrows and clucked. He lit another cigarette. "Not too bad an idea," he said, "if you think paper money is actually worth a damn."

"It's cheap in the United States," said Colonel Garovsky. "We want a bargain as well as the leverage Espensheid spoke of."

"Why didn't you pick France, for God's sake? The franc is worth a hell of a lot more than the dollar. I imagine it would've been just as easy to loot the national lottery."

"Oh, don't play naive with us, Headlight," snapped Colonel Garovsky. "What good would it do to control France? I mean—"

"Who do you think owns *us*? The French, the West Germans, the Japanese. The Dutch are leading the pack."

"We don't care a damn about *owning* the United States. We simply want some leverage here."

"You don't think you have leverage now? The state of Israel runs one of the most active legislative lobbies in Washington. You people make the labor unions and the civil rights people look rinky-dink."

"We what?"

"I'm saying that you're risking an awful lot of money to buy something you don't need."

"*We* need it," snorted Major Espensheid.

"Headlight," said Colonel Garovsky, "I've known you for a number of years. I think we first met in nineteen fifty-four or fifty-five. I've never known you to be perversely stupid. Surely you don't need me to explain this further. If this were your operation, you wouldn't think it odd in the least. You've bought more countries than I can easily name, Israel included."

"I would say Israel was up for sale, wouldn't you, at the time we bought it?"

"We needed the weapons," Colonel Garvosky replied heatedly. "We needed official U.S. help. Otherwise we'd all be dead."

"I would say that Israel isn't in the same condition now as when we bought it."

"I couldn't agree more. And I can assure you it never will be again.

This operation, for example, will guarantee that Israel will never again have to agree to terms—on *anything*—that are decided by a lot of simple-minded politicians in Washington."

"Here, here!" said Major Espensheid.

"The local police might have other plans," Headlight said calmly.

Colonel Garovsky thrust his hands onto his hips. He cocked his head. "What have the local police to do with it?"

"A little matter of some unsolved murders," Headlight said. He drew on his cigarette. "The 'Finger of God' killings. They've been in all the papers. What do you suppose would happen to all this if the police got word that the man they want is one James Edward Dolan, a member of Espensheid's Uitmoormag. What do you think the police would say if they knew that Dolan was using Espensheid's personal hunting rifle? What do you think they'd say if they knew Dolan was being run by a Mossad officer named Eli Zanin?" Headlight narrowed his eyes. "And what do you think they'd say if they found out that Mossad and BOSS have fifty kilograms of explosives in an apartment out in Brooklyn? Monday morning would look a little different if the police heard about that, wouldn't it?"

Colonel Garovsky and Major Espensheid looked at each other and then turned and looked out the window. Presently Colonel Garovsky turned around and said, "Your contract, how much is it worth?"

Headlight shrugged. "Not bad. Not beyond the dreams of avarice," he said; his lips tightened back over his teeth, "but not bad."

"Not bad," Colonel Garovsky said meditatively, "but not so good, either. Am I right?"

"What are you driving at?"

"Oh, come now, Headlight. Let's presume at least that we understand each other. You're here on contracted assignment because your Counter Intelligence isn't up to standard. Everyone knows that. Do you think we'd have mounted this operation if your Counter Intelligence worked the way it did in the old days?"

Headlight said nothing. His mouth turned up in a small grin.

"We all know that men who have been drummed out aren't paid the top wage," Colonel Garovsky continued, "even if they're known to be better at their work than the men still doing the official job. It's one of the conceits of intelligence work. The quality of the product falls off, a new regime takes command, any number of things happen, and heads must roll. But above all, mistakes must not be admitted. If your service—or mine or Espensheid's—admitted mistakes, how could we ever protect ourselves when occasionally we succeed?"

"Are you asking me to make allowances for you? To overlook your mistakes?"

"It would be worth your while."

"How much is that in dollars and cents?"

"We will match your contract."

Headlight threw back his head and laughed. "Hell, Yakov," he said; his drawl thickened, "I wouldn't let you go to bed with my sister for three times the amount of my contract. Not after what I saw downstairs."

Colonel Garovsky raised an eyebrow. "How much then?"

"This is your show. You name a figure."

"A half million dollars. Cash."

Headlight whistled and looked at the ceiling. "That would get me through the weekend," he said and smiled. "All right. Tell you what I'm going to do. I'm going to keep all this to myself. For the time being, I mean." He looked at his watch. "I'll let you know in two hours. In the meantime you've got a clear road. How does that suit you?"

"Not at all," said Colonel Garovsky. "I'm afraid we can't allow you to leave. Unless, that is, we're able to reach a mutual accommodation."

Headlight shook his head. He was still smiling. "Uh, uh," he said. "I've got a reporting schedule, remember? If I miss a call, people will start looking for me. At least one man knows exactly where I am. So if you'll excuse me, I'll be running along. I'll get in touch with you in two hours."

"Let me give you a number," said Colonel Garovsky. He and Major Espensheid stepped aside.

"Don't trouble yourself."

"How will you reach us?"

"I have the number."

"You have the number *here*?"

"Sure do."

Headlight left the room and descended the stairs.

Colonel Garovsky and Major Espensheid watched from the window. They saw Headlight make his way across the soggy park.

Mr. McManus opened his eyes. He was aware of a noise. He blinked several times. He looked around. He was dazed and confused. Gradually he recognized where he was. He felt something. He looked at his hand. It was his cigar. He was still holding it. It had gone out. He let it drop to the floor.

The noise persisted. He took a tentative breath. His chest and left arm were locked in a dull, leaden ache. He took another breath. The ache deepened. He recognized the noise. It was pounding on the door and someone calling his name.

"All right. I'm . . . " He listened to his voice. It was faint and quaky. With an immense effort he hauled himself from the chair. He trudged to the door. He unlocked it.

"Mac!" shouted Lula. Standing behind her was a bellhop with an armload of parcels. "Great God in the morning! Get yourself in yonder and get in the bed!"

She turned to the bellhop. "Put that stuff down and tell what's his name, Ranier or René or whatever his name is, the God damned manager, tell him to get a doctor up here!"

The bellhop just stood there.

"You better move, boy!" Lula shouted.

The bellhop dropped the parcels. He fled down the corridor.

Mr. McManus slumped against the wall. He closed his eyes. "Jacket pocket," he croaked. "Pills."

Lula fished the aspirin tin from his pocket. She crammed one of the digitalis tablets into his mouth. The muscles in Mr. McManus's throat constricted as he swallowed. The veins in his temples bulged.

"I'd've been here quicker," she said; she took Mr. McManus by the arm, "but those motherfuckers at the store had the security man following me around. Me in there spending a thousand dollars on one thing and another and that fool following me around like, like I was going to *steal* something."

In perfect unison, slow step by slow step, they walked toward the bedroom. As they crossed the threshold Mr. McManus tugged Lula's arm. She bent her ear close to his mouth.

"Call Billy," he said, barely above a whisper. "Tell him . . . Fifth Avenue lobby . . . Noon . . . The money . . . Half million . . . Two-fifty for you . . . Plane reservation . . . Tonight . . . Grand Cayman . . ."

They dragged on toward the bed. Mr. McManus stopped again and whispered, "Man named Coombes . . . Taft Hotel . . . Call him, too . . ."

Lula carefully sat Mr. McManus on the edge of the bed. She

moved to ease him onto his back. He made a noise. He gestured weakly with his finger. She leaned close to him.

"The other money . . . Hooples . . . Fifty-five million . . . Billy knows . . . Tell him . . ."

"Tell him what, Mac?"

"Philadelphia."

She loosened his clothes and took off his shoes. She laid him on the bed. She tucked the pillows under his head. She took a blanket from the closet and covered him.

"Call Billy," he said softly. "Now . . . And Coombes."

She disappeared into the living room. Mr. McManus opened one eye. He wondered how close he really was. Pretty damned close, he guessed. Maybe not, though, he thought. The one back in August was worse than this. Or was it? Maybe it just seemed worse because it was the first one. What is it with these heart attacks? Do you get used to them or do they kill you or what?

He could hear Lula on the phone.

". . . I don't give a shit what you think, Billy Light. Mac said Philadelphia. . . . No, he can't come to the phone. He's lying in yonder about to die. . . . Course I know what it means. Any damned fool see that. . . . Uh, huh . . . He's getting his, too. Noon. That's how come he wants you to come up here. . . . Don't give me that shit. How's he going to fuck an old nigger woman when he ain't got the strength to go downstairs and pick up a suitcase with a half a million dollars in it? . . . Uh, huh. Noon . . . Did I hear about what? . . . In Brooklyn . . . Oh, Lord that's awful. . . . Don't I know it. Well, it ought to teach people not to mess around with that stuff."

A moment later. "Mr. Coombes? You don't know me. I'm calling for a Mr. McManus. Said to call you and tell you Philadelphia. Said you'd know what he's talking about. . . . No, he can't come to the phone. He's sick . . ." She slammed the phone onto the cradle. "Rude motherfucker."

She walked back into the bedroom. Mr. McManus had thrown back the blanket.

"Mac!" cried Lula. "You know damned well you can't—"

He nodded and grinned in a minor way.

She stepped up to the bed. She placed her hands on her daintily fleshy hips. She looked striking in her new soft dress. "All right," she said, smiling gently. "Just a little flip-flop 'til the doctor gets here. Nothing else."

*   *   *

The manager gave up knocking. He shrugged to the doctor and sent the bellhop to fetch the key. He returned presently and unlocked the door.

"Mr. McManus!" the manager called out as they entered the living room.

A muffled, gurgling sound came from the bedroom.

The manager and the doctor exchanged glances. They raced to the door. They stopped short. Their mouths fell open at the same time.

They saw the naked body of Mr. McManus stretched out on the bed. His hands, arthritic thumbs extended, clutched the head of Lula to his groin.

"My God!" shouted the manager.

The doctor quickly put his stethoscope to Mr. McManus's chest. He stood up and shook his head. Then he took a pair of scissors from his bag. It took several minutes to cut Lula's hair away from Mr. McManus's stiffening fingers.

Detective Second Grade Tedesco turned a corner in the Flatbush section of Brooklyn. He parked a block away. Ambulances were everywhere. Attendants were lifting bleeding, moaning bodies onto stretchers. The police were evacuating the neighborhood. Officers talked into their walkie-talkies out of the sides of their mouths. Television men with mini-cameras jostled each other.

"This better be worth it," said Detective Lieutenant Burns. He slammed the door on the passenger side. "There's more paperwork when you try to retire than any in case you'll ever try to clear. And don't forget you owe me twenty bucks."

They hung their gold detectives' shields from their breast pockets and walked around the corner. They had to mince their way over a tangle of fire hoses.

The street—or rather what was left of it—came into view.

"Jesus Christ," said Burns.

It was a short block. Midway up one side of it was a crater. On either side the houses had been almost totally shattered. The houses next to them were blackened with smoke and knocked to perilous degrees off their foundations. The street and sidewalks were strewn with masonry, chunks of brick, and broken glass. Cars that had been parked along the street at the time of the explosion were severely dented and burning. Windows were broken in every building on the block. Most were afire. Firemen were at work extinguishing the blazes.

Burns and Tedesco found the bomb squad detective in charge. He was wearing a suburban jacket. His face was smudged.

"We're working like hell on the gas mains and we're still rounding up all kinds of shit," the detective said, "but what I called you about is over there on the sidewalk. It's pretty well beat up, but there ain't no doubt about what it is."

"An arbor cartridge press?" said Burns.

The detective nodded.

"We'll take a look in a minute," Burns said. "What else?"

"Five bodies from the point of the blast. Believe it or not, they're the only fatals so far." The detective sighed. "They're pretty interesting."

"How so?"

"Three of them were wearing shoulder holsters. All but one of them, every stitch they had on was blown off. For some reason, one of them is blown to bits like the others, but the concussion leaves him wearing an old black raincoat. Shoes, pants, shirt, everything blasted off him but that old raincoat. It's like the thing was made of asbestos or something. They're ripped to shit, though, all three of them, but them holsters are still strapped on them. Pieces still in them, too—.22 caliber Berettas."

Burns scowled. "That's mob stuff," he said. "What the hell are—"

"That ain't all," the detective went on. "The other two"—he lowered his voice, although the noise on the street made it impossible for him to be overheard—"they got holes all in them. One of them shot ten times at least. The other, fifteen or twenty. Of course, that's just an eyeball. Some of the entry and exit wounds might be from the same slug. Have to wait for the ME."

"What the hell happened?" Burns said. He shook his head and gestured at the scene of destruction.

"They were fucking around with some high-powered shit," said the detective. "Smells like blasting gelatin, but I don't know yet. All we've found so far is a fragment of an old-fashioned timer. One of the old kind, you know. You never see them much anymore. They're okay, if you know what you're doing."

"Obviously these clowns didn't," said Burns.

The detective shrugged. "Oh, one other thing. I took a look at one of the .22 cartridges. The three of them must've reloaded after they blasted the other two. The cartridge, I opened it up. Got one of them small powder packs, you know, professional rub-out type of equipment."

"The two that got iced, where're they?"

"Over there," the detective said. He pointed to two covered bodies on the opposite sidewalk. "They're still recognizable. Clothes burned and that. But they're recognizable."

Burns and Tedesco walked over to the bodies. A uniformed patrolman stood guard. They knelt down and pulled back the weatherproof cover.

"Oh, Christ," said Tedesco.

One of the bodies had an acne-scarred face and a black-and-blue right shoulder. The other was vaguely handsome. The only damage above the neck of the second body was the badly singed dark hair.

"Know who that one reminds me of?" Burns said. He pointed to the second body.

"Who?" said Tedesco. He looked at the brilliant sky and sighed.

"Charlie Dolan."

"Who the hell is Charlie Dolan?"

"Used to be my partner. You remember him, Charlie. I introduced you to him the other night."

They examined the arbor press.

"What do you think?" asked Tedesco.

"About that cartridge press?" Burns said. "I think you could make a cartridge with it. Even one for a whatchamacallit .375 magnum rifle. Other than that I don't think nothing at all. I'm retiring. I don't think about things like that anymore. Get one of your buddies in ballistics to check it out. Maybe they'll turn up something, ballistics. See where it gets you. Grab that thing and let's get out of here."

"I want to speak to Katz," Nathan Leitstein said through clenched teeth.

"May I say who's calling, please?"

"Nathan Leitstein."

"I'm sorry. We don't have anyone by that name at Provi—"

"You stupid prick! Put Katz on the fucking telephone!" He heard his voice break and he swallowed hard to fight back tears.

Presently Colonel Garovsky said, "This is Mr. Katz. What can—"

"How come this line's been tied up for the last forty-five minutes, you fucking hoople? I been trying to get through to you, God damn it!"

"Just one moment!"

"Just one moment yourself, pal. I'm giving you the skinny—"

"Connect me with McManus. My business is with McManus."

"McManus is dead!"

There was a pause. Then Colonel Garovsky said, "I'm sorry to hear that."

"I'll bet you are. Now pass this along to your buddy, the other hoople, Espensheid. The other fifty-five million, you put that on Philadelphia. On the nose."

"*Philadelphia*? Have you seen the point spread? I mean, New Orleans is a one-point favorite now."

"So what? You put that fifty-five million on *Philadelphia*. To *win*. You got that? *Philadelphia*. Oh, yeah. You tell Espensheid to deliver my dough the same time you deliver McManus's. Same place. Same everything."

"Who'll be representing McManus?"

"I will. Me and a lady friend of his."

"I don't think we'll be able—"

"You'll be able, pal. If you ain't, you're finished. You'd be surprised how easy it is to fuck something up in this town with just a couple of phone calls."

"Very well."

"You bet very well . . . you hoople."

He hung up and quickly dialed a New Jersey number.

"This is Nat Leitstein. Give me Solly."

After a moment, "Yeah, Nat?"

"Solly, I got something I want taken care of. Usual terms."

"Five K up front?"

"Yeah. See Sid tonight. He'll give it to you, Sid."

"*Tonight*? What the hell is this shit? Christ, I can't do nothing *tonight*!"

"I don't want you to do nothing tonight. I want you to get things rolling. I want you to take the five K so the thing don't slip your mind. Couldn't be done tonight, anyway. Certain people ain't available. Might not be available for a couple of months. I don't care about that. I just want to get things rolling."

"Anybody in particular you want me to see?"

"Guy by the name of Dolan. Charlie Dolan."

"Hey, ain't that the guy works for you? Ex-cop and that?"

"Yeah."

"That's the guy you want me to get in touch with?"

"That's what I just told you, Solly."

"Jesus, an ex-cop. That's a tough one, you know. I mean, ex-cops are tough to talk to."

"Ten K up front."

"I'll check around and that. Guy like this Dolan, he might be tough to get in touch with."

"I don't care when you get in touch with him, Solly. Long as it's sometime before Passover."

"Hey, it ain't even Christmas yet."

"So you got plenty of time, right?"

Coombes joined Headlight for a late lunch at a restaurant in Rockefeller Center. He declined a drink. Headlight sipped a vermouth on the rocks.

"You should try one," Headlight said. "Refreshing but not alcoholic to speak of."

"Coffee," Coombes said to the waiter.

"With your lunch or later?" the waiter asked.

"Now," Coombes said with a snarl.

When the waiter had gone, Coombes said, "They're betting Philadelphia for the final go-round. I heard from McManus this morning."

"Oh," said Headlight. "How is Mac?"

"Christ," Coombes muttered. "Look. The call came from some woman. She said she was calling because McManus was sick."

"Sick?"

"Yes."

"Another heart attack?"

"Maybe. She didn't say. I'll check the hospitals this afternoon. If he—"

"You needn't bother. Unless you're interested personally of course."

"Well, he was with us at the Ridge. And Burma. Don't you think—"

"Of course. Excuse me a moment. I have to make a phone call."

Headlight returned after a few moments.

"Garovsky and Espensheid are a bit confused," he said. "About betting on Philadelphia, I mean. Up 'til now they've played nothing but New Orleans. They asked *me* if the Philadelphia bet sounded right. Can you imagine?"

"What did you tell them?"

"I told them it sounded right—and I told them I'd report that as far as you and I could find out Mossad and BOSS were conducting some kind of training exercise."

"*But—*"

"McManus is dead, by the way."

Coombes's hooded eyes widened. His mouth turned down at the corners.

"Look," said Headlight, "we've earned our money. Why do you think McManus bothered to call you?"

"I don't know."

"Oh, open your eyes, Coombes. It's as clear as a spring day. . . . You know, Mossad and BOSS are very ingenious in some ways. In others they're pathetically obtuse. Do you know that they've bribed me?"

"*They've what?*"

"They've bribed me," Headlight said cheerfully. "Of course it's an absolute waste of money."

They finished their lunch and walked together for several blocks down Fifth Avenue. The sidewalks were jammed with Christmas shoppers. The break in the weather had brought them out in droves.

"I'm flying back to Washington this afternoon. Do you want to go with me?" Headlight asked.

They paused under a clock at Forty-fourth Street. Coombes bit at a fingernail. "I think I'll stay on for a few days. I'll probably go to the funeral."

"McManus's."

Coombes glared at him briefly. He turned abruptly and stalked back up the street.

That night Nathan Leitstein called Lula.

"I been thinking about it," he said, "and I got to tell you the truth, Lula. I hope you don't take offense, but it ain't safe, you and all that money up there by yourself."

"Billy, sometime you sound awful dumb for a Jew. Who in the hell would ever think *anybody* in Harlem except a dope pusher got five-hundred thousand dollars? In cash? You ain't going to tell, are you?"

"No, but—"

"Then don't worry about it."

"What I'm telling you is, I'm flying to Basel in the morning. Nice trip if you like that kind of scenery. What I'm going to do with my half million is put it in the bank."

"What bank?"

"Our bank. Mine and Kid's."

"Oh, that's right. Y'all got a bank. I remember now. That's the thing to do with it, put it in the bank. Them Israelis and South Africans see that ball game tomorrow, they liable to want their money back."

Nathan Leitstein laughed. "What do you think it's going to be?"

"New Orleans seven and Philadelphia six."

"That close, huh? I figure New Orleans'll take it by at least three."

"Whatever it is, Philadelphia ain't going to win and OTB still be in business on Monday. It's going to be a big payoff, but that's all. Ain't going to break them. They ain't going to get caught in no middle. And you know what else? Hips going to get what he needs."

"He's going to break fifteen-hundred yards again? I didn't think he was even going to dress out, Hips."

"Uh, huh. He called me a little while ago. Said his toe's still sore as a rising, but he had that dream again. The one about the new suit with the flower in the buttonhole. Said he figures he can run two or three times. He don't need but seventy-four yards, you know, and he could do that sitting down."

"Yeah, Hips'd dance in the half-time show to get that fifteen-hundred yards."

"Oh, Billy. Let me ask you about something. You still going to try and figure the line?"

"I might give it a try. Jesus, I don't know if I can do it by myself. I mean, Kid's brain was half the edge. More than half. The rest, I don't know, it was you and the dreams and stars and that, and—"

"And you."

"And me. And Kid's ma and what the hell ever she calls them things."

"Life pulses. Biorhythms."

"Something. Anyway, most of it, the edge, was that brain of his. Figure anything out, Kid could."

"Well, reason I ask is, I got home—after I got done to the hairdresser's—and I find this note stuck in the door. Know what it said? It said the man who wrote it is the seventh son of a seventh son's seventh son. Ain't *that* something?"

"Is it?"

"Oh, Lord, yes, honey. It's just a damn shame Mac had to punch out before we could play one using a seventh son."

"It's that good?"

"Billy a seventh son is like something you ain't ever seen. Won't beat Mac's brain, like you said, but it'll give us *some kind* of edge. You watch,"

"Who is he?"

"I couldn't make out the name. Said he's going to call on Monday. If he's for real, I'll let you know."

"Take care, Lula."

"Take care, yourself, Billy."